LADY AT ARMS

LADY AT ARMS

A Medieval Romance

A "clean read" rewrite of *Warrior Bride*, published by Bantam Books, 1994

TAMARA LEIGH
USA Today Best-Selling Author

ISBN: 1942326114
ISBN 13: 9781942326113

TAMARA LEIGH NOVELS

CLEAN READ HISTORICAL ROMANCE
The Feud: A Medieval Romance Series
Baron Of Godsmere: Book One 02/15
Baron Of Emberly: Book Two 12/15
Baron of Blackwood: Book Three 2016

Medieval Romance Series
Lady At Arms: Book One 01/14 (1994 Bantam Books
bestseller *Warrior Bride* clean read rewrite)
Lady Of Eve: Book Two 06/14 (1994 Bantam Books
bestseller *Virgin Bride* clean read rewrite)

Stand-Alone Medieval Romance Novels
Lady Of Fire 11/14 (1995 Bantam Books best-
seller *Pagan Bride* clean read rewrite)
Lady Of Conquest 06/15 (1996 Bantam Books best-
seller *Saxon Bride* clean read rewrite)
Lady Undaunted Late Winter 2016 (1996 HarperCollins
bestseller *Misbegotten* clean read rewrite)
Dreamspell: A Medieval Time Travel Romance 03/12

INSPIRATIONAL HISTORICAL ROMANCE
Age of Faith: A Medieval Romance Series
The Unveiling: Book One 08/12
The Yielding: Book Two 12/12
The Redeeming: Book Three 05/13
The Kindling: Book Four 11/13
The Longing: Book Five 05/14

INSPIRATIONAL CONTEMPORARY ROMANCE
Head Over Heels: Stand-Alone Romance Novels
Stealing Adda 05/12 (ebook); 2006 (print) NavPress
Perfecting Kate 03/15 (ebook); 2007 (print)
RandomHouse/Multnomah
Splitting Harriet 06/15 (ebook); 2007
(print) RandomHouse/Multnomah
Faking Grace 2015 (ebook); 2008 (print edi-
tion) RandomHouse/Multnomah

Southern Discomfort: A Contemporary Romance Series
Leaving Carolina: Book One 11/15 (ebook);
2009 (print) RandomHouse/Multnomah
Nowhere, Carolina: Book Two 12/15 (ebook);
2010 (print) RandomHouse/Multnomah
Restless in Carolina: Book Three Mid-Winter 2016
(ebook); 2011 (print) RandomHouse/Multnomah

OUT-OF-PRINT GENERAL MARKET TITLES
Warrior Bride 1994 Bantam Books
*Virgin Bride 1994 Bantam Books
Pagan Bride 1995 Bantam Books
Saxon Bride 1995 Bantam Books
Misbegotten 1996 HarperCollins
Unforgotten 1997 HarperCollins
Blackheart 2001 Dorchester Leisure

*Virgin Bride is the sequel to *Warrior Bride*
Pagan Pride and *Saxon Bride* are stand-alone novels

www.tamaraleigh.com

Prologue

England, 1152

"GILBERT!" HEEDLESS OF the brigands ransacking her dowry wagons, Lizanne Balmaine pulled free of her maid and rushed past the torn and blood-strewn bodies scattered over the ground. The old woman called to her, but Lizanne ignored her desperate pleas.

Dropping to her knees beside her brother, she reached to him. Though his face was shuttered, she could not—would not!—believe he was gone from her. She shook him. "Pray, open your eyes!"

His head lolled.

Whimpering, she forced her gaze down his body. His hauberk lay open, its fine mesh brilliant with the blood seeping through its links. And his leg...

God help his leg.

With trembling fingers, she tried to seam the flesh back together, but his blood only coursed faster and made the bile in her belly surge. Swallowing convulsively, she raised her hands and stared at the wet crimson covering her palms.

Dear Lord, he cannot be—

She was wrenched upright, hauled back against a coarsely clothed chest, and lifted off her feet.

"Nay!" She reached for Gilbert but grasped only air.

The one who held her chuckled. Feeling the wicked sound move his chest, she knew he would do things to her she had only heard whispered about. And could not have more quickly thanked God when she was shoved into the arms of her old maid. However, as she knelt in the dirt, clinging to Hattie and weeping with a twisted mix of grief and relief, the villains began a boisterous argument over who would have her first.

Lord, I can bear it. I shall bear it. Just do not let Gilbert be gone from me.

It was Hattie's trembling, so savage it shook her brittle frame, that pulled Lizanne from the heavens and dropped her back to earth. Amid the sudden hush, she lifted her face from her maid's bosom and peered past the old woman's shoulder at muddy boots.

"Nay, milady." Hattie tried to press her mistress's head down. "Be still."

Lizanne pushed aside the hands that had delivered her from her mother's womb five and ten years ago. With daring she had not known she possessed, she lifted her gaze up the lean, muscled body that stood over her. The man was uncommonly tall—nearly as tall as Gilbert and every bit as broad.

Hatred, more intense than any she had known, suffused her and set her own limbs to quaking. Here was the one who had dealt the final blow to her brother.

Making no attempt to keep loathing from her face, she slid her gaze from a generous mouth, up over a long, straight nose, to glittering eyes as dark as his hair was light.

Aye, that hair. Not quite flaxen, not quite white, it fell about a deeply tanned and angular face. As she stared at him, she could not help but question God's wisdom, for He had wielded no foresight in bestowing such a handsome face on this spawn of the Devil. Doubtless, many women were rendered agape by the sight of him. But not she. There was nothing captivating—

That was not true. The streak of blood matting a length of his hair was fascinating. Gilbert's blade had done that.

"God's teeth, what delights have we here?" he said in the coarse English of a commoner. As his men guffawed, a slow grin spread his lips and revealed straight but discolored teeth. He reached down and lifted a lock of her black hair. "Aye," he murmured, pulling his fingers through the heavy strands. "Yer a beauty, lass—a fine prize."

His eyes met hers, their fathomless depths charging her with fear she did not wish to feel. Hate was so much more comforting.

Hattie clutched her young charge nearer. "Take that which ye came fer and leave the child be," she said.

Laughter rumbled from the man, and the other brigands answered with more of the same.

Finally, he sobered. "Aye, hag, I'll take what I came fer." He drew back an arm and landed a fist to the old woman's temple.

With a gasp, Hattie loosened her hold and toppled backward.

Lizanne screamed, reached to her, but hardly had she touched her maid's rough woolen tunic than she was hauled to her feet and forced to face that evil visage.

Grinning, the man dipped his gaze to the neckline of her gown and ran a hand down her chest.

"Do not!" She struck out at him.

He pinned her arms and dragged her near. "Ye will bend to me, my beauty." He lowered his head toward her untried lips.

The brigands' laughter paining her ears, Lizanne jerked her chin aside and strained away from the hands that roamed her.

Dear God, I shall die! Pray, let me die!

As tears fell to her cheeks, she felt other hands touch and pinch her flesh.

"She is mine," the man growled, then swept her into his arms and shouldered his way through the throng.

Breath coming in great, choking gulps, Lizanne gripped his tunic as he carried her past those terrible, leering faces.

They had only just cleared the gathering when her captor lurched and dropped to one knee. Keeping hold of her, he shook his head as if to clear it, and she saw blood still flowed from his head wound. It was no mild injury as she had first thought, and it occurred to her God might not have abandoned Gilbert and her after all—that the miscreant might simply drop dead.

However, neither the Lord, nor her captor, seemed of a mind to oblige.

Amid mocking laughter, the man surged to his feet and swung around to face the others. "Do ye laugh again, I'll see the lot of ye gutted," he snarled, then strode from the camp toward the moonlit wood.

"When ye finish with 'er, Darth," one called, "I'd like a taste meself."

As his words were met with more jeering, Lizanne silently repeated *Darth* until she found a niche for the name in the turbulence of her mind. Then, with fear and trembling, she turned her thoughts to her desperate circumstances that were about to become more desperate.

She did not doubt he intended to steal her virtue that was to have been the privilege of her husband, Philip. He would defile her. But was that all? Might her fate be the same as her beloved brother's?

Do not just let it happen! You are more than this!

She did not know if it was her brother's voice or her own she heard, but she acted on it, bucking and letting her hands fly. When her nails raked her assailant's rough, unshaven face, he dropped her to her feet and repaid her with a slap so heavy she nearly fell over.

Covering her stinging cheek with one hand, she looked up at the devil in moonlight. He stood so rigid, face nearly deformed by anger, that she knew his slap would not be retribution enough.

Lizanne took a step back and glanced left and right. The castle of her betrothed lay less than five leagues to the west. If she ran and hid in the wood until the sun rose to guide her…

She turned to flee. An instant later, she found the needled ground at her back, and looming over her was the man called Darth.

His lips fell to her throat, and she squeezed her eyes closed and tried to go deep inside herself.

'Tis but my body, she told herself once, twice, three times, desperately willing her soul to rise above her.

But it was his weight that rose from her.

Merciful Lord! she called praise to the heavens. However, when she lifted her lids, she saw it was no angel come to her rescue. The man had pushed up onto his knees to remove his tunic. She started to look away, but her gaze was drawn to a long, jagged scar that slashed across his lower abdomen.

"Fight it, and 'twill go worse fer ye," he growled, only to shake his head and press a hand to it.

Realizing he still suffered from his injury, Lizanne threw herself to the side but got no further.

He thrust her onto her back and, gripping her throat, lifted her face toward his. "Listen well! I prefer not to spoil yer beauty, but I will. Do ye understand, wench?"

She understood, but it did not stop her from prying at fingers that denied her air. What did still her was the pain that lanced across his brow.

Do something!

She swung a clumsily bunched fist upward and, to her amazement, connected with his head wound. However, there was no moment to rejoice, for a blinding pain shot through her hand and wrist.

When the man slumped atop her, she only distantly noticed his weight as she sucked in precious air and whimpered over the shards of light dancing against the backs of her eyelids.

Why did it hurt so? What was this pain that made it feel as if she had laid her hand upon a fire?

As the lights began to recede, she opened her eyes and focused on the pale head upon her shoulder. Except for the shifting of hair by the meandering breeze, there was no movement about the man.

Was it possible? Had she, who had never struck another being, knocked the man unconscious?

Question not, Lizanne! Run!

Biting her lip, drawing blood as she tried to distract herself from the pain in her hand, she twisted beneath the man and used her forearm to push him off. As he rolled onto his back, he groaned.

Run! Now!

Holding her hand to her chest, she stumbled to her feet and looked one last time at her assailant. Had she a weapon—and the courage—she would put an end to him.

Skirts gripped high, she plunged into the wood. Deeper and deeper she went, oblivious to the sharp rocks and pine needles that tore at her feet, the branches that tangled her hair and scratched her face.

How far or how long she ran, she did not know. Only when she tumbled into a narrow ditch, lungs raw from exertion, did she notice light had begun to seep into the sky above the wood.

Panting, she squeezed her eyes closed and listened for the sounds of pursuit. All she picked out were the innocent noises of an awakening wood—the buzzing of insects, the twittering of birds, the gurgle of water.

Would they come? She raked her fingers through the hair falling about her face and shoulders, prayed she had outdistanced them.

Knowing she should continue on, she tried to stand, but her legs would not hold her. She would have to stay awhile. For fear her clothing would reveal her amid the greenery, she burrowed deeply into the undergrowth and promised herself she would not sleep. But her body had other plans.

With her last presence of mind, she dug her uninjured hand into the loose soil beneath her, unearthed a rock, and clasped it to her chest lest she find herself in need of a weapon.

As fatigue dragged her under, images of the night past tumbled through her mind, the worst being her brother's ravaged body. "Ah, Gilbert," she whispered, "'twill not go unavenged. This I vow."

1

England, 1156

BY DEGREE, RANULF Wardieu became cognizant of his surroundings. A fetid, musty odor assaulted his senses first, the taste of it on his indrawn breath making his throat constrict.

Lord, I thirst!

Swallowing hard against the parched tissues of his mouth, he lifted his chin and put his head back against cold, weeping stones. Where his head settled, he felt an aching throb, but before he could ponder the cause, he became aware of lowered voices.

He opened his eyes and peered into the dimly lit room. Though it was too dark to be certain, his wakening senses told him he was in a cell. As his eyes slowly adjusted, he watched indistinct shadows move in and out of the light cast by a single torch.

'Tis but a dream, he told himself. Still, he leaned forward to catch the conversation, and it was the rattle of chains on either side of him that brought him fully awake.

Though his senses screamed with shock and outrage and his mind protested the pain in his outstretched arms and the numbing chill throughout his body, the warrior in him forced him to stillness.

Unfortunately, the protesting chains had already alerted his shadowy companions that he had regained consciousness, for the voices had gone silent and the flickering torch was the only movement to be seen.

His own face in shadow, Ranulf peered at the dark figures through narrowed lids. Why did they not show themselves? Who were they?

Then they were moving again, speaking again—though not loud enough for their words to have form. Would they draw near?

A door was thrown open on the far side of the room, the light that shone through transforming the figures into three men who filed out.

Dear God, I truly am in a cell!

The last of the men pulled the door closed behind him, returning the cell to its state of near-darkness.

Although Ranulf's eyes and ears confirmed he was alone, his senses said otherwise. Someone was yet within.

Resenting the torch that cast its dim light across the floor and illuminated little save the lower half of his body, he determinedly set about assessing his situation.

He was imprisoned, stripped of tunic and boots, his only clothing undertunic and chausses. Chained upright to a wall by manacles that bit into his wrists, his arms were stretched out to the sides. Beneath him, his knees were buckled, his arms having carried the weight of his slumped body for...How long?

Though he felt the grip of manacles around his ankles, there was no tension between them. He lowered his chin and peered at the chain that ran from one ankle to the other, the excess of which lay pooled between his feet.

Grinding his teeth to keep from giving voice to the pain in his limbs, he searched for an answer to his predicament and, gradually, memories unfolded.

He had been at Langdon's Castle. Full of wine and ale and against his better judgment, he had succumbed to the beckoning of a comely maid and followed her down a narrow corridor. She had teased him, allowing glimpses of slender calves as she danced ahead—always just out of reach.

Upon rounding a corner, he had been set upon. Though he had delivered a retaliatory blow, his assailant had struck again—this time to the back of his skull—and it had dropped him to the stone floor. He had only a moment to focus on the darkly hooded figure bending over him before darkness dragged him away.

Now, most acutely aware of the injury to his head, he moved it, and the ache trebled. Still, it did not equal the discomfort in his burning joints that tempted him to get his legs under him and take the weight off his arms.

Trembling from the effort to contain his spiraling anger, he turned his head and searched the darkened cell. The cloaked corners revealed nothing he had not seen before, but he continued to feel another presence.

He remained unmoving several minutes longer. Then, with raging resentment, he lowered the heels of his bare feet to the cold earth—and brushed something soft and warm that shrieked and scuttled away.

Straightening, he peered at the manacles overhead. Thick bands encircled raw wrists darkened with blood. As he was large-boned, they intimately tested his flesh, nearly cutting off the laborious upward flow of blood.

He opened and closed his hands until he was rewarded with a prickly warmth that spread from his aching shoulders to the tips of his fingers. With the return of feeling came a measure of strength and, eager to test it, he thrust his arms forward. The restraints held, drawing fresh blood as their clatter violated the silence.

When the noise died away, he caught the sound of movement to his left. "Show yourself!" he demanded, his voice echoing around the stone walls.

Nothing.

'Tis a game we play, then.

Straining to the right, Ranulf put all his strength into his left arm and wrenched it forward. The manacle bit more deeply, causing blood to trickle down his wrist. Where was he, and who dared chain him like an animal? With his bare hands, he would crush the miscreant!

Fury, fueled by imaginings of revenge, intensified until there was nothing to do but release it. He propelled his body forward and, ignoring the pain in his shoulders and wrists, fought the chains until his strength drained. With hoarse curses, he collapsed against the wall.

"What ails you, my lord?" a sweetly sarcastic voice cut through his stream of expletives.

He snapped his chin to the left. A darkly clad figure stood an arm's reach away. It was impossible to make out the features of the upturned face amid the shadows of a hood, but the woman's eyes caught the barest light and glittered coldly.

He swept back to the moment before he had lost consciousness at Langdon's castle. It had to have been her.

"A lord, indeed," she murmured. "I never suspected as much."

Though size and gender could be deceiving, Ranulf did not doubt this woman was his captor. "Who are you?" he demanded.

"An old acquaintance." She stepped nearer, rose to her toes, and boldly tested his chains.

Maddening! Close enough to smell the sweetness of her woman's body, but he could not so much as touch her. He curled his fingers into fists.

"They hold well," she said, and her gloved hand grazed his as she stepped back. "Best you not waste your strength so foolishly...my lord."

Ranulf jerked the chains. "I demand to know the grounds for my imprisonment!"

She turned away.

Forcing himself to a calm he was nowhere near to feeling, Ranulf followed her progress across the cell. When she stopped before the wall sconce with its single torch, he saw she was not clothed as the lady her voice proclaimed her to be. Visible beneath the hem of her cloak were the chausses and boots of a man.

As he watched, she removed the torch and used it to light others around the cell. Soon, every corner stood out in sharp contrast to its former self, confirming the two of them were the only occupants.

Immediately, he imprinted every detail upon his mind. He was chained to the wall of the main room where guards could be stationed. To the left, beyond an iron-banded door with its grate set at eye level, was a row of individual cells. To the right, stood a corridor that stretched into nothingness, and from which he detected the sound of running water.

When he returned his attention to the woman, she faced him, and he almost laughed at her bold stance, legs spread and hands clasped behind her back. Unfortunately, he still could not make out her features, and he wondered if she had good reason to keep them hidden. After all, what kind of woman dressed as a man and tended a cell with such ease?

He felt the tug of a smile. Never had he been intimidated by a woman—not even his strong-willed mother—and this woman's display sparked humor in him despite it being an entirely humorless situation.

Shaking off the emotion, he asked, "Am I to be told of the charges against me?"

The woman traversed the earthen floor and once more came to stand before him. The hood continued to hide her features, though he could now make out the line of a straight nose and the curve of full lips. More intriguing was a pair of keys on a thin leather thong about her neck. Surely worn to taunt him, they would fit the manacles.

"You are here, Baron Wardieu"—she pushed the hood back—"to atone for sins visited upon others."

He narrowed his eyes on her pale, familiar face, shifted his gaze from her intensely green eyes that regarded him with loathing, to the blackest hair he had ever seen—like the starry night of a new moon.

His captor was Lady Lizanne, though he knew her only from the one time he had made inquiries after catching a glimpse of her at Lord Bernard Langdon's castle. Shortly after his arrival, while he and his vassal, Sir Walter Fortesne, had been seated with Lord Langdon and his steward in the hall, a commotion at the opposite end had interrupted their discussion. Exhausted after two days of riding in the constant drizzle of the season, Ranulf had been annoyed at the intrusion and turned in his chair to observe the perpetrator.

There she had stood, all that unconstrained black hair about her shoulders as she berated a servant who, it seemed, had dared lay a hand to her maid. Despite the drab bliaut the lady had worn ungirded, Ranulf had been intrigued.

"Lady Lizanne!" Lord Langdon had arisen so abruptly he upended his chair.

The lady had turned and looked across the hall, eyes wide with surprise.

"Apologies, my lord, I did not realize…" The moment her gaze lit upon Ranulf, her words fell away.

Swiftly, he had risen from his chair and, towering over Lord Langdon's plump figure, smiled and dipped his chin.

Her eyes had widened further and mouth gaped as the color drained from her face.

Wondering if he should take it as a compliment, Ranulf had stared as she stepped toward him. Then, with a strangled gasp, she had pivoted and fled as if evil itself were at her heels.

Grunting, Lord Langdon had reseated himself in the chair his steward had rushed to upright and said, "My apologies for Lady Lizanne. Would that you knew what a trial she is to me."

"Your daughter?" Ranulf had asked.

"God's mercy, a daughter such as that?" Lord Langdon guffawed. "No worse curse could be visited upon me. Nay, she is my wife's cousin. It will be a blessing when she returns to her brother, Baron Balmaine, on the morrow."

"The lady is not wed, then?"

Lord Langdon's smile had disappeared. "Take my advice, young Ranulf, and stay away from that one. She is mean-spirited."

Ranulf's curiosity had only increased. However, the lady had not appeared in the hall for the evening meal, and he had not seen her again. Instead, he had followed the skirts of an enticing maid straight into an ambush.

But why? Atonement for what sins? Desire? He pulled himself back to the present and said, "The Lady Lizanne."

Her dark eyebrows rose. "My lord knows me?" she said in mock disbelief, then stepped nearer and once more rose to her toes so her face was within inches of his and he felt her warm breath.

Forcing an indifferent expression, Ranulf searched for an advantage to her being so near, but there seemed none. If he lunged forward, he would do no more than push against her.

"I do not know you," he rasped, "but I know of thee."

A corner of her mouth lifting, she set herself back on her heels and began peeling the gloves from her hands. "My good cousin Bernard has been wagging his tongue." She clucked her own, then lowered her eyes over Ranulf. "I wonder...do you not remember our first meeting?"

Did her voice break, or was it only imagined?

She lifted her head and pinned him with those impossibly green eyes.

Reflecting on her improper display in Lord Langdon's hall, he said, "Aye, and most memorable it was."

Her head snapped back as if he had slapped her.

Despite the circumstances, Ranulf was beginning to enjoy the game. He smiled. "Tell me, are you in the habit of imprisoning men you desire?"

She blinked. "Do you not deny it, then—that first meeting?"

He was baffled by her refusal to rise to the bait. "Deny it? Why should I? 'Twas you, not I, who made a spectacle of yourself before Lord Langdon."

Color suffused her face. "That is not the meeting I speak of!"

Ranulf lowered his own face near hers. "I recall no meeting other than our brief one in Langdon's hall—could that be called a meeting."

She gave a bitter laugh, then reached up, touched the fingers of her gloves to the base of his throat, and trailed them down his collarbone.

Ranulf stiffened.

"I shall never forget our first meeting," she said. "'Twould seem, though, you have." She caught her bottom lip between even white teeth and lowered her gaze to the chain between his bound feet.

Though a frown drew her eyebrows near, it did nothing to diminish how lovely she was—like a rose. Unfortunately, though her petals would be soft and fragrant, her nasty thorns could prove a man's undoing. Still, he longed to be the one to strip away her prickly defenses—

Disgusted at the realization his initial attraction to this woman had not abated, he snarled, "I demand to speak to the lord of this castle."

She continued to consider the ground at his feet. "Hmm, well, if you refer to Lord Langdon, I must disappoint you. You are no longer under his roof, Baron Wardieu. You are under mine."

He was not surprised. "As told, I would speak to the lord of *this* castle."

She sighed. "Regrettably, 'tis not possible. It will be a sennight ere he returns. And then…"

Her gaze flew to his and, in that moment, Ranulf realized why the chain so aroused her interest.

Once more giving his arms his full weight, he thrust his legs out before him and captured her waist between his thighs, causing the length of chain between his feet to strike her shins and buckle her knees.

She cried out as her head slammed into his chest and black tresses spilled from the collar of her man's tunic.

"Now," he growled, "take those keys from 'round your lovely neck and release me."

She tossed her head back. "'Twill do you no good." With the back of a hand, she wiped at the blood trickling from her nose. "You will not be allowed to leave alive."

"Do it, else I will crush the life from your accursed body." He tightened his legs.

She gasped and, swift as a cat, raked her nails across his face.

Ranulf held, for a scratch, no matter how deep, was nothing to one who had survived bone-deep cuts.

She strained backward, clawed and pried at his thighs, but it would take far more to escape him. And from somewhere, she produced the means to do so. He caught the flash of silver and identified it as a dagger a moment before she sank the blade into his thigh.

Ranulf's shout of pain was followed by her release.

Propelled backward, his captor threw her hands behind her to break her fall. Still, she hit the earthen floor hard, her arms going out from under her and landing her flat on her back. Surprisingly, she almost immediately regained her feet.

Clutching her ribs, she staggered toward him. "You! I will see you in hell for this."

He glanced at the dagger protruding from his thigh. "Am I not already in hell? Witch!"

Unexpectedly , she startled at the sight of her bloody handiwork, then spun around and ran from the cell.

Drawing deep breaths through clenched teeth, Ranulf fought the darkness that once more threatened to pull him under. Though never in his one score and seven years had he considered doing physical harm to a woman, he would not trust himself were he loosed upon Lizanne Balmaine. With one such as she, mean-spirited as Lord Langdon had warned, it would be too easy to forget women were meant to be protected rather than set upon as he now plotted.

The thick shadow that fell across the floor heralded the arrival of a large man who hesitated before stepping into the cell.

He crossed to Ranulf's side and splayed enormous hands on his hips. "Me name's Samuel. I be yer jailer." His eyebrows pinched as he leaned near to look upon the injuries his mistress had scored into her prisoner's face. "Hmm." Lowering his great, bald head, he next inspected Ranulf's thigh. "She got ye good, she did. Ye must have made her right angry."

"I require a physician!"

Samuel straightened, placing himself eye-to-eye with Ranulf. "Well, now, Lady Lizanne ain't ordered no physician. But I've had some experience if ye'd like me to give it a try."

"I have no desire to lose my leg!"

The big man shrugged. "Mayhap that be what she wants. She do seem to hold a mighty grudge again' ye."

Ranulf calmed himself enough to ask the burning question. "Why?"

"Milady's reasons I ain't privy to."

"Then do not speak to me of them!"

Samuel's face split with a grin, showing a full set of teeth. He leaned over again and tapped the dagger's hilt. "It ain't such a deep wound," he pronounced and strode across the earthen floor and out the door.

Some minutes later, he returned with a fistful of rags. With one swift movement, he pulled the dagger free and tossed it aside. Immediately, he pressed a rag to the wound to stanch the blood.

Ranulf groaned. The dagger's removal was worse than the getting of it. Squeezing his eyes shut, he gnashed his teeth as Samuel continued his clumsy ministrations.

"Now hold still!" the man commanded and made quick work of applying a tourniquet.

Drawing deep breaths, Ranulf considered his bandaged leg. "'Twill take more than that to save my leg."

"Ungrateful, are ye?" Samuel's lips twitched. "Well, now..." He put his head to the side. "...methinks it'll do fine."

At Ranulf's thunderous expression, he said, "Don't ye worry. After the nooning meal, I'll have me missus come and clean it right for ye. She knows plenty 'bout tendin' wounds." Another grin and he was gone, returning moments later to secure the forgotten door behind him.

Imposing though he might be, Ranulf knew this Samuel was no jailer. Perchance, an ally.

He searched his gaze across the dirt floor until he spotted the carved hilt of the dagger the man had carelessly tossed a short distance away.

Balancing on his injured leg, he twisted his other foot into the hard, packed dirt of the floor and kicked a spray of granules toward the weapon. It took time and effort, but when he was done, the dagger was no longer visible. In its place stood a loosely mounded pile of dirt.

Ranulf leaned his head back and, through a haze of pain, began plotting. He would not leave this place without Lizanne Balmaine.

2

IGNORING THE SHOCKED faces of the castle folk she rushed past, Lizanne barely reached her chamber before giving up the simple meal of which she had partaken that morning.

Kneeling, she held her head in shaking hands and rocked her body. "Why?" she groaned. Why should she suffer remorse at having defended herself against that beast? Why had it bothered her to look upon the wound she had inflicted? It was no less than he deserved—a ruthless man who had taken from her nearly all she held dear. Still, it sickened her.

She drew a long, shuddering breath and stood. On legs that felt as if they might fold, she traversed the chamber, barred the door, and crossed to the large window from which she had earlier removed the oilcloth to let in the light of a cloudless day—a blessed reprieve from the past six days that had been cursed with overcast skies and constant drizzle.

The sun's descent into the west had begun, but it was still high, casting a warm column of light over her. She closed her eyes and savored the heat upon her icy skin, but though she warmed outwardly, she could not shake the chill at her core, one that she had carried with her for four years.

She slid into the window embrasure and peered down into the inner bailey, noting but paying little heed to the young squire engaged in swordplay with a man-at-arms.

Clasping her hands against her mouth, she began chewing the edge of a thumbnail. For the first time, the implications of her abduction of Ranulf Wardieu began to burden her. Previously, she had given little thought to what the consequences of her vengeful act might be, filled as she was with the need to free herself from years of painful memories and to avenge Gilbert.

Such a surprise it had been to discover Ranulf Wardieu was of the nobility. However, she had put that aside, telling herself it mattered not that he had been personally sent by King Henry to preside over a dispute between Lord Langdon and one of his vassals.

Of course, it would have been much simpler had he been but the common villain he had portrayed years ago. But now...

Dare she believe her taking of him would leave her and her brother, Gilbert, unscathed? Though she knew little of Ranulf Wardieu, he would surely be missed. And soon.

Unbidden, his image forced itself upon her. His rank of nobility, with its accompanying speech, mannerisms, and clothes might have thrown another off his scent, but Lizanne would know him anywhere. That long, shockingly pale hair. The large, powerfully muscled frame—a bit huskier, perhaps. And those eyes that had stared at her with such anger. They were as black as she remembered, yet different as if—

"Curse him!" she rasped. It was he. Could be no other. Drawing her knees to her chest, she wrapped her arms around them.

The revenge she had envisioned these past years while honing her body and weaponry skills to a level that vied with her brother's men, was so close that she had but to raise a hand to bring it down upon Ranulf Wardieu's head. But could she? Dare she?

If only Gilbert had not been waylaid in his return from court. Surely, he would have challenged the man properly and seen justice done. After all, had he not more reason to hate Ranulf Wardieu? Was it not he who bore the marks of that fateful night upon his lame body?

Her weakening resolve found strength in the memories that had driven her these years, and she called to mind the image of her brother and his pronounced limp…his agony…the lost laughter that had once lit eyes now rendered empty of nearly all but suffering. Wardieu had done that to him.

And what of her? Had she not also suffered? Had not her betrothed, a man with whom she had believed herself in love, broken the marriage contract, citing she was no longer chaste? Aye, she had suffered, but not as much as Gilbert.

Now nibbling the inside of her bottom lip, she searched for a means to exact her revenge. For exact it, she must. But what to do?

Tears of frustration welling, she tossed her head and, out of the corner of her eye, caught another glimpse of the duel in the bailey below. The young squire had backed his opponent into a corner and was taunting him as he prepared to deliver the mock thrust that would name him the victor.

She stared as he thrust gracefully forward, withdrew, then laughed joyously and waved his sword heavenward. *Foolish*, she told herself as the idea came together. *Terribly foolish.*

"Nay," she murmured, "perfect."

A knock at the door brought her head around. "Milady!" Her maid's voice floated into the chamber. "Ye are needed."

As distinct as her words were, Lizanne knew the girl was on her hands and knees in the corridor outside, mouth pressed near the large gap between floor and door.

"Can it not wait?" Lizanne called.

"'Tis a child, milady. She is hurt."

Lizanne jumped up and hastened to the chest that contained her medicinals—a chest that had been her father's. "A moment, Mellie," she called, dropping the lid back against the wall. As happened each time she delved within, memories visited her.

Though more often a woman's domain, her father had been fascinated with the healing properties of herbs. He had encouraged his daughter's interest in healing, taking her "herbing" with him from a young age. In the end, though, nothing could save the old baron from the terrible sickness that had feasted upon his body. And the attack on Lizanne and Gilbert's camp had wrested from him his last hold on life. Another reason Wardieu must pay.

Blinking away tears, Lizanne gathered the pots she might need, her fine sewing needle, and strips of clean linen. Then she ran across the chamber and threw open the door.

"Where is the child?" she asked as Mellie straightened from the floor.

"Belowstairs, milady. A dog bit her." Relating the details of the attack, the maid kept pace with Lizanne all the way to the hall where the child's weeping mother sat upon a bench, her precious one clutched to her bosom as the servants clustered around.

At Lizanne's approach, all stepped aside to allow her access to the sobbing child. "Send for Lucy," she instructed Mellie as she sank to her knees.

"She has been sent fer, milady."

"What is keeping her?" Gently, Lizanne pried away the mother's arms and turned the child about. She was a pretty little thing, perhaps four years of age.

Lizanne pushed aside the bloodstained cloth on the child's arm and leaned near to examine the injury.

Mellie bent down so no others might hear and whispered, "Lucy is tendin' that other one's wound, milady."

Other one? Lizanne stretched out the child's arm and gently wiped away the blood. The bite was not as bad as she had feared, but it would require stitches—

She snapped her chin around. "Other one, Mellie?"

The maid shrugged apologetically and nodded, confirming it was Wardieu whom Lucy tended.

Lizanne's anger was short-lived as the healer in her pushed it aside. Evil though the man was, he had been wounded and it would be unseemly to leave him uncared for, even if she could not bring herself to see to his needs. After all, not even a vicious animal deserved to be left bleeding and in pain. Nay, her revenge would be carried our properly, Wardieu given the opportunity to defend his person.

She returned her attention to the child. "And what is your name, little one?" She pushed damp hair back from tear-swollen eyes.

The little girl's bottom lip trembled. "A-Anna."

"Anna," Lizanne repeated, forcing out all thoughts of Wardieu in order to summon a genuine smile. "You are a brave girl."

A smile tugged at Anna's mouth. "I-I am?"

Lizanne reached for her medicinals. "Aye, you fought that mean old dog and won, did you not?"

Sniffling, Anna turned questioning eyes upon her mother. "Did I win, Mama?"

The woman met Lizanne's gaze. Gratitude shining from her eyes, she smiled, then looked to her daughter. "You did."

"Now," Lizanne said as she unstoppered a bottle, "I wish you to tell me the whole story."

Anna looked uncertainly from Lizanne to the bottle that wafted a pungent odor. "Will it hurt?"

Lizanne touched Anna's cheek. "Mayhap a little, but you are brave, hmm?"

After a brief hesitation, Anna nodded.

3

❧

IT WAS NOT merely the cold that awoke Lizanne with a jerk, but the nightmare. Although it visited her less often with each passing year, it had taken this most recent opportunity to return with a vengeance—frighteningly vivid in every detail.

She was huddled again in the window embrasure, having returned there after stitching little Anna's arm. While she had plotted revenge, the afternoon and evening had slipped away and, eventually, she had fallen asleep.

Drawing a hand across her face, she was surprised to find it damp with tears. As she brushed them away, she looked out at the dark night and shivered when a cool breeze buffeted her face.

Though unwilling to admit her fear, she searched for and finally spotted the dark, shadowy figure that slowly traversed the parapet of the inner bailey's wall. Disconcerted, she looked for more men-at-arms but saw none. In all likelihood, there were no others.

It was a relatively peaceful time under the reign of King Henry II, and Gilbert, having seen to his sister's safety by placing her under the protection of Lord Langdon, had nearly divested the castle of its defenses, taking the bulk of his men with him to court. He had left behind only a minimum capable of offering a token resistance in the unlikely event the castle was set upon. Unfortunately, he had not anticipated the delays that had resulted in her return ahead of his own. And he most certainly could not have foreseen her recent venture. Thus, should Ranulf's presence at Penforke be discovered and a campaign undertaken to free him, the defense of the castle was less than questionable. It was nearly nonexistent.

Shifting her cramped muscles, she grimaced at the chill that had settled in her limbs—more, in her right thumb. Having broken it when she had knocked Darth—rather, Ranulf Wardieu—senseless, it had never set properly and was wont to bother her from time to time.

She eased her feet to the floor and stuck out a hand to feel her way across the darkened room. Familiarity guided her, and she found her bed without mishap. She began to disrobe, but not until she stood in her thin shift did her woolly mind register that something was missing—the precious dagger given to her by Gilbert. She shook the last of the cobwebs from her mind and tried to remember what she had done with it.

Wardieu. She had used it against him, but what had become of it afterward? Surely, Samuel had put it aside for safekeeping. Still, she was bothered by its fate. Not only was it of sentimental value, but if it fell into Wardieu's hands—

She pulled on a robe, crossed to the door, and stepped out into the dimly lit corridor. After retrieving a flickering torch from a wall sconce, she hastened down the corridor and descended the stone steps to the great hall.

Moving quietly so she would not awaken those sleeping on the rushes and benches, she crossed the room and hurried down a narrow passageway, then a long flight of stairs to the door of the main cell.

Although she had ordered that a guard be posted, there was no sign of one. Stamping down anger, she peered through the grate into the darkened room. The torches had long since expired, leaving the cell pitch-black.

She unbolted the door, opened it and, carrying the torch before her, stepped inside.

Her heart leaped when her gaze fell upon the still figure across the room. Not only was her captive fully clothed, but he sat on the earthen

floor, chin resting on his chest where he slept. Though he remained man-
acled, his arms were comfortably suspended by chains mounted lower in
the wall on either side of him.

"Curse you, Samuel!" she hissed, then strode to the tables and
benches on the far side of the room. The light from the torch illuminat-
ing the bare surfaces, she soon resolved that Samuel must have taken the
dagger with him.

Though reason told her she should leave, she crossed to her prisoner
and looked from the pale crown of his head to his bandaged wrists to his
left leg where the material of his russet chausses was torn open to reveal
his bandaged wound.

Would he be forever constrained by an ungainly limp like that suffered by Gilbert? It would certainly be fitting.

Taking stock of her defenses and concluding the man was of less
danger to her sitting, she knelt beside him and lowered the torch to better see his leg. The bandages were not bloody, nor were they damp to the
touch as they might have been if the wound had begun to fester.

It was the handiwork of Lucy, Samuel's wife. How had they had
managed Wardieu? Even injured, he would be a worthy adversary. But
then, Samuel was strong and had likely brought armed men with him
for the task.

Determining the wound had not been deep and, now that it was
properly cared for, would likely heal fine, she lifted her head. And looked
into the blackest eyes.

Lurching backward, she lost hold of the torch. It dropped to the
earthen floor and flickered uncertainly. As she scrambled to retrieve it,
harsh laughter sounded around the cell. Heart pounding, she swept the
torch high and was relieved when its flame sprang upward again.

Wardieu sat with his head back, a thin smile stretching his lips as his
laughter subsided.

The silence that followed lengthened as he began an insulting perusal
of her inappropriately clad figure. When his eyes finally returned to

hers, she hated herself for the fear that raced limb to limb and, abruptly, turned away.

"Nay!" he bellowed.

Clutching the torch in one hand, the lapels of her robe in the other, she looked around.

"Come here!"

Why she should feel vulnerable—childish—before this man, she did not understand. After all, he was *her* prisoner.

"Surely, I can do you no harm." He rattled his chains.

Lizanne lifted her chin and returned to stand over him. "Aye, my lord?"

"Sit."

"I prefer to stand."

He shrugged. "I have a boon to ask of you."

"A boon?" Disbelief pitched her voice high.

"I would know the grounds for my imprisonment and where I am held."

She considered him, then slowly lowered to her haunches. "Would it give you comfort, my lord?"

By the light of the torch that shone full upon his face, she saw his jaw shift and the muscles tighten. "Mere curiosity bids me ask," he said, then added, "*my* lady."

Lizanne stiffened. "Do not call me that!"

"My lady?" He arched an eyebrow. "'Tis but a polite form of address—respect for your station."

"I am not your lady!"

"Indeed. You are not a lady at all, are you?"

His words cut more deeply than she would have thought possible. There were others who would agree with him—especially Gilbert's knights who thought it unseemly for a woman to bear arms and clothe herself in men's garments. It did not seem to matter that, more often than not, she dressed appropriately and acted as lady of the castle, a role for which she had been trained from an early age. They saw her only through the eyes of men threatened by her ability to protect herself.

"And I..." Wardieu continued, baring even, white teeth, "am not your lord. Yet."

A cold hand closed over her heart. How was he able to arouse such misgivings? Had she not resigned herself to the task ahead? Was she not the one in control?

She stood and released the lapels of her robe. "I have a proposal for you. If you can best the opponent of my choice in a duel of swords, I shall set you free."

His lids narrowed, but not so much that she could not see the ominous emotion rising in his eyes.

She steeled herself. "'Twill be a fight to the death."

After a long moment, he said, "Who is this witless man who would die for you?"

"That need not concern you, Ranulf Wardieu. All you need know is that I have chosen a worthy opponent."

"Witch!" he shouted, anger surfacing like a stab of lightning. "Do you truly believe you will escape retribution once I have killed this man who shall die needlessly for you?"

"I have faith in my choice. And even if I did not, 'tis not as if it will require the most proficient warrior to best one in your condition, for what good is skill without speed?" She looked at his bandaged leg. "A decided disadvantage, my lord."

"His will be a bloody death! Then you and your family will suffer as well."

There was a chance he would be the victor, but she had already considered that. "That is part of the bargain. The duel is to the death. If you are successful, there will be no further retaliation against my family."

He slammed his body against the wall, once more testing his chains.

Lizanne observed his struggles but drew no pleasure from them. As difficult as it was to admit even to herself, she was frightened.

Ranulf hardly knew himself, for he was accustomed to being in control of his person—thinking first and well before acting—but this was no ordinary foe. This was a woman who had reduced him to a level no man had ever done. Thus, it was no easy thing to talk his emotions down from the violent ledge they had stepped out upon.

When he finally settled himself, he dropped his head back and pinned his gaze to his captor.

"So much anger," she murmured.

He frowned. Her eyes were flat, as was her voice that lacked the sarcasm he would have expected. It was as if she had gone someplace else. Might she be mad? If so, it would certainly explain some things.

When she spoke again, her voice was softer yet. "I, too, know such anger. 'Tis the reason you are here." She nodded as if to herself. "My family and I have suffered greatly for your crimes. Thus, we will have our revenge."

"What are these crimes you put upon me?" Ranulf demanded. "What have I done to you, Lizanne Balmaine?"

She blinked and, for a moment, appeared confused. Then her mouth pressed into a tight line. "That is the bargain I strike with you. I will have your word on it. Now."

He shook his head. "Neither will I be cheated of revenge, for it is more my due than yours."

In the glare of torchlight, he saw color suffuse her face, her shoulders move with shallow breaths. "Give me your word," she snapped, "else die the death of a coward on the morrow."

He frowned. Though doubtful of her threat, he found himself reconsidering her challenge and wondered if what she proposed was simply a way out of the mistake she had made in imprisoning him.

Likely, for the woman who stood before him now was not the same one who had been so arrogantly confident earlier in the day. Indeed, it was possible she had even shed tears, for he had seen that her eyes were red and slightly swollen.

Deciding her proposal was not without merit, especially as he had no desire to remain chained in this cell a moment longer than necessary, he slid his gaze over her soft white neck and down her robe that revealed a glimpse of the undergarment beneath its hem. "Very well, I give you my word. Of course, it remains to be seen whether or not I keep it." He smiled. "Though I am inclined to leave your family be, know that you may not be so fortunate."

He expected her to protest, but she said, "'Tis enough. On the morrow, then."

"On the morrow, *my* lady."

Her nostrils flared, but she swung away and came as near to running from the cell as one could come without actually putting to flight.

When the door slammed shut and darkness once more descended, Ranulf considered the dagger that pressed against the backside of his thigh where he sat upon it, certain it was the reason the lady had ventured to the cell in the middle of the night.

After devouring the dinner Samuel had brought him earlier, he had succumbed to whatever had been added to his food or drink to render him impotent. Fortunately, it was an offense that served him well, for not only had his tunic been returned to him and his leg skillfully bandaged and curiously painless, but he was no longer chained upright. Seated upon the floor, he had been able to retrieve the dagger with his right foot and, with some difficulty, work it up beneath his left leg.

Of course, it was of no use to him now, but once he could bring it to hand...

4

Ranulf was awakened the next morning by Samuel's ungainly clamor and the smell of food. He watched as the big man, two men-at-arms following, traversed the cell.

"You," Samuel addressed the men, "light the torches."

With a murmur of assent, the men moved away.

"Yer awake bright and early," Samuel greeted Ranulf as he lowered a tray to the floor. Straightening, he planted his hands on his hips and frowned as he peered into Ranulf's face. "It does not appear ye slept well last night, an' after all me trouble to make ye comfortable."

"It was unkind of you to drug me."

Samuel lifted a palm heavenward. "'Twas but a mild sleeping draught. Seeing as I had only me wife's help, it was the easiest way to tend yer wound and clothe ye."

"Surely, you are not frightened of me?"

The great man scowled. "Ain't no man frightens big Samuel. 'Twas me wife, Lucy, who insisted. Saw that bloody nose ye gave our lady and wouldna come down till ye were out fer certain."

Ranulf made no attempt to suppress his smile. "Forsooth, I am grateful to you, Samuel—and your Lucy. My leg does not pain me as it did, and I am certainly more comfortable sitting than standing."

Samuel's chest puffed with pride. "Lucy's good with medicines and herbs. Taught by the lady herself."

"Lady Lizanne?" Ranulf could not keep disbelief from his voice.

"Aye. Fer all her wildness, that one has a gift fer healin'. Takes care of everyone, she does."

Ranulf attempted to fit this odd bit of information among his other impressions of the woman. After a few moment's deliberation, he lumped it with a growing number of oddities.

"Here now!" Samuel raised his voice and crossed the cell in a half-dozen strides. "Do I have to do it meself?" He took the torch from the men and quickly lit the others.

"Simpletons," he grumbled when he returned to stand before Ranulf. "'Twill be a relief once Baron Balmaine returns. Gone to court and took his best men with him, he did. And now him delayed." He heaved a sigh.

Ranulf pretended an interest in the food as he pondered Samuel's words. The man was proving a good source of information. Perhaps he could learn more.

Samuel did not disappoint. "Highly improper, I say, to allow Lady Lizanne to come home to Penforke with all this disorder. And she only makes matters worse with all her lordin'."

Penforke. Ranulf searched his knowledge of the southern lands in an attempt to determine his location. It was not far from Langdon's castle.

Samuel leaned down and removed the manacle from Ranulf's left wrist. "Knows she can get away with it, of course. Ain't a one ceptin' her brother that'll tell her nay, and even he usually gives in to her. I ain't ne'er understood it. Been that way since me Lucy and I came here."

Ranulf accepted the warm, freshly baked bread Samuel shoved into his free hand.

"He knows better 'n to leave her to her own devices. That one needs supervision, I tell ye. And look what she's done bringin' ye here. Can't say as I like it. Nay, canna say as I do."

Ranulf was tempted to insert his own comments on that subject but, fearful of alerting Samuel to his loose tongue, squashed the idea. He bit into the bread and glanced at the other men. Bent over a table, they were engaged in a game of dice.

Samuel loosed another sigh. "Have a taste o' that brew. 'Tis the best fer miles around."

Ranulf lifted the pot of ale and took a deep swallow while he waited for Samuel to speak again.

He did not. Hearing a cry of triumph from across the cell, the bald man looked over his shoulder to the others, one of whom tossed his newly won wealth from one hand to the other. Samuel grunted, shot Ranulf an apologetic smile, and trotted off to join the game.

Ranulf was satisfied with what he had gleaned from the man's grumblings, and now that he was forgotten, the need to secure the dagger was uppermost in his mind. Keeping his eyes on the three men, he retrieved it from beneath his leg, lifted the hem of his tunic, and slid the keen-edged weapon into the top of his chausses.

Attired in men's garb, Lizanne sat atop her gray palfrey and peered through the trees bordering the meadow. On a baldric passing from her right shoulder to her hip hung a two-edged sword. In a scabbard attached to the saddle was a second.

Beneath her, the mare shifted restlessly, throwing its head to the right and straining against the reins Lizanne held in her gloved hands.

"Shh, Lady." Lizanne leaned over the mare's neck and stroked the favored spot between the pert ears. "'Twill not be long now."

The mare was only recently saddle-broke, but she had a spirit and grace that had immediately caught Lizanne's eye. In spite of Gilbert's misgivings about the animal's flighty temperament, he had gifted the horse to his sister for her eighteenth year that had come and gone a twelvemonth past.

Lizanne straightened and glanced at the sun's position, wondering not for the first time if Samuel had misunderstood her instructions, perhaps intentionally.

But then she heard the thunder of hooves.

Three horsemen entered the meadow from its southernmost corner. At the fore rode Samuel, and pulling up the rear was the armed escort. Ranulf Wardieu rode between the two, a long mantle about his shoulders, short boots on his feet.

Lady whinnied in welcome. Thankfully, the noise went unnoticed, eclipsed by the beating of hooves. At its mistress's command, the mare pranced backward and assumed a detached stance to await the next instruction.

Lizanne watched as the horses were reined in at the center of the meadow and held her breath while Samuel scanned the bordering wood.

He had made it clear he did not like the orders she had delivered at noon and had suggested they await her brother's return before doing anything further. Lizanne had been adamant, instructing him to escort the prisoner to the meadow east of the castle and release him. With a suspicious gleam in his eyes, Samuel had agreed.

Shortly, Ranulf Wardieu dismounted with an ease that belied the injury he had suffered the day before. He tossed the reins to Samuel and said something that made the other man laugh. More words were exchanged, then a sack was handed down—provisions, no doubt.

Lizanne drew a sharp breath. Samuel had disregarded her orders again. It was small wonder he was not also providing the cur with a horse.

Lady must have felt her mistress's mounting tension, for she tossed her head, and her great, soulful eyes rolled back. With whispered words of assurance, Lizanne soothed her while never taking her eyes from Ranulf Wardieu.

Pale hair lifting in the warm breeze of early summer where he stood in the long grass, he turned to watch his escort depart, but even when the riders disappeared and the pounding of hooves faded away, Lizanne did not move. Less than eager to finish what she had started, she gripped the mare's silky mane and fought the panic that, if she did not beat it down, would send her back to the safety of the castle.

It was Lady who decided the matter, lunging from the cover of trees into the meadow.

Providence, Lizanne concluded. As she spurred the mare into a gallop, the hood of her short mantle slid off her head.

Ranulf turned and stared at the horse and rider, felt the ticklish vibrations of their approach through the thin soles of his borrowed boots. Though he tried to assess his opponent, the man was too distant, and the sun was at his back.

When the glint of steel caught his eye, he grimaced at the grisly task before him. A vision of the lady safe behind the walls of her castle while she sent another to his death only served to deepen his anger and resolve.

He did not want this man's life. He would be satisfied only with avenging himself upon Lady Lizanne. And though he would keep his vow to hold her family blameless, he had determined to take her as she had taken him. If that meant doing battle with the brother, so be it.

Thus, it was with astonishment that he found himself staring up into the flushed countenance of that lady when she brought her horse to a halt before him. It was the first time he had seen her face without the cover of her unkempt hair, it now being confined to a thick braid, and he was pleased by the flawless oval above a slender throat.

"Welcome, Baron Wardieu. 'Tis a fine day for a duel."

He inclined his head. "Forsooth, I did not expect you to attend this bloodletting. I must needs remember you are not a lady."

Her jaw hardened. "I assure you, there is naught that would keep me from this."

He looked at the weapons she carried, then past her. "Where is this man who would champion your ill-fated cause?"

"There is no man."

Ranulf lifted an eyebrow. "You were unable to find a single man willing to die for you?"

She leaned forward and smiled faintly. "Alas, I fear I am so uncomely none would offer."

Suspicion creeping in, Ranulf said, "What of our bargain?"

"It stands."

"You think to hold me 'til your brother finds his way home?" He shifted more of his weight onto his uninjured leg and took a step toward her. "I vow you will not return me to that vile cell."

The mare snorted loudly and pranced sideways until the lady brought it under control.

"Nay," she said, gaze unwavering, "your opponent is here before you now."

It took Ranulf a moment to comprehend the incomprehensible, then he laughed. As preposterous as it was, a woman challenging an accomplished knight, her proposal did not surprise him—though it did amuse him—for it fit the conclusions he had wrestled with regarding her character.

Had she a death wish, then? Even if that spineless brother of hers had shown her how to swing a sword, it was inconceivable she would be proficient with such a heavy weapon. A sling, perhaps, and he mustn't forget a dagger, but a sword?

He blinked back tears of mirth as she edged her horse nearer, indignation evident in her bearing.

"I find no humor in the situation," she said. "Mayhap you would care to enlighten me, Baron Wardieu?"

"Doubtless, you would not appreciate my explanation, my lady."

Her chin went up. "You think I will not make a worthy opponent?"

"With your nasty tongue, perhaps, but—"

"Then let us not prolong the suspense." She removed the sword from its scabbard and tossed it to him.

Ranulf pulled it from the air and closed his hand around the cool metal hilt. He was taken aback as he held it aloft, for inasmuch as the weapon appeared perfectly honed on both edges, it was not the weighty sword to which he was accustomed. Indeed, it was so light that it felt awkward in his grasp.

"What is this? A child's toy?" He twisted it side to side.

In one fluid motion, Lady Lizanne dismounted. "'Tis that which will determine whether you live or die, my lord." Advancing on him, she drew her own sword, one identical to that which he held.

He lowered his sword's point. "Think you I would fight a woman?"

"'Tis as we agreed."

"I agreed to fight a man—"

"You agreed to fight the opponent of my choosing. I stand before you now ready to fulfill our bargain."

"We have no such bargain."

"Would you break your vow? Are you so dishonorable?"

Never had Ranulf's honor been questioned. For King Henry and, when necessary, himself, he fought hard and well, and he carried the battle scars to attest to his valor. Still, her insult rankled.

"'Tis honor that compels me to decline," he said.

"Honor?" She halted a few feet from him. "Methinks 'tis your injury, coward. Surely you can still wield a sword?"

Feeling his jaw tighten, he acknowledged this woman was expert at stirring the depths of his anger. "Were you a man, you would be dead now."

"Then imagine me a man." She raised her sword.

The very notion was laughable. Even garbed as she was, Lady Lizanne was wholly woman.

"I fear I must decline." He leaned on the sword. "'Twill make a fine walking stick, though." He flexed the blade beneath his weight.

She took a step nearer. "You cannot decline!"

"Aye, and I do."

"Then I will gut you like a pig!" She leaped forward.

Instinctively, Ranulf swept his sword up to meet hers. The strength behind her controlled swing surprised him. Had he not been prepared, her blow might well have landed across his neck.

Still, he was confident she presented no real threat. It would be easy enough to disarm her, but perhaps he would humor her a few minutes until she tired.

He smiled and, with a shove forward, pushed her sword off his.

She fell back a step and countered with a wide, arcing swing. A moment later, the point of her sword found its mark just shy of his right eye.

Ranulf clapped a hand to the thin tear that ran up into his hairline.

"Do not underestimate me!" she spat and resumed her attack.

Although he was more angry with himself than her, Ranulf's tolerant disposition altered significantly. He had indeed underestimated her ability—and her conviction. It was ages since an opponent had landed him a blow, and to have a woman do so was an insult.

Castigating himself for his former nonchalance, he assumed a proper dueling stance and thrust his sword forward, easily knocking her next blow aside.

She recovered and, with an unladylike snarl, came at him again.

She was swift and accurate, taking full advantage of his disability, just as she had promised. Though she was well practiced and proficient with a sword, her chief advantage lay in the ease and grace with which she maneuvered. One moment she was fully to his right, the next she attacked from the left. Even so, with Ranulf's body mass and years of experience, he easily deflected her blows, wearing her down beneath the forceful impacts with which he countered.

When she stumbled, he pressed the advantage and slashed his sword across her chest. It could have meant her death, but he was too precise for such an error. Instead, he cleanly opened her tunic and scored a thin, neat line across her collarbone.

She spared a brief glance downward before raising her sword and swinging near his midline.

Ignoring the protests of his injured leg, Ranulf sidestepped, then advanced on her. With deliberate acceleration, he drove her back, but still she fought, her tenacity sustaining her in the face of failing strength. Even when she labored for breath, now using both hands to guide her swings, she pressed onward.

With growing satisfaction, Ranulf watched her sword grow heavier, noted the perspiration on her skin and the frenzied look that entered her eyes as he forced her out of her offensive posture into one of pure defense. She was his.

Deciding it was time to end the senseless exhibition, he hoisted his sword a final time, put his whole body behind it, and brought it forcefully down upon her steel.

The unthinkable happened. At the juncture where blade fused with hilt, his sword snapped.

He looked up to find Lizanne with her own sword frozen midair. She stared, cheeks flushed, lips parted, hair loosed from its braid, rivulets of moisture meandering down the flawless skin of her face and neck and over her scored collarbone.

He heaved a sigh. "Inferior steel," he pronounced and tossed the hilt aside.

Feeling her dagger where it pressed against his abdomen and knowing he might have to use it to subdue her, he stepped forward. "I am resigned to my fate, witch. Have mercy and be quick about it."

Sword before her, Lizanne took a step backward. Though her moment was surely at hand, thoughts of revenge began to desert her. She had never killed a man. For that matter, she had only ever taken small game—and with her bow. In the next instant, she accepted what Wardieu knew. She could not take his life.

"To the death," he said, lengthening his stride. "Was that not our bargain?"

She bolted for her horse. Though she heard Wardieu give chase, each time she glanced around, she was assured of a chance to escape. He was never far behind, but his injury slowed him enough to gain her the time needed to reach Lady.

Hastily, she sheathed her sword, hoisted herself onto the mare's back, and gathered the reins. She pulled hard, causing the horse to rear and cleave the air with its hooves. And bring her pursuer to a halt.

"I give you back your life, Ranulf Wardieu," she shouted above the mare's agitated cry. "'Tis finished!" Veering away, she pressed her heels into Lady's sides and galloped across the meadow without a backward glance.

Ranulf watched her go. "Nay," he breathed, "it has only begun, Lizanne of Penforke."

5

"Ah, Mellie! 'Tis my brother who comes, not a suitor," Lizanne protested as the young maid pressed her down onto a stool and began combing her hair.

"Aye, but ye've not seen him nigh on two months." Mellie tugged at a troublesome snarl. "Ye know he prefers it when ye look the lady."

"I do look the lady."

"Ah, but such an occasion warrants more effort than simply droppin' a veil over your hair, especially as you've donned your finest."

Mellie was right. Though Gilbert did not speak against his sister's preference for hiding her mess of hair beneath a veil or wrestling it into a sloppy braid, she knew he liked it when she gave herself into Mellie's capable hands. Thus, for him she would do this, but none other. She only hoped it would not be in vain and he would, indeed, return on this, the sixth day since she had released Ranulf Wardieu.

Her insides churned at the thought of that man. As each uneventful day passed, she grew increasingly confident her brother would return in time to quell any retaliation Wardieu might undertake. However, in the event she was wrong, she had seen the castle's defenses strengthened as much as possible. But Wardieu had not come, and now it seemed unlikely he would.

When the torturous tugging finally ended, Lizanne stood, only to be urged back down. Glowering, she squirmed as Mellie applied hot irons to her hair, creating orderly curls that flowed down her back. Last, a light veil was placed upon her head and secured with a silver circlet.

She would have left her chamber then, but Mellie pressed a small mirror in her hand.

As Lizanne viewed her reflection from different angles, she was ashamed at her twinges of pleasure. Arrayed in her best bliaut, an embroidered garment of green samite slit up each side to reveal a saffron-colored chemise beneath, she looked every bit the lady—the picture of femininity that, as a gawky girl, she had dreamed of attaining. Thoughtfully, she fingered the ornamental girdle settled loosely upon her hips.

Vain, she reproached, but could not refrain from staring. Gilbert would be pleased.

"You are lovely, milady," Mellie said.

Feeling heat rise in her face, Lizanne swatted at a lock of hair that fell across her cheek. "And now to be certain all is in order for my brother's return," she said.

Shortly, she descended the stairs. As she stepped into the hall, a lad of a dozen years rushed into her path. When he looked up at her, he appeared momentarily dumbstruck, then his head jerked as if he had been smacked.

His reaction to her appearance was almost enough to cause her to throw off the veil and drag fingers through her curls, but his words trampled the thought.

"Riders approach from the east, milady!"

Lizanne ran, unmindful of appearing unladylike as she hastened from the hall and out into the inner bailey. She sped over the inner drawbridge and across the outermost bailey and, at the gatehouse, threw the bulk of her skirts over one arm and ascended the stone steps two at a time. As she shouldered her way between the gathering of men on the roof, she looked out between the crenellations to the large group of riders descending upon Penforke.

Though they were still too distant for her to make out the pennants they flew, she knew it was Gilbert.

The riders disappeared as they plunged down a distant hillside and reappeared when they crested another hill.

Charged with a mixture of excitement and uncertainty over her brother's return, Lizanne shaded her eyes against the sun's glare and leaned out over the stone wall.

These many long weeks had not been easy. In spite of her disdain for court life, she would gladly have accompanied Gilbert if not for fear the king would once again undertake to match her with one of his knights. He had done just that the previous year, and she had caused a most unpleasant scene. In fact, so great was Gilbert's humiliation that he had not spoken to her for days thereafter.

Once she revealed her abduction of Ranulf Wardieu and his subsequent release, what would be her brother's reaction? For certain, it would not be good. She'd had too many days to reflect on her deed and accept the truth that, in her impatience to exact revenge, she had acted rashly.

Again, the riders disappeared.

In the lull, she turned to find Robert Coulter, the captain of the guard, behind her. A frown marred his aged countenance as he looked past her, his squinting more from failing eyesight than the sun's glare.

"Lower the drawbridge," she ordered.

"But, my lady—"

"Do not argue. Prepare a proper welcome for my brother."

Grumbling, he turned on his heel and strode opposite.

Lizanne returned her attention to the hills. Over the next rise, the lofty pennants were visible before the riders, their vivid blue, red, and gold colors backlit by sunlight that glinted off armor.

She beamed—until she looked again at the pennants. A denial tore from her lips at the same moment the drawbridge began its descent with a rattle of enormous chains. She rounded on the man nearest her. "Send word to raise the bridge. Run!"

Assisted by a thrust from his mistress, he sprinted to the stairs.

The drawbridge was three-quarters lowered before it came to a wrenching halt. Moments later, it began its laborious ascent. Amid a flurry of confusion, Lizanne swept her gaze back and forth between the drawbridge and the approaching riders.

On level ground now, the army of what appeared to be a hundred strong spurred their horses forward, the thundering of hooves rising above the land to strike fear in the castle folk who, having realized something serious was afoot, were making themselves scarce.

Though Lizanne did not know the colors of Ranulf Wardieu, she did not delude herself into believing the pennants belonged to any other.

He had returned.

She searched among the riders for their leader, eliminating those whose horses were devoid of the trappings emblazoned with the same colors as the pennants. Shortly, she settled her gaze on one who rode before the others, a man large even from a distance. Though his telling hair was covered by a mail hood and helmet, it had to be him.

Her skin pricked with a chill that raised every hair on her body and threatened to buckle her knees. Grasping the ledge of the stone wall, she squeezed her eyes closed in the silly hope that, when she opened them, a far different sight would greet her.

It did not.

Struggling for composure, she began weighing the alternatives she would soon be forced to choose among. Repeatedly, she came back to one—Gilbert. If she could keep Wardieu at bay, her brother's return would send the miscreant running. And surely Gilbert would appear this day. He must.

As Wardieu's men flanked the castle's curtain wall, reining in at a distance beyond the range of arrows, the drawbridge completed its return journey. Silence, save for the labored breathing of the great warhorses, fell.

Mounted astride an enormous destrier as dark as he was light, Ranulf raised his gaze to the top of the wall and searched out the scant men-at-arms visible there.

As he had expected Gilbert Balmaine to precede his own arrival, he was taken aback by the seemingly inadequate defenses. Still, appearances could be deceiving. He shifted his attention to the drawbridge that had been raised against him.

"What make you of this?" Sir Walter Fortesne asked as he urged his mount alongside Ranulf's.

Ignoring the question, Ranulf continued his inspection of the castle's fortifications. Although they appeared solid and in good repair, the stronghold would be difficult to defend if it lacked an adequate supply of well-trained men. One by one, he considered the avenues of attack available to him should one be necessary. There were several.

"'Twould appear the lord of the castle and his men have not yet returned," Walter said.

Ranulf smiled and was reminded of the healing cut near his right eye where the chain-mail hood grazed it. "If 'tis so, I shall have that which I came for ere the noon hour."

He lifted his gaze farther up the gatehouse and counted half a dozen men-at-arms stationed between the crenellations of the tower. Was she there? He searched for unruly black hair. As he considered each person, a lone figure to the left caught his attention.

He had only to shift his eyes to see the richly garbed woman who stood on the roof of the tower, motionless except for a white veil shifting in the breeze. Who was she? He had it from a reliable source there were no ladies at Penforke other than Lizanne Balmaine.

Deciding the woman was unworthy of his attention, Ranulf averted his gaze, but not before the air stirred briskly and lifted her veil. Then he knew.

Though he could not be certain from this distance, he thought her attention was fixed on him as well. And at that moment, he would have given much to be able to see her face up close. She would know it was he, although from her manner of dress, it was her brother she had expected. Most assuredly Gilbert Balmaine had not returned. Thus, it would take little effort to capture Penforke.

"My lord, is she the one?"

Ranulf turned his head toward Walter and saw his man had also picked out the lone woman. "Aye, Lady Lizanne."

A true friend and fiercely loyal, Walter was the only one Ranulf had entrusted with a recounting of his disappearance. Only he could guess at the emotions beneath his lord's composure—and just as easily disapprove of them.

The day following his release, Ranulf had met up with the search party Walter had organized to find him. Forcing logic to dictate his actions, he had temporarily set aside his plans for revenge and returned to Langdon's castle to conclude his business there.

He had offered no explanation for his absence to the overwrought Lord Langdon and had set to working day and night to resolve the differences between the lord and his vassal. However, at meals, he had made a point of engaging Langdon's wife in conversation. Initially, she had been close-mouthed on the subject of her cousin, Lizanne, but eventually she had been coaxed into enlightening him.

Of particular interest was the close relationship between Lizanne and her brother. The two were practically inseparable, and it was not uncommon for Lizanne to accompany Gilbert on his campaigns. That bit of information helped explain her facility with weapons, but it did not explain why the man allowed his sister to conduct herself in such a manner. By all rights, he should have wed her off long ago and been done with her. Thus, Ranulf wondered if Gilbert Balmaine would appreciate the favor that was about to be done him.

When he returned his gaze to the gatehouse, Lizanne was no longer visible. Motioning Walter to accompany him, he urged his mount forward.

A select portion of his retainers took up their bows and followed until they were just within arrow range.

Ranulf and Walter paused to accept the shields their squires passed to them, then proceeded to within feet of the arid moat.

"I am Baron Ranulf Wardieu," Ranulf shouted. "I command you to surrender and lower the drawbridge."

Silence.

"Who speaks for this castle?" he demanded.

"I do!"

Of course she did. Catching a flash of green fabric between the crenellations of the gatehouse, Ranulf called, "Do you yield?"

Her answer was an arrow that pierced the cool morning air and cleaved the ground before his destrier. Startled, the horse reared and would have bolted if not for his master's firm hand.

At once, Ranulf's men loosed a barrage of arrows.

With an angry shout and a throw of his arm, Ranulf suspended the counterattack and searched out Lizanne, but once again she had gone from sight. Had she taken cover? Or had an arrow found its target?

"That was but a warning, Wardieu," she shouted. "The next will find your heart."

He resented the relief that swept through him. After all he had suffered at her hands, he should not care that she was unharmed.

"I would not test her were I you," Walter said, peering at Ranulf from behind the cover of his shield.

Just as he would not have had his lord undertake the task of righting this injustice. Ranulf cast him a look to silence further advice and called, "Show yourself, Lady Lizanne."

"I regret I must decline."

"I vow no harm will befall you."

"Ha!"

Ranulf fought down his anger. "Blood need not be spilled over this."

"'Tis your blood that will spill. Even now, my brother rides to defend his home."

"In that you are wrong!" Though Ranulf had not considered such a deception, it rose so easily to his lips he could not refrain.

His words achieved the desired effect. Lizanne moved into the open, the drawn bow with its nocked arrow trained on him. She stood alone among the crenellations, her men-at-arms having disappeared from view.

Ranulf suppressed the smile that tried to turn his lips. Though she was suitably attired as the lady of Penforke, the picture she presented of soft femininity was at odds with her defiant bearing, made even more prominent by her state of dishabille.

He studied the face behind the bow. A dark smudge slashed diagonally across her brow and disappeared beneath the hand grasping the bow's string. One eye was leveled down the arrow's shaft at him, her mouth was grimly set, and much of her curled hair sprang free of the veil that, having slipped from the restraining circlet, hung unevenly.

"Shield yourself, Ranulf!" Walter exclaimed. "She means to run you through."

Refusing to break eye contact with her, Ranulf remained unmoving.

"What have you done with my brother?" she demanded.

"He is alive," Ranulf said, ignoring Walter's startle of surprise.

Lizanne's arm wavered. "Where is he?"

"He is safe. For now."

Her gasp was audible. "Tell me where he is!"

He urged his mount nearer the edge of the moat. "Mayhap I will take you to him."

"I shall go nowhere with you!"

"And I shall go nowhere without you, even if it means the lives of your people." He allowed his words to sink in before continuing. "Their fate, and that of your brother, is in your hands, Lizanne of Penforke. Yield, and I give you my word there shall be no bloodshed."

She maintained her offensive stance and Ranulf began to worry about the arrow trained upon him. Not that he thought she meant to shoot him, but the sustained effort of keeping the string taut was surely wearing on her. In readiness should she unintentionally loose the arrow, he tensed his shield arm.

When she spoke again, he had to strain to catch her words.

"I would bargain with you."

He thinned his lips into a hard smile. "I know all about your bargains, Lady Lizanne." Had he not been forced to raise a sword against her? "Not only am I done bargaining, but you are in no position to ask such."

"Would you have me dead or alive?" she threw back, her veil slipping farther.

"Naturally, I would prefer you alive."

"Then you will honor my terms."

He did not like being forced to make concessions, particularly to her, and certainly not in front of his men, but he said, "What would you ask of me?"

"I will come with you. In exchange, you are not to enter these walls."

He almost laughed, for it was more than agreeable. "And?"

"You will release my brother and hold him blameless for my actions."

"And?"

"'Tis all."

Then she would make no demands for her own safety—a miscalculation on his part, for it would have pleased him to refuse at least one of her demands. He looked to Walter. The man was clearly amused. Ranulf was not.

"My quarrel is with you, Lizanne Balmaine," he called. "Hence, I shall honor your terms. No harm will befall those of Penforke."

"And my brother?"

"Gilbert as well."

"I would have your word."

He grasped the hilt of his sword. "I give you my word."

She began to lower the bow, only to swiftly raise it and release the arrow. It found its target, rending the fabric of a raised pennant.

"I will not make this easy for you, Ranulf Wardieu," she shouted and disappeared from sight.

"I did not expect you would," he muttered. Nevertheless, he had won.

Alone atop the gatehouse, Lizanne dropped her bow and knelt behind the battlements. Steepling her hands before her face, she struggled to summon a prayer in the hope God had not set her aside as she had very nearly done Him four years past, but all she could manage was, "If You are there…" She shook her head, opened her eyes.

The very thought of what Wardieu would do to her made her knees quake and heart skip. When she gave herself into his hands, he would surely take what she had wrested from him four years past—and more. And when he finished with her, would he give her to his men? Kill her?

She felt the sting of tears. Her thirst for revenge had brought her to this moment. Was this why it was said vengeance belonged to God?

With feet that dragged, she descended to the outer bailey where the castle folk had gathered before the gatehouse. Silently, she looked from one to the next.

They were frightened, the women wringing their hands and clutching their children against their sides, the men ashamedly bowing their heads and looking anywhere but at her. Even Robert Coulter could not meet her eyes.

"All will be well," she said. "My brother will return shortly. He will know what to do."

A murmur of opposition rose from the gathering, but died when Samuel and Lucy pushed their way through.

"Milady." Samuel lifted her hand and enveloped it in his much larger one. "Surely ye canna be thinkin' of giving yerself over?"

"There is no other course, Samuel. I must consider the welfare of our people—and my brother."

"Methinks it a bluff, milady. Baron Balmaine wouldna allow himself to fall prey to that man."

"I cannot be so sure." She pulled her hand free. "'Tis too great a risk." She turned to the captain of the guard. "Robert, lower the drawbridge."

He nodded and moved away.

"And raise the portcullis no more than is necessary for me to slip beneath. Once I am through, secure it."

"'Twill be done."

Mellie rushed forward and threw her arms around Lizanne's waist. "Nay, milady, ye cannot!"

Lizanne returned the girl's hug and disengaged herself. "I must."

"Then I will go with ye."

"Nay, I go alone."

Emotions flitted across Mellie's face as if she pondered a matter of grave importance, then she said, "Ye will have need of protection." She lifted her skirts, rummaged beneath them, and produced a meat dagger.

After a brief hesitation, Lizanne accepted it and concealed the weapon in the top of her hose as, for the second time that morning, the drawbridge began its descent. She smoothed her skirts. "Thank you, Mellie."

The girl reached up and straightened Lizanne's veil. "If ye look the lady, he will have no choice but to treat ye as one."

Lizanne did not think so, but she did not have the heart to disillusion her. She allowed Mellie to adjust the circlet and smooth her hair. However, when the girl began to rub at the smudge on her face, Lizanne stepped away and drew the back of a hand across the mark.

"Ye did not get it all." Mellie reached again.

Lizanne waved her off. "'Twill do." As the drawbridge neared its end, she turned and crossed to the arched portal. Standing before the portcullis, she once more tried to pray, this time by silently reciting a paternoster. However, the words that had been banished to the farthest reaches of her memory would not properly order themselves.

As the drawbridge revealed, bit by bit, the two mounted warriors before the moat, her heart quickened, then lurched when the immense, planked device joined with the stationary bridge that spanned half the moat.

Lizanne lifted her chin and stared straight ahead.

The portcullis groaned as it was raised, shuddered when it stopped at the level of her waist. Drawing a deep breath, she ducked beneath it and stepped out onto firm wooden planks. As directed, the iron gate immediately descended.

Lizanne met Wardieu's gaze across the breadth that separated them, then stepped forward. However, upon reaching the bridge's threshold, she stopped, determined he would have to meet her part of the way.

He dropped the reins and dismounted. With the metallic ring of his great hauberk echoing before him, he strode toward her.

Though he seemed a bit stiff in the leg, it appeared he had suffered no lasting ill effects from the wound to his thigh. But then, it had not been deep.

He halted before her. Though she was tall, he towered over her, and she reflected that he had not seemed as large chained to a wall. Was the armor responsible?

Determined to conceal the fear that made her feel so light of head that her consciousness was threatened, she crossed her arms over her chest and studied the face partially concealed beneath chain mail and the nasal guard of his helmet.

Ranulf was struck by the incredible bit of femininity before him. Though Lizanne Balmaine was tousled and rebellious, she was all woman. He did not want to like the sparkle of her very green, very candid eyes, the thick fringe of lashes that threw shadows beneath her delicately arched eyebrows, her perfectly bowed and rose-hued lips. But he did. And fought the desire to touch the sable hair that fell past her shoulders and which did not begin to resemble the wild mane of all those days past.

Was this truly the same woman? He lowered his eyes over her fitted bodice and saw that her chest rose and fell with the force of short, rasping breaths. Lower still, the ends of her curling hair caressed her hips.

He returned his gaze to her face, yanked the veil from her hair, and sent it and the circlet plummeting to the dry bed of the moat.

Lizanne could not control the startle that propelled her backward, but Wardieu did. His large hands fell to her shoulders and wrenched her forward, bringing her face within inches of his. Here were the cold, angry eyes that had haunted her nights, so dark it was impossible to distinguish where color ended and pupil began.

"Surely, you are not frightened of me?" he said, his breath stirring the hair at her temples.

She narrowed her lids. "Does not your flesh bear my mark, Baron Wardieu?"

His hold tightened and tension appeared around his lips.

"I will never fear you," she lied, "and lest you forget, I give fair warning. Do not show me your back."

Or what? You will put a knife in it? Coward. Even when you held him at the point of a sword, you could not finish what you had begun.

"You are fortunate we are not alone," he warned.

"You would not beat me in front of your men?" She raised her eyebrows. "You are truly gracious, *my lord.*"

He caught her chin in his leather-gauntleted hand. "I truly *am* your lord now. And you would do well to remember that."

She started to refute him, but his next words made her swallow hers.

"Are you armed?"

She hesitated, perhaps too long. "You need not worry. I left my bow behind." It was the truth, after all.

He dropped his hands to her waist and slid them over the material of her garments, searching his way down her body.

"Oh!" She twisted out of his grasp and jumped back when he reached to recapture her.

He straightened, removed his gloves. "I would see what you have hidden beneath your skirts. Lift them."

"I will not!"

He took a step toward her. She took a step back.

"Obey me, else I will tear the clothes from you."

"You would not!"

"I would," he said, then bridged the distance with a single stride.

Though she longed to refuse anew, the look on his face told her she did not dare. With a deeply held breath, she hiked up her skirts to her knees.

Wardieu bent and ran his hands up from her ankles.

Warmed by humiliation, Lizanne trained her eyes on his companion where he sat astride his mount. The man looked thoughtful, even troubled, but when he met her gaze, whatever had shown on his face passed and he raised his eyebrows as if he was amused by her disgrace.

She scowled and turned her attention to the mounted soldiers who flanked the moat. They also appeared to be enjoying the spectacle.

When Wardieu's hands turned around her thighs, she gasped and looked down.

Ranulf was not surprised to discover the lady was armed, though he certainly did not expect her weapon of choice to be the puny meat dagger he pulled from the top of her hose. He looked up, smiled wryly at her wide-eyed expression, and straightened.

She thrust her skirts down, muttered, "I had to try."

"*This* is trying?" He glanced at the dagger, raised his eyebrows. "I am almost disappointed."

Her nostrils flared. "As you ought to have learned from your last visit to Penforke, the particular weapon is of less consequence than the person behind it."

Ranulf caught back the anger she seemed intent on rousing. Though he had not expected her to grovel, he had believed she would be sensible enough to suspend her hostilities. Any other woman would have used her beauty and charm to soothe him, but not Lizanne Balmaine. She was unlike any woman he had encountered.

"As you say," he said, "'tis the person behind it." He tossed the dagger aside and stepped nearer. "Three times, Lizanne of Penforke, you had the chance to slay me, once with a dagger, once with a sword, and today an arrow. Three times you failed."

"A mistake I intend to remedy."

"I am sure you will try." He grasped her arm and pulled her toward his destrier.

She dug her heels in, forcing him to half-carry, half-drag her across the short distance.

"What of my brother?" she demanded when he halted before Walter.

Ignoring her, Ranulf looked to his man. "She shall ride with you."

Walter's face shone with distaste. Unfortunately for him, Ranulf did not trust himself with Lizanne. Though it was not in his nature to strike a woman, he had felt near to it these last few minutes. Doubtless, if she rode with him, she would continue her verbal assault and, at the moment, he needed respite from her waspish tongue.

He lifted her onto the back of Walter's mount, but she immediately scooted backward and nearly unseated herself, causing the great destrier to prance sideways.

Grinding his teeth, Ranulf transferred her to the fore of the saddle.

Reluctantly, Walter encircled her waist with one arm and drew her back against his armored chest.

When she strained away from him, Ranulf gripped her thigh. "You would do well to remember these are your terms, Lizanne. You keep your side of the bargain, and I shall keep mine. Now accept your fate and show some dignity."

She was slow to still, but when she did, that chin of hers went up. "I would have you take me to my brother that I might see no harm has befallen him."

As it was neither the time nor place to disabuse her of her brother's capture, for he did not doubt she would prove far more difficult when she learned the truth, Ranulf turned away. Disregarding the questions and demands hurled at his back, he swung into his saddle and spurred his destrier away from Penforke.

Walter stared after his lord, then turned his horse's head. As he did so, the woman given into his care snapped her chin around and peered at her home with moist eyes. Moved as he knew he should not be, he was once more beset with doubt over the course Ranulf had set himself.

As the drawbridge chains sounded behind, Lizanne Balmaine slid her gaze to Walter's, and he felt as if he looked into the eyes of a frightened girl. However, in the next instant, the angry woman who had abducted and subjected his lord to degradation gave him a hateful glare.

Good, she deserves no pity, he told himself. But as he set his horse to a gallop amid the thunder of hooves that sounded the army's retreat, she was forced back against his chest and he regretted the silent sobs that moved her shoulders.

Oh, Lady, what have you done? And what am I to do about it?

When Ranulf had revealed his encounter with her at Penforke, Walter had understood his lord's desire for revenge. But revenge it was. Though it was agreed the lady should not go unpunished, Walter had encouraged Ranulf to find a better way to see justice served, especially since she had professed to have a good reason for abducting him. But regardless of what that crime was, she had to be mistaken, for Ranulf Wardieu was a man of honor. Walter had seen to that himself, training him up in arms as well as faith.

Unfortunately, Ranulf had refused to be dissuaded from repaying abduction with abduction, which had surprised Walter—until he had pondered the brief and distant encounter between his lord and the lady in Langdon's hall. Clearly, Ranulf had been captivated by the shrew. And he still was.

Walter shook his head. For all of his lord's talk of making the lady suffer as he had suffered, there was more than revenge behind the taking of Lizanne Balmaine. Ranulf surely did not realize it, but it was more likely he was looking for a bride than a settling of scores. If so, it was upon Walter to make him see sense.

6

LIZANNE HAD NOT intended to sleep and was astonished that she had been able to considering the pace set by Wardieu.

Muddled by her abrupt awakening, she yielded to the hands that lifted her from the horse's back and allowed them to support her when her knees buckled and toppled her forward onto an armored chest. Cheek smarting from its brush with the rough links of armor, she lifted her head.

Wardieu had removed his helmet and unbuckled his chain-mail hood so that it hung loosely over the collar of his hauberk and revealed his pale hair, the length of which remained tucked beneath the neck of his armor.

Lizanne was captivated by the effects of the setting sun behind him. Like a halo, it surrounded him and gave color to his colorless hair. She lowered her gaze. Had his eyes softened? Was that a smile tucking up the corners of his mouth? Without thinking, she reached up and traced the cut above his eye into his hairline.

"'Twill not even scar," she murmured.

His eyes reflected surprise at her boldness, and only then did she realize what she did and snatch her hand away.

What had she been thinking? The man was evil—could not possibly put aside a past such as his. Horrified that she had willingly touched him, she thrust her hands against his chest and began to struggle.

Immediately, he set her back from him, and when she looked up, his face was hard again.

"Come!" He turned on his heel, retrieved his horse's reins, and led his destrier toward where the others tethered their horses.

Lizanne folded her arms over her chest and stared after him.

"I will drag you if needs be," he called over his shoulder.

The thought of that humiliation gained her capitulation. She followed, maintaining a safe distance as they crossed the meadow where a camp was being erected for the night. A half dozen wagons that had not been present earlier were grouped near the horses, and she guessed they had joined the party while she slept.

Leveling her gaze on a spot between Wardieu's shoulder blades, she sidestepped the soldiers in her path. For each interested look she received, she lifted her chin a degree until it was so high she stumbled and nearly fell over an exposed root.

She glared at the chortling group of men who had paused in the midst of raising a tent to witness her clumsiness. They grinned wider.

"My lord," Wardieu's squire called, hurrying forward. "I've the rope you asked for."

Wardieu accepted it and lowered his head as the animated young man spoke to him. Their words were hushed, and Lizanne could not make sense of them across the distance. Curious, she took a step nearer, then another, and pulled herself up short when Wardieu straightened.

"See he is given plenty of oats and water, Geoff," he instructed, stroking the horse's neck.

"Aye, my lord." The squire stole a glance at Lizanne and led the horse away.

Wardieu watched their departure, then turned to Lizanne, looped the rope beneath his belt, and raised his eyebrows.

She turned her back on him and pretended an interest in the flurry of activity.

Shortly, a hand closed over her upper arm.

As Wardieu pulled her behind him, she searched for scathing words to toss at his back. Then she saw where she was being led—a copse of trees. What he had tried to do to her four years past when he had taken her deep into the wood came thundering back to her and she dug her heels in and wrenched at her arm.

He gripped her tighter and increased his stride, forcing her to match his pace to keep her feet beneath her.

Dear God, this cannot be happening. Not again!

Shockingly, he released her at the edge of the meadow and pushed her forward. "Relieve yourself, and be quick else I shall interrupt your privacy."

Then he did not mean to...?

She expelled her breath, ducked beneath a low-hanging branch, and hurried into the wood. Though it occurred to her she might be able to outrun him given the extra minutes' lead she would have, she grimly accepted that, until Gilbert was released, escape was not an option.

Not wanting to give Wardieu an excuse to humiliate her further, she finished quickly and hurried back.

"You try my patience," he said. "Another minute and I would have come after you, regardless of your state."

"'Tis not so easy for a lady," she snapped.

"Were you one, I would make allowances."

Though she wanted to argue the matter, she knew it would be folly to attempt to persuade him that she was, indeed, a lady. "Nevertheless," she said, "there are differences."

"I assure you, I am aware of them."

She tilted her head to the side. "I do not believe you are."

Ranulf knew better than to act on impulse, but he caught her arm, pulled her into the shelter of trees, and drew her against him. "If you would like a demonstration of my knowledge," he said, "I am willing to oblige."

As she stared up at him, he felt his annoyance ease. He liked the feel of this wild-haired vixen and the glimpses of femininity beneath the hardened exterior she hid behind.

It unsettled him to admit it, even if only to himself, but the attraction he had felt the day he had first seen her at Langdon's castle had not diminished though he had tried to convince himself it had. Having spent every spare moment planning his revenge, he was surprised by the intensity of his feelings and, once more, tried to push them down, but to no avail.

He shifted his gaze to her parted lips, told himself he should not, then lowered his head and covered her mouth with his. At the taste of her, his annoyance receded further and he drew her nearer. It was some moments before he realized she was completely unresponsive.

He raised his head. Wide-eyed, but otherwise expressionless, she held his gaze.

Nay, he amended, she gazed through him. The infuriating woman had removed herself from the present. In fact, she would likely crumple to the ground if he released her.

It had not occurred to him she might be frigid and, even now, with the evidence before him, it was difficult to accept. There was too much fire and spirit in her for it to be anything other than a defensive ploy—a means of cooling a man's ardor.

"Lizanne!" He gave her a shake.

Pulled back from the scenes that had burst upon her mind, Lizanne blinked, and the past and present melded as she focused on the face above hers. It was the same one that plagued her dreams, yet somehow different. The realization unsettled her, and she instinctively knew that something more than the intervening years was responsible for the discrepancy. It went deeper, and it confused and alarmed her.

Wardieu was smiling now, though the expression did not reach his eyes. "I think 'tis you who does not understand the difference between the sexes," he said. "You have much to learn, but I shall enjoy instructing you."

It was just what she needed to snap her out of her stupor. She flew at him with hands, feet, and angry words, but his only response was to pull her tight against him and hold her until she was overcome with exhaustion.

When she stilled, he lifted her chin and touched a corner of her mouth with his thumb. "First, I will teach you to kiss."

She gasped. "Never!"

With a laugh that echoed around the wood, he released her and swung away.

Grudgingly, Lizanne lifted her skirts and tramped after him. When she emerged from the thicket, it was to find him uncoiling the rope.

He motioned her forward.

"Nay."

He looked up. "'Twill not bode well if I must needs collect you."

Mouth dry, she remained unmoving.

He grumbled something, and she flinched when he strode toward her. However, he merely said, "Your hands."

"'Tis not necessary for you to fetter me."

He caught her wrists together and wound the rope around them.

She tried to pull free. "You bind them too tight."

"I but repay in kind." He glanced at his own wrists that bore the marks of healing flesh.

She averted her eyes. "Surely you know I will not attempt an escape as long as you hold Gilbert."

He knotted the rope and led her to a tree where he eased her down into a sitting position with her back against it. "'Tis precisely the reason I do this," he said.

Lizanne frowned.

"Moreover," he continued as he began lashing her to the trunk, "I do not want you causing mischief among my men. There is much to be done ere nightfall, and you would surely distract them."

When he sat back on his heels, she considered the rope that bound her and defiance once more raised its head. "You think I cannot work my way out of this?"

His eyes narrowed, then momentarily closed. "You may try, but 'twill only waste your strength." He stood.

"What of Gilbert? You agreed to release him. Have you done so?"

He hesitated, then lowered to his haunches, rubbed a hand over his mouth and chin, and slowly shook his head. "Nay."

Lizanne groped for words to express her outrage.

"You are turning an unbecoming shade of red," he noted.

"You gave me your word!"

"I did—that no harm would come to the people of Penforke or your brother. None has."

She shook her head. "You agreed to release Gilbert. You vowed this before your own men!"

Ranulf considered his knuckles. He would have liked to avoid the subject of her brother a while longer, for the leverage afforded by the deception was appealing in its simplicity. It had, after all, delivered her to him without bloodshed. However, she would have to be told, for it was not in her nature to be satisfied with evasive answers.

He returned his gaze to her. "I cannot release a man I do not hold, Lizanne."

Her eyes widened a moment before her face contorted with such fury it was almost laughable. "You deceived me!"

He shrugged.

Bound to the tree, her only recourse was to strike out with her legs, stirring up a cloud of dust and scattering stones in his direction. "Dishonorable swine!"

He held up a hand. "Lest you forget, 'twas you who assumed I had captured your brother. I neither confirmed nor denied it."

"You deliberately misled me!"

"I did." He stood. "It seemed best to use your assumption in order to protect your people from foolishly risking their lives for such an unworthy cause."

"Unworthy?" Her voice was strained.

"Aye. You are not worth dying for, Lizanne of Penforke."

To his surprise, he glimpsed vulnerability on her face before she masked it with a sweep of long lashes and a tightening of lips. A moment later, she dropped her head back against the tree and pinned him with eyes full of hatred.

Were it possible to lay a man down with such a look, he was certain he would be dead. There was far too much hate in Lizanne Balmaine.

"When you come to my tent tonight," he said, "I shall expect you to have worked through your anger."

"Then you had best not send for me!"

"But I shall." He pivoted and started across the meadow.

She threw angry words at his departing back, and though he had no intention of reacting, a particularly vile word turned him back. "If needs be, I will gag you," he warned and resumed his course.

Lizanne clamped her mouth shut. Only when he went from sight did she give in to the emotions that hammered at her temples with such intensity it seemed her head might split open.

She dropped her chin. "Ah, Gilbert, what have I done?"

There was no one to answer her, no one to offer hope for the wrong she had sought to right. A great sorrow, rooted in years of anger at the injustice suffered by her brother and her, descended, so thick she feared it might smother her.

"Now that you have her, what will you do with her?"

Walter's question was not unexpected, nor new to Ranulf, for he had asked it of himself numerous times since departing Penforke. Still, he resented it, and especially that he felt obliged to further discuss Lizanne Balmaine—so much that, rather than collect his prisoner himself, he had sent his squire and Walter's for her.

Confident the young men would follow his instructions and heed his warnings, he turned from their retreating backs and met the gaze of the man who stood at the center of the tent. "I shall teach her a much needed lesson."

"Methinks already you have done that, my lord."

"There is more she must learn."

"And there is more you must needs consider, Ranulf." Walter's familiar use of his name was a reminder that Ranulf had not always been his liege, but a young man in need of guidance. "You have abducted a noblewoman—"

"A favor repaid in kind."

Walter sighed. "For that, none would fault you, but are you prepared to defend your actions by revealing hers—that she knocked a warrior senseless, chained him, and forced him to cross swords with her?"

It was not a thing of which a man would boast, Ranulf allowed, but it was an offense that pride demanded not go unpunished. "I will deal with that when I come to it."

Walter took a step toward him. "You cannot have prayed about this."

Ranulf did not dare, for he was familiar enough with God to know revenge was not pleasing to Him. "I have not." He firmly held his gaze to the other man. "Nor shall I."

Disappointment staggered across the older man's face. "Then you will put aside all I taught you—all you know to be true."

"Lizanne Balmaine is my prisoner and will remain such."

Walter shook his head. "I shall be bold then and tell you what I see."

"What is that?"

"In spite of all that has gone between you and the lady, you desire her."

Ranulf knew he should not be surprised, for Walter knew him better than any. He pivoted, crossed to the tent opening, and came back around. "I know I should not, that she gives me no reason, but it is true."

Walter narrowed his eyes. "And?"

"And what?"

"You will further stir this hornet's nest by making her your leman?"

It *had* been a consideration—even before he had kissed her—and, in his anger, he had allowed her to believe he might be of such a mind.

Ranulf lifted a hand to his neck and kneaded the muscles there. "You know me, Walter. The lady would have to be willing, and this lady is not."

"In that I believe you are right."

He was, but if only he knew the reason! "She thinks me capable of all manner of ill and yet refuses to reveal what I have done to earn her wrath."

Walter closed the distance between them and gripped his shoulder. "Whatever it is, she is wrong. This I know."

Ranulf inclined his head. "I thank you, friend."

Walter lowered his arm. "And now I would advise you."

As Ranulf did not wish to be advised, but he did not send him away.

"Lizanne Balmaine is a noblewoman and will one day wed a nobleman. Even if you do not give in to temptation, 'twould be folly for you to share quarters with the lady."

Ranulf jutted his chin at the far side of the tent. "As you can see, there are two pallets, each in its own corner."

When he looked back around, disapproval compressed Walter's lips. "Folly, Ranulf," he repeated. "Unless you think to wed her yourself."

Had Walter struck with a fist rather than words, he could not have landed a harder blow. "I do not," Ranulf growled. "There is a world between desire for a shrew and spending one's life with one."

Walter sighed, crossed to the tent opening, and looked over his shoulder. "Still, you have not told me what you will do with her."

Ranulf clenched his hands. "When she reveals the crime of which I stand accused, then I will decide and not before."

"Let us pray 'tis not too late." Walter stepped outside and dropped the flap behind him.

It was dark and growing cold before anyone came for her. Her tears having dried, Lizanne squinted at the two sent to fetch her to Wardieu.

Their torches revealed youthful, somber faces. However, the one she recognized as Wardieu's squire was clearly trying to mask a grin.

Though the deception she was about to work made her want to retch for the severe punishment they would surely receive, she favored each with a smile and flirtatiously swept her lashes down.

Both youths broke into grins.

The taller one stepped forward. "I am Geoff, Baron Wardieu's squire. This is Roland, Sir Walter's squire."

"Geoff and Roland." She forced her smile wider. "You may call me Lizanne."

Blushing, Roland moved closer. "B-Baron Wardieu has instructed us to escort you to him."

She angled her head, feigning bewilderment. "Two of you? Why, I am honored."

Geoff nudged Roland and winked, then handed his friend his torch and dropped down beside her. There ensued a struggle to untie the rope that bound her to the tree, but at last it fell away. A hand beneath her elbow, Geoff assisted her to her feet.

"Thank you." She entreatingly thrust her joined hands forward.

Geoff shook his head. "Baron Wardieu did not say we could."

She widened her eyes. "Then how am I to relieve myself? Surely, he did not set you that task as well?"

The young men shifted uncomfortably.

"The baron told that we are to bring you straight to him," Geoff said.

Lizanne bowed her head. "I fear I shall not make it that far. Mayhap one of you can accompany me—though you must vow not to look."

Though they were obviously ill at ease, they agreed and Geoff unsheathed his dagger.

Fearful of losing a finger to the young man's clumsiness, Lizanne held her breath as he cut the rope from her wrists and sighed when she was freed without mishap.

To her chagrin, it was Geoff—the larger of the two—who volunteered to accompany her into the wood. He retrieved his torch from the other squire and led the way.

Rubbing her wrists, Lizanne followed.

"There." He pointed to a row of low-lying bushes several feet away.

She shook her head. "They are poisonous. Did you not know?" She walked past him and headed deeper into the wood.

"This will do," she announced when they were out of sight of Roland's torch. Peering around a large oak tree, she motioned for him to turn around. He obliged.

Lizanne could hardly believe her good fortune when he began to whistle, the noise masking her movements as she groped along the ground in search of a weapon. Hefting a decent-sized branch, she weighed it for ease of swing. Though she did not like that leaves clung to it, for they would rustle, it would have to suffice.

Verifying Geoff's back was turned to her, she crept from behind the tree and winced as the leaves crackled beneath her feet.

The young man did not hear her approach, perhaps did not even realize he had been struck when he fell at her feet.

She retrieved his fallen torch, thrust its tip into the ground, and knelt beside him. His pulse was strong, indicating she had not struck too hard, but the lump on his skull would be of good size when he returned to consciousness.

"Forgive me," she said and began to disrobe him. Within minutes, she was outfitted in his garments, his dagger belted at her waist.

Turning away, she fled deeper into the wood and, though there was not much moon to guide her, made do with what there was.

7

WITH CONTAINED ANGER, Ranulf stared at the unconscious young man. In spite of the long years of training, first as his page and most recently his squire, the lad had failed him. He had ignored an order and, as a result, Lizanne had escaped. Mayhap he had overestimated Geoff's ability—

Nay, he had underestimated Lizanne's. And not for the first time. He clawed a hand though his hair and over his scalp. He was more angry with himself than the gullible squires he had sent in his stead. Foolishly, he had believed two nearly grown men would have no difficulty bringing one woman to him. The lads would be disciplined for disregarding his orders, but he alone must take responsibility for what Lizanne had done.

Impatiently, he wondered at the time it was taking Roland to alert the camp and assemble a search party. He had sent the cowering squire for them minutes ago. If they did not arrive shortly, he would go for them himself.

When Geoff groaned and raised his head, Ranulf stepped closer and flung Lizanne's bunched-up bliaut at him.

The dazed squire emerged from the garments and, rubbing the back of his head, looked up.

After realization came horror. "My lord!" He scrambled to his feet, then pitched forward onto his knees. Only then did he notice his state of undress. Wearing only braies, every other garment having been stripped from him, he forced himself upright and bowed his head.

Ranulf knew well his discomfort. Had Lizanne not done the same to him? Still, it was necessary to impress upon the squire the seriousness of his error.

"What say you?" he demanded.

"My lord, the lady claimed she had need of privacy—"

"And you believed her?"

"She deceived me."

"Nay, you allowed yourself to be deceived. What did she do? Smile at you?"

Geoff shuffled his feet in the fallen leaves, and Ranulf pivoted away.

Shortly, his men entered the wood. Leading Ranulf's horse, Walter arrived ahead of the group with shamefaced Roland riding behind.

Bearing torches, the men assembled before Ranulf and awaited their instructions. Though their eyes reflected amusement at the sight of Geoff, they wisely held their tongues.

Ranulf took the reins Walter passed to him and mounted his horse. "Geoff, you shall ride with Roland," he said, then frowned. "He has brought clothes for you. Be thankful I do not make you don Lady Lizanne's."

As the squire turned away, Ranulf issued his orders and divided his men into two groups. With himself leading one group and Walter the other, they rode in opposite directions.

Ranulf guided his men through the densely wooded region. Their progress was frustratingly slow, but there was comfort in knowing they covered ground more rapidly than Lizanne would be able to on foot.

Throughout, Ranulf silently cursed the night and the weak sliver of moon. Under cover of darkness, it would be easy to overlook her were she hidden among the trees.

Had she truly escaped him? Why had he told her about Gilbert? Why had he not waited? As long as she had believed he held her precious brother, this would not have happened.

He ground his teeth. If she eluded him all the way back to Penforke, he would bring her out again—even if he had to topple the walls around her.

"My lord!"

Ranulf reined in and eyed the horse speeding through the trees toward them. A moment later, one of the men from Walter's party halted before him.

"We have found her!"

Relief swept through Ranulf. "Where?"

The man hesitated. "She has gone over the side of a ravine."

Ranulf's chest tightened. "She is unharmed?"

"For the moment. Sir Walter has sent someone down to bring her up."

The ride was a short one, though for Ranulf it seemed without end. When he spotted the glow of torches atop a rise, he overtook the messenger and covered the remaining distance alone.

Walter hurried forward as Ranulf dismounted. "Kendall is with her, my lord."

The men who peered into the ravine moved aside at their lord's approach.

Leaning over the edge of the sheer drop, Ranulf looked down and heard the rush of water before he caught the play of light over its surface. It was a long way to the bottom. Worse than expected.

It took his eyes a moment to adjust to the shadowy scene below. When they did, he first saw the knight who had been lowered thirty feet down the side. Then, following the man's progress to the right, he located Lizanne. She appeared to have a firm hold on an outcropping of vegetation, but she was practically vertical against the cliff, suspended who knew how many feet above the breaking water.

When she lifted her head in response to the commotion above, the light from the torches danced over her features.

Ranulf saw the mass of hair strewn across her filthy face, but what held his attention was her expression. She looked furious when she ought to be screaming, weeping, pleading—anything but defiant. She ought to be terrified!

"You certainly took the long way here, Ranulf Wardieu," she called through the chill night air.

Was she truly chastising him? He dragged a hand across his eyes. At least he could be fairly certain she was unharmed.

Kendall, having worked his way along the wall, was now beside her. "My lady, give me your hand."

"Nay!"

"I would help you." He reached for her arm.

Ranulf watched in amazement as she jerked away. "I do not ask for your help!"

"Lizanne!" Ranulf bellowed. "Give Sir Kendall your hand—now!"

She looked up. "Leave me be. I shall find my own way up."

The knight reached for her again but pulled back when her struggles sent rocks showering from beneath her feet. An instant later, the undergrowth to which she clung snapped.

A gasp went up as she slid farther down the wall and scrambled for another hold. Miraculously, she grasped a root and her descent was arrested a few feet below her original position.

"Bring him up!" Ranulf shouted.

When Kendall was pulled over the side, Ranulf cut the rope sling from him and fashioned another for himself. Without delay, he was lowered over the edge.

As he drew near, Lizanne turned her face away.

Taking her silence as further defiance, he felt his ire rise. Refusing to waste time arguing with her, he reached out, turned an arm around her waist, and pulled her toward him. Though her lower body followed, her upper did not.

"For the love of God, Lizanne, let go!"

When she did not comply, he clamped her legs between his thighs and tried to pry her hands free. The tenacity of her hold amazed him, and he silently cursed the disadvantage of having only one free hand, the other occupied with steadying the rope.

"Release it, Lizanne!"

She turned to him and he saw tears had forged paths down her mud-streaked face. "I cannot," she croaked.

She *was* terrified.

He removed his dagger from his belt and slashed at the root. A moment later, still grasping it, she fell against him.

"Put your arms around my neck," Ranulf said, though he did not expect her to obey.

She pressed her head more deeply beneath his chin, slid her hands up his chest, and encircled his neck.

He stared at the top of her head. Would he ever understand this beautiful, wild creature?

They began a slow ascent, during which neither spoke. At the top, Ranulf's men assisted him over the edge, but though he set Lizanne down, she immediately fell back against him. Thus, he supported her while his men extracted him from the sling.

He was baffled. From what he knew of this woman, he would have expected her to have recovered from the ordeal by now, but she continued to cling to him. Of course, she might be feigning helplessness in hopes of avoiding punishment.

He swung her up against his chest and carried her to his destrier. There, he ducked from beneath her arms, lifted her onto the saddle and, while Geoff steadied her, mounted behind.

When he pulled her back against him, she turned and slid her arms around his waist. Then she buried her face in the soft wool of his tunic. Nay, he did not think she was acting at all.

The ride back was torturous. His awkward baggage clung to him, pressing her body so tightly against his that he became far too aware of the differences between them. By the time they reached the camp, she was asleep though she continued to hold fast to him.

Ranulf carried her into his tent and lowered her onto a pallet. Though he tried to remove the root from her white-knuckled hand, he finally gave up for fear of awakening her. He did, however, remove the belt upon which Geoff's dagger was fastened.

Fatigue setting in, he crossed to the squat table that held a platter of meats, cheeses, and bread, but dismissed the food and lifted a tankard of warm mead and drained it.

Upon returning to the tent opening, he spotted Walter across the way delivering instructions to the man chosen to ride north to Chesne to warn of the possibility of retaliation from Gilbert Balmaine. Although Ranulf's impression of Lizanne's brother was less than flattering, it was best to exercise caution.

Lizanne awoke slowly. For a moment, she thought she was at Penforke, but her eyes told otherwise, opening the window of her consciousness to remind her exactly where she was—and with whom. She turned her face toward the soothing breeze that wafted through the tent.

Wardieu stood at the opening. Though recollection of her escape was hazy, she remembered the riders descending upon her and the soul-wrenching moment when she stepped into empty space. She remembered a strong arm encircling her, carrying her to safety. Ranulf Wardieu's arm.

She made no attempt to delve further, for it was disturbing to dwell on the comfort her enemy had provided—and that she had accepted it.

Hate being her best defense, she drew on it in the hope it would help her through the violation Wardieu intended to visit upon her this night.

He lowered the tent flap and turned, removed his belt and tossed it aside, then bent and pulled off his boots. As he reached to the hem of his tunic, his gaze fell upon her. Straightening, he folded his arms over his chest.

When Lizanne sat up, something dropped from her hand, and she saw it was the severed root and remembered how she had clung to Wardieu and pressed tight against him. And had wanted never to let go.

What a fool you are! This man is your enemy, and yet for the comfort of his arms, you traded strength for weakness—made yourself into a pitifully useless woman to be taken advantage of and ground underfoot. And be you assured, he will grind you underfoot. And worse.

In response to the emotions Lizanne made no attempt to keep from her face, Wardieu's countenance darkened. "Have you nothing to say for yourself?" he demanded.

She drew a deep breath and pushed to her feet. "I did warn you."

"Warn me?"

She smoothed Geoff's tunic over her thighs. "I told you 'twould not be easy to hold me." Realizing something was missing, she looked down. The belt was gone and, with it, the dagger. She snapped her chin up.

His smile greeted her. "Missing something?"

She squared her shoulders, stepped near him, and reached to the tray of food. After some consideration, she chose a chunk of hard white cheese and popped it in her mouth. Though her hunger had been a pretense to avoid confronting Wardieu head-on, the taste of food suddenly made it very real. She swallowed and reached for another morsel.

"You cause a lot of trouble, woman! Did you truly think to so easily escape me?"

She shrugged. "Actually, I thought it would be more difficult. Mayhap the next time you ought to send four to fetch me. I do enjoy a challenge."

His nostrils flared. "There will not be a next time. I shan't underestimate you again."

She turned away. "Aye, you will."

"Then you have learned naught from your failure—and do not forget you did, indeed fail."

With her back to him, she drew her teeth across her bottom lip and forced a shrug. "I would have made it if not for that little ravine."

"Need I remind you that you nearly broke your neck in that *little* ravine?"

She rounded on him. "If your men had not chased me down like common game, I would not have lost my footing!"

"You ran from them?"

"Certainly! Did you think I would simply throw up my hands and surrender? I went to a lot of trouble to escape you." She snatched up a strip of dried meat and lifted it to her mouth.

Wardieu's hand closed over her wrist, denying her the food.

She looked up. "Do you mind? I am hungry." When he did not release her, she leaned forward and brought her mouth to the meat.

He muttered something and pushed her away. "Will you give me no peace, witch?"

She sank onto his wooden chest and clasped her hands between her knees. "I will not. As you do not play fair, why should I?"

He turned slowly to face her. "You are the one who does not play fair, Lizanne. I but follow the rules set by you."

"There was nothing unfair in what I did!"

"Nothing?" He gave a bark of laughter, then closed the distance between them. "You attacked me downwind, abducted me, chained me, and stabbed me. You think that is fair?"

She jumped to her feet, a mistake that brought her within inches of him. "I had my reasons!" Reasons that, strangely, were no longer as clear as they had been a sennight past.

"Reasons you prefer to keep to yourself," he reminded her.

She could hardly breathe for the heat his body radiated between them.

"Tell me"—his eyes bored into her—"what sin have I committed that is so terrible to warrant such hatred?"

Not for the first time, she considered revealing her knowledge of his marauding exploits, but she was certain that to do so would place her in greater danger. Still, she asked, "If I tell you, will you release me?"

The anger in his eyes flickered and, for a moment, he said nothing, then he reached up and drew a thumb across her lower lip. "I make no promise."

She could not move. Though she tried to fathom the strange feeling his caress evoked, she knew only that it was not entirely unpleasant as it should be.

Thankfully, he lowered his hand and stepped back. "When you and I are done, I will send you back to your brother. Not before."

When they were done…

Lizanne closed her eyes so he would not see her fear. When he was finished bedding her, perhaps even getting her with child, he would allow her to return to Penforke. A fortnight? A month? A twelvemonth? When?

"Then I have nothing to gain by enlightening you." She stepped past him to a corner of the tent where a washbasin was set on a stool, snatched up the thick cloth beside it, and dipped it in the water. Alert to Wardieu's movements about the tent as she fought for a composure that had slipped so far that she did not think she would recapture it this night, she took her time scrubbing her face clean.

When he moved behind her, it took all of her self-control to not react.

"Have a care," he said near her ear, his breath stirring her hair and sending shivers up her spine. "I would not want you to rub away your beauty."

Though she knew she was acting like a child, she scrubbed more vigorously.

He yanked the cloth from her hand.

She whipped around and tread upon his toes. "Give it to me!"

Holding it out of reach, he swept his gaze over her face. "You are clean. Now remove those filthy clothes and lie down."

Even before fear leapt in her eyes, Ranulf knew he had poorly chosen his words.

She backed into the stool, nearly upsetting the basin of water.

He sighed. "'Tis late, Lizanne, and we rise early come morn. I but meant that you cannot sleep in that tunic, nor those boots—look at them."

Her face paled, and she protectively folded her arms across her chest.

Not so long ago, the thought of owning her fear had appealed to him, but no more. "I give you my word, you will not suffer my attentions." He motioned to the pallet he had laid her upon following their return to camp. "You have your bed, I have mine. Providing you do not leave yours, neither shall I."

Warily, she looked to the far side of the tent, and he saw her surprise when her eyes shifted from her pallet to his.

"You will, of course, be bound."

Her gaze sprang back to his. "Why?"

He nearly laughed. "As already told, I have no intention of underestimating you again. And I will have a good night's sleep."

She rubbed one wrist, then the other. "I do not like being bound."

"I certainly sympathize." Indeed, the time he had spent as her prisoner was still so fresh he could feel the manacles' bite. "Nevertheless, it shall be done—unless you prefer my arm about you through the night."

She caught her breath, and her eyes swept left and right as if in search of a way past him. But this time there would be no escaping him. Shoulders slumping as if the last of her defiance had run out of her, she said, "You may bind me."

Though tempted to remind her he did not require her permission, he said, "Go to your pallet and remove your tunic and boots. I will come to you when you are done."

She complied, and he turned away to give her privacy.

Shortly, she said, "I am ready."

Ranulf retrieved a rope from his chest and crossed to where she had pulled the blanket up to her chin. He dropped to his haunches. "Give me your hands."

She slid them out from beneath the blanket and pressed them together.

As he reached to apply the rope, he saw the abrasions on her wrists caused by her own struggles against imprisonment. Though rope did not cut as deeply as manacles, she was surely sore.

Resenting that he should care for her comfort, he pressed the rope into her hands. "Put it around your waist."

"Why?"

"It will suffice."

"I do not understand."

"And I am tired." Not that he would get the good night's sleep he had hoped for. "The other end I shall hold to."

Something he did not like glittered in her eyes before she blinked it away.

"I warn you," he said, "I shall feel every move you make through the rope. If it does not remain taut, I will take up the slack—even if it means you end up in my bed."

Whatever had come and gone in her eyes did not come again. She turned the blanket back, revealing thin undergarments, and quickly threaded the rope around her waist.

"I will knot it," he said.

She flinched when his hands brushed hers, and he heard her teeth grind when he knotted the rope a second time. And a third.

"Do not test me," he said and straightened. He tossed the end of the rope onto his pallet and began to douse the candles about the tent.

"Would you leave one burning?" Lizanne called when only one remained to be put out.

He peered into the shadows that had fallen over the pallets. Was she plotting again? If so, of what use was candlelight when the absence of light would surely serve her better?

"It was…dark in the ravine," she said.

Ranulf smiled grimly. *Walter will not like it, but methinks you will be in my bed tonight, Lady.*

He left the candle burning, crossed to his pallet, and removed his tunic and boots, then he laid down and wound the rope around one hand. As he pulled the blanket over him, the rope loosened.

He took up the slack—and more.

Lizanne gasped.

"Keep it taut," he growled.

"I but turned over."

"Taut, Lizanne!"

Lizanne stared across the space between the pallets and picked out Wardieu's pale hair. She had not been testing him. Indeed, she was not even sure she could now that it was dark but for the one candle. She knew she had raised his suspicions in asking him to leave it burning, but she did not mind, for it was better that he think ill of her than he know the deepening fear that had gripped her as he extinguished each candle. The darkness was far too eager to return her to her flight from Wardieu's men. Worse, as she had darted among trees and scrambled over rocks and roots, her fear mixing with the smell of damp earth, she had returned to the first time she had fled this man—the night he had cut down Gilbert and tried to ravish her.

Had he?

She startled.

And the devil snapped the rope. "Be still!"

He had. Of course he had.

His speech might be as fine as his clothes, but he remained the villain of four years past who had pillaged and wounded and murdered.

And yet you lie untouched when there is naught to prevent him from stealing your virtue. Indeed, he has not so much as raised a hand against you when none of his men would think it untoward for him to beat you.

"Quiet," she whispered. And winced.

But though Wardieu surely heard, he said naught.

For what seemed hours, she lay unmoving and listened to his breathing, but it never changed—as if he were also awake. Only when the candle went out, taking with it the small measure of comfort, did she close her eyes.

8

Iᴛ ᴡᴀѕ ɢʀᴏᴡɪɴɢ light when Lizanne opened an eye and peered at her
shadowy surroundings. She sighed and turned her face into what should
have been a pillow but was not. Raising her head, she frowned at what
appeared to be the ground. She scraped her fingers across it and confirmed it was, indeed, dirt upon which she had made her bed. Why? And
how?

Memories of the night past returning in a rush, she looked to the left
and saw her empty pallet. To the right, Ranulf Wardieu slept on his own
pallet, the five feet that had separated them reduced to two.

Had she truly forced him to take up the rope's slack to such an
extent? More, how had she slept through it?

Mayhap the same way he now sleeps through your awakening.

Had his watch over her through the night so exhausted him? Or
did he sleep? She studied his face that seemed less familiar than before.
His chiseled features appeared softer, hard mouth fuller, lips retracted
slightly to reveal even white teeth.

She frowned as something tugged at her memory, allowed a frustrat-
ing glimpse, and receded. What was it?

Squeezing her eyes closed, she tried to retrace her thoughts, but
the answer was gone. When she looked again at the man who was too
near for comfort, it struck her that he had kept his word that he would
not violate her. The enemy she had known would suffer no remorse in

breaking his vow. He would not even have given his word in the first place. Had Ranulf Wardieu truly changed? If so, what force was so great it could turn a man from a path as evil as his? Faith?

It did not matter. What mattered was that he slept and she did not. Of course, neither did those outside the tent sleep, the sounds of their stirring growing louder.

Though this was not the time to attempt another escape, it did not mean she could not put distance between herself and Wardieu. Five feet was hardly acceptable, but two?

Slowly, she raised herself and eyed the rope around her waist. It was not taut, but neither was it slack. She followed it to where it looped several times around Wardieu's hand. When had he last moved to draw her near?

Again, it did not matter.

Careful to disturb the rope as little as possible, she eased onto her side and pushed up to sitting. She considered the knots Wardieu had tied, reached up, and traced them. They were tight and would not easily be loosened, but—

"Once again you test me."

Lizanne yelped and jerked back, but gained only inches before the rope stretched tight.

"What was your plan this time?" Wardieu asked in a voice not fully shed of sleep.

Suppressing the urge to slap a hand to her heart, she met his gaze. "I but wished to return to my pallet."

He sat up, and when the blanket fell away, she was relieved to see he not only wore an undertunic but chausses. "I am to believe you, Lizanne Balmaine?"

"'Tis not my custom to be dragged through the dirt, nor to sleep in it!"

"I took up the slack as I warned you I would. Unfortunate for you, it seems you are a restless sleeper."

She stiffened. Had she been visited by a nightmare? She did not remember having had one, but if so, had she cried out and jabbered as her maid, Mellie, told she was wont to do? Had she revealed anything about that terrible night?

She searched Wardieu's face, but it was unreadable. Forcing herself to relax against the straining rope, she shrugged. "Mayhap I was merely working trickery on you."

He raised his eyebrows. "I considered that, but you were unawares."

"That is what you think."

"That is what I know. Twice, near thrice"—he jutted his chin at where she sat in the dirt—"you were close enough that I was tempted to pull you into my bed that I might gain more sleep."

Lizanne caught her breath.

"But"—

She did not like the slant of his smile.

—"there was also the possibility I would gain even less sleep with you in my bed."

Meaning he would have ravished her. He had not changed, after all.

"Therefore, both times I carried you to your pallet."

She startled. Did he lie? It was difficult enough to believe she had slept through the pulls of the rope, but that she had not known his arms were around her?

"And," he continued, "on neither occasion did you object. Indeed, you were most receptive to my embrace."

"Indeed not!" Lizanne burst. "Though I yield that I may have been unawares when you returned me to my pallet, I would *never* be receptive to you."

He released the rope he had wound around his hand and shrugged. "Then I know you better than you know yourself."

She struggled against anger that aspired to outrage, fearful of how far it might push him. After all, they were both clad in little more than undergarments.

Determined she would not further fuel the fire, Lizanne sealed her lips and lowered her gaze.

She felt Wardieu's stare, but finally he rose from his pallet and she heard the crack of his stiff joints.

"In one thing you spoke true," he said.

When he did not elaborate, she hurried her gaze to his to avoid looking too near upon the rest of him. "More than one thing, but to what do *you* refer?"

"That you would not make it easy to hold you."

As evidenced by the fatigue written in the lines of his face. "And still I will not."

He considered her, nodded, and thrust out a hand. "We must make ready to depart."

Lizanne ignored his offer and started to rise, but he closed his fingers around her arm and pulled her to her feet. To her surprise, he immediately released her. To her further surprise, he grasped the rope at her waist and began to free the knots.

Staring at his bent head, she struggled to suppress her response to each brush of his fingers across her midriff for fear he would misinterpret any quake or tremble. However, when he dropped the rope from her waist, she could not keep her breath from coming out in a rush.

Wardieu lifted his head. "For someone who professes to loathe me, I am surprised I should so deeply affect you."

Though there was nothing holding her to him now, she could not move. "You affect me only insomuch as I do not like you near."

"You are certain?"

"I am."

His gaze fell to her mouth, and once again she could not breathe. "Should we test if you are, indeed, receptive to me?"

It had to be a game he played, advancing one moment, retreating the next, looking for the right moment to pounce. It made her want to scream—and gave her back her breath. "If you intend to ravish me," she hissed, "pray have done with it that I might sooner return home."

Her words doused the amusement in which Ranulf had foolishly indulged. "Ravish?" he bit.

She stared at him out of eyes that had gone so dark they could no longer be called green. "'Tis the only way you will ever know me, for I care not what your men think of you. I will not come willingly to your bed. I will not be your leman."

"I would never take a woman by force," he growled.

Her laughter was cold. "Would you not?"

Once again distrusting himself so near her, he took a step back. "I would know the reason you think so ill of me."

As if she could breathe more easily with the added space between them, her rigid shoulders eased. "I can say only that you have given me good cause."

Lord, grant me patience! "And I am to defend myself knowing only that?"

She raised her chin. "I have not asked you to defend yourself, for you can have no defense that will satisfy me."

Denied his request for patience, Ranulf took back the step he had allowed and looked down upon her. "Tell me of that first meeting, the one you spoke of when you held me at Penforke."

She looked up. "I will not, but this I shall tell you—I would rather slip a blade between your ribs than suffer your touch."

Ranulf would have liked to laugh, but his insides were too tightly wound. "I know it, just as I know you could no more do it than you could cut me down when you had me at sword's end."

She opened her mouth as if to deny her lack of resolve, closed her mouth, and averted her gaze. "I should have cut you down," she whispered.

"And yet, you could not. What does that tell you, Lizanne?"

Slowly, she shook her head.

Hoping he might finally reach her, he said, "You are not entirely certain I am guilty of whatever sins you have laid at my door."

When she did not respond, he curved a hand beneath her chin and lifted it. "What do you see when you look at me?"

She searched his face. "I..." She raised her gaze to his hair and frowned. A moment later, she jerked her chin free. "I fear you would not be pleased by my observation."

And so they were back to where they had started.

"I will discover what you hide from me," Ranulf said and strode past her.

"My secrets are my own," she called after him. "I share them only with those I choose. I do not choose *you*, Ranulf Wardieu."

He turned. "I weary of your mockery. Henceforth, you will address me as 'my lord,' for that I am now. Do you understand?"

She glared. "'Tis not a matter of understanding but of compliance, and I am hardly of a mind to comply."

He knew he ought to let her defiance pass but could not. However, as he once more moved toward her, she sprang to the side, skirted him, and darted toward the tent flap. He could have lunged and caught her before she slipped outside, but reason prevailed and he let her go.

At his leisure, he stepped from the tent.

She had not gone far. Ranulf's men, who had paused in the dismantling of camp, gawked at the barely clothed woman in their midst.

Dawn's light falling softly around her, Lizanne stood unmoving with her arms crossed over her chest. And there was Geoff, bearing a tray surely meant for his lord, his jaw nearly upon his chest.

Ranulf turned a hand around her arm. "Methinks you have forgotten something," he said. He drew her back into the tent, led her to her pallet, and pushed her down onto it. Though he intended to berate her for behaving without a thought for modesty, he saw tears in her eyes before she lowered her chin.

Frustration at finding her escape thwarted was what he expected, not...

What? Mortification over her state of undress? Was she truly so troubled? Regardless, it was of her own doing.

"That was not well thought out," he said and reached for a blanket.

"'Twas not thought out at all," she muttered. "I am sorry."

He paused. An apology was the last thing he expected from a woman who wielded weapons and challenged men to duels. Would he ever make sense of her? And why did he care?

He draped the blanket over her shoulders, and she gripped the edges and clasped them closed.

Shaking his head, Ranulf crossed to the tent opening and beckoned Geoff inside.

"Greetings, my lord." His face yet flushed from his unexpected encounter with Lizanne, the young squire kept his gaze turned from her as he carried his burden across the tent. Deftly, he removed last night's supper tray and replaced it with the smaller one.

Ranulf retrieved the belt and dagger Lizanne had taken from his squire and handed them to the blushing young man before sending him on his way. When he turned back, he saw that Lizanne stared at the food. Meaning she was coming back to herself.

Though he sensed she would be easier to handle in her shaken state, he was strangely relieved by her return.

He broke off a piece of bread, grabbed a small apple, and returned to her pallet.

She accepted his offering. "Thank you."

And still she was civil. Of course, it could not last. As she bit into the apple, he turned and crossed to the chest. Though it was Geoff's duty to keep the contents in order and to make ready the garments his lord wore, it seemed the squire had been remiss. After some rummaging, Ranulf extricated a clean undertunic, tunic, braies, and chausses. And became aware of the silence at his back.

He looked over his shoulder. Lizanne leaned forward, gaze intent on the chest, though only for that moment before she realized she was watched.

"You will find naught in here to *slip* between my ribs," he warned.

She shrugged and took another bite of the apple.

Ranulf lowered the lid, dropped the clean garments atop it, and whipped off the undertunic he had slept in.

As he reached for the fresh undertunic, he heard a terrible wheezing. He turned and found Lizanne bent forward, a hand to her throat.

In three strides, he was beside her. He wrenched her upright, spun her about, and thumped her on the back.

She wheezed, coughed, coughed again, and expelled a piece of apple.

Drawing a deep breath, she straightened and looked over her shoulder. "Bad apple," she said and smiled.

Ranulf nearly informed her he saw no humor in the situation but that smile dispelled all thoughts of a reprimand. It lit her face, turning her eyes a shade of green shot through with gold, bringing a glow to her cheeks, curving her mouth into a bow that showed pearly teeth, and revealing for the first time a single dimple in her left cheek. He was mesmerized. Who would guess that such a canted smile could be so lovely and captivating?

"I would have you smile more often," he murmured and reached up and touched the indentation.

She startled, and when her eyes shifted to his bare shoulder, he heard her breath catch as it must have done when he had removed the dirty undertunic—hence, the apple she had sucked into her airway.

"Is that an order?" she asked, once more her old self.

Firmly, he set her away from him. "But a suggestion."

"Good." She retrieved the blanket that had fallen to her feet, tossed it over a shoulder, and crossed to the tray of food.

As she stood with her back to him, picking at the morsels, he changed into the clean garments. Then he joined her in breaking his fast.

A short while later, Geoff returned and handed a bundle to his lord. After the young man had removed the tray and departed, Ranulf strode to where Lizanne had retreated to her pallet and extended the bundle. "Your clothes."

She frowned at the folded bliaut, chemise, and slippers. "I much prefer tunic and chausses. Those are far too cumbersome." She flicked her fingers at the garments but did not take them.

"A fact I am well aware of," he said, "and one I find convenient where you are concerned."

She scowled.

He dropped the bundle beside her. "If you are not properly clothed when I return, I will dress you myself."

Following his departure, Lizanne wasted the first few minutes vacillating between defiance and grudging capitulation. In the end, she threw off the blanket and hurriedly pulled the chemise and bliaut over her head. She was struggling with the laces when Wardieu returned.

Wordlessly, he pushed aside her hands and pulled and knotted the laces. Then he stood back and perused her top to bottom.

Lizanne lifted her chin. "Do I meet with your approval?"

He shook his head. "Hardly."

As she held in words better kept behind her lips, he went to his chest and tossed back the lid. Shortly, he pressed a comb and small mirror into her hands. "See to your grooming. You are a mess."

She lifted the mirror before her face. "I see nothing amiss." It was a lie, for her appearance was staggeringly shoddy. As usual, that accursed hair!

"Do it," he ordered. "We depart within the hour." Then he was gone again.

Ignoring his command, Lizanne waited for sufficient time to pass to ensure his absence, then crossed to the tent opening and poked her head out.

Leaning against a tree across the way was Wardieu's squire, Geoff. He smiled thinly, then nodded at the men-at-arms positioned on either side of the tent.

She retreated from the opening. With naught to do but pace, her mind slipped to the place she had gone when she had run from the tent and found herself in the midst of Wardieu's men. When they had looked upon her in her meager garments, their eyes had not been feral, unlike the brigands' eyes of four years past, but she had been drawn back to that terrible state of helplessness—of being a woman at the mercy of men.

Most disturbing, though, was how desperately grateful she had been to the one who had pulled her back inside the tent, a man she should fear above all.

With a growl of frustration, Lizanne retrieved the comb and began yanking it through her hair.

An hour later, Lizanne found herself seated before Wardieu on his destrier.

Although curious as to their northern destination, she maintained a rebellious silence despite her captor's comments as they passed through the changing countryside.

Fortunately, the ride was less rigorous than that of the day before. Unfortunately, it was a strain to hold herself apart from Wardieu. When they paused at a stream to water their horses at noon, her muscles were crying for ease. Grudgingly, she allowed Wardieu to assist in her dismount and grimaced as her body creaked when he set her to the ground.

"You are a stubborn woman, Lizanne Balmaine," he said and turned and stalked away.

Kneading the muscles of her shoulders, she looked around. To her left and right stood the two men who had guarded the tent entrance that morning, their eyes trained on her. Squire Geoff also watched as he fed oats to his horse.

Once again, Lizanne felt the weight of regret over having worked deception upon the young man on the night past. Doubtless, he had suffered terrible humiliation. Most assuredly, none disliked her more than he.

She sighed, turned aside, and came face-to-face with Sir Walter.

Mouth grimly set, much as it had been when he had been forced to carry her upon his horse the day before, he thrust a skin of water at her. No greeting. No acknowledgment. Just this—and grudgingly given.

Lizanne could not help but be offended. "Am I to take it you would lower yourself to offer me a drink?"

His face darkened.

"'Tis a kindness I would not expect, Sir Walter."

His nostrils flared. "I assure you, it is not out of kindness I offer, my lady."

She blinked. Though she had resorted to sarcasm in hopes of forcing him to speak, thereby establishing some control over their encounter, she had not expected him to be so blunt. It seemed the tolerant dislike he had shown her on the day past had turned to animosity, surely the result of her escape attempt.

I was wrong. Here is one who has even less of a care for me than Squire Geoff.

She accepted the skin, took a swallow of cool, sweet water, and returned her gaze to the knight who looked upon her as if she, not his lord, shouldered all the evil in the world. "You do not like me."

His jaw shifted. "I bear no affection for vipers, my lady."

She was taken aback, not only at being likened to a viper, but by the vehemence with which he did so. Struggling to suppress the outward expression of her hurt, she stared at the man who was older than Wardieu by at least a dozen years, his dark hair threaded through with silver. Though his face was marked by the ravages of a childhood illness, he was attractive, his piercing blue eyes like chips of ice beneath dark eyebrows. Very much like Gilbert's eyes.

She took another swallow of water and returned the skin to him. "Methinks you mistake fear for dislike, Sir Knight."

His brow lowered. "Fear?"

"Aye. It seems to me men are frightened by what they do not understand. And you certainly do not understand me. But then, misplaced loyalty does cast shadows upon one's good judgment."

A flush creeping up the man's face, he turned on his heel and stalked away.

Telling herself she did not regret the words she had spoken in response to his insult, Lizanne heaved a sigh, strolled to the stream, and squatted at the edge.

She considered her rippled reflection, then pushed back the long sleeves of her bliaut and dipped her hands in the water. After the long, hot ride, it was wonderfully refreshing. She scooped up handfuls of water and splashed it on her face. Even as she gasped at its cold bite, she reached for more and carried it to her neck, unmindful that she also wet the bodice of her gown.

She sighed, lifted her skirt, and patted her face dry on the material.

"What did you say to Sir Walter?"

She startled so violently she nearly toppled into the stream. Thinking that, for such a large man, Wardieu moved with incredible stealth, she peered over her shoulder. "Naught of import. We simply agreed to dislike each other."

His lids narrowed. "I will not have you causing strife among my men. Henceforth, you will refrain from speaking to them."

"I have done nothing wrong."

"Have you not? I have seen how you treat your inferiors, and I warn you, if you think to treat my men the same, you will see how very intolerant I can be."

Lizanne searched backward for an occasion when he might have witnessed her dealings with servants. There was only one. Though she rebelled against explaining her unseemly behavior, she could not help herself. "You speak of the servant at Lord Langdon's castle."

"I do."

"I would have you know that miserable woman slapped my maid."

He held up a hand. "I will not argue with you."

Resentment gripping her, she scooped up another handful of water and slung it at him.

Ranulf sidestepped, avoiding most of the spray, then caught her arm and pulled her to her feet. "More and more," he said, "I wonder whether you are woman or child."

She gasped, and he let her wrench free. Then she put that chin of hers into the air.

Albeit tempted to give her the slight push that would land her in the stream, Ranulf turned away. "Follow me." After the requisite hesitation, he heard her footsteps.

He led her to a secluded area away from the others and pointed to a grove of trees. "You may relieve yourself there."

Her eyebrows rose. "How thoughtful of you."

"Do not try my patience," he warned and turned his back on her. As her footsteps receded, he focused on his squire. It was obvious his pride had suffered a grievous blow and Lizanne would not easily dupe him a second time. So what task might be set him that would allow him to redeem himself?

When several minutes passed without Lizanne's reappearance, Ranulf grew uneasy. He turned and scanned the area for a glimpse of her green garment, then silently cursed. He had not thought how easy it would be for her to blend in with the surrounding vegetation wearing that color.

"Lizanne! Do not dawdle!"

Receiving no answer, he momentarily closed his eyes. Had he once more underestimated her?

He called again, and again she did not answer. He strode forward, then broke into a run.

"Lizanne!" he bellowed when he came to the place he had last seen her and still there was no sign of her.

He stilled. Though she made no sound to alert him to her whereabouts, he instinctively raised his head, squinted against the sun's glare, and scanned the trees. And there she was, perched on a limb midway up an ancient oak.

How had she managed to climb so high, especially hampered by skirts? She was like a boy, a contentious, uncontrollable little boy constantly getting into trouble.

He strode to the base of the tree.

"You are not very quick, are you?" she said, jolting him with a mischievous grin. "Had I known you would take so long, mayhap I would have tried to escape after all." Her legs dangled amid her skirts, offering a tantalizing glimpse of firm calves and fine-boned ankles.

"What do you up there?" he demanded, unsettled that she had placed herself in danger.

"'Tis a lovely view." She swept a hand before her. "Why, I can see—"

"Come down."

She looked back at him. "I like it here. Mayhap you should come up."

To Lizanne's surprise, he unbelted his sword and began to scale the gnarly tree. Watching him, she could not help but admire the ease with which he accomplished the feat. Even without her burdensome garments, she could not have made the climb appear so effortless.

Shortly, he heaved himself onto the branch upon which she was balanced partway down its length. She watched as he assessed the situation and was not surprised when he reached for her rather than venture out on a limb that would likely snap beneath his added weight. "Give me your hand. I will help you down."

Lizanne frowned. "You are not angry?"

"Nay. You hoped to make me so?"

"I did."

"For what reason?"

She opened her mouth but, for once, regretted the words before they were spoken. To say she had climbed a tree to make it appear she had attempted escape for his having questioned whether she was a woman or a child would only prove he had good reason to do so. And he would not be the first, for hardly a fortnight passed without her brother grumbling over something she had done that did not "reflect well" on one her age. As much as it hurt to admit it, Ranulf Wardieu's observation was well-founded.

"Why?" he asked again.

She glanced at the hand he offered. "I fear it would reflect poorly on me were I to share my reason for trying to vex you."

"Lizanne," he said softly, "you do sometimes act like a child."

And he was too perceptive. Though she did not want to look at him for what she might find in his eyes, she gave him her gaze.

"You are impulsive," he said. "You think first with your anger and seem not to consider the consequences of your actions."

As when she had abducted him. But she was hardly going to discuss her regrets with the man responsible for setting the story in motion. Though she longed to tell him there were also consequences to his actions, she lifted her face to the sky. "It was a miserable ride."

After a long moment, he said, "You made it so. If you relax, 'twill be more comfortable."

"Of even greater comfort would be a horse of my own." She turned her head so quickly that she teetered on the branch.

He drew a sharp breath. "We will speak of this when we are on the ground. Now take my hand."

She glanced at it. "As I got myself up here, I will get myself down."

"You will break your neck is what you will do!"

"Would you care?" She had not meant to ask it, and yet it had passed her lips as if in need of an answer.

At his protracted silence, she said, "I have been climbing trees, shooting bows, and engaging in swordplay for years. I do not need to be rescued."

To her surprise, Wardieu lowered his hand and eased back against the tree trunk. When he spoke, his tone was gentle. "Tell me of your childhood, Lizanne."

She frowned. "Now?"

He shrugged. "Unless you are ready to climb down."

She mulled his request. Deciding there was no harm in the telling, she said, "Though you may not believe it, I was brought up to be a proper lady. At one time, I could even sew a fine stitch." She grimaced. For the first time since she had set aside that womanly skill, she felt a pang of loss.

"Still, I was always interested in those things considered the privilege of men." She nearly smiled. "Once I even challenged Gilbert to a duel—my stick against his sword. He was not amused."

Ranulf was intrigued. One question after another came to mind, but he remained silent for fear she would not continue.

"When I was fifteen, shortly after my father's death…" Her voice caught and he heard her swallow. "Gilbert finally relented and began secretly instructing me in arms."

Wondering what kind of man would allow himself to be coerced into something so dishonorable, Ranulf asked, "Why?"

She stared at her hands. "So that I might defend myself."

Ranulf shook his head. "That is the responsibility of men, Lizanne."

She turned sorrowful eyes upon him, whispered, "But sometimes they fail."

Who had failed her? Feeling a need to comfort her, he asked "Who? Was it Gilbert?"

Her eyes widened, then that mask of indifference dropped into place. "I am ready to climb down."

Ranulf was not ready, but he extended his hand.

She scooted along the limb, placed her fingers in his, and allowed him to draw her against him.

He tilted her face up. "What am I to do with you, Lizanne?"

"Let me go home."

He shook his head. "I cannot. 'Tis done."

A smile of bitter proportions curved her lips, and when he lowered his head and set his mouth upon hers, she did not resist. He kept the kiss light and brief, and when it was over, she buried her face against his neck.

9

GILBERT BALMAINE SWEPT the long table clear with one stroke of the arm. Pitchers of ale, platters of viands, and tankards flew across the room. Those within range either ducked or fled in search of cover.

Bellowing curses he had forbidden his sister, Gilbert swung around to face the captain of the guard and the steward where they stood before the assembly of knights at the edge of the hall.

Resentfully aware that his limp was more pronounced than usual, he strode across the rush-covered floor. When he reached the two men, he hauled them up by the fronts of their tunics. "I will have both your necks if ill befalls my sister!" The blast of his breath stirred their hair. "Best you pray to your God for her safe return."

He thrust them aside and set off on a new tangent, scattering his knights as he went. A sideboard burdened with pastries went crashing to the floor, and a bench toppled beneath a well-placed kick.

In search of further means of venting his anger, Gilbert swung around. And stilled.

Shock hung from the faces of those in the hall. They were unaccustomed to seeing their lord alive with emotion, especially an emotion that gripped him so violently he had not a care for the fear he was surely striking in their breasts. They knew him as a just and honorable lord, albeit one who was more often sullen. But he had good reason for that, the humorous and enthusiastic young man he had been prior to inheriting the barony long gone—just as the innocent, light-hearted Lizanne was gone.

The events that had led to the changes in brother and sister, though vague in detail, were common knowledge among most of the castle folk, but never spoken of. It was forbidden.

Gilbert drew a deep breath and returned to tower over the men who had earned his wrath. "Who is this black-hearted knight who holds my sister?"

Robert Coulter stood taller. "He called himself Wardieu. Baron Ranulf Wardieu, my lord."

Gilbert considered the name and found it recently familiar. He remembered the large, fair-headed man who had sat at the king's table more than a fortnight earlier. The White Knight, the ladies had whimsically named him.

Not one for women's prattle or gossip, he had turned his attention elsewhere, but it had been impossible to ignore the speculation the man raised among those at court. Still, Gilbert had gleaned little from the snatches of conversation he had been privy to. He knew only that Wardieu held vast lands to the north—Chesne—and he was said to be a formidable adversary.

A group of younger ladies had twittered over the recent death of the man's wife and unashamedly vied for his attention. However, the man had not seemed to notice.

Gilbert clenched his hands at his sides and tried to make sense of the events that had led to the taking of Lizanne. Why had Wardieu carried her away? What could have possessed him to undertake such an action? His sister might be beyond lovely, but her belligerent disposition was easily recognized, and most men found it far outweighed her looks.

"My lord?" Ian, the steward, apologetically broke into his thoughts. "Samuel knows more. 'Twas he who tended the man when Lady Lizanne held him prisoner."

Gilbert jerked. "Prisoner? My sister held Wardieu prisoner? A baron?" At the stewart's nod, Gilbert shouted. "Bring Samuel to me!"

"I am here, my lord." The huge bald man skirted a group of knights and came to stand before him.

Gilbert knew the man well. He and his wife were favorites of Lizanne's. "Samuel," he said, fighting to regain control of himself, "I would speak with you in private." At the man's nod, he looked again to Ian. "Send for Mellie," he ordered, then motioned for the others to clear the hall.

The horse-weary knights withdrew, taking with them the captain of the guard and the few servants skulking about.

Rubbing his aching right leg, Gilbert crossed to the raised dais and dropped heavily into his high-backed chair. He lifted his good leg, pressed his booted foot against the edge of the table, and tilted the chair onto its two back legs.

Samuel lowered onto the bench alongside him.

"Tell me everything," Gilbert commanded.

The man began his narrative, commencing with the return of Lizanne from Lord Langdon's castle and her giving of the unconscious prisoner into his care.

Halfway through the telling, Mellie crept into the hall and approached the raised dais.

Gilbert, leaning precariously toward Samuel, his chair on the verge of overturning, acknowledged her by jabbing his finger at the bench upon which the bald man was perched.

She sank down on the edge and, clasping her hands in her lap, bowed her head and stared at her nibbled nails.

"She did what?" Gilbert roared, his outcry so startling Mellie that she slipped off the bench.

"Aye," Samuel said as the maid regained her seat. "She faced 'em alone and loosed her arrow on the man."

"Did she wound the miscreant?"

"Nay, though had she meant to, I do not doubt she would have. As you know, her aim…"

Gilbert waved the man to silence. "So she went willingly, without breach of the castle walls?"

Samuel nodded, his bare pate gleaming in the midday light that streamed through the upper windows. "She had no choice, milord. We were greatly outnumbered, and the knight claimed he had taken you captive."

"Deceitful villain! I—" Gilbert halted his words as a thought that had been niggling at the back of his mind sprang forward. "Curse King Henry!" Well he remembered the monarch's seemingly innocent inquiry into his sister's whereabouts.

With a resounding crash, Gilbert returned his chair to its four legs. Leaning forward, he turned his hands into fists. He had told the king of Lizanne's stay with her cousin at Landgon Castle. Henry had smiled, then he had said he would find a worthy man to take her in hand. Was Wardieu the one Henry had in mind?

One delay after another had been thrown into Gilbert's path over the next fortnight until, finally, he and his retainers had been allowed to return to Penforke. At the time, Gilbert had seen it as a coincidental nuisance. Now he thought it more likely he had been the victim of delay by design—the king's.

"He is behind this," Gilbert said. "But how did my sister take Wardieu prisoner? And why?"

The knight was a man of immense proportions, after all. How had she managed to fell him? Most importantly, why would his man-hating sister go to such lengths?

"Milord?" Mellie said softly.

Gilbert looked at her. "What know you of this?"

"'Twas I who lured the baron into the trap."

"You?" He sat straighter. "Why?"

"I did it at my mistress's bidding," she wailed and looked away.

"Make sense, girl!"

Bottom lip trembling, the young maid looked back at Gilbert. "Lady Lizanne did not tell me her reason, milord, but she had me lure the man down a darkened corridor at Lord Langdon's castle. He was near upon me when she sprang out of the shadows and dealt him a terrible blow."

"Single-handedly?" Gilbert knew well his sister's abilities, but he could not reconcile the size and apparent strength of Wardieu with that of hers.

"Aye." Mellie bobbed her head. "He was well sated with drink, milord. Though he tried to fight, milady was too quick for him and knocked him unconscious with a second blow. 'Twas like a great oak he fell."

Gilbert imagined the scene and could not help but smile. What had possessed Lizanne? "How did she deliver him to Penforke without alerting Lord Langdon? Surely he was suspicious?"

"We hid him in one of the wagons and left before dawn the following morn. He was not missed at that time, milord."

"And he did not awaken? 'Tis a day and a half's journey to Penforke."

A mischievous twinkle entered the maid's eyes. "Each time he stirred, I but waved one of me mistress's potions beneath his nose and"— she snapped her fingers—"he went right back to sleepin'."

Gilbert groaned and tugged at his new growth of beard. "Did Lady Lizanne reveal what cause she had for abducting the knight?"

Mellie shook her head. "All's she said was he had greatly wronged your family, and she intended to punish him for his sins."

It sounded like her, but what had Wardieu done to warrant his abduction? Was it possible he had tried to tread where no other men dared? Mayhap tried to steal a kiss from Lizanne? Or worse? He growled low and said, "How many days does this Wardieu have on us?"

"He rode north three days ago, milord," Samuel answered.

Three days? Was he returning to Chesne?

Suddenly exhausted, Gilbert ground the heels of his palms against his eyes. He would need to allow his men to rest before giving chase, but give chase he would. The thought of failing Lizanne a second time burned like molten steel.

"We are done," he said and heaved his body out of the chair. He strode across the hall and mounted the stairs. Inside his solar, he ignored the discomfort of a belly that gnawed with hunger and began to pace.

"Why, Lizanne?" He lengthened his stride until his leg protested, shooting pain up his hip. Grimacing, he threw himself into a heavily worn chair. As he massaged his impaired limb, he considered his sister's abduction from Penforke.

Never had he known Robert Coulter to back down from a challenge. The man had, after all, held his esteemed position as captain of the guard for nigh on twenty years. He had served Gilbert's father well during the time of King Stephen's reign when conflicts between neighboring barons had been commonplace events. And yet he had allowed Lizanne to surrender herself without putting up a token resistance. Had he gone soft in the intervening years of relative peace? It *was* possible Penforke could have held out long enough for Gilbert to return and do battle with the miscreant. Why had none gainsaid her?

Because you allowed her too much rein.

It was true. He had indulged nearly every whim she put to him, even to the point of instructing her in arms. Though the castle folk frowned and shook their heads, none dared question their lord. Perhaps someone should have.

Gilbert closed his eyes. There would be changes when he brought his little sister home. For too long they had allowed their futures to be governed by the forces of past aggressions. It was time they both assumed their rightful roles at Penforke. What had happened four years past—

Struck by remembrance of that grisly night when his blood had spilled, he opened his eyes wide in an attempt to turn back the memories. And would have succeeded if not for a sense of impending discovery that bade him revisit every detail of his failure.

A full score strong, the brigands had swept down on the camp, their blades already seasoned with the blood of slain guards. Gilbert and his men had awakened and reached for their swords, but even as they gained their feet, weapons rose and fell against them.

All around, Gilbert heard the cries of his men as they fought, their shouts of agony as they fell. He had tasted blood that sprayed the air and flecked his clothing, but had not paused in his fight to defeat those who would see him put down.

Blade sheathed in blood, the first who had challenged him dead at his feet, he had turned his attention to the two advancing on him. Rage was his ally, lending him the strength to match blows as they simultaneously fell upon him.

Refusing to surrender ground to the assailants, he had forced them back. However, the satisfaction felt at burying his sword in the flesh of the smaller man's neck was short-lived. The other's blade sliced through Gilbert's chausses, flaying open skin and muscle and driving him to his knees.

Though the pain was excruciating, his need to protect Lizanne was stronger. He struggled to his feet and swung his sword high to deflect a blow intended for his neck. However, torn by escalating pain and weakened by the loss of blood, he was unable to stand again and was forced to fight from the ground.

As he defended himself, he caught a glimpse of another swiftly approaching—pale hair that slashed light across the night. However, he had not had time to fix his gaze on this new adversary, for his assailant was upon him.

Though his thrusts grew labored and his vision dimmed, his warrior's mind rebelled against his body's weakening and bade him continue to seek the other's steel. He did so almost blindly, his other senses guiding his arm.

Once again, his sword made contact, though he could not say with what. Then he felt a white-hot pain explode within his chest. He collapsed, still gripping his sword. As consciousness fell away and a dark hand urged him to explore the depths of a void theretofore unknown, he heard a scream that cleaved his soul.

Lizanne!

He struggled to rise above the darkness, but it was stronger than his mangled body. Even as he was dragged under, he clung to a single thread of life—that he had promises to keep.

Gilbert groaned and sat forward in the chair, his knuckles white where he gripped the padded arms.

The pieces fit. Although he had caught only a glimpse of the man who had led the attack on their camp, Lizanne had been adamant about his appearance. Could it be? Such colorless hair was not common.

He shook his head. Why would a landed nobleman disguise himself as a common villain? It was preposterous, but he could think of no other explanation for Lizanne's actions. Had she not vowed to one day unleash vengeance upon the one who had mortally wronged her family?

For this, had Wardieu stolen her away? If so, what did he intend to do with her?

Gilbert feared the answer—that she could not be allowed to live. Did she still?

He shoved to his feet, strode from the solar, and descended the stairs two at a time. This night he and his men would ride.

10

"You have never tended a wound?" Ranulf asked, ignoring Lizanne's silent plea to be excused from the task.

"Mayhap a scratch or two."

He frowned. "'Tis not uncommon for the lady of a castle to be accomplished in such things."

She did not meet his gaze. "I gave up those duties long ago."

Ranulf knew otherwise. Samuel had been very clear on this. Still, he would play her game—for a while. "Then I will have to teach you."

He was amused by the indignation that flitted across her face. "I take to fainting at the sight of blood," she said, backing away. "You would not want me swooning, would you?"

He caught her hand and pulled her down onto the pallet beside him, then placed her palm on the bandages covering his bared thigh. "It is nearly healed. 'Twas a clean cut. Do you not remember?"

She looked away. "It would not have happened had you not attacked me."

"Nay, 'twould not have happened had you not imprisoned me."

She sighed, pressed her lips together, and began removing the bandages. When the evidence of her attack lay before her, she seemed to forget she was not a healer and leaned forward to examine the wound. "It is, indeed, nearly healed. Lucy made fine work of her stitches, and I see no redness or swelling—good signs."

Ranulf pushed a small pot beneath her nose.

She took it, removed the lid, sniffed the creamy salve. And caught her breath. "Where did you get this?"

He smiled. "Lord Langdon's wife gave it to me. Her cousin, whom I understand to be a lady with a gift for healing, prepared it for her household."

Her eyes flashed and she sat back on her heels. "What else did my cousin tell you?"

"You concede too easily, Lizanne. I had thought we could play this game a while longer."

"You did not answer my question."

He leaned toward her. "I will not repeat her exact words, but I must say the lady appears to have no great affection for her cousin."

Color bloomed in her face. "You are despicable. And deceitful!"

He grasped her chin. "'Twas you who sought to deceive me, Lizanne. Now, I want your word you will cease with these lies and start behaving like a lady."

She pushed his hand away. "I will do what I must to protect myself, even if it means behaving in ways you do not approve of."

He narrowed his lids. "I want your word."

"I am sure you do, but do you truly believe I would keep vows made under order?" She laid her hand to his chest and pushed him back. Then she dipped two fingers in the salve, scooped up a generous amount, and worked it into the wound.

"I require fresh bandages," she said.

He handed her strips of clean cloth, and she quickly wrapped his leg—a bit too tightly. "There. I will remove the stitches in two days."

"Then you are not planning another escape?"

After a moment's hesitation, she shook her head. "I plan for naught. I simply await another opportunity, which you are bound to give me."

"There will be no more opportunities." He pushed the leg of his chausses down and stood. "You will not play me for a fool twice."

She rose to her feet. "Is it only once, then?"

Ranulf's patience was pulled thin, though mostly because of disappointment. After she had let him kiss her up in the tree, then pressed herself against him, he had thought things would be better between them, but once again she swung her barbed tongue in the absence of a sword.

He took a step toward her. "That is enough, Lizanne."

"My lord!" called a voice outside the tent.

Ranulf shot her a warning look, then moved past her. "Enter, Sir Walter."

The knight threw back the flap and strode inside. He spared Lizanne a cursory glance before turning his attention upon Ranulf. "The patrol has returned."

"And?"

Walter sent a meaningful look in her direction. "No sign, my lord."

"No sign of what?" Lizanne asked.

Ranulf looked over his shoulder. "'Tis none of your concern."

"I would know if my brother rides for me!"

"You are in no position to know anything, Lizanne."

She put her hands on her hips. "Does he ride for me?"

"Be silent!"

Her jaw shifted, but just when he was certain she intended to further challenge him, she retreated to his wooden chest, lowered onto the lid, and drew up her legs to sit crossed-legged.

Suppressing the urge to instruct her in the proper behavior of a lady, Ranulf turned his attention to the remains of the meal brought earlier. Between bites, he discussed with Walter provisions, disputes, and preparations for the next day's ride.

"Where are we going?" Lizanne asked when mention was made of King Henry and his Eleanor.

Ignoring her question, Ranulf accompanied Walter to the tent opening.

"Your home?" she suggested.

Walter gave Ranulf a pitying look. "I shall leave you to her," he murmured and turned away.

"Is that our destination?" Lizanne pressed.

Ranulf dropped the tent flap and swung around. "You will show me respect in front of my men!"

She put her head to the side. "Aye, *my lord*—when you earn it."

He was across the tent in seconds. If not for her reaction to the force of his arrival—shoulders shrugging up to her ears, eyes wide—he would have yanked her off the chest.

Flexing his hands to keep from curling them into fists, he said, "Regardless of what you think I did, Lizanne, I would never beat you."

She lowered her gaze over him, paused on his hands, and looked up. "Why?"

Having never before considered his aversion to hitting a woman, he did not immediately answer. It was simply something he did not do. "Though I have had to kill many men, I have never hurt a woman."

Before Lizanne could rethink her words, she demanded, "You do not consider forcing yourself upon a woman harmful?"

Wardieu frowned. "You know I desire you, though I do not understand how it can be when you hate me with nearly every look and word that passes your lips, but I have not forced myself on you. And I will not."

She averted her gaze. She had wanted answers to the questions she had posed in Sir Walter's presence but had knowingly pushed Wardieu toward anger in search of further proof that the man whose kiss had caused something traitorous to move inside her was the same who had done terrible things on that night years ago. It had seemed worth the risk of physical harm to return herself to the singleminded place she had been when she had imprisoned him at Penforke. But he denied her that proof—as if there was no proof at all.

"I would like some fresh air," she said.

She felt the bore of his gaze, but he said, "I will escort you."

Outside, the sky was deep purple, pinpoints of light sprinkled upon its canvas. Did Gilbert see the same sky?

She paused to search the gathering darkness. Three days had passed since she had been taken from Penforke. Surely, he had arrived home by now and, finding her absent, gone in search of her.

"Hurry, Gilbert," she whispered, then lifted her skirts and hastened after Wardieu.

Directly ahead, a group of men who were gathered around a fire halted their conversation at the approach of their lord and his captive.

Lizanne lifted her chin in an attempt to project dignity in an otherwise undignified situation. Once she and Wardieu were past, the men's talk resumed.

At the outskirts of the camp, Wardieu leaned against a tree and watched as his men broke into boisterous song.

Standing a short distance away, Lizanne clasped her hands behind her back and savored the rare moment of peace between her and this man.

"What is it they sing?" she asked after several minutes. "I have not heard it before."

"I am surprised you do not know it. 'Twould seem your brother finally did something right by you."

She turned to him. "You have no right to speak against Gilbert. Unlike you, he is honorable."

Wardieu sighed, pushed off the tree, and strode away.

Regretting the harsh words that had shattered their peace, Lizanne followed and drew even with him as they neared the group of men. This time she did not look away from them but favored each with a level stare.

The men ribbed one another and exchanged winks, then one of the younger knights began a bawdy song that told the story of a great baron and his mistress. The others quickly joined in.

It was a song with which Lizanne was familiar, having heard it during the late-night watches at Penforke, but then it had been an earl, not a baron. She squared her shoulders and plodded ahead. Though Wardieu might not understand the relevance of the choice of song, she certainly did.

At the edge of the group, she pivoted and, almost immediately, the raucous voices faded away.

When all eyes were on her, she put her hands on her hips and finished the lyrics. "Ere he goes afightin' on yon green hill, she will clasp him to her and he will take his fill!"

Silence, save for the crackling fire.

Lizanne curtsied. In the next instant, she was being pulled toward the tent.

Wondering from which fount she drew such scandalous spirit, Ranulf pushed her in ahead of him and yanked the flap closed.

She turned to face him, smiled broadly, and loosed joyous laughter.

He could only stare. Never before had he seen such true expression of humor from a lady. But then, he must remember she was not much of a lady.

"Are you mad?" he bit.

Eyes bright, she shrugged and, amidst laughter, said, "Do not tell anyone...but methinks I am."

"Have done with this foolishness!"

She sighed long and high, pressed her shoulders back. "Pray do not lecture me, Ranulf."

He nearly startled over her use of his Christian name, having only ever heard her pair it with his surname—and a good dose of sarcasm.

"'Tis the only enjoyment I have had in a long time," she said. "Did you see their faces?"

"Clearly, I did."

"Oh, you make too much of it." She waved a hand. "I suppose now you will tell me how dishonorable Gilbert is—his one redeeming quality proven false."

"Should I ever meet this brother of yours, I fully intend to have words with him regarding your upbringing."

She sobered. "You will meet him. That I can promise."

Ranulf was as certain of it as she. "I want no more improper displays. Do you understand?"

"You have no humor," she said, then shrugged. "Very well. I give you my word I will not sing with your men again. Is that all?"

"It will do for the time being." He jutted his chin in the direction of her pallet. "Now remove your bliaut and go to bed."

"But it is too cold not to wear it." She clasped her arms about herself.

"Remove it, Lizanne." He strode to his chest and lifted the lid. When he turned and found she remained fully dressed, he glared.

She held up her hands. "I know. If I do not, you will." She blew out a long breath, loosened the laces, and tugged the bliaut over her head. Clad in her chemise, she hurried to the pallet and quickly slid beneath the blanket.

Ranulf followed and dropped the tunic he had removed from the chest beside her. "If you require more warmth, wear that."

He saw her surprise a moment before she looked away.

"I have business to which I need to attend," he said and crossed the tent. "Get some sleep. Another long day lies ahead."

"When will you return?"

He looked around. "Shortly, but do not worry. Aaron and Harold will be just outside should you require anything." He hoped it was all the warning she needed.

Hours later, Ranulf returned. Light-headed from one tankard too many of ale, he paused just inside the tent. Only one candle still burned, though it flickered uncertainly in its puddle of hot, melted tallow. Still, it was enough to see that Lizanne lay on her pallet with her back to him.

Knowing it best not to think in her direction, he made his way across the tent, pulled off his tunic, and started to lower to his own bed.

She whimpered.

"Lizanne?"

When she did not answer, he crossed to her and touched her shoulder. She was warm, her garment damp. A moment later, she quaked and made a low, miserable sound.

Ranulf turned her onto her back and saw she had donned the tunic he had given her. Why it should please him that it covered her as it had last covered him, he did not delve.

"Lizanne?"

She gasped and shook her head, but did not awaken.

He touched the hair upon her brow. It was damp as well and, when he brushed it back from her face, she cried out and slapped at him. However, before he could restrain her, she slumped and began sobbing.

He grasped her shoulders and gave her a firm shake.

"Nay!" She tried to pull away.

He shook her more forcefully.

Once more, she struck out, and this time her ring caught the flesh of his lower jaw.

Merciful Lord, she has done it again!

Wondering at the likelihood of further wounds gained at this woman's hands, he lowered himself onto her pallet and lifted her onto his lap.

Weeping now, she gripped his tunic.

"Lizanne, you are safe."

He could not be certain, but he thought she shook her head.

Crooking a finger beneath her chin, he raised her face toward his, murmured, "Safe," and pressed light kisses to her temples and damp eyelids.

Long after her weeping subsided and the candle had burned its last, he held her and, throughout, struggled against the temptation to lie down with her and give his body its rest. He knew that though she clung to him now, her response at awakening in his arms would surely be far different from this. Thus, when he was certain she was clear of whatever terrible thing hunted her in her sleep, he eased her onto the pallet, pulled the blanket up over her, and left her none the wiser that she had needed him.

11

Dᴜʀɪɴɢ ᴛʜᴇ ɴᴇxᴛ day's ride, Ranulf pondered Lizanne's nightmare. He had not spoken of it, for she seemed to have no recollection—so far removed from it that she had inquired after the small cut on his jaw. Rather than reveal her ring had put it there, he had shrugged off her question.

By early afternoon, they reached the castle of Lord Langdon's vassal, Sir Hamil Forster. It was a formidable structure, constructed of stone and rising against a backdrop of craggy, barren slopes.

Though Ranulf wanted nothing better than to return to his own lands, he was obliged to finish the king's business and, thus, determined to swiftly conclude the negotiations between the two parties.

Recently, Sir Hamil had taken it upon himself to claim this, Lord Langdon's property, as his own. If not for the vassal's close familial ties with King Henry, Langdon could have resolved the dispute simply enough with a show of force, likely resulting in Sir Hamil's capture and possibly his death. But Langdon had wisely appealed to the king to assist him in removing the errant knight from his lands. Occupied elsewhere, Henry had sent Ranulf in his stead after arriving at a compromise he felt would appease both parties.

Since they were expected, Ranulf and a fair-sized retinue were allowed entrance within the castle walls, but most remained without.

"I expect your complete obedience, Lizanne," he said once they had dismounted. He beckoned to Geoff who came alongside her, then turned his back on the two and took a step forward.

Lizanne frowned at Wardieu's back, leaned to the side to peer around him. However, no sooner did she catch sight of the short, stocky man who confidently strode forward than Sir Walter positioned himself beside his lord, once more blocking her view.

"Baron Wardieu," their host called, "welcome to Killian."

Wardieu strode forward to meet the man. "It has been a long journey, and my men are tired and hungry. I would see them settled quickly."

"They will be tended to forthwith, as I have set the cooks to preparing an early meal. As for your reception, I must apologize. We expected you days ago and had nearly given up on your visit."

"I was delayed," Wardieu said curtly.

"All is well with the negotiations?"

Wardieu's disapproving silence hung upon the air, then he said, "We will speak of them later. Now I would like a bath."

"Then come, I will show you inside."

As Wardieu and Sir Walter followed the man to the donjon steps, Geoff said, "Not a word, my lady," then lightly gripped her upper arm and urged her forward behind the others.

The main hall of the donjon was impressive and Lizanne found herself appreciatively eyeing the tapestries hung about the room.

"My daughter, Lady Elspeth," Sir Hamil announced. "She will see you to your chamber, Baron Wardieu."

Still held by Geoff, Lizanne craned her neck to better see the woman whom Sir Hamil had drawn forward. Though the lady was half-obscured by Wardieu's bulk, Lizanne did not need to see more to know the woman-child was beautiful.

Smooth, flowing brown hair that sparked envy in Lizanne framed a heart-shaped face dominated by large, liquid eyes. Though well-proportioned, she was petite—the top of her head falling short of Wardieu's shoulder by an inch or more—and so incredibly feminine it annoyed Lizanne. Not that she cared if Wardieu found the lady appealing.

"I trust your journey was without mishap, my lord?" Lady Elspeth's voice was so sweet Lizanne was certain there must be a hive nearby.

"Would that it were." Wardieu bent over her hand and pressed his lips to it.

Lizanne felt a strange, tight sensation in her chest.

"Jealous?" Geoff whispered in her ear.

She looked around. "Better she suffer the attentions of your lord than I."

He grinned. "Oh, she shall suffer naught, for that one is a lady."

His words wounded nearly as much as Sir Walter's that had equated her with a viper. Hating that they should tempt tears to her eyes, she looked forward again.

"My lord, you travel with a lady?" Sir Hamil's daughter asked.

As if he had forgotten Lizanne, Wardieu turned and swept his gaze over her. "Nay." He turned back to Lady Elspeth.

"Then who is that?" She crooked a finger at Lizanne.

All eyes turned to Lizanne. In that moment, painfully aware of her disarray—and grateful it was not made worse by having slept in her bliaut on the night past—she would have liked nothing better than to seek a dark corner.

"That is a servant," Wardieu replied after some consideration.

Lizanne gasped, but the tightening of Geoff's hand upon her arm served as a reminder that she was not at liberty to express her outrage. She set her teeth, stared at the woman.

Elspeth blinked prettily and returned her regard to Wardieu. "You must be a great baron if you are able to clothe your servants in such finery."

Sir Hamil moved forward. "Elspeth, show Baron Wardieu to his chamber—and take a girl with you to attend his bath."

"'Twill not be necessary," Wardieu said. "My servant sees to all my needs."

Elspeth's eyebrows rose as she glanced from Wardieu to Lizanne. Then, smirking, she turned and led the way to the stairs.

Geoff followed with a seething Lizanne in tow.

"'Tis not large," Lady Elspeth was saying when Geoff and Lizanne came down a short corridor, "but well-appointed as you can see, my lord."

Wardieu inclined his head. "It will do nicely."

Near the threshold of the chamber, Geoff stepped to the side and drew Lizanne alongside him.

"I will send hot water for your bath," the lady continued. "Should you need anything else, send word and I will do my best to accommodate you." Followed by Wardieu, she quit the chamber, swinging her hips and flashing a satisfied smile at Lizanne.

At least my teeth are even, Lizanne comforted herself, having noticed the lady's overlapped quite a bit.

"Lizanne," Wardieu said, "come inside."

Geoff gave her a slight push forward.

Lizanne strode past Wardieu and, upon reaching the middle of the chamber, turned and crossed her arms over her chest.

"How dare you," she said when Wardieu closed the door behind him.

"How dare I what?"

She longed to launch herself at him, but contained the impulse, determined she would not give him another reason to question whether she was woman or child.

"You know of what I speak. You not only called me a servant but insinuated that I am your leman."

Ranulf eyed the woman before him. She was angry, just as he had known she would be.

She took a step toward him. "I am as noble as that…woman who must swing her hips that a man might even know she has any!"

Was she jealous?

"Deny it you may, Ranulf Wardieu, but I am a lady."

He smiled wryly. "Since what time?"

Her eyes flashed, the high color in her face swept higher, and she took another step toward him.

Ranulf knew he pushed her and should not, but he was curious about the inner battle she waged—one he did not believe she would have bothered with on the day before. Had his questioning of whether she was woman or child hit the mark?

She drew a deep breath, pressed her shoulders back. "No matter that I once bested you at your warrior's game, I am and will ever be, Lady Lizanne Balmaine of Penforke."

Now *she* pushed *him*—or tried to. "Though by your behavior, methinks you have renounced that title, I acknowledge you are a lady. However, I am not so fool to announce your person to our hosts. For both our sakes."

"Both?"

"Just as I do not wish to explain my reason for holding you, Lizanne, I do not think you would like it any better—if not for how it would reflect upon you, then how it would reflect upon your brother who himself denies you are a lady by instructing you in the things of men."

She blinked.

"And since I do not trust you too long in the care of others, there must be an accounting for the reason we share this chamber. Hence, you have become my servant, and if 'tis believed you are also my leman since a squire can well tend to his lord's grooming..." He shrugged.

He heard her exhale and saw the color in her face recede. "I still do not like it."

"I did not think you would."

As they stared at one another, a knock sounded. "Enter!" he called.

The door opened and three servants scurried in, each toting a large, steaming pail. Eyes averted, the girls emptied the water into the wooden tub that was set before the brazier, then quickly withdrew.

"You should rest." Ranulf jerked his chin in the direction of the bed.

Lizanne glanced at it, and he felt her unease, for it was far too intimate a setting for a lady who was not, indeed, his leman. "Nay," she said, "I am fine."

"You intend to watch me bathe? Perhaps assist?"

"I do not!"

Nearing the thinnest portion of his patience, Ranulf said sharply, "Then you had best seek yon bed and draw the curtains."

Lizanne glared at him and wrestled with her longing to continue the argument. However, finding no room in which to do so, she turned on her heel and stalked toward the bed.

"When I have finished my bath and gone from the chamber," he called, "you may also bathe."

Though tempted to retort that she had not and would never bathe in another's dirty bath water, Lizanne busied herself with yanking the curtains closed. Before she slipped inside, she stole a glance behind and saw he watched her.

Over the next quarter hour, she sat in the center of the bed in the near darkness created by the curtains and listened to the servants return thrice more to finish filling the tub. When Wardieu thanked them the last time, she caught the sound of their girlish giggles and imagined he had smiled at them. Then the door closed.

She did not have to strain to hear the rustle of discarded clothes, the lap of water against the sides of the tub, nor the rasp of a body being scrubbed clean. But despite her discomfort at knowing what was happening beyond the curtains, made unseemly by her presence in the very same chamber, she began to long for her turn at the bath—no matter that the water would be little better than warm and less than clear. As had become obvious in Lady Elspeth's presence, these past days had been far from kind to Lizanne's appearance.

She startled when another knock sounded and tensed in anticipation of being ordered to open the door for whoever stood without.

"Enter!" Wardieu called.

Rather than giggling girls, it was grunting men who tread the wooden planks, the cause of their strain evident when one said, "Your chest, my lord."

He directed them where to set it and, shortly, the door closed again.

Lizanne waited, refusing to lie back lest she liked it too much and fell asleep only to awaken to chill bath water.

At last, she heard a great rush of water, evidence Wardieu rose from the tub. Now he would don clean garments.

"Be quick about it," she whispered. "And be gone!"

The chest lid groaned as he raised it, and once more she caught the rustle of clothes being picked over.

She counted the minutes it took him to dress, then a couple more during which silence fell and did not lift. What did he do? Yielding to curiosity, she quietly moved to the mattress edge and peered between two curtain panels at where he stood in profile before the tub, fully clothed.

A moment later, she caught her breath when she saw what held his attention—her dagger, the one with which she had defended herself at Penforke. Slowly, as if giving it great thought, he turned the weapon in his hand, causing the light to flit in and out of the recesses of the ornately carved handle.

Not once since that night she had gone to the cell in search of it had she thought of it again. But he had likely had it then, and certainly in the meadow where they had battled with swords. Recalling the look in his eyes when, his sword broken, he had advanced on her and demanded she fulfill their bargain, she understood. And felt anger surge when he slid the dagger into a scabbard on his belt.

Before she thought to draw another breath, she found her feet on the floor and the distance between her captor and her covered without the slightest regard to stealth. Therein lay her downfall, for he turned, caught the wrist of the hand with which she reached for the dagger, and whipped her around in front of him.

Pushing off the tub that was now at her back, she lunged forward and reached with her free hand to retrieve the dagger.

"Cease, Lizanne!"

She did not. Thus, she came up against the tub again. However, before she could launch herself off it a second time, he gave the push that decided the battle.

She grasped for something to keep from going where she was not ready to go, but only the air obliged. And the water, warmer than expected, parted for her.

Her out flung arms that caught upon the tub's rim saved her from going completely under, but there was nothing to save her from the sloshing water that doused her.

Face streaming, drenched gown billowing around her where she knelt in the tub, she looked up at Wardieu. Beneath toweled hair that gleamed pale again, his black eyes were hard, nostrils flared, and mouth compressed, all of which made the emotions that had found their pause the moment she hit water, surge anew.

"That"—she pointed to the dagger—"belongs to me!"

Shoulders rising with a breath deep, he unsheathed the weapon. "Nay, it belongs to me now." He ran his gaze down the blade, then looked back at her. "And I shall not soon forget how I came by it."

His threat hung on the air some moments before she laid her tongue to the only words to be found. "I detest you!"

Up went his eyebrows. "You are sure?"

"I could not be more certain!"

Nor could you tell a greater lie, taunted a little voice within.

Wardieu returned the dagger to its scabbard, set his hands on the tub's rim, and leaned toward her. "You would do well to remember, Lizanne, hate is as strong an emotion as love." A corner of his mouth lifted. "Be careful lest you mistake one for the other."

Though there was certainly air in the few inches between their faces, she could not breathe, unsettled as much by his words as his proximity. Then, mercifully, he straightened and turned away.

What had he meant in speaking such? Did he think her in love with him? Did he think she could ever feel such an emotion for a man she had once thought to see dead? Never could she love one like him. But if he were not such a man...

She squeezed her eyes closed. If only he had not wreaked such pain upon Gilbert and her. If—

"You look like a wet rat," he said, and she lifted her lids to find him peering at her from where he had halted alongside the door.

Even if he had warranted the same observation—and he certainly did not, the dust and grit of the long ride washed away and dressed as he was in fresh clothes—she did not think she could have tossed the words back at him. She was too tired. Indeed, if she did not know better, she might think herself drained of her last drop of blood.

"Bathe yourself and get into bed," Wardieu ordered. "I do not wish to find you sitting there when I return."

If only holding one's tongue were always so easy, she marveled.

A moment later, he pulled the door open, allowing a glimpse of two guards posted outside, then closed her inside.

Ranulf paused outside the door. Ignoring the curious stares of his men, he strained to catch a sound from within the chamber that might prove Lizanne was capable of the same emotion of other women, that of tears—conscious tears, not of the sort she had shed amidst her dreams.

A moment later, he caught her muffled sob. Though he had no liking for such expressions of a woman's misery, especially were he the cause, it heartened him to know she did possess such vulnerability. He had begun to think her made only of anger, hate, defiance and a fear she refused to allow more than a glimpse of.

He opened the door and stepped back inside.

Lizanne did not appear to hear him, head buried in her arms that were crossed on the rim of the tub.

Ranulf eased the door closed and stared at her dark head and shoulders that shook with emotion. Twice he heard a miserable, mewling sound escape her lips, but it seemed neither was allowed to give full vent to her sorrow.

When another sob broke from her, he strode forward and lowered to his haunches beside the tub. Knowing she would likely react violently to him bearing witness to her tears, he held his breath as he lowered a hand to her damp head. Though she stilled, she did not throw off his touch.

Lizanne was too stunned by Wardieu's return to react. Opening her eyes wide, she stared at the water below her and searched for some semblance of composure. Why had he returned? That he might witness the humiliation of her suffering? To taunt her? Was he pleased to know he had reduced her to such weakness?

As much as she wanted to believe it, she did not think so. The hand upon her head was comforting, not threatening, and the compassion emanating from him was so tangible that she was certain it brushed her skin through her clothes.

Curse his patience! The anger to which she had driven him was far too short-lived for the kind of man he had once been. Where was that heartless being who had uprooted her world?

She drew a shuddering breath, slowly lifted her head, and met his gaze.

They stared into one another, and then he smoothed a tear from her jaw. "Is it really so bad?" he asked, a smile lifting a corner of his mouth.

Bad? It was not bad enough, and therein lay her dilemma. "I do not detest you," she whispered. "Not anymore."

The other corner of his mouth lifted. "I know. Though I do not understand exactly what you are, Lizanne Balmaine, this I do know— you are not what you try so very hard to be."

She frowned. "Nor do I understand you. You are not at all as you should be."

"How should I be?"

She knew she should say no more but could not keep the uncertain words from her lips. "Evil. Without conscience. Bent on taking pleasure no matter the pain of others. That is the kind of man you should be. The kind I—" She pressed her lips, broke free of his penetrating gaze, and stared at her knuckles that had grown white where she gripped the tub.

"The kind you imprisoned to exact revenge upon," he finished for her, then uncurled her fingers from the rim and encased her hands in his. "Tell me what you believe I did to hurt you."

She lifted her face and contemplated his eyes, nose, mouth and, lastly, pale hair. So handsome...

Halfheartedly, she chastised herself for her traitorous feelings. Changed or not, he was the same man. If only she could convince her heart of it, but it would not accept what her eyes demanded it recognize.

And since when did your heart become involved in this dangerous web spun by your thirst for revenge, Lizanne?

She shook her head. "I cannot say."

Anger made a brief appearance in his eyes, then he drew her against him and pressed her head to his shoulder. "One day you will come to me," he said. "You will trust me."

She breathed in his scent through the weave of his tunic. "I know," she murmured. "'Tis what I fear most."

How long she let him hold her and let herself savor being held, she did not know, but too soon he pulled away. "I am expected in the hall."

Avoiding his gaze, she sank back on her heels in the water.

He straightened. "I shall send a servant with your meal."

She nodded. "I thank you."

Then, once more, he left her alone. But she did not cry again.

The lack of warmth brought Lizanne fully awake. Opening her eyes, she found morning had come after the long dark of the night when Ranulf Wardieu had not returned—at least, not while she lay awake.

Fearful he might have, indeed, joined her, she lifted her head and peered over her shoulder. She was the only occupant of the bed. There had been no other.

Relieved, but also unsettled in a way she did not care to reflect upon, she sat up. And was immediately reminded of her state of undress. Having soaked her garments and found Wardieu's chest locked on the night past, the only covering available to her had been a sheet from the bed. Around and around she had wound it about herself, and though it had held through the night, it had loosened considerably.

Dragging the makeshift garment higher and clasping it at the base of her throat, she surveyed the chamber. Bathed in the first light of morning, the shadows gradually receded as the sun rose outside the window. Colorful prisms of light, like those that arched against the sky after a long rain, fell across the floors and ever so slowly slid up the walls.

Confirming she was, indeed, alone, she pondered Wardieu's whereabouts and his reason for not returning to the chamber. Had he spent the night with one of the maids, perhaps Elspeth?

Feeling a constriction about her chest, she chastised herself for the emotion she refused to name jealousy, thrust thoughts of the man aside, and scooted to the edge of the mattress.

Grateful for the thick rushes beneath her feet, the absence of which would have made the chill in the room less tolerable, she straightened from the bed, drew the sheet tighter about her, and securely tucked the end of the cloth into the layers beneath her collarbone. Then she crossed the chamber, passed between two chairs that had been placed in front of the hearth following the removal of the tub on the night past, and halted before the mantel over which she had draped her garments to dry.

Though the bliaut was yet damp, owing to the demise of the fire while she slept, the undergarments and chemise had dried completely.

Recalling the sorry state of her clothing upon her arrival at the castle, she delighted in their renewed crispness and pressed her face to them. As she had applied soap to them as vigorously as her body, they smelled and felt clean again, something she had not realized she missed until that moment.

She shook out her shift and, leaving the bed sheet in place lest Wardieu returned without warning, pulled it over her head. Next came the chemise. She smoothed it down her hips, made quick work of the laces, and eyed the bliaut, the damp of which would surely seep into her dry undergarments. Unseemly though it was to eschew it knowing she might not be alone much longer, she reasoned there was nothing at all seemly about her relationship with Ranulf Wardieu. The bliaut could wait. In the meantime, she had her sheet.

Plucking at it through her chemise and shift, giving herself a good shake, she loosened it. It fell and pooled about her feet, whereby she snatched it up, pulled it around her shoulders, and tied it at her neck—a mantle of sorts. Then she addressed her hair by combing her fingers through it. As she tugged at a particularly vile knot, she wondered if Wardieu had put the comb in his chest and grimaced in remembrance of her struggle on the night past when no amount of effort had budged the lock.

Once she worked the last of the tangles free, she turned from the hearth, swept her hair over her shoulder, and began braiding it. She was halfway down its length when sunlight, having left its timidity behind, shifted and shone upon the nearest chair—and its occupant.

Suppressing a yelp, Lizanne released the braid and moved her gaze along an outstretched leg, over a slowly rising and falling chest, and into penetrating black eyes.

He had not spent the night with another, then? Her grudging relief was short-lived by the realization he had witnessed her morning antics. The only good of it, and it was a great good, was that she had not bared herself as it would have been easy to do believing she was alone.

For some moments, Wardieu remained unmoving, chin propped in the palm of a hand, one leg thrown over the arm of the chair. Then he said in a tone thick with what seemed more than sleep, "As ever, morning wears well upon you, Lizanne Balmaine."

She struggled to summon anger at him for not alerting her to his presence. Would he have done so had she made to remove the sheet before donning her undergarments?

They continued to stare at each other, the air fairly vibrating with emotions she did not know the name of and that sought to distract her from expressing indignation—and, in the end, succeeded. Instead of her enemy, she saw the one who had come to her yestereve and offered comfort. She saw he who not only made her body warm but had somehow touched her heart.

Still, she fought the treacherous waters that tried to drag her under and backed away.

You desire him, her mind named what she did not wish to name. *But look at him! He is the one. Your enemy!*

Coming up against the hearth, she splayed her hands against the stones behind.

He is responsible for all the pain. He is the one who tried to ravish you. He is the one who spilled Gilbert's blood.

And yet her body and heart saw another—a man capable of tenderness, of honor and word, who would never take what was not given freely.

Dear God, how can he look exactly like he who haunts my dreams and yet be another?

She caught her breath when Wardieu dropped his head back and reached a hand to her.

Do not, I tell you!

In the thrumming quiet of the chamber, her breath grew shallow and her heart beat so frenetically she felt sure he could hear it.

Though her mind rejected his invitation, her legs had no such misgivings and carried her toward him.

Eyes never leaving her face, he slid his leg off the chair arm, leaned forward and grasped her hand, urged her down.

Kneeling before him, Lizanne read the emotion in his eyes that she did not doubt was in her own.

Who have you become, Lizanne? This is not who you groomed yourself to be. Think swords and daggers, not kisses and caresses. Think the games of men, not the games of simpering females whose bodies are easily used and discarded. Think!

"I cannot," she breathed and knew he heard her from the frown that crossed his brow.

"Should not," he murmured, then drew his hand from hers and raised it toward her face. For a moment, his fingers hovered a hair's breadth from her flushed skin, and then he touched her.

Lizanne accepted the light caress that moved over her cheek, across the curve of her jaw, down her neck, then back up to trace her mouth.

Nearly overwhelmed by the feeling she was falling from a great height, plunging toward a destination she could not guess at but desperately wanted to reach, she swayed toward him and felt his warm breath against her lips. And then his mouth.

It seemed the most natural thing to close her eyes, to simply feel, and feel she did when he entwined his hand in her hair, drew her nearer, and deepened the kiss.

Lizanne did not realize she had lifted her own hand until she felt the strands run between her fingers and the heat of his scalp beneath them.

When he pulled his mouth from hers, she startled at the loss of intimacy, but next his lips found her jaw, then a breathtakingly sensitive spot beneath her ear.

She dropped her head back and whispered, "Ran."

Ranulf stilled, certain he could not have heard right, but again she said, "Ran." Not *Wardieu* or *RanulfWardieu* as ever she scorned. Indeed, only once had she simply called him *Ranulf*. And now *Ran*. Did it mean what it sounded like?

He opened his eyes upon her blackest hair that his fingers had loosened from its unfinished braid and which he longed to bury his face in. And that was not all he longed to do.

Walter would not approve—and rightly so.

Ranulf pulled his hand from her hair and drew back.

After a long moment, she lifted her lids.

"Say it," he said.

Confusion flit across her features, but then she slid her hand up his lightly whiskered jaw and leaned forward as if to press her mouth to his again.

He drew further back. "Lizanne, say what you feel."

She shook her head. "I...do not know what it is." She frowned. "Only that I should not feel it."

"Why?"

As soon as he asked it, he knew he should not have—at least, not at that moment—for her expression told that she was returning to a place of undisclosed accusations against which he could not defend himself, a place he did not wish to be with her ever again.

Desperate to recapture the soft, yielding Lizanne of minutes earlier, he gripped her waist and lifted her onto his lap. To his relief, she eased her stiffening, sank back against him, and lowered her head to his shoulder.

Looking down at her, he was drawn to the part in the sheet that she had tied around her shoulders and saw the faint, thin line his blade had drawn across her collarbone when she had forced him to swords.

He reached up and, as he traced its path, heard her catch her breath. "It seems," he said, "we each bear the mark of the other."

He heard her swallow. "I do not understand why you stopped," she said and hastily added, "Not that I am ungrateful."

Dare he tell her he wanted more from her than a moment of passion? That he wanted her to long for him as constantly as he longed for her? That he wanted her thoughts so preoccupied with him she could barely function as, more and more, his thoughts were fixed upon her? That even if he set aside all Walter had taught him and made her his leman, it would not be enough?

She tipped her head back and met his gaze. "Why did you stop?"

Liking too well the feel of her skin, he drew the sheet over her collarbone and lowered his arm. "Do not doubt that I would have more from you than kisses," he said, "but just as I do not take what is not my due or has not been given to me, neither do I take that which should not be given to me."

She narrowed her lids. "Then this is not your revenge? To lure me in with kindness and sweet kisses that I might want what I should not want—what I should rather die for?"

He pondered that. He had not regarded what he had allowed to happen between them as a means of retaliating against her for the humiliation of his capture and imprisonment. However, it was, indeed, a better revenge than any he had previously entertained.

"Though 'twas not intentionally set in motion," he finally said, "forsooth, 'tis a good revenge. But if it comforts you, know this—you do not suffer alone."

Lizanne searched Ranulf's face that was framed by the pale, pale hair that told he was the one. Somewhere, written upon it, there must be evidence of some secret pleasure at having unraveled the warrior she had woven into her being, at having her cling to him like the weak, love-sapped girl of ten and five who had ached for the day she would wed her Philip, at seeing the woman who had wielded a sword against him now wield only the keen edge of tears.

She moved out of his unresisting arms, lowered her feet to the floor, and went to stand before the hearth. Keeping her back to him, she said, "I do not know what has become of me, why I cannot hate you anymore, why my body betrays me." She shook her head. "How can it be?"

She heard the chair sigh as he leveraged out of it.

"Do not fight it," he said. "You will only fail, as I did, for you are a question never before asked of me."

As *he* was a question never before asked of her.

His footsteps retreated across the rushes, and she knew he meant to leave her alone with her misery again. But then a key rattled in a lock and hinges creaked, revealing his destination to be the chest that would yield up clean garments for the day ahead.

As the shush of cloth sounded, Lizanne felt the chill of the room that had been forgotten the moment Ranulf had touched her, fool that she was. Keeping her back to him, she yearned for a dark hole in which to wail out grief over her body's illicit longings. It was wrong for her to desire Ranulf. But though she dredged up his crimes, she could not help but wonder if his black heart had, indeed, healed, if it was possible to have done the things he had done and now be the man he appeared to be.

Was it by faith he had changed? She had heard it said that anything was possible with God.

"Lizanne," he called, "finish dressing and you may accompany me to the hall for the morning meal."

There was nothing she wanted to do less. She needed time to sort her thoughts and feelings, to take her body in hand and exorcise its infernal longings and misplaced loyalties—

"Now, Lizanne."

She turned and saw he was fully clothed, tunic to boots. "I cannot. My bliaut is not yet dry."

With furrowed brow, he strode forward, pulled her gown from the mantel, and shook it out. "'Tis mostly dry," he said. "Remove the sheet and lift your arms."

Wanting to argue but having no energy, she pulled the sheet off over her head, raised her arms, and pushed them into the sleeves when he lowered the bliaut over her. She stood still as he tugged the damp, resistant bodice into place and smoothed the skirt down her hips. Then he pulled the laces tight and tied them off.

"Slippers," he said, gesturing to where they sat upon the hearth.

She stepped into them.

"You are ready." He turned toward the door.

"My hair," she protested and pulled it over her shoulder to start anew that which his hands had undone. Throughout, she felt his impatience, but finally she knotted her hair to end the braid.

"Have you no ribbon?" he asked.

Glancing at him where he leaned against the door with arms folded over his chest, she almost laughed. "I do not, but have not a care, for it will not come undone. 'Tis the nature of my hair."

"Aye, were it fine like Elspeth's, it would unravel quickly."

Lizanne was glad she had not laughed, for she would have noticeably swallowed her mirth at being so unfavorably compared to that woman. Unfortunately, there was nothing she could do about the color heating her cheeks.

Still, there was good to be had in Ranulf's words, for they hauled her out of her miserable ponderings and back to a semblance of anger that would serve her far better for what lay ahead. And, when she stepped past Ranulf into the corridor and glimpsed the turning of his lips, she wondered if that had been his intention.

12

LIZANNE'S DISPOSITION DETERIORATED further when, upon entering the main hall, Elspeth materialized at Ranulf's side and placed a familiar hand upon his arm. Her short veil perfect upon smooth hair that could not possibly hold a knot, she looked entreatingly at Ranulf. "You will sit next to me again, will you not, Baron?"

"I would be honored, my lady." He turned to the dais at the far end of the room.

Lizanne stared after the couple, uncertain as to whether she should follow or retreat.

A touch on her arm brought her around, but the smug smile on Squire Geoff's face faded when he caught sight of her expression that she should not have allowed to linger.

He cleared his throat. "You may sit with Roland and me." He indicated the long table behind.

She nodded and followed him.

Though Squire Roland refused to more than glance at her, he moved down along the bench to make room for her.

Seated between the squires, uncomfortably aware of the damp embrace of her bliaut, Lizanne bowed her head as the chaplain said a hasty grace. Immediately following, the hall erupted with the sounds of fifty or more voracious men and women.

Picking at the simple meal that was placed before her, Lizanne found her gaze far too often drawn to where Ranulf was seated between Sir Hamil and the man's daughter. Each time, she felt her color rise, and each time she regretted the weakness that impelled her to gaze in his direction. The woman fawned over him, touching his sleeve as often as possible and giggling at his every word.

Lizanne grabbed a piece of cold, overcooked meat and popped it in her mouth. *She* did not giggle—had not since she was ten and five.

She looked again at Elspeth and disliked her all the more for the beguiling smile she turned upon Ranulf, and yet more for the taunting smile the petite woman pulled when she looked straight at Lizanne.

Lizanne smiled tightly back, refusing to be the first to look away.

With a tinkling laugh that carried across the hall, Elspeth tossed her head and leaned toward Ranulf.

Lizanne chewed and chewed until she pulverized the tough meat well enough to swallow. It went down like a lump. Pushing away the remainder of her meal, she sat back and folded her hands in her lap.

Moments later, she felt a telling prickle along her spine and looked around to find Squire Geoff watching her.

She swept an errant lock of hair from her eyes and raised her eyebrows. "I do not suppose that if I smiled at you, you would think it genuine?"

He shook his head. "Save your smiles for Baron Wardieu. He will appreciate them more than I."

She glanced at the subject of their discourse, grimaced, and looked back at the squire. "I do not think so."

"Then you are wrong."

She raised her eyebrows again, but Geoff gave her a dismissive look and peered past her. "Mayhap we can practice with slings this morn, Roland," he suggested.

The other squire leaned forward to get a clear view of his friend without having to look at Lizanne. "I would prefer swords."

Geoff grinned. "You will never master the sling if you do not try."

"It is but a toy. Now a sword…"

It was as if Lizanne had vanished. Neither squire acknowledged her, even when she leaned forward and blocked their view of each other. They simply leaned opposite and continued their conversation behind her back.

"I am still a better shot than you," Roland boasted.

"Ha!" Geoff countered.

Lizanne looked from one to the other. "I can help," she said and, at last, gained their attention. "I am quite adept with a sling. Have you one along?"

They exchanged looks, then turned their attention back to the meal.

Lizanne laid a hand upon Geoff's arm. "I speak true."

He glanced down, then raised to her a face tight with disapproval.

She drew her hand back. "'Twill hurt naught for me to show you."

"Have a woman instruct me in the use of arms?" He snorted.

She put her head to the side. "Were you not at Penforke Castle when I put an arrow through one of your lord's pennants?"

His eyes widened.

"I assure you, Squire Geoff, it was not by chance I did so."

After a long moment, he said, "You would trick me again?"

"Nay, I vow 'tis not my reason for offering to instruct you."

He studied her, abruptly rose from the table, and stalked away.

Dejected, Lizanne watched him depart the hall, then turned her attention to the other occupants.

Unequally, they consisted of Sir Hamil's and Lord Ranulf's men, each group set noticeably apart from the other. Though Ranulf's men were generally better mannered than Sir Hamil's, they were coarse—the lot of them.

She shifted her gaze from a disgusting old man who was making obscene gestures at a young serving wench, and her gaze fell upon a handsome, flame-headed man seated at the far end of Sir Hamil's table.

Surprisingly, his attention was set upon her. Having caught her eye, he smiled wide.

Pleased to see one friendly face among the many, she returned the smile and inclined her head before moving on. For the first time since her arrival in the hall, her eyes met Ranulf's. And his expression told that he had seen the exchange with the other man and was not pleased.

She glared. Having abandoned her, there he sat with that harpy practically in his lap and thought nothing of it. But a mere smile between strangers and he looked fit to strangle them. A blight on Ranulf Wardieu!

"Here," Geoff said, resuming his seat and discreetly dropping a strip of leather in her lap.

Lizanne lowered her chin and stared at the sling, then at him.

He smiled as he picked up a piece of cheese and handed it to her. "No stones," he said. "I would not trust you to refrain from launching one at Lady Elspeth."

She glanced across the hall. Ranulf had returned his attention to that lady and she thought that, had she a stone, she might, indeed, be tempted.

She ran her fingers over the smooth leather. "'Twould be easier to instruct you out of doors."

"Surely you needn't cast a stone to show us how to use it?" Roland challenged.

"'Tis the best way," she said as she moved back so he could see as well.

After rolling the cheese into a compact ball, she pressed it to the center of the leather. "Assuming this to be a stone, you must place it so."

The squires exchanged looks of amusement and Roland snickered.

Lizanne raised a finger. "The placement is important. You want your stone to find its mark, do you not?"

They rolled their eyes, nodded, and leaned nearer.

"Place your fingers through the loops...see?" She slid her own through them and turned them over to demonstrate. "Not too tightly, for when you arc it..."

Nodding at something Elspeth was saying, Ranulf glanced toward Lizanne and frowned at the sight that greeted him. Roland and Geoff sat close to her, heads bent over her lap, nodding as she spoke animatedly.

When she lifted her hand above the level of the table, he caught a glimpse of something long and narrow before it disappeared. He did not know the object of their intense discussion, but he did not like it.

He grew even more annoyed when he heard Lizanne laugh minutes later and turned to find her smiling squire to squire. Geoff and Roland beamed back, under her spell once again.

For the remainder of the meal, Ranulf kept a close eye on the far table but never discovered what Lizanne hid. When the annoyingly long repast was concluded, he excused himself and headed straight for her, only to be brought up short by Walter.

"I must needs speak with you, my lord," his vassal said.

Ranulf tore his eyes from where Lizanne was being assisted to her feet by the squires and glared at Walter. "What is so urgent it cannot wait?"

Walter looked knowingly at the object of Ranulf's agitation. Jaw hardening, he stepped closer. "King Henry's negotiations, my lord."

Ranulf scowled. "First I must see to another matter. I will meet you at the stables shortly."

Walter inclined his head and strode opposite.

Geoff, followed by Lizanne and Roland, met Ranulf hallway across the hall. "Godspeed, my lo—"

"You have enjoyed yourselves?" Ranulf asked.

Geoff's smile fell. "My lord, Lady Lizanne was merely showing us how to hold a sling. She knows much about—"

"A sling! Did you learn naught from her first deception? Did it not occur to you she might turn it on you?"

Lizanne came out from behind Geoff and placed herself directly in front of Ranulf. "Unlike some men," she said, "your squire is not a fool twice." She snatched up his hand, pressed the sling into it, and stepped aside.

Ranulf looked down and felt his lips twitch when a ball of cheese rolled from his hand to the floor. Immediately, it was snatched up by a scraggly dog that scurried off to a corner to enjoy its booty. "It seems you have learned well, Geoff, but in future, leave your training at arms to men."

A grin surfacing, the squire nodded and took the sling his lord held out to him.

"And do not call her 'lady,'" Ranulf added. "She is no more." Certainly not in this place. But elsewhere? He met her narrowed gaze, then strode forward, took her arm, and drew her stiff figure across the hall.

It was good neither spoke as they traversed the stairs and the corridor, for with each step, Ranulf sensed a lightening of Lizanne's pique. Indeed, by the time they reached their chamber, she strode almost easily alongside him. Once inside, she pulled her arm free, crossed to the bed that had been put to rights in their absence, and sat down upon it.

"What are you up now, Lizanne?" Ranulf asked where he had halted just inside the chamber.

She crossed her ankles, clasped her hands before her, and shrugged. "Naught to say?"

She pressed her lips together, shook her head, and raised her gaze to the ceiling.

Wondering where the woman he had held in his arms this morn had wandered off to, he said, "'Tis just as well, for I haven't time to discuss this with you. But I assure you, we shall later."

She sighed.

"I shall set men at the door," Ranulf said, then turned on his heel and quit the room.

The moment the door closed behind him, Lizanne flopped back on the bed and tried not to think about the woman with whom Ranulf would likely be spending time—she of fine hair that could not possibly hold a knot.

"Her loss," she muttered and turned her thoughts to what she could do with the hours that surely yawned before her. As she mulled, she plucked at the bodice of her bliaut, the dampness of which continued to irritate her skin though it no longer chilled her as deeply. Of course, that had much to do with the warmth of the hall and, now, the chamber.

She sat up, eyed the hearth where a fire once more burned, and was off the bed in a moment and out of the bliaut minutes later. Once she had secured the garment upon the mantel where it might finish drying in Ranulf's absence, she undertook an exploration of the chamber. Not unexpectedly, it yielded little of interest. However, what did hold her interest was what drew her to the window—the din of squires tilting at a battered quintain in the bailey below. That lasted for, perhaps, an hour, and when it was done, there seemed nothing left to do but pass the time with a nap.

She laid down with her head at the foot of the bed and, hoping her lids would soon grow weighted, considered a scene depicted on the ceiling to floor tapestry that stretched the length of the wall behind the bed—a romantic scene that wove together a lady and her knight in various states of mutual adoration.

Lizanne started to close her eyes against the foolery, but then she glimpsed a flutter of movement from the left-hand side. Though she knew it was likely just the breeze come through the window that had gone to play behind the tapestry, a thought struck her and she slid off the bed.

She drew back the tapestry. Dust particles flew into her face. Rubbing at her prickling nose, undeterred by the accumulation of dirt and the solid stone wall facing her, she went behind the tapestry and, in the darkness, slid her hands over the stones. Near the bed's poster, she felt the breath of air that moved the tapestry. A moment later, her seeking fingers found the groove of a portal.

With quick, short breaths, she searched for the hidden catch and located it near the floor. When pressed, the door creaked inward to reveal a deeper darkness.

Lizanne nearly obeyed the impulse to go directly into it, but the blast of chill air reminded her of her state of undress and she hurried out from behind the tapestry. With hands that so trembled with excitement it seemed they sought to thwart her, she dragged on her nearly dry bliaut and sloppily did up her laces.

Shortly, she entered the exceedingly narrow passageway and placed her hands on opposite walls to assure her safe descent in the absence of a torch to light the way. She came upon two other landings with doors but, eager to find what lay at the end, moved past them, assuring herself she could explore them on her return.

That last thought made her pause. She laughed and shook her head. If she found a way out of Killian, there would be no need to return.

There were things in the passageway that did not bear thinking about—the moist, diaphanous threads of spiders' webs, scuttling around and over her feet, the stench of mold and rot. Thus, when she glimpsed a thin line of light ahead, she released one of many breaths she had held.

Taking the final steps with reckless excitement, she came to the last landing and pressed her face to the crack in the door. Through the narrow opening, she glimpsed greenery.

She released the catch and slowly pulled the door open, revealing a wall of thick rosebushes. Stepping cautiously into the bright, glorious sunshine, she eased the door closed and stood silent for several minutes to listen.

Naught.

She pressed herself against the donjon's wall and moved along it until she spotted a break in the overgrown bushes. She bent low and peered out at an enclosed, unkempt flower garden and, with an eye to escape, surveyed the possibilities. The walls were high, but not so much that they could not be scaled.

When there appeared to be no one about, she carefully eased herself between the thorny branches and straightened on the opposite side. After brushing away the cobwebs and leaves and loosening the thorns from her skirts, she began an exploration of the grounds.

Quickly, she discovered it was laid out like a maze, its paths winding, merging, and often ending abruptly.

Momentarily forgetting her plans for escape, Lizanne plucked a rose and wove it into her braid as she rounded a corner.

She halted. There, on a bench in the middle of a grassy, rectangular courtyard, was the redheaded man who had smiled at her during the morning meal.

She retreated a step, but not before he looked up.

"I am sorry," she said as he jumped to his feet. "I did not mean to intrude."

"You are not." He took a step toward her. "Indeed, I would be honored if you would join me." Smiling warmly, he gestured at the bench.

She shook her head. "I thank you, but I must return to my chamber."

"Of course," he said with disappointment, then asked, "How came you to be in the garden? There is but one entrance." He nodded at the door across the courtyard.

Only one entrance, and it led back into the donjon. So, she would have to scale the wall after all…

Deciding it best to change the subject, she said, "May I ask your name?"

He strode forward and gallantly bowed. "Sir Robyn Forster, eldest son of Sir Hamil."

That surprised her. Unlike Elspeth, he did not resemble his father. "Lady Lizanne Balmaine of Penforke," she introduced herself with a curtsy.

His smile slipped. "Lady? I understood you to be the…servant of Baron Wardieu."

She had momentarily forgotten she bore that distinction. "I suppose I am that, too," she grudgingly conceded.

Robyn put his head to the side. "Forgive me if I appear dull-witted, but I do not understand the situation." Lightly, he gripped her arm and pulled her toward the bench. "Perhaps you can explain it."

Lizanne's annoyance flared at his handling of her person for, of late, it seemed she was always being pulled along after a man. And she was weary of it. However, she suppressed the impulse to jerk free when she realized that here might be one whose aid she could enlist. Thus, she allowed herself to be drawn down beside him upon the cool stone bench.

"I would like to know more about you," he said, enfolding her hand in his and raising it to his lips.

Such was the scene Ranulf Wardieu happened upon.

13

"GOD ALMIGHTY, WHAT is this?"

Startled to their feet, Lizanne and Sir Robyn stared at the man who filled the doorway.

He looked fierce, muscles bunched in readiness, challenge—as evidenced by his hand gripping his sword hilt—hanging upon the air.

Protectively, Sir Robyn stepped in front of Lizanne.

"Robyn of Killian," Ranulf growled, "take up your sword, for I would have you feel the bite of mine."

Lizanne peered around the young man who stood unmoving before his opponent, the likes of which she was certain he had never faced. After a long moment, he raised his hands, palms up. "I am unarmed, Baron Wardieu."

"Then get you a sword!"

Sir Robyn lowered his arms. "What manner of transgression am I accused of?"

"Trespass!"

The young man gave a short laugh. "If you refer to my being with Lady Lizanne, you are mistaken. We have but talked. No insult have you suffered from our innocent meeting, nor was one intended."

"Do you think me blind and dim-witted?" Ranulf strode forward. "Get your sword, man."

Loathing the role of helpless, shrinking female, Lizanne stepped from behind Sir Robyn and hastened forward to meet Ranulf. They halted with barely a foot between them.

Up close, Ranulf appeared even more wrathful. The muscles of his jaw worked, his nostrils flared, and his eyes were like slick, bottomless pools of pitch.

She raised her chin. "There will be no bloodletting. If you must blame someone, blame me, for 'twas I who intruded upon Sir Robyn's sanctuary."

"Do not doubt for one moment I hold you responsible for this treachery, Lizanne, but I will see to you after I have dealt with this whelp." He pushed her aside and advanced on Sir Robyn.

Lizanne spun around, saw the young man's gaze shift nervously between Ranulf and her.

"Aye," Sir Robyn said, voice strained, "I will fight you."

"Nay!" Once more, she inserted herself between the two.

Ranulf halted. "Do not make a coward of a man who has earned his spurs, Lizanne!"

She turned a hand around his arm and said low, "Ranulf, he speaks true. 'Twas naught but a kiss upon the hand. And naught else would it have been had you not come upon us. I beseech you, do not hold him accountable for the sins of one who but thought to use him to further her means of escape."

Sensing his hesitation in the barely perceptible easing of his muscles, she added, "I am not worth dying for."

Ranulf nearly jerked at hearing her speak the words that had first passed his own lips and, with their casting, he had meant. No longer, though. In spite of her maddening nature and stubborn resolve to hold him accountable for something so terrible that she had sought his death, he wanted her more than he had ever wanted anything, and if it meant fighting for her, so be it.

Sensibilities stunned by the admission, he said, "I do not plan on dying, not even to please you."

Her lids flickered as she searched his face, and then she whispered, "It would not please me. But you know that, for as you have told, you know me better than I know myself."

It was what he had said that morning in the tent when she had stated she would never be receptive to his embrace.

"Please, Ranulf."

He looked to where Sir Robyn watched warily and felt a rush of shame at having challenged one who was not much beyond the age of a boy. And for a mere kiss upon the fingers.

Lord, what this woman does to me!

Though poised to accede to her beseeching, he realized there was something to be had from the moment. And he intended to take it, even if only for his peace of mind. "Very well. I shall withdraw my challenge—providing you give your word you will attempt no more escapes."

He heard her swallow and saw the color recede from her face.

"Your word, Lizanne."

She jerked her chin. "I give it. No more escapes. But if Gilbert—"

"Not even if he comes for you."

She removed her hand from him and tightly clasped it with the other at her waist. "Not even then. You have my word."

But would she keep it?

Ranulf returned his gaze to Sir Robyn. "The challenge is withdrawn. Leave us now."

The young man shifted his gaze to Lizanne. "My lady?"

She looked over her shoulder. "All is well, Sir Robyn. Pray, leave us."

He inclined his head, then stalked to the donjon and disappeared inside.

In the ensuing silence, Lizanne crossed to the bench and sank down upon it.

Ranulf followed but remained standing as he considered the flower woven into her braid.

He reached forward and plucked it. "Did he give this to you?"

Her hand came up to snatch it back, but when she grasped only air, she blew a breath up her face and lowered her chin to consider the pink ovals of her thumbnails. "I picked it."

Ranulf looked around. "How came you to be here? I would not believe you single-handedly outwitted the men posted outside your door." In the next moment, he silently scoffed at the absurd statement. To his detriment, he kept forgetting she was like no other lady he had encountered. "Or maybe I would," he muttered.

She shook her head. "I doubt they even know of my disappearance."

He turned and looked up the vertical face of the donjon. "You cannot have climbed from yon window," he said, though it would not have surprised him to see knotted bed linens hanging from the sill.

"'Twas by a secret passageway I came to be in this place."

Of course. Ranulf berated himself for not considering the existence of one. It was not uncommon for hidden stairways to be incorporated into a donjon as a means of escape should it come under siege, though they were more often used for trysts among nobles.

Unnerved by how careless he was becoming, he leaned near and tilted her face up. "And you thought to escape."

She shrugged. "It was too good an opportunity to waste."

"Our new understanding precludes any more escape attempts, Lizanne."

Her lashes swept down. "You are not likely to let me forget that."

"Verily." Briefly, he touched his mouth to hers. "Now show me this secret passageway."

Lizanne stood and strode past him. She led him along paths so jumbled and wound around one another that he began to think she had lost her way, but then she called over her shoulder, "Through there," and pointed to a narrow opening in the rosebush wall. A moment lower, she disappeared through it.

It was a tighter squeeze for Ranulf, but he caught up with her just as she was stepping through the hidden doorway.

"Our chamber lies three flights above," she said as he closed the door behind him, throwing the landing into darkness.

He reached out and caught her arm. "Did you not bring a torch?"

"I did not think to, but the dark does not frighten me so much."

Then she was no longer haunted by her fall into the ravine. "I am not thinking of your fear, Lizanne," he said. "You have little enough of that. 'Tis your neck that concerns me."

"Oh, that..."

He stepped ahead of her, threaded his fingers with hers, and drew her up the winding steps.

They reached the first landing, but as he started up the next flight, she entreated, "Just a peek."

He knew what she wanted, his hand having recognized the shape of a door, and started to refuse her. However, the thrum of excitement that had supplanted her dismal mood stopped him. "Very well."

She slipped her hand from his and, a moment later, he heard the click of the catch she had located. Dim light filtered into the passageway as she quietly opened the door a crack and peered at the back of a tapestry. As she pulled the door wider, voices fell upon their ears.

"'Tis enough," Ranulf whispered and drew her back. However, as he started to ease the door closed, Sir Hamil's voice rose loudly from within.

"You are betrothed to another, Elspeth!"

"That old codger!"

"He will make you a good husband. He is wealthy—"

"As is Baron Wardieu. He would make me a better husband. I would marry him."

Ranulf hesitated, though he knew he should not.

"He will offer for me, Father. I know he will."

"I do not believe it, Elspeth. Methinks he is well satisfied with the lady who shares his bed."

"That harlot is no lady! He has said as much himself. Have you not seen how brazenly her eyes follow him everywhere?"

Beneath his hand, Ranulf felt a tremor go through Lizanne.

"And that hair of hers! And the state of her clothes! And the way she mucks about with his squires. Nay, if ever that wanton was of noble birth, there is good reason she no longer bears that distinction."

"Elspeth, you know not what you speak of."

"Do I not? She is but a bed warmer. Soon he will take another wife and throw her back whence she came."

Lizanne pulled out of Ranulf's hold and leaned back against the stone wall alongside the door.

"Enough, Elspeth! The man is recently widowed, and I doubt he is ready to assume the burden of another wife. I know I would not."

"Aye, but you have your heir. He does not."

It was true. And now Lizanne likely knew more about him in these last minutes than he had revealed in the past four days, for there had been no occasion or reason to talk of his marriage. Was there now?

"We will speak no more of this, daughter," Sir Hamil said. A moment later, a door slammed loudly, its vibrations felt through the stone.

Ranulf eased the door closed, captured Lizanne's arm. "Come." He pulled her after him up the steps.

He was heartened that she was able to keep pace despite emotions that were nearly as tangible to him as his own. However, as he reached the landing of their chamber, she stumbled. Glad he had kept hold of her, he tightened his grip and pulled her up beside him and into his arms.

Hearing her muffled sob, he drew her nearer and breathed, "Shh."

She swallowed convulsively.

He tucked her head beneath his chin, said softly, "'Tis rare any good comes from listening in on conversations not meant for one's ears."

She did not reply but, after a while, drew a shuddering breath, lifted her head, and said, "I lied."

"Again?" Ranulf could not keep the amusement from his voice.

"Again. I do fear the dark."

"Why? There is nothing there that is not also present in daylight."

"In that you are wrong, Ranulf. Dreams and memories lurk there, ones I cannot escape no matter how far or how long I run."

Recalling the nightmare he had witnessed and sought to pull her free of, he said, "What haunts you, Lizanne?"

Just when he thought she did not mean to answer, she whispered, "I fear someday Gilbert will be taken from me, and then I shall truly be all alone."

Ranulf was surprised at the jealousy engendered by her words. Her brother possessed that part of her he did not dare hope he ever would—devotion. Aye, and love. But was that really what he wanted? Her love?

He rejected the idea, but it came back to him.

"Most of all," she continued, "methinks I fear you, Ranulf Wardieu."

He knew that. Despite her bluster, he had seen fear in her eyes on more than one occasion, but until that moment he had not realized its true depth. It went beyond reason. And the answer lay in that which she held back.

"What of the past?" he asked, knowing there lay the key to the mystery of her.

"You *are* the past and, by my foolish actions, I have made you my present...my future. You are everywhere, and I cannot seem to escape you."

He drew his hand up her arm and set it upon her cheek. "You have spoken of a previous meeting between us. I pray you will tell me of these sins you cast upon me, for I do not recollect ever having seen you before that day in Lord Langdon's hall, and 'tis not likely I would forget you if I had."

He felt her waver as if she might speak of what she held close, but then he felt her spine stiffen and jaw tighten beneath his fingers.

"I cannot," she said, "for then I would have more to fear from you."

Patience, he reminded himself, but he had too little left. "God help me," he muttered and released her. He bent, found the catch, and dragged the door open.

"Go," he said.

She stepped inside and, when he came out from behind the tapestry, he saw she had gone to stand before the window with her back to him.

Ranulf strode across the chamber and threw open the door.

The two guards outside turned, their tolerant grins wiping clean the moment they beheld their lord.

"My lord!" one gasped. "But…how…?"

"Send for Geoff," Ranulf said and slammed the door.

When he turned back into the chamber, Lizanne faced him, her expression solemn.

"I have much business to complete this evening, and 'tis best if you are not underfoot. Geoff will stay with you to ensure you do not find yourself in any more mischief."

Her eyebrows rose. "I have given my word I will not attempt to escape again."

"That you have but, regrettably, I will not feel able to trust you until you feel able to trust me."

"I see."

"I am glad you do."

He stalked to where a basin of water sat upon a table. "God willing, we will depart this place on the morrow," he said, then splashed his face.

"Where are we going?" Lizanne spoke from directly behind.

He turned and saw she held a hand towel. "That need not concern you."

She nodded, then reached up to blot the moisture from his skin.

He was too shocked by the gesture to do anything but accept it.

"There." She stepped back.

He studied her, then said, "I do not require your complete submission, Lizanne. I would simply have less arguing between us."

"I am not submitting. I but perform the duty of a servant."

What was she up to now?

"You should take a comb to your hair," she suggested.

He stepped past her, unlocked the chest with a key from a purse on his belt, removed the comb, and once more locked the chest. Lowering to its lid, he beckoned to her. "Another duty a servant performs."

He saw her jaw shift and heard the grind of her teeth, but she took the comb.

"Gently," he instructed.

Lizanne steeled herself, then stepped alongside him and pulled the comb through the ends of his hair, working her way up to his scalp. Unlike her own hair, his easily gave to the persuasive tugs and fell into place. It was an almost pleasurable task.

But it was also dangerous, she learned a short while later when he caught her around the waist and pulled her onto his lap. Finding his face near hers, her heart tripped over itself.

"I have been wondering about this." He took her right hand in his and ran a finger down her crooked thumb. "How came you by it?"

She tried to pull her hand free, but he held fast. "An accident," she said, attempting to close her mind to the flood of memories. She did not wish to dwell on that particular incident any longer, for it was too unsettling in light of the battle she now waged between body, heart, and mind.

"Tell me of your wife, Ranulf," she said, hoping to change the topic.

His lids lowered so that his eyes were dark, narrow slits. "You already know more than I would have you know."

"I know only that she is no longer living."

"Which is sufficient."

"But—"

A knock sounded.

Ranulf lifted Lizanne off his lap, set her on her feet, and crossed the chamber. "Do not test the boy overly much," he said over his shoulder before opening the door.

"Godspeed, my lord," Geoff greeted him.

Ranulf motioned him inside. "You shall remain with Lizanne until I conclude my dealings with Sir Hamil."

Confusion lining the squire's brow, he turned his head to view the two men posted in the corridor.

"You see," Ranulf continued, "she has discovered a secret passageway that leads from this room to the gardens below. I would not have her undertake any further explorations."

Lizanne scowled.

Geoff nodded. "I will see no harm or mischief befalls her, my lord."

Ranulf charged her with a look of warning, then quit the chamber.

"Would you like me to show you how to use that dagger?" Lizanne asked when several minutes had passed and neither had spoken.

Geoff fingered the weapon on his belt. "Methinks a game of chess would be safer."

She grimaced. "Moving a bunch of funny little pieces around a checkered board? If you ask me, 'tis a waste of time."

The squire's eyebrows rose. "You do not know the game, do you?"

"I am familiar with it. I just have never been interested enough to engage in a match."

"Then I shall teach you." He stepped to the door, opened it, and spoke with one of the guards. When he turned back, he wore a smile. "With any luck, Aaron will locate a board for us."

Lizanne shrugged. "Very well, but I warn you—I am a fast learner."

14

THEY LEFT KILLIAN before the first light of dawn spread its tentative fingers across the night sky.

For reasons unknown to Lizanne, Ranulf kept his distance over the next three days' ride. On the second day out, he even allowed her an old packhorse that, in the end, made her rides with him seem like too much comfort.

More than once, as she urged her horse to a quicker pace, she caught herself dwelling on how Ranulf's arms had felt on either side of her and the comfort of his broad chest against her back. It was, however, more than just her body's comfort she missed.

Though Ranulf was generally kind, he seemed to have detached himself emotionally, and she guessed he wearied of her. And tried to feel pleased.

In the late afternoon of the third day, they set up camp on the outskirts of London where peddlers, eager to sell their wares, descended upon them offering sweetmeats, new wine, cloth, buckles—anything and everything. It was a sight to behold.

Perched on a boulder, Lizanne watched the good-natured haggling between a knight and purveyor of small pastries. In the end, it was the purveyor who held out and obtained a price just below that which he had originally asked. Still, he grumbled as he exchanged three of the little pies for the coins the knight dropped in his palm.

A large, aproned woman approached Lizanne, holding up a handful of colorful ribbons, her toothless smile entreating. Lizanne felt a small thrill as she beheld the assortment, but she had no coin with which to purchase one.

With regret, she shook her head and turned her attention to Ranulf who stood with Walter near the horses. Although they were too far off for their conversation to be heard, she surmised they spoke of matters of importance. She had noted Walter's return from the city earlier and thought it likely he carried word from the king.

"Milady," the large woman persisted, tugging at Lizanne's sleeve, "this 'ere one would look nice with yer pretty black 'air."

Lizanne opened her empty hands. "I am sorry, but I have no coin."

The woman pressed her lips tightly and trundled away.

Laughter drew Lizanne's gaze to Geoff and Roland, and when she grimaced, they winked.

Deciding the day was done, she scooted down the smooth face of the boulder and went to Ranulf's tent where she stretched out on her pallet. After the long day of riding, it felt wonderful.

It was fully dark outside when Geoff arrived with the evening meal. In comparative silence, he and she ate a sumptuous variety of foods bought from the purveyors. When they finished, he brought out a small chess set, and they played a game on the floor of the tent. Not surprisingly, she lost again—for the fifth time.

"You are improving," Geoff said as he scooped the pieces into a pouch.

She shrugged. "It seems such an easy game. I do not understand why I continue to struggle with the moves. There are too many pieces, do you not think?"

Grinning, he stood and reached out a hand. "Practice," he said as he assisted her to her feet. "Much practice."

She smiled. "One day I will beat you at this game, you know."

"Then you plan to remain a long while with Baron Wardieu?"

She looked away. "I have not much choice in the matter."

"Methinks you have more choice than you realize, my lady."

Lizanne absorbed his words. However, as they were too worrisome to contemplate, she pushed them to the recesses of her mind and said, "Then I will have to defeat you soon."

He chuckled, threw back the tent flap and, as he stepped out into the cool night air, put over his shoulder, "I do not doubt you will."

Clasping her hands behind her back, Lizanne disciplined herself to mentally retrace the moves he had used to place her in checkmate. He had been so cunning!

Shortly, Ranulf entered. "You have eaten," he said with a glance at the cluttered tray.

"Geoff and I, but we left plenty for you." She turned and crossed to the washbasin.

Ranulf stared at her back and wondered at the impulse that had cost him several coins—more, how his gift would be received. Rethinking it, he seated himself and removed his boots.

As he picked over the leftovers, he watched Lizanne move about the tent as she prepared for bed and, as was best, looked elsewhere when she removed her bliaut.

Clothed in her shift and chemise that covered her well enough though they were quite creased and limp from days of wear, she sat upon her pallet and began the nightly ritual of bringing order to her wild hair. When the comb became caught in a great tangle, she muttered and tugged until the teeth came free, then continued with the task.

Ranulf pushed his food aside, stood, and crossed the tent.

Dropping her head back, Lizanne frowned up at him, and more deeply when he held out his hand. With a suspicious light in her eyes, she yielded the comb.

He stepped to her back, lowered to the pallet, and drew her into the vee of his thighs. She stiffened, but he ignored her discomfort and began drawing the comb through her thick tresses that were of no better mind to accommodate him. Still, he persisted and felt her relax as he gently worked out the tangles. Not until her hair shone and fell thick and smooth down her back, did he return the comb to her.

"I thank you," she said, and he liked how breathless she sounded. She started to rise, but he pulled her back.

"I am not done," he murmured and swept his fingers from her chin and back over her jaw, loosely gathering her hair at the nape of her neck.

"Ranulf?" she said, uncertainty and something else in her voice.

"Patience, Lizanne." He spread his purse strings. First he tied a bright green ribbon around her hair, lower a vivid blue one, and inches from the ends, a red one the color of ripe pomegranates.

"Now I am done," he said.

He thought she would look around. Instead, she reached a hand over her shoulder and touched the green ribbon. "Oh." She slid her fingers over the loops he had made into a lopsided bow. "'Tis very soft. Is it red?"

"Green."

"I like green."

"The next is blue."

"I like blue too."

"The last is red."

She gave a short laugh. "Red I especially like." She drew her bound hair over her shoulder and fingered the ribbons. "Oh, Ran, they are lovely."

So he was *Ran* again—better than he had hoped for.

She looked over her shoulder, and the smile with which she gifted him once more revealed that mesmerizing dimple in her left cheek.

He returned the smile, wanted the one she wore for him to never fade, for the light in her brilliant green eyes to shine only for him, and to hear from her the words women spoke to ensnare a man's heart. Aye, that was what he wanted—for Lizanne to declare herself his. If she did, he would not let her go. Would not surrender her when her brother came for her—

She turned into him, said, "Thank you," and lightly touched her mouth to his.

Her initiation of intimacy baffled him. For days he had longed to hold her again. But, determined to give her time and space to sort out her feelings, and for him to better examine his own, he had repeatedly denied himself.

Whether or not she had discovered anything in the intervening days, he knew not. All he was certain of were his own riotous feelings and the way they defied intense scrutiny. And that her lips were yet upon his.

He drew a hand up over her spine, pushed his fingers through her splendidly thick hair, and cupped her head to draw her nearer.

She allowed it, sliding her arms around his neck, but though he was tempted to see how much more she would allow, they were not alone. Walter was in his head, reminding him of honor, of the rights and wrongs espoused by their faith, of the trust Lizanne had yet to give, of the innocence that was not his to take, of the regret that would be felt by both on the morrow.

Thus, he pulled back and, as she opened her eyes, gently disengaged her arms. "I am pleased you like your ribbons," he said and rose from the pallet.

Lizanne stared after Ranulf's retreating back, hardly able to breathe as she searched to recall how she found herself in a place such as this— body thrumming, lips longing for what was lost to them, heart clenched so tight it ached. Worse, it was she who had first kissed him, and all for a handful of silly ribbons that she had delighted in as if she were, indeed, the child he accused her of being. Worse yet, not once had she thought to stop him from taking her where she should rather die than go. Had *he* not stopped…

Why had he? Because it was wrong? Or because Lady Elspeth was right about Lizanne Balmaine? That she was no lady, a harlot whose traitorous eyes were ever seeking a man who refused to play the part of an enemy?

Suddenly weary, she lowered her chin. And there was the red ribbon upon her pallet, doubtless having come free when Ranulf had pushed his hands through her hair.

She picked it up and, seeing it still held the bow he had tied, was momentarily tempted to toss it and the others upon the dirt floor between their pallets. Instead, she curled her fingers around it, laid down, and pulled the blanket over her.

She meant to close her eyes—to close out Ranulf—but she watched him move around the tent, readying himself for a night's sleep. Thus, when he crossed to his pallet and drew his tunic off over his head, causing the undertunic to rise with it and bare his muscular abdomen, she again heard Lady Elspeth's pronouncement that she was a wanton who could not keep her eyes from Ranulf.

She dropped her lids, but behind them arose an old memory that did not fit the one she had just made—far from it.

"Where is it?" she said, and opened her eyes to search it out. However, Ranulf's undertunic had fallen back in place and covered his belly.

He met her gaze. "Where is what?"

She swallowed. "The scar. Where is it?"

His laughter was dry. "I have many scars, including the one you cut into my flesh. That is the one of which you speak?"

She pushed up onto an elbow. "Nay, the one upon your abdomen."

He considered her a moment, lifted the undertunic. "Thankfully, you will find none here."

Lizanne wanted to explain away its absence as merely a result of poor candlelight, but it had been too hideous...too long and jagged... too distinctly angled across his lower abdomen to not show itself in the barest of light as it had done that night.

"I do not understand. I cannot—" Her voice broke. "I cannot have been mistaken." It was he, for it was not possible another should look so much like him. After all, there was nothing common about Ranulf Wardieu—his height, build, eyes, and especially that hair!

Had her childish imagination conjured the scar of the man who had nearly killed Gilbert and tried to ravish her? Vicious memories of that night rushed back and she groaned. There *had* been a scar!

"Lizanne, what is it?"

Eager to throw off the crimson-stained images, she opened eyes she had not realized she had closed and found Ranulf on his haunches beside her. "It makes no sense," she whispered and dropped her head back to the pallet.

"What makes no sense? And what of the scar you speak of?"

"I should not have spoken of it."

"But you did."

She searched his face—the same face—and shook her head. "I want to go home. Pray, allow me to return to Penforke."

Silence fell between them, and then he said, "Would that I could, but not yet."

One day he would, though. He would discard her just as Lady Elspeth had said. "When?" she pressed.

"When it is done between us."

"'Tis done!" She winced at the near screech of her voice. "I want no more of your kisses or caresses, Ranulf Wardieu. I want only to be gone as far from you as possible and to never see you again."

Slowly, he straightened. "You lie, Lizanne Balmaine. And not well. Now sleep, for on the morrow we go to see the king."

She felt as if punched. "We?"

"Aye, you shall accompany me."

"Before the king, you would exhibit me as your captive? You would be so bold?"

"'Tis not my purpose, nor would I be so foolish. It is the king who has requested you attend him."

"But how does he know of my presence?"

"This city has many eyes and ears. Your accompaniment was noted upon our arrival. I should have kept you hidden."

A thought occurred to Lizanne, and she could not keep herself from voicing it. "Think you King Henry will approve of your abduction of me?"

"Think you he will approve of your abduction and imprisonment of my person, Lizanne—the wounds you inflicted upon one of his barons? That your actions are responsible for delaying the negotiations to which he set me?" At her silence, he continued, "Do not think you will escape me by appealing to him. You may be his subject, but I doubt he would hesitate to mete out punishment for your inappropriate behavior. He is not an especially tolerant man."

"How will you explain my presence, then?"

"With only as much detail as I need to in order to ensure you remain with me," he said, then more softly, "Do not forget the vow you made me. Even the king cannot release you from that."

Nearly overwhelmed with foreboding, she rolled over and gave her back to him. "I shall do my best to remember it," she murmured, "but you would do well to remember that not even you can refuse a king... or God."

"Nor can you, Lizanne."

15

∽⤳❊⤳∾

NEITHER HAVING SPOKEN a word to the other since the night past, silence yawned between Lizanne and Ranulf as they rode side by side through the gates of Westminster Palace.

Feeling the curious looks cast upon her by the bustling castle folk, Lizanne raised her chin and sat straighter in the horrid sidesaddle Ranulf had insisted upon.

Shortly, they drew to a halt and, out of the corner of her eye, she watched Ranulf dismount. When he strode toward her, no doubt to assist her down as befitting a lady, she took the matter in her own hands and dropped to her feet a moment ahead of his arrival.

As she straightened her attire, she smiled tightly at him and told herself she delighted in his glittering gaze that spoke what he would not allow to pass his lips.

He gripped her forearm.

Trying not to think about the man beside her as he led her up the steps of the palace, for his simple touch was disturbing enough, she looked up at the building before her.

During her visit with Gilbert the year before, Henry and Eleanor had been in residence at Bermondsey Castle, located at the busy east end of the city. Thus, this was the first time she had seen Westminster up close. Recently restored and refurbished following King Stephen's reign, which had seen it fall into a sorry state of neglect, it shone like a jewel.

Inside the palace, Ranulf exchanged words with a soldier. Then, following the man, he led Lizanne up a staircase and down a long corridor. Near the end of it, the soldier threw open a door and stood aside to allow them to enter.

Ranulf urged Lizanne ahead of him into the lavishly appointed apartment, spoke in hushed tones with the soldier, then stepped inside and closed the door.

"What is this?" Lizanne asked from where she had gone to stand on the far side of the chamber with her back to the large fireplace.

"Your apartment for the duration of our stay," he said and strode forward.

She raised her eyebrows. "Our stay? Will we be long at Westminster?"

He shrugged, his muscled shoulders rolling beneath the fine weave of his dark blue tunic. "For as long as the king decrees 'tis necessary."

That last word sent a shiver up her spine. "Necessary?" she repeated and, for the dozenth time, wondered why King Henry had specifically requested her presence. She was, after all, hardly noteworthy, much less held in high regard. What warranted such esteemed treatment?

She peered past Ranulf where he had halted before her and swept her gaze over the furnishings a second time. They were much too fine.

In the next instant, she put a finger on the significance of her surroundings. "Ah, nay."

"What is it?"

She laughed, a cracked sound that held not the slightest portion of joy. "The king intends to wed me."

"Wed you?" Ranulf scoffed. "He is wed to Eleanor—"

"He intends to wed me to another!" She stepped around him and crossed to the large four-postered bed.

"What speak you of?"

"Do you not see?" She threw her hands up to encompass the room, then dropped back onto the coverlet and glared at the beautifully draped fabric overhead. "Last year, he tried to wed me to Sir Arthur Fendall. But I did not wish to wed the man and…the king was greatly angered."

"You refused him?" Ranulf asked, coming to stand alongside the bed. "You defied the king?"

She pulled her bottom lip through her teeth. "Not exactly."

"How exactly?"

She pushed up onto her elbows. "I made it so that Sir Arthur, that most esteemed nobleman, changed his mind about taking me to wife."

"*How?*"

Were the situation not so dire, Lizanne thought she might enjoy the color that had seeped into Ranulf's face.

"I wrestled him," she said, then stood from the bed.

Eyebrows nearly touching, Ranulf dropped his face near hers. "You what?"

"I wrestled him." She moved to step around him.

He caught her arm. "You will make sense, Lizanne."

She sighed. "Shortly after King Henry announced he would give me in marriage to Sir Arthur, that awful little man began publicly boasting about bedding me. I overheard one particularly lewd description of how he was going to...you know. And so, somewhat by accident, I struck him in the nose."

Ranulf's look of horror fascinated her, so much that she impulsively reached up to smooth his brow and just barely caught her hand back. "Do not look so concerned. He could hardly retaliate in front of the king, though he did try later. And when he did, he ended up on his backside with me astride."

Ranulf blinked. "You wrestled him to the ground?"

Momentarily forgetting her more immediate problem, she smiled as she recalled the man's utter embarrassment. He had been pompous and arrogant, and she had bettered him without much effort.

"I did," she said, "though, in all fairness, he was not large like you. Indeed, he was much shorter than I and slight of build. Hardly a challenge."

Ranulf shook his head. "I am sure."

"Needless to say, he thought better of wedding me and bid the king to release him from the obligation. Fortunately, Gilbert spirited me away that evening before the king could attempt another match."

Ranulf shook himself out of his stupor, not understanding why he should be surprised by her disclosure. It was, after all, the kind of behavior she had indulged in up until their departure from Killian.

"And so you think he intends to try again?" he concluded, not caring for the implications, for he had no intention of letting her go to another man.

She heaved a sigh. "'Twould seem likely."

"You suspected as much yestereve?"

"The possibility crossed my mind. Now, I am nearly certain of it. Why else would he place me in a nuptial chamber?"

For the first time, Ranulf more than glancingly looked about the apartment. Then he strode to the door and pulled it open.

"Where are you going?"

Gripping the doorjamb, he looked around. "'Twould be inappropriate for us to share this room."

"That was not my question."

"My quarters are just down the hall, Lizanne. Should you need me, I will be there."

"I will not need you."

He shrugged. "I have asked that hot water be delivered for your bath. Freshen yourself, and I will collect you for the midday meal."

"I will be ready."

Ranulf inclined his head and closed the door on her.

Attired in the borrowed garments Ranulf had sent to her chamber, Lizanne walked beside him as they entered the great hall for the midday meal. At the far end, on a raised platform, sat King Henry, and beside him, his queen. Noting their approach, the king motioned them forward.

Lizanne looked first to Queen Eleanor. The woman was a dozen years older than her husband, a man who had been crowned king of all England less than two years before. Despite having attained thirty and more years of age, Eleanor was still the legendary beauty of whom the troubadours sang, and though she had recently given Henry their third child, the princess Matilda, the birthing appeared to have laid no waste to her. She was so incredibly feminine and strong at the same time that Lizanne could not help but envy her, especially the intelligence that shone from her eyes.

Lizanne offered Eleanor a tentative smile, then shifted her gaze to Henry's square, bearded face. He looked much the same as she remembered, though she had forgotten the intensity of the close-cropped red hair that matched his freckled complexion. Still, he was a handsome man.

When she met his large gray eyes, she inwardly cringed at the look of disapproval he leveled upon her. No doubt, he remembered their last encounter. And was plotting this one. What would Ranulf do if she were given to another man? He could hardly hope to claim her for himself without also offering marriage...

Breaking eye contact with King Henry, she looked farther down the long table, quickly dismissing each face she did not recognize—until her gaze stopped upon a man whose eyes shifted between Ranulf and her.

She felt color rise in her cheeks, not from embarrassment or any other mild emotion, but anger at the cruel irony of finding herself in the presence of both Ranulf and Philip Charwyck, the two men she had so long hated.

Six years had passed since last she had seen her formerly betrothed— two years prior to the wedding that had never taken place—and yet her memories of him had remained relatively intact. Except for premature graying at his temples, he was as boyishly handsome as ever.

The heat in her face having spread to the pit of her belly, she wondered if he recognized her. But only for a moment, for in the next, she stood before the king and queen and Ranulf's tug on her arm had her kneeling beside him.

After a short, uncomfortable silence, they were commanded to stand.

"Baron Wardieu and Lady Lizanne, you are most welcome at my court," King Henry said, then leaned toward Ranulf. "I trust you bring me worthy news."

"I do, Your Majesty."

Henry grinned. "Then let us enjoy the meal and speak of it. Come." He motioned them toward the empty chairs to his right.

Lizanne and Ranulf had to walk the length of the table to reach the proffered seats on the other side. Thus, as Lizanne approached Philip, she boldly met the eyes he turned up to her and let the full weight of her animosity shine through.

With a crooked smile, Philip swept a degrading look down her figure that Lizanne realized Ranulf had witnessed when his grip on her arm tightened as he led her past.

"Mayhap you would like to set yourself upon his lap?" he rasped.

She met his disapproving stare but kept her lips sealed against the thoughts that were attempting to transform themselves into inflammatory words. She only hoped Ranulf appreciated the effort she made to not cause a scene.

"Behave yourself," he warned as he helped her into her chair. Once seated beside her, he turned to King Henry and became engrossed in their conversation.

Feeling excluded, Lizanne tamped down the temptation to look along the table to where Philip sat and lifted her goblet that had been filled to brimming with warm, dark wine. It was surprisingly sweet, and she let it sit in her mouth several moments before swallowing. The next sip was just as flavorful. Thus, before she considered touching a morsel of the food set before her, she had drained the goblet. Directly, it was refilled.

As she turned her fingers around the stem, she acknowledged the persistent sense of being watched and swept her gaze around the hall. More than a few pairs of curious eyes were turned her way, and she did not doubt their owners pondered her relationship with Ranulf.

Leaning forward, she peered down the table and encountered the gaze she had most particularly felt. She raised her chin and narrowed her eyes at Philip Charwyck. She was fairly certain he did not recognize her, for he had never looked at her *that* way. Indeed, he had only ever been mildly tolerant of her.

Ranulf's hand closed over her clenched one upon the table, bringing her head so quickly around that she felt the effects of the wine. However, her senses were not so dulled that she did not feel his anger or miss the look of warning he directed at Philip.

"Remember, Lizanne," he whispered as he stared down the man he surely perceived as a rival, "you are mine."

She lifted the goblet to her lips and boldly leaned into his line of vision, breaking the staring duel between the two. "For the moment," she murmured and returned her attention to the meal.

With a low rumble, Ranulf drew his hand from hers and turned back to the king.

When, at last, the meal was finished, Lizanne felt light-headed from the two goblets of wine she had consumed without benefit of adequate food and was content with silence as Ranulf led her across the hall to where Geoff awaited them.

After passing Lizanne into the squire's care, Ranulf strode opposite.

From a shadowed alcove outside the main hall, Philip watched the transfer, noting again the possessiveness the baron exercised over a lady who was certainly not his wife. Like the others, he was deeply interested in their relationship.

The moment he had laid eyes upon her, he had determined he would have her, no matter her association with the king's favored baron. Her wild beauty set her apart from the other ladies of the court, from her blackest hair to her bold gaze, from her self-possessed bearing to her pleasing figure.

But it was not only the lady who occupied his thoughts. More, he was intrigued—and unsettled—by Baron Wardieu's striking likeness to another. He had seen that pale hair before, those eyes, and the imposing stature. And he knew exactly where.

As he had sat at the table, he had considered the possibilities for such a resemblance that could not be coincidental and had been gladdened, for there was power to be gained in the knowledge. He did not yet know how he would use it. But he would.

Emerging from the alcove, he hastened after the lady and her escort and, disregarding tact, placed himself squarely before them just as they reached the stairway.

"I am Sir Philip Charwyck," he announced to the squire. "And you are?"

The young man straightened to his full height so that he was nearly level with Philip. "I am Geoff, squire to Baron Wardieu."

Philip shifted his attention to the lady.

She stared at him out of eyes so fiery he felt as if burned and might have recoiled if not for the promise of what such passion portended.

Grasping her hand and drawing it to his lips, he purred, "I would have the pleasure of your name, my lady."

A moment later, he clutched air. Pricked by her rejection, he straightened and met her green eyes that plucked a chord of familiarity within him. Was it possible he did know the lady?

"Ah, but we have met before, Sir Philip," she said as she made a show of wiping her hand upon her skirts.

Philip frowned more deeply. "Forgive me, but I do not recall."

She gave a scornful laugh, curtsied, and said, "Lady Lizanne Balmaine of Penforke, formerly your betrothed."

Philip was ashamed by his violent startle and the step he retreated, though he was not the only one to react to the revelation, for the squire jerked and caught his breath.

Mouth bowing beautifully despite the enmity out of which it was formed, she said, "Though it pains me that you could so easily forget your commitment, I daresay I am not surprised. Indeed, it puts me in mind of something I owe you."

She swept a hand up and, if not for what appeared to be drink-induced sluggishness, she might have struck him across the face. However, fathoming her intent, the squire caught hold of her wrist.

"Nay, my lady," he said with urgency. "'Tis not prudent."

Something like hurt flickered across her face, but she nodded and allowed him to draw her away and up the stairs.

They were a half dozen steps ascended when Philip's former betrothed stopped and looked around. "I regret I cannot say it has been a pleasure to meet you again," she said, then gave her back to him.

When they were out of sight, Philip contemplated the encounter. Lady Lizanne was fortunate the young squire had stayed her hand, for he was not sure he could have refrained from like retaliation had he been struck by the one who obviously bore a grudge against him for his refusal to wed her.

With some difficulty, he dredged up memories of the gangly, dark-haired girl who had continually vexed him during his squire's training at her father's castle. Never had he imagined she would become a beauty.

He shook his head. He had thought himself fortunate to escape marriage to her, but now he was not so sure he should have put forth the effort required to forego the obligation set to him by his father.

But it was not too late. If she could play leman to the enigmatic Baron Wardieu, she could entertain him as well. The thought cheered him considerably.

Ranulf found Lizanne facedown on the bed, feet dangling over the side, one shoe on, the other amid the rushes.

He lowered to the mattress edge and leaned over her sleeping figure to examine her face. A fist curled against one brightly flushed cheek, her features were relaxed as the eyes beneath her lids traveled side to side.

She did not look as if she had been weeping as he had expected. Indeed, she appeared content, likely a result of the wine she had consumed.

He eased his shoulders. When Geoff had brought word of her encounter with Charwyck, Ranulf had been greatly unsettled by the news that the two had once been betrothed. But he had also been reassured by the hostility that Geoff reported Lizanne had displayed toward the man.

He fingered the ribbon that bound her freshly washed hair and was pleased she had chosen to wear his gift in spite of their most recent quarrel. Perhaps she truly was growing up.

When she stirred but did not awaken, he decided to let her sleep off her stupor.

Though he knew he ought to seek a chair, he laid back upon the mattress, stared at the draped material overhead, and considered his meeting with the king.

Henry had been receptive to the bargain struck between Lord Langford and his vassal—pleased, in fact. Oddly though, he had been less interested in the mission he had sent Ranulf on than the circumstances surrounding Lizanne's accompaniment.

Although Ranulf had been brief in telling the story the king had demanded of him, he had been honest. With creeping suspicion, he had quickly become watchful, catching the glances exchanged between Henry and Eleanor throughout the accounting.

When Henry had asked whether or not he had bedded Lizanne, Ranulf had been shaken by the forward inquiry and declined to answer. Surprisingly, the king had not pursued the matter.

Ranulf's greatest shock came near the end of his interview with the young, mischievous king when Henry had asked whether or not he intended to wed the lady. Ranulf's immediate response had been to deny any such consideration.

The king had looked disappointed but had set himself to ticking off the names of eligible nobles with whom he could match Lizanne, including this Charwyck.

The accuracy of her prediction, coupled with his imminent loss of her, had shaken Ranulf.

Prior to his dismissal, Henry had slyly suggested he reconsider his decision to offer for Lizanne and informed him a choice would be made soon if no offer was forthcoming.

Had the man not been king, Ranulf would have throttled him, but he had withdrawn with his head still firmly in place.

Of a sudden, Lizanne rolled onto her back and threw an arm across his chest. She groaned and turned her head to peer at him through narrowed eyelids. "Oh, 'tis you."

"Did you expect Philip Charwyck?"

"What?" She blinked, then her eyes widened. "Geoff told you."

"Naturally."

"Naturally." She raked a hand through her rumpled hair and leveraged up to sitting.

"Tell me of your broken betrothal to Charwyck," Ranulf said.

Disbelief rose upon her face. "'Tis none of your concern."

"You are wrong." Amazed at the firm grip he maintained on his composure, he sat up. "The king does intend to see you wed, Lizanne, and this Charwyck is among the candidates."

She caught her breath.

"Since you are under my protection, I would know."

Fear, anger, uncertainty, disgust, and a flurry of other emotions tripped across her features before she bowed her head and stared at the hands she had turned into fists.

Overwhelmed by the longing to embrace her and offer solace, Ranulf crooked a finger beneath her chin and lifted it.

She met his gaze, asked, "And were you considered a candidate as well?"

He was surprised by her directness. "Aye, but I have declined."

Abruptly, she drew back, dropped her feet to the floor, and crossed to a window.

Ranulf followed. "Are you disappointed?"

She swung around to face him where he had halted an arm's reach away. "Think you I would want to marry you?" she demanded, tears in her eyes. "That I would want to marry any man? Lest you do not yet understand who I am, I will tell you—I do not like men. They are the pestilence of the earth."

He took a step nearer. "What of your brother? You hate him as well?"

"Nay! Gilbert is different—"

"Different from other men? How can that be?"

"He is my brother. And a good man."

"Ah." Ranulf slowly nodded. "And Geoff?"

Her eyes widened. "He…he is…"

"What of Roland? You do not hate him either."

"They are boys! They have not yet learned the treachery of men."

Ranulf stepped nearer. "And treachery…Is it an exclusive trait of men? What of women, Lizanne?" He was remembering the one to whom he had been wed for five miserable years. "Methinks the fairer sex can be far more treacherous than men."

She was breathing hard now. "I do not speak of matters of the heart but of pillaging and murder and…ravishment." She flinched, pressed a hand to her temple.

Staring into her pain-drawn features, likely as much a result of the events of this day as the wine, Ranulf shuffled through the pieces of Lizanne's character, analyzed them, and attempted a fit that would give him the insight that constantly eluded him.

And then came realization. Focusing again on her face, he saw fear had risen there. "Some man tried to steal your virtue." Or had stolen it. "That is what this is all about, is it not?"

Her eyes dilated, the muscles of her jaw contracted, blood flushed her skin.

"Who was it?" he asked. "Charwyck?"

"Philip?" she cried. "He is far more honorable than the one who tried to ravish me. He is the one I wanted more than anything to wed!"

Ranulf winced. She had loved Charwyck—at least, thought herself in love with him. "Why did you not wed him?"

She raised her chin higher. "Believing I had lost my virtue, he determined I was no longer worthy to be his wife."

Ranulf ground his teeth. Philip Charwyck was every bit the miscreant he appeared to be. Though he longed to put his arms around Lizanne, he drew no nearer, certain his touch would not be welcome. "If 'twas not Charwyck, then who, Lizanne?"

She drew a deep breath. "'Twas you—Ranulf Wardieu."

16

HEAD POUNDING, THROBBING, releasing arrows against the backs of her eyes, Lizanne struggled to keep from squeezing her lids closed as she watched Ranulf transform from inquisitor to the accused. But unlike Philip when he had learned of her identity, the man before her did not startle or stumble back.

Anger drained from his face and was replaced by disbelief, bafflement, and, slowly, understanding. "It explains much," he murmured, staring at her out of eyes that did not seem to see her—at least, not here and now. "My imprisonment. Your hatred. Your shame at responding to my touch."

Was that an admission? It seemed so and yet not. "Do you know what you have wrought?" she asked past the tears in her throat. "No matter who you have made yourself into these past years, you destroyed everything dear to me—my father, Philip, Gilbert...Aye, Gilbert! You might as well have killed my brother when you attacked our camp, for he is lost to me and everyone else."

Another arrow struck the inside of her left temple, and she pressed a hand to it. "Now will you deny it was of your doing?"

His gaze having risen back to the surface of her, he said almost wearily, "I am not in the habit of admitting to crimes for which I am not responsible, Lizanne. And, I vow, I am not the one who should pay the price for that which you lay—nay, *throw*—at my feet. So terrible a thing I could never do."

Lizanne did not think twice about the impulse that struck her. Indeed, she did not even think once. She heard the crack of flesh on flesh, felt the sting across her palm, saw the bright color that marked his face.

"'Twas you!" she hissed.

His jaw convulsed. "It was another."

She laughed bitterly. "I am not surprised you deny it, for it cannot have sat well with a warrior such as you to be bested by a woman."

"Again, I know not of what you speak, Lizanne."

"This!" She swept up her right hand, this time to show, not strike. "You wanted to know about this." She flexed the crooked thumb. "Foolish. I should have had it on the outside rather than the inside of my fist when I struck you. But I can hardly complain, for it achieved the same end and stopped you from taking what I would not give. Now do you remember?"

He shook his head. "Until I saw you at Lord Langdon's, never had I laid eyes upon you."

Trying to ignore the pain behind her eyes, she reached forward and grasped a handful of his hair. "There is no other with hair the color of new snow." She moved her gaze to his eyes. "Nor eyes so black they are but one color." She dropped her hand and stepped back. "And your size is unmistakable. I have not erred."

"Aye, you have," he said sharply. "I am not this man you speak of."

"You lie. You may not have the scar I was certain I had seen, but you are one and the same."

Ranulf glowered. "Tell me about the scar."

She put her lips together, raised her chin.

He stepped so near there was hardly the space of a hand between them. "You will tell me, Lizanne—"

She brought her knee up, but he sidestepped her attempt to unman him. And before she could try again, he swept her up into his arms.

"Put me down!"

Unmoved by her flailing, he carried her across the chamber and dropped her on the bed. When she scrambled to raise herself, he pushed her back and thrust his face near hers.

"The man who tried to violate you would not have been as patient I have been, Lizanne. He would not have stopped at kisses. He would not have slept on another pallet. He would have taken everything that first day and every day thereafter until there was naught left of you."

Lizanne stared into his eyes. It was the same argument she'd had with herself over and over again, trying to reconcile *that* man with this one.

"And if I were that man, never would you desire me as you do," he said softly and lowered his mouth to hers.

Lizanne pressed her lips together, squeezed her eyes closed, tried not to feel the warmth of lips that coaxed a response from her, struggled to focus her thoughts and senses elsewhere. However, they were not going anywhere without Ranulf.

Keen, unnerving sensations in the small of her back spread up and outward like a warm breeze, and though her mind protested, she began to relax, to feel what she was not meant to feel, to accept his kiss and give it back.

A moment later, his mouth lifted from hers.

She raised her lids and watched the lips that had battered her defenses take a bitter turn.

"Though you refuse to accept the truth of who I am and am not, Lizanne Balmaine," he said, "your body knows."

He straightened from the bed, turned, and strode to the door. "Think on it," he said, then was gone.

She released the breath she had not realized she held. The last thing she wanted to do was think on it more, for it hurt too much to be at war with a heart adamantly resistant to the belief Ranulf was responsible for that horrible night.

"Later," she whispered. "Much later."

As Ranulf had expected she might, Lizanne pleaded illness and did not put in an appearance for the late meal. In her place sat Walter, his expression dour as, in a confidential tone, he related to Ranulf the information obtained about Charwyck.

Ranulf leaned closer at the mention of Philip's knight service to the king—rather, lack of it.

"He pays the shield tax to avoid military service," Walter said.

"So he is a coward as well," Ranulf murmured and looked to the subject of their discussion. Charwyck did not notice, engrossed as he was in staring at a curvaceous serving wench.

"It would appear so," Walter said, "but I am also told he is not inexperienced. The first three years following knighthood he did fulfill his service. 'Tis just in recent years he has declined to do so."

"What else?"

"Shortly after Philip broke the marriage contract with Lady Lizanne, he wed a landed widow, nearly doubling his family's holdings."

Ranulf lifted an eyebrow. "She is no longer living, I presume?"

Walter drew nearer his lord. "Two years ago, she died under suspicious circumstances. Sir Philip says she fell down the stairs and broke her neck, but 'tis gossiped her neck was broken prior to the fall."

Ranulf reached for his wine goblet. "Do you think it merely lurid gossip?"

The vassal shook his head. "I fear 'tis likely true. The rumors of his cruelty abound such that there must be some substance to them."

Raising the goblet to his mouth, Ranulf looked again at Sir Philip. As he swallowed a mouthful of the warm liquid, he met the icy blue of the other man's stare over the goblet's rim. Without breaking the contact, he took another drink and watched Charwyck's lips slowly curl.

They understood each other, then. Excellent. Ranulf lowered the goblet and returned his gaze to Walter. "I will not allow Lady Lizanne to wed him."

His vassal showed no surprise. "Then you will marry her yourself?"

Inwardly, Ranulf sighed. He had delivered Lizanne unto this, and he would deliver her out of it. Whether or not she liked it, she would be his. "Aye, I will offer for her."

Almost shockingly, Walter grinned. "Though the woman bedevils you, my lord, methinks you will not soon tire of the novelty of her company."

Ranulf frowned. "I gathered you did not care for her."

"I did not, but I have watched her closely since we left Killian and think I may have misjudged her—though only because she wished to be misjudged."

"Then what of your agreement to dislike one another?"

Walter drew back slightly. "Did she tell you that?"

"She made it clear you had reached some sort of understanding."

After a long moment, Walter chuckled. "I suppose we did reach an agreement, though 'twas certainly not spoken."

"Ranulf," the king broke into their conversation.

"Your Majesty?"

Henry leaned toward him. "I have made my choice, and a fine one at that."

Knowing with dread certainty that Henry spoke of the man who would be Lizanne's husband, Ranulf stiffened and felt a similar tension emanate from Walter. "I would speak to you on that, my liege. I have reconsidered and would offer to wed Lady Lizanne myself."

Henry looked surprised, then regretful. "I fear 'tis too late. I have approached Charwyck, and he has agreed to take her to wife. Did you know the Balmaine and Charwyck lands adjoin?"

Struggling to keep from turning his hands into fists, Ranulf stared at the king.

"Curious thing," Henry continued, "but I have learned Lady Lizanne was once betrothed to the man." His eyes drifted upward as if he searched for the details.

"I would ask that you reconsider," Ranulf said low.

The king raised his goblet and drained the contents. "There is naught to reconsider. The decision stands."

Patience, Ranulf silently counseled, nearly overwhelmed by the desire to strike out. Determinedly, he redirected that urge to Lizanne's newly betrothed. He would personally deal with the man.

Eleanor leaned forward and, smiling beautifully, placed a hand on her husband's arm. "Mayhap you should allow Lady Lizanne to choose for herself," she suggested. "After all, 'twould seem either man would be a suitable match."

Surprisingly, Henry was a long time considering the suggestion. "Aye," he finally said, "Lady Lizanne will herself decide on the morrow."

He favored Eleanor with a lazy smile. "'Twill make for an interesting diversion, hmm?" He laughed. "Though I do not know that she will be any more agreeable than she was the last time."

Ranulf was not pleased, but there was nothing else to be said, for the king shoved to his feet and signaled an end to the meal.

As Ranulf pushed his chair back, he swept his gaze over the hall and located Philip Charwyck among the throng of nobles eager to depart. Then he headed toward the man, and only Walter, who sprang in front of him and barred his way, stopped him.

"My lord," his vassal entreated, "do not."

"You are too presumptuous," Ranulf growled and reached to set the smaller man aside.

Sir Walter raised a staying hand. "Pray, listen to me. As the king has decreed what will be, you will only do yourself and your family disservice if you defy him. Thus, you must let Lady Lizanne decide her own fate, which is as it should be."

Ranulf narrowed his gaze on him.

"And this I know…" Walter gripped Ranulf's arm. "…you will gain what you seek. She will choose *you*."

Ranulf was jolted by the conviction in his vassal's voice. *Would* Lizanne choose him? After the accusations she had made against him and affirmation of the feelings she had once had for Philip? He did not believe it.

"Unhand me, vermin!" Lizanne strained against the two men on either side of her who held her arms, but resistance was useless. Expressionless—or nearly so, for neither man was entirely successful in keeping a smirk from his lips—they pulled her through the wide doorway, pushed her forward, and retreated.

As the doors behind came together with a resounding thud, the king's booming voice reached her from across the hall. "We thought, perhaps, you had decided to leave us early, Lady Lizanne."

She drew a long breath, looked across the expansive floor to where King Henry sat in an elaborately carved chair high upon a raised platform. Beside him sat Eleanor, arrayed in a gown the color of sapphires. To the queen's left stood a stout priest, a psalter clasped between his hands. To the right of the platform were Ranulf and Philip.

Lizanne looked between the two men, but it was Ranulf her eyes came to rest upon. Though he was some distance away, she saw the tight-lipped expression he wore and the hard glint in his eyes. Something bad was afoot. And she was not at all surprised.

"Come, Lady Lizanne," Henry ordered. "You have kept us waiting too long as it is."

No doubt, for the younger of the two soldiers who had come for her while she strolled the gardens this morning had grumbled over the amount of time expended to find her. And, when she had refused to accompany them unless they revealed her destination, they had lost all patience and dragged her into the palace.

Squaring her shoulders, she walked forward and silently counted her steps two by two in an attempt to distract the anxious thoughts she did not wish to show upon her face.

She halted in front of Henry whose thunderous expression nearly made her forget what was expected of her. Lightly lifting her skirts, she knelt before him.

"Enough," he said.

With a sidelong glance at Ranulf, she straightened.

"'Tis time you wed, Lady Lizanne," Henry began in a tone similar to the one her father had used when she misbehaved.

Dear Lord, I have not much hope of escape this time, do I?

"For too long, you have been a burden to your brother. Thus, 'tis time that burden was passed to another." He smiled at that.

And he could, for he was not the one made to suffer a bad marriage, which was surely what hers would be if she was forced to exchange vows with Philip Charwyck. But surely there were others with whom the king might match her.

"Once again," Henry continued, "I have taken it upon myself to find you a suitable match. This time"—he pointed at her—"you will not defy me. I will see you wed this day and, henceforth, I expect to hear no more of your unladylike behavior."

This day. Lizanne swung her gaze to the priest. The reason for his presence suddenly clear—worse, the reason for Philip's presence and only Philip—she felt a terrible weight fall upon her.

No hope at all, Lord...

"Is that understood, Lady Lizanne?"

She looked to Ranulf who, it seemed, was prepared to hand her over to Philip himself.

I am going to be sick.

She swallowed hard, shifted her weight to counter the wave of dizziness, and looked to the man who would, this night, claim marital rights over her.

Philip Charwyck smiled slowly and raised his eyebrows above triumphant eyes—as if he were about to gain a prize he very much wanted. But how could he want her? Why consent to a marriage he had years ago refused?

Heart beating hard and fast, Lizanne returned her gaze to the king. "Your majesty, I beseech you—"

"Is it understood, Lady Lizanne?" Angry color rose in his face.

She cast her eyes down, nodded.

"You will look at me when I speak!"

Lizanne lifted her head. "Aye, your Majesty. It is understood."

He considered her, then smiled. "I am pleased we are finally in accord. Indeed, it puts me in a generous mood." He leaned back in his great chair. "You would like me to be generous, would you not, Lady Lizanne?"

In what way? Allow her to drink herself into oblivion before being tossed upon the marriage bed? Provide a few more feather pillows to soften the violation she would be made to suffer this night by a man she would be made to suffer the remainder of her life?

At her continued silence, the king grunted. "Despite your most recent behavior, I will, indeed, be generous. As the queen believes it would be fitting to give you a choice in the matter of whom you wed, I present these two knights." He jutted his chin in the direction of Philip. And Ranulf.

Lizanne jerked. Ranulf was offering for her as well? Why? He had said he had declined to be numbered among those who might take her to wife and now...

The king had forced him to it. That had to be it.

Feeling heavier yet, she looked to Ranulf and met those unwavering black eyes. Even at a distance, she recognized the anger there that confirmed he was no willing participant in the king's game. Next, she turned her regard upon Philip who looked self-assured and wore a charming smile. Though she had once thought him the most handsome of men, she could not help but compare him to Ranulf beside whom he paled.

"Well?" the king pressed.

She turned back to him. "I cannot," she whispered and heard a sharply drawn breath she knew must have come from Philip.

Henry leaned forward. "I have given you a choice you do not deserve, and still you test me. So now I test you. Choose one of these men or make ready to enter a convent."

A convent? That or Philip who, for some reason, wanted her though she did not want him. That or Ranulf who did not want her though she...

She put her chin up. "I choose the convent."

Once again, the king's face brightened, this time so much that it was difficult to discern where skin ended and hair began.

Nerves bunching, she sought out the queen, but the woman had turned her attention elsewhere as if uninterested in the discord that hung thick upon the hall.

The king heaved a sigh, and when she looked back at him, she saw he had regained most of his natural color. He rubbed a hand over his beard. "Then I withdraw the option of the convent."

Lizanne took a step forward. "You cannot—"

"What?" He shot to his feet. "You question my authority?"

She quickly stepped back. "Forgive me, Your Majesty. 'Tis just that the other options do not so much appeal to me."

He turned his head sharply toward Ranulf and Philip. "I see before me two worthy men for whom you can bear children, Lady Lizanne. Choose now or I will do it for you."

For whom *she* could bear children. That was all she was to this man—a womb to bring forth more subjects in need of ruling.

Watch your temper, Lizanne! You have lost and will only lose more if you continue to defy him. The ability to choose between these two may be all you have, but it is everything.

She drew a deep breath that did little to calm her, inclined her head. "Very well, I will choose." And make certain she was not the only one to suffer such humiliation and degradation.

She crossed the floor and halted before Ranulf. She stared at him, he stared at her, then she leaned in and whispered, "'Tis out of your hands now."

His eyes narrowed.

She stepped back, appraisingly ran her gaze down him, then circled him. When she once more faced him, he was utterly still. However, his eyes belied his calm, warning of consequences for having been subjected to consideration reserved for gauging the worthiness of a horse.

Lizanne moved to Philip who smiled lazily at her as if they shared a secret. They did not.

She inclined her head, then appraised him in the same manner as Ranulf. He, too, grew still and, when she was done with him, his eyes also warned of consequences. But from the depth of outrage that shone from them, she knew his consequences would be much different from those doled out by Ranulf, and in that moment she was grudgingly grateful to have been given a choice of the man for whom she could bear children.

She crossed her arms over her chest, asked, "Do you wrestle, Sir Philip?"

She almost smiled, not because of the confusion that momentarily displaced his anger, but the suppressed choking sound made by Ranulf who obviously recalled the story she had told of her encounter with Sir Arthur Fendall.

"Enough of your games!" King Henry roared. "Choose!"

Lizanne placed a hand on Philip's arm, turned to face Ranulf, and shrugged.

To her surprise, anger filled his eyes rather than relief. She had meant for him to think she had chosen Philip, and it seemed he did. But why should that displease him when he did not want her himself?

The game at its end, and none too soon, she looked to the king and gave words to her choice.

Philip Charwyck roared for clarification.

17

"I CHOOSE," LIZANNE repeated, turning away from Philip, "Ranulf Wardieu." She stepped before him, curled her fingers around his arm, and looked to the king.

"A fine choice," Henry proclaimed.

Ranulf stared at the profile of the woman before him. Now it was he who was dumbfounded, Charwyck who was infuriated. He whom relief ran through like a river, Charwyck whom umbrage turned rigid.

When Lizanne had taken such humiliating measure of him, he had berated himself for being a party to such antics, especially as he had been certain she would not choose him. Was it possible she hated Philip more strongly than she hated the man she believed Ranulf Wardieu to be? Or had she realized the error of her accusations? Accepted his disavowal of the odious thing done to her brother and her? Regardless, Walter was proven right.

The face Lizanne turned to him no longer reflected the devilry with which she had made a show of choosing between Charwyck and himself. Instead, there was sorrow as if of deepest regret. "I have kept my vow to you," she said softly. "I only hope you do not rue it as much as I."

In the presence of God, King Henry, Eleanor, and a modest gathering of Ranulf's men, Lizanne and Ranulf stood before the priest an hour later and exchanged vows. It would have been sooner, but the queen had been adamant about the attire such an occasion warranted, and Lizanne's borrowed garments had been deemed unacceptable.

Three seamstresses had quickly altered one of Eleanor's gowns, a cream-colored samite heavily embroidered with silver and gold threads to which a flounce had been added to accommodate Lizanne's height. Despondent, she had sat still while her hair was tamed and arranged beneath a light veil secured to her head with a garland of flowers.

When she had been escorted across the hall, she'd had no notion of the comely picture she presented until she met Ranulf's gaze. She did not think she would ever forget the way his eyes settled upon her. It was as if he were seeing her for the first time.

Throughout the ceremony, she stared at her fisted hands amid the voluminous skirts, looking up only once to repeat the vows given her. Increasingly pained at having forced Ranulf into this travesty of a marriage, she knew it had been wrong of her, but she could not have chosen Philip. What her childish eyes had been blind to years ago, she now saw clearly.

When Ranulf lifted her chin to drop a kiss on her lips, she did not have time to respond before he drew away. She swayed, steadied her feet, and focused on the smiling faces that moved in from all sides.

Geoff was the first to reach her side. Grinning broadly, he gave her a quick, affectionate squeeze and said, "You are truly my lady, now."

She tried to smile but, instead, felt her eyes pool with tears.

A hand emerged from the throng and extended a square of cloth. Glancing in that direction, she saw it was Walter. Although the corners of his mouth were only slightly curved, he was smiling.

At her? Why? He could not be pleased. Did he not dislike her?

The cloth fluttered beneath her nose.

She tried again for a smile, this one of gratitude, and accepted the offering and dabbed at her eyes. As she lowered her hand to the folds of her skirt, crumpling the soft linen between her fingers, Ranulf turned from the well-wishers and drew her against his side.

Swallowing convulsively, she looked up.

His smile seemed so genuine that her heart tumbled over itself. And again when he pulled her closer, turned her body into his, and touched his lips to her temple. "Let us make the best of this, hmm?" he whispered, the warm sweep of his breath raising the hairs along her arms.

She nodded. "I shall try...Husband."

A moment later, they were swept along to the main hall where a hastily prepared but worthy feast was laid out to celebrate their marriage.

Lizanne was overwhelmed by the number of people who awaited them. It seemed as if all of London had turned out for the occasion.

The men were quick to congratulate Ranulf, slapping him on the back, cuffing him on the shoulder, and muttering words in his ear that Lizanne could only guess at.

In contrast, most of the women were less enthusiastic, especially the younger ladies who gazed at the handsome groom with what seemed longing and regret. And which made Lizanne look closer upon the man who was now her husband.

Considering his strong profile, she tried to see him in a different light from the one corrupted by the anger and hate of the past. Not only was he peculiarly handsome with that shock of long pale hair, but he was young and virile—a baron held in high regard by the king. He was honorable, patient, kind.

Most certainly it was envy that held the other women apart from her, each one likely believing herself more worthy than Lizanne with her wild black hair and bothersome height that topped the majority by inches.

Her musings were hauled up short as her last observations of Ranulf returned to her with such force they seemed to turn her world upside down. Honorable, patient, kind?

She had acknowledged it herself, and once more the foundation upon which she had built her case against him was shaken. Whence had come these beliefs? The man who had tried to defile her had not possessed any of those qualities, yet the one she had wed truly seemed to.

"Lizanne?" Ranulf's voice reached her as if from a great distance.

She lifted her gaze to his. "Hmm?"

"All is well?"

She forced a smile. "I am fine."

He opened his mouth as if to press her further, but then the king appeared.

"Come, Baron Wardieu, do not keep your bride to yourself. Share your good fortune." At Ranulf's hesitation, Henry laughed. "I vow I shall not keep you long. I would but have your opinion on a matter that vexes me."

Ranulf gave Lizanne an apologetic smile, then followed the king.

Dismayed, she watched the two men disappear among the crowd. Alone and under intense scrutiny, she edged her way among the people in search of the friendly comfort of Geoff and Roland.

She did not find them, but Walter found her.

"My lady," he said, "your husband has not so soon deserted you, has he?"

Lizanne was grateful to see a familiar face, even though it belonged to the redoubtable Sir Walter. "I fear business with the king has taken him away."

He grimaced. "A pity, it being his wedding day. Perhaps you would suffer my company a while?" He offered his arm.

"You do not trust me alone?" she asked as he led her out of the press.

"Truly, I had not considered that," he said, and spoke no more until they reached an unoccupied corner of the hall. "But, since 'tis you who broached the subject"—he released her arm and leaned back against the wall—"mayhap you would tell me if you intend to continue bedeviling my lord now that you are wed?"

Feeling her smile falter, she said, "Though you will not believe me, Sir Walter, 'tis not evil that drove me to transgress against Ranulf. At the time, I felt my actions were more than justified."

"And now?"

She lowered her eyes, stared at the toes of her shoes. "Now I am not so certain. Mayhap I have erred, though logic dictates otherwise."

"Which will you follow?" he asked. "Your heart or your head, my lady?"

Surprised by his question, she looked up. "Perhaps both," she finally conceded.

A brief tightening about his mouth showed he was not pleased with her vague answer. "At least lead with your heart," he suggested.

Warmed by his concern, she said, "I will think on it. But tell me, Sir Walter, do you lead with your heart?" After all, it seemed more than casual advice he offered.

He looked away, shifted his stance, and cleared his throat. "You would like something to drink?"

She laughed. "Your heart or your head, Sir Walter? You have not answered me."

"And I do not intend to."

"Very well," she conceded, "but it seems hardly fair that you expect me to take advice that you yourself have not proven worthy."

"I did not say I have not…" His voice trailed off.

Realizing he would reveal no more, Lizanne folded her arms across her chest. "Why, of a sudden, are you so kind to me?"

"Am I?"

"Aye. As I recall, you not so long ago took great pleasure in calling me a viper."

He pulled a face. "I suppose I did."

"What has changed your opinion?"

"I have not said it has changed."

She raised her eyebrows. "You still think me a viper?"

He chuckled. "Nay, I do not."

"I am pleased to hear that."

In the ensuing silence, her stomach rumbled. Embarrassed, she pressed a hand to it.

"You have not eaten, have you?"

"Not since yesterday."

Sir Walter motioned to the tables laden with every delight imaginable. "There is food aplenty here. Wait here and I will bring you a plate."

Alone again, Lizanne looked around. Geoff and Roland were nowhere to be seen, although she recognized many of the Wardieu knights. Idly, she watched as they vied for the attention of the serving wenches and unwed ladies who were far outnumbered by men in the hall.

It was interesting, this ritual, she thought as she studied the beautifully clothed ladies who wove in and around the groups of men.

Lizanne looked down at her wedding gown and was suddenly grateful for the queen's foresight in providing such finery. The garment was splendid, emphasizing her narrow waist and flattering—

Disturbed that she should appreciate feminine attire with such depth of feeling, she drew a sharp breath. It was years since she had taken any real interest in her appearance. Was this what marriage did to a woman?

Nay, it was what a man like Ranulf did to her. She groaned inwardly. She should be wishing for a loose, comfortable tunic and the freedom of chausses and boots, not this.

"All alone?" a derisive voice asked.

She snapped her head around and her eyes came level with Philip Charwyck's glacial stare. He stood two feet to her right, his expression one of resentment and contained anger.

Feeling a prick of fear, she said, "I am not. Sir Walter has gone to fetch me food."

Though her announcement was meant to be more of a warning than informative, Philip deigned to ignore it. "Not your husband? Ah, but mayhap he is as averse to used goods as I."

Lizanne turned to fully face him. That he had thrown into her face the reason for his rejection all those years past was cruel, but though her first instinct was to launch herself at him, she squeezed anger into her fists to keep from making a spectacle that would surely shame Ranulf.

Philip grinned. "Do you think he is seeking his pleasure elsewhere?"

Knowing that if she did not put distance between this man and herself the wedding celebration would come to a crashing close, Lizanne straightened to her full height and started to step past him.

His hand shot out, captured her wrist, and yanked her near. "Do you think I wished to wed a woman who so freely gives herself to another?" he hissed. "Be assured, I am grateful for your consideration in choosing Wardieu."

Staring into his face that was too near her own, Lizanne said between clenched teeth, "You sound as if you are trying to convince yourself of that, Sir Philip." Pleased by how shot with red his eyes were, she pressed on. "You seemed all too willing to take me to wife earlier, and more than a little disappointed when I rejected you."

His grip tightened so cruelly she was certain there would be bruises. "Do not mistake my desire for your body as anything other than that," he spat. "Just because you are wed to another does not mean you cannot share my bed as well—and I will have you in it."

"Release me!"

Fingers biting more deeply into her wrist, he put his mouth near her ear. "Not a soul would notice if we slipped away. Come with me, and I will teach you things—"

She brought her chin around so quickly their noses brushed. "Truly? Even though I am far less pure than I was the day you broke our marriage contract?"

His gaze flickered. "Then 'tis true you were first Baron Wardieu's leman."

Never would she have thought she would wish anyone to believe such a lie about her, but she did. "I am proud to have been, and to now be his wife."

The color in his face deepened.

"Thus," she continued, "I have no desire to lower myself to your canine slaverings, Sir Philip. And even if I did, I daresay there is naught you could teach me that my husband has not already done."

His breathing turning shallow. "I will have you, Lizanne Wardieu, and when I have disposed of your husband, 'twill not be marriage I offer."

Although pierced by his deadly threat, she forced her face to remain impassive. However, he was no longer looking at her, having shifted his attention to something beyond her.

"Release me," she said again and was surprised when he thrust her hand away. A moment later, she saw the reason—Walter, and beside him strode Ranulf, the latter's expression thunderous as he stared at her and Philip.

"Your husband," Philip murmured, "does he not remind you of someone?"

Lizanne swept her gaze to him.

He gave a wicked smile. "A common villein, perhaps?" Then he stepped quickly away.

As Lizanne stared after him as he immersed himself among the celebrants, she felt the walls close in, their thickness suffocating as anger was replaced by the weaker emotions she had earlier discarded.

A common villein...He who had been called Darth?

As the floor began to shift beneath her feet, she tried to pull air into her lungs, but her throat would not open.

Dear Lord, I cannot faint. Pray, not here.

A chill breaking over her, she turned her head and searched out Ranulf.

Through the narrowing field of her vision, she saw he was nearly upon her, his face no longer reflecting anger but alarm.

He blurred, and though she blinked rapidly to return him to focus, he disappeared altogether. Amid her darkening consciousness, she felt strong arms come around her. Then nothing.

18

⤜⦶⤛

"'T is a fine night for a raid, my lord," the squire, Duncan, said, voice pitched higher than normal at the prospect of adventure.

A fine night, indeed, the young man's liege thought as he assessed the situation.

He and his men stood on the edge of a glade across which a warm wind howled, churned the water of a wide moat, and buffeted the stone walls of a stronghold that rose against a night sky.

Though the moon was near full, it more often disappeared than reappeared in the blue-black spaces between intermittent cloud cover that had stolen in just before dusk—a Godsend for the raiders whose furtive negotiation of the hilly terrain before the castle would be more easily facilitated. Not so for the men who walked the parapet along the crenellated walls and would not see what came their way until it was too late.

Still, the lord concluded, caution would have to be exercised, for the castle appeared to be in a state of readiness for attacks such as the one planned this night. There could be no mistakes.

With much restless shifting amid the excitement that had been building since their arrival, his men watched as the chosen few were given final instructions and their weapons secured fast to prevent them from making noise.

Not until the moon was obscured behind a long bank of clouds did they set off, and when next it appeared, they were halfway to their destination. They threw themselves facedown in the long, waving grass and waited for the protection of darkness to return. It was a long time coming, but at last they were moving again and made it to the bank of the moat.

At the most likely point of vulnerability—the southernmost wall—they gathered before the slapping water and knelt in thick undergrowth just moments ahead of the moon's reappearance. While they waited, they searched for signs of movement among the crenellations. And found it.

When darkness returned, the lord was the first to enter the chill, muddy water. Steeling his mind against the discomfort that penetrated his clothing and pierced his skin, he led the way forward.

Their progress was mercilessly slow, the mud sucking at their feet as if to pull them down into the murky depths. At the midpoint, the ground dropped sharply from beneath their feet, and they began to swim. To avoid losing the benefit of their blackened faces, they paddled, struggling to keep their heads above the agitated water.

At the sloping base of the great wall, they once again found treacherous purchase for their feet and dragged themselves up the side. Water swirling about their hips, the wind whipping around their wet torsos, they waited and listened for the sound of the guard who patrolled the stretch of wall. Finally, they heard him, his boots scraping the walkway as he passed overhead.

When the footfalls faded, the young squire was urged forward and two men-at-arms held him steady in the shifting mud.

Duncan fit his bow with the prepared arrow, to which a padded hook was attached. Trailing behind this was a coil of light, albeit wet, rope that one of the knights laid across his arms to ensure a smooth ascent.

None could dispute Duncan's skill. It was the reason he had been chosen for this task. Although not particularly skilled with other weapons, he was nearly unrivaled with the bow.

He drew the string taut, raised the weapon, gauged the air's erratic movement, and waited for the momentary stillness that would best ensure the arrow's accuracy. When he released the string, the arrow sailed upward, struggling to maintain its course as the wind revived and shifted direction. Almost miraculously, the feathered shaft dived over the wall and fell with a dull thud.

The lord was the first to go. Arms strong and able, he wasted no time scaling the wall and, shortly, lowered himself to the parapet on the opposite side. Crouching low, he secured the rope, then yanked on it. He felt it grow taut as the first of his men began the journey upward.

The torches placed about the outer bailey gave him a good idea of the castle's layout, though he had already gathered much from the man he'd had slip through the walls earlier with a group of peasants. The news that the baron had not yet returned had baffled him, but it had also offered a rare opportunity to capture the stronghold with the least amount of resistance.

One by one, his men came over the wall and scattered to take up their positions. The squire was the last. He dropped down beside his lord, and the two promptly made their way from the parapet to the bailey below. It was no simple task, for there were many guards about, and thrice they had to silence one in their progress toward the donjon.

Leaving the squire to watch outside, the lord entered the great, darkened hall, dagger in hand. The sound of sleeping men, women, and children guided him over the dimly lit, rush-covered floor. Warily, he mounted the stairway, grimacing at the sound of his sodden advance that seemed to bounce off the walls of the narrow passageway. At the first landing, he peered around the corner and studied the wide, torch-lit corridor stretching before him.

All was quiet.

Too quiet? He crept to the door of the chamber he had been informed was occupied by the lady in residence. Ear to the door, he listened. Silence.

He eased the door inward, revealing a room softly lit by the glow of a dying fire, and fixed his gaze upon the bed where the still figure of his prey lay. Quietly, he closed the door, returned his dagger to its sheath, and moved forward.

On a pallet at the foot of the bed slept the lady's maid. He subdued her first, shoving a wad of cloth in her mouth as she stared up at him out of eyes wide with terror, then trussing her hand and foot. As she grunted and wriggled, he crept around the bed.

Suddenly, the lady beneath the coverlet sat up, snapped her chin around, and drew a breath to scream.

He launched himself across the bed and thrust her back upon the mattress. As if the breath had been knocked from her, she wheezed, giving him just enough time to fit a hand over her mouth and stop the sound that would have called others to her aid.

As she struggled beneath him where he straddled her, he listened. And heard the alarm being raised. If all had gone as planned, his men were in position and the reinforcements were riding to cross the lowered drawbridge. Soon the castle would be under his control—with or without this woman.

In the next instant, her hooked fingers clawed at his face and neck. Since he did not yet dare release her mouth, he captured hold of one hand and suffered the other, the scratches that marked his flesh nothing compared to the other injuries he had sustained throughout his life. But what did compare was the sharp thrust of her knee into his bad leg.

He clamped his mouth closed on the shout of pain that strained to be loosed from his chest and, though he'd had no intention of getting any nearer the woman, stretched his damp length out upon her to prevent her from landing another near debilitating blow.

When she finally stilled, he drew his head back and looked closer upon her dimly lit face.

Nostrils flaring with the breath she dragged in through them, the lady stared at him, dark eyes glittering with outrage. And fear.

For her age, Baron Wardieu's mother was still a lovely woman, her skin relatively smooth and clear, the figure beneath him slender—not skeletal but softly rounded. Her long hair was nearly as light as her son's, but interspersed with darker strands of gray. There the resemblance to the miscreant ended, for her features were delicate and refined, and she was nowhere the height or breadth of the one she had birthed.

It was difficult to believe this petite woman could have borne such a son. But her hair was testament to that unfortunate distinction.

"If you behave, you need not fear me, Lady Zara," he reassured her, though he did not know why he bothered. "I come only to recover that which is mine. And to repay your son a very old debt."

Her eyes widened in silent question, but he would waste no time enlightening her further.

"Now..." He released her wrist, retrieved his dagger, and touched its tip to her throat. "No screaming, hmm?"

Her eyes lowered to the weapon, and he slowly lifted his hand from her mouth.

When she did not utter a sound, he moved off her, gripped her arm, and pulled her from the bed. Keeping her tight to his side, he led her across the chamber and out into the corridor.

The other members of the household who had spilled from their rooms could only stare in horror as the great, blackened man made for the stairs with their lady.

In the main hall that had been lit by torches, the invader halted and waited for all eyes to fall upon him. Beyond, through doors thrown wide open, came the sound of thundering hooves as his men descended upon the inner bailey. There would be resistance, but his men would soon put everything in order. Fortunately, the threat to Lady Zara would mean far less bloodshed.

Once his presence was noted by all, a great hush fell over the people and they looked from him to their lady and the dagger at her throat.

"Send word to your garrison leader that I hold Lady Zara," he shouted. "If he agrees to an unconditional surrender, no harm will befall her."

"My son will slay you for this injury," the lady spat.

"Not if I slay him first," he returned.

As if having forgotten the blade at her throat, she turned sharply, drew back a hand, and struck him across the face.

He was as startled by the slap as he was by the lack of blood upon her neck. Though his reflexes were honed and he had not hesitated to adjust the position of his blade, she should not have escaped unscathed.

And as if she did not know how close she had come to a lethal injury, she began to tug and jerk to free herself. "Unhand me, villain!"

He dragged her closer. "You mistake me, Lady. I am no villain. I am Baron Balmaine of Penforke."

She dropped her head back, slid her narrowed gaze over his face, and sneered. "I know who you are, though I would not deign to bestow so esteemed a title upon one such as you."

Gilbert laughed—or something like it. "Then you *were* forewarned. I thought it possible, but considering how easy it was to breach your walls..." He shrugged. "I do not think much of the defenses of this holding."

"You are vile! Had you come a day earlier, 'twould be a far different ending to your attack."

"Then it was foolish of you to let your guard down so quickly."

She raised her eyebrows. "Ah, but one would not expect a seasoned warrior to dally so long. You are seasoned, are you not? Or did you obtain that limp chasing about your mother's skirts?"

She could have no way of knowing how close to the edge she pushed him—so close he had to reach deep to find the strength necessary to pull back from the precipice.

19

RANULF LAID A palm on the stonework framing the window and looked out at the starry night. It was hours since Lizanne had collapsed in the hall, but still she slept.

He was angry with himself for having let the king persuade him to leave her side. He had known better. She had been in no state to fend for herself among those people.

He had been disturbed—and jealous—when he had seen her conversing with Charwyck, their bodies so close as to nearly touch. The other man's swift retreat and Lizanne's subsequent faint raised questions that, as yet, remained unanswered.

His men had been unable to locate Charwyck, but word had finally come that the man had left the palace forthwith, taking his small retinue with him. Though Ranulf had longed to go after him, he had chosen instead to stay with Lizanne.

He looked over his shoulder to the bed. Candlelight flickered over a face made even more pale by the tumble of black hair spread around her. Listening intently, he heard her slow, even breathing.

Queen Eleanor's personal physician had shrugged off Ranulf's concerns. He had said that when she was ready to awaken, she would, and it was merely a matter of exhaustion, excitement, and a disregard for proper nourishment.

That last had bothered Ranulf. Although he'd had a tray sent to her the night before, the chambermaid had reported to the physician that nothing had been touched. Knowing the state Lizanne had been in when he had left her yestereve, Ranulf upbraided himself for not making certain she ate—especially after the way she had picked at her midday meal.

Still, he knew there was more to it than the physician's diagnosis, that the exchange he had witnessed between her and Charwyck had played a part.

He rubbed a hand over his face, crossed to the bed, and lowered into the chair he had earlier dragged beside it. Leaning forward, he brushed the hair from Lizanne's face.

Her lids flickered, and she made a sound low in her throat.

He bent nearer, ran his knuckles over her jaw, and brushed his thumb across her softly parted lips.

Her lashes lifted, revealing the sparkling slits of her eyes. "Ran..." She sighed, then reached up and touched his face.

As relief flooded him, he turned his mouth into her palm and kissed her cool skin. "How do you feel?"

"Tired," she breathed, her lids beginning to lower. "Why am I so...?" Her eyes opened wide. "I fainted."

He lifted her hand in his, rubbed a thumb across her pulse. "You did."

Emotions shifted across her face, while beneath his thumb, he felt her blood course faster. Doubtless, she remembered her meeting with Charwyck. "Tell me, Lizanne."

She startled as if unexpectedly returning from some other place. "Forgive me for embarrassing you."

"Forgive me for not being there to keep that knave from your side." Still her pulse raced.

"Tell me what happened."

"I...am not sure."

She lied. Was this to be yet another battle? "Are you not?" Ranulf said, struggling to keep irritation from his tone.

"I suppose I should have eaten more," she lamely confessed, "and I did not sleep well yestereve."

Inwardly, he sighed.

"And then the wedding." Her brow furrowed. "For which I am also terribly sorry."

Though it was Charwyck he wished to discuss, he momentarily set the man aside and asked, "You are?" only to recall she had preferred entering a convent over marriage to either of those presented to her.

"Aye," she said and struggled to rise.

He assisted her, placing pillows behind her back and lifting her to sitting. As she leaned back, the covers down around her waist revealed how thin her shift was.

Determinedly, Ranulf raised his gaze to hers.

"I should not have forced the marriage upon you," she continued, "and I would not have had there been another way. You understand, do you not?"

He did not, but he intended to. "There was another way, Lizanne. The king gave you a choice—Charwyck or me."

She shook her head. "That was no choice. Never would I marry Philip, even if there had not been you. Methinks I would have died first."

"Why?"

She opened her mouth, closed it, drew her arms nearer her sides.

Ranulf leaned close. "I am your husband now. You must share these things with me. You must trust me."

She was silent a long moment, but just when he was certain she would say no more, she nodded. "If there was anyone I hated as much as you, Ranulf, it was Philip. I grew up loving him. I idolized him, followed him everywhere. In my eyes, he was perfect and so handsome." She dropped her head back and stared at the canopy.

Ranulf waited, his insides twisting at the emotion in her voice and the jealousy that surged through him over her admission of love for another man.

"He was never very kind to me, though. I was tall for my age—awkward—and cursed with this black horse's tail for hair. Doubtless, he found me less than appealing." She sighed. "Beneath my nose, and that of my father's, he trysted with the women servants of our castle. Though it hurt to see him behave as he did, I told myself it did not matter since, in the end, he would belong to me. As arranged by our parents, one day I would become his wife and bear him children."

She returned her gaze to Ranulf. "For two years, I had not seen him but had thought of him every day. I was on my way to the wedding, escorted by Gilbert and our father's men when our camp was attacked." She exhaled deeply, inhaled deeply. "Blood was everywhere, and though I did not wish to believe it, I feared Gilbert was dead."

"But he lived."

"Aye. He is strong-willed, even more than I." A faint smile touched her mouth, then was gone. "When Philip refused to wed me, it killed my father."

"Still you think 'twas I who maimed your brother and tried to take your virtue?" Ranulf asked, his voice harsh as he did not intend it to be.

She averted her gaze, pulled her hands from his, and covered her face. "I do not know anymore," she choked. "I was certain 'twas you, but now…"

Hope surged through Ranulf.

She let her hands fall to her lap. "Trust is not easy for me. I have lived too long with these memories to so quickly discard them, though I want to. More than ever."

She did not offer as much as he wanted, but he told himself to be content in that it was more than she had previously allowed.

Ranulf stood and strode across the chamber to the hearth. He returned moments later and placed a tray of viands on the mattress beside her. "You are to eat everything," he said and lowered into the chair.

Lizanne reached for a meat pie.

Not until she had consumed a good portion of it did he return to the question uppermost in his mind. "I would know what Charwyck said to upset you."

She stiffened.

"Lizanne, do not think to tell me he said naught, for I will not believe you."

She so roughly pulled her bottom lip between her teeth that he winced. "'Tis not important."

Ranulf sat forward. "I will judge whether or not it is important. Now tell me."

She stared at her fingers as she worked them over the edge of the coverlet. "He was angry, said it mattered not that I was wed to you, that he would...have me." She looked up.

"And?"

"That he would dispose of you."

Ranulf nearly laughed. "He intends to kill me?"

"I am sure of it."

"What else?"

Lizanne stared at Ranulf—her husband, the man to whom she ought to be able to tell anything. And there *was* more to tell.

Your husband, does he not remind you of someone? A common villein...

She had been shocked by Philip's parting words, so deeply that everything had gone black. But though she knew she should not withhold this last piece from Ranulf, the implications of which so terribly frightened her, she was reluctant to speak of it. She would have to think on it some more.

"'Tis all," she said and slipped down beneath the covers.

Ranulf sat unmoving some moments, then stood, bent, and briefly touched his lips to hers. "Sleep, then." He turned to leave.

Lizanne caught his hand. "You are not staying?" It was, after all, their wedding night, and he had every right to claim it.

He looked back at her. "Were you well, Wife, I would be pleased to take what your eyes offer, but 'tis better you not suffer my attentions. We will have our wedding night when we reach Chesne."

What her eyes offered? Her indignation flared but honesty quickly doused it. She truly did not want him to leave. "I do not wish to be alone," she said softly. "Will you not stay?"

His eyebrows gathered. "Where would you have me sleep, Lizanne?"

Feeling heat rise to her face, she said, "Here, beside me."

He smiled. "You think it safe?"

"You could just hold me."

"Ah, torture." His dark eyes twinkled. "Is that what you have in mind?"

"'Tis not my intention," she said. "Would it really be so bad?"

"It would, but so long as you do not plan on chaining me to a wall, I am willing."

Hiding her smile, Lizanne folded back the covers and invited her husband to share her bed.

20

"CHESNE," RANULF SAID as he looked out across the land spread before him. The three days' ride from London had seemed like a dozen, not only because he longed to be home, but because he had yet to exercise his husband's rights over Lizanne. At Chesne they would finally know one another and their life together would begin.

"What do you see, Lizanne?"

"Land," she said where she sat before him. "Fertile land." She peered over her shoulder at him.

"And?"

She looked again. "What would you have me see, my lord?"

He caught her chin and brought her face back around. "'Tis not Penforke. It is Chesne, and it is your home now. That is what I would have you see. And accept."

Her gaze momentarily lowered to his mouth. "I have accepted it, Husband."

He studied her face. Finding no lie there, he murmured, "That pleases me," and pressed a kiss to her lips.

When he started to draw back, Lizanne followed, sliding an arm around his neck and bending his head back to hers.

He lingered over her mouth, then reluctantly ended the kiss, leaving her staring disappointedly up at him. "Your heart knows the truth," he said, then settled her back against his chest, took up his destrier's reins, and led the descent toward Chesne.

The sun was nearing its zenith when one of the men from the small party Ranulf had sent ahead broke from the trees and rode wildly toward them.

Ranulf and his men halted their horses, and the ring of swords being drawn from scabbards echoed all around.

"My lord!" the man gasped when he reached them.

"What has happened?" Ranulf demanded. "You have seen my mother?"

"Nay, my lord." He drew a deep breath. "Chesne has been taken and all within held prisoner."

Feeling Lizanne stiffen, Ranulf forced himself to think calmly and rationally as called for in all situations where blood was to be spilled. "What of the rest of your party?" he asked.

"We were set upon, my lord, and taken within the walls. I was sent back to deliver a message."

Ranulf nodded for the man to continue.

"I was told to inform you 'tis Baron Balmaine who holds Chesne—"

"Gilbert!" Lizanne once more turned her face up to Ranulf.

He narrowed his eyes on her. "It changes naught," he growled, then commanded the messenger to continue.

"He said if you wish to see your mother alive again, you will return his sister to him and hand yourself over forthwith."

The man fell silent, but Ranulf knew there was more. "And?"

The messenger pulled a cloth pouch from beneath his tunic and extended it. "He said this would convince you of his intent should you think to refuse his demands."

Ranulf took it. Feeling heat move through his every vein, he stared at the object, tested its weight. It was light. Something small. He met his wife's gaze. "What kind of man is your brother?"

Fear scampering through her on clawed feet, Lizanne turned over and again what the messenger had told. She had heard of sending body parts of an adversary's loved ones to mark the seriousness of the captor's threat, but she could not believe Gilbert capable of such a terrible thing. It was preposterous.

"He is not an animal," she said and reached to take the pouch from Ranulf.

He closed his hand around it. "If he is, Lizanne, I will have to kill him like one."

His words slashed at her and, without thought, she flung at him, "He will not give you a second chance to do so."

"I do not ask for a second chance," he ground out, muscles bunching every place they touched, "only a first."

Either way, I shall lose. And that thought finally made her admit what she had refused to acknowledge for days. *I love Ranulf Wardieu.*

Pure madness, but what she felt for him could have no other name. Never before had she felt such depth for another. And it hurt. She closed her eyes, felt the moisture of tears gather behind her lids, but when she returned her gaze to Ranulf, he stared as if unmoved.

"Open it," she whispered.

The world seemed to stand still as he peeled back the folded cloth and unveiled what Gilbert had taken from Ranulf's mother.

It was Walter who first came to life amid the tense silence. "Almighty!" he exclaimed.

Lizanne released her breath. It was hair. Only hair. A long, pale lock against dark cloth. She looked up at Ranulf, but her smile of relief that she had expected to be matched by his own quickly retreated.

Eyes once again that terrible black, he said, "How dare he lay a hand to her. I will kill him for this."

"'Tis but hair!" Lizanne gripped his arm. "He is my brother."

"And she is my mother!" He lifted her hand from him, beckoned to his squire. "Take my lady wife up before you," he commanded.

"What do you intend?" Lizanne demanded as she was lifted from her place before Ranulf and settled on Geoff's mount.

Ranulf pinned her with his steely gaze. "You are my wife, Lizanne, and you will remain so."

"What of your mother?"

"I will have her back shortly. And Chesne."

She shook her head. "Pray, let me speak to my brother. Blood need not be shed over this. I can make him see reason."

"Aye, but whose?" He turned his mount aside.

"Ranulf!" she cried, but she had lost him.

Tears unchecked, she watched as the men donned chain mail in preparation for battle. They were efficient, remounting minutes later and following Ranulf who, wearing his great hauberk, set the course for the short ride to the castle.

Squire Geoff said not a word as he held Lizanne before him and brought up the rear.

Shortly, the fortress that was Chesne came into sight. It was made entirely of stone, the gray rectangular donjon rising high above walls that bordered on a wide expanse of wet moat. Although the drawbridge was lowered, the gatehouse's portcullis was firmly in place.

At such a distance and from behind the ranks of Ranulf's men, Lizanne could only just make out those who dotted the crenellated walls. For certain, Gilbert was among them, likely atop the gatehouse. Which one?

Out of range of fire, Ranulf and his men gathered at the far end of the glade surrounding the stronghold. With a pervasive restlessness, each man readied himself for that for which he had been trained.

Lizanne experienced her own restlessness, knowing it was only a matter of time before many of these men, and her brother's, lay bloodied upon the ground.

She had to speak to Gilbert, to show him she was well and convince him she was with Ranulf of her own free will. Surely, it would make a difference once he learned she was wed.

"Geoff..." She shifted around. "Take me to my husband. I must needs speak with him."

"Nay, my lady, he would not want you any closer. You are safe here."

"They are going to kill each other," she said as levelly as she could manage. "Can you not see that?"

Regret grooving his mouth, he said. "'Tis my lord's decision, this. Your brother has done great offense in taking his home and threatening his family. He has a right to defend both."

She clenched her hands. "And what of the offense done my brother?"

Geoff's face hardened. "I know not the details, my lady, but 'twas you who began this. You dealt the first offense."

She longed to refute his claim, to explain why she had done it, but she knew it would be futile. Geoff seemed fond of her, but it was nothing compared to his loyalty toward Ranulf.

Lizanne turned back to survey the scene. Through the ranks, she glimpsed Ranulf and Walter whose heads were bent toward each other as they conversed. Shortly, the messenger of earlier spurred his horse toward the castle.

"What is happening?" Lizanne asked.

"I know not, my lady," Geoff answered tightly, clearly frustrated at being relegated to the outskirts.

The messenger was not allowed within the walls, though he was permitted to cross the drawbridge to deliver the message through the portcullis. Minutes later, he turned and started back across the glade.

As the man drew near, Geoff urged his horse forward until he was as near the rear of the ranks as he could draw.

"He will meet you, my lord," the messenger's voice carried to Lizanne. "He has agreed upon swords."

"Nay!" Lizanne cried and gave Geoff the trouble he surely feared, pleading and crying as he prudently turned his mount aside and, finally, attacking him with every available part of her such that it was questionable whether or not they would remain astride.

When an arm came around her and dragged her from atop Geoff's horse, she hardly noticed she had changed hands, but when she saw it was Ranulf, she stilled.

"Do not do this," she pleaded as he lowered her to her feet. "Do not fight Gilbert. He is an excellent swordsman—"

"You are worried for me?" His face softened slightly.

She reached up and laid a palm to his cheek. "I am worried for both of you."

"'Tis your chance to free yourself of me," he said, "and gain that which you intended all along—without soiling your own hands."

She gripped his chain mail. "I do not wish your death anymore. I do not think I ever did."

His eyebrows drew together.

"Don't you see?" she pressed. "Gilbert does this only in retaliation for you taking me from Penforke."

Ranulf released her, took a step back, and thrust a hand through his hair. "The insult has been given and the challenge issued, Lizanne. I have done naught against your family without provocation but have borne another's punishment. Now 'tis time your brother paid for the wrong he has done me."

"Let me talk to him first. I am your wife now. There is nothing he can do to change that. I will make him understand."

"Nay, 'tis done." He reached for her, pulled her to him and, with his back to his men, lowered his head and captured her lips. The kiss was breathtaking in its intensity, as if it might be their last, and then it was over. As he set her from him, their eyes clashed. A moment later, he was walking away.

Lizanne watched as he remounted his great destrier and nosed it through the ranks, Geoff following. When she could no longer see him, she became aware of another nearby and turned to find Roland to her left. He beckoned her forward.

Forcing down panic that would only hinder her, Lizanne walked slowly toward him, setting in motion the workings of her mind in hopes of solving this deadly dilemma. As Roland offered a hand to her, she hit upon an idea. It was not a good one, but she had so few options and no time to search out another. Still, she was grateful it was not Geoff she must take advantage of this time.

Sitting before Roland, she searched out Ranulf and found him at the outermost margin of his men.

'Tis all in the timing, she told herself as she measured the distance to the castle. "Roland, can we not move closer?"

"Lord Ranulf would not wish it."

"Then just to the outer edge so I might better view the duel. I would see for myself 'tis fairly fought."

Roland shook his head. "You can see well enough from here, my lady."

"I cannot." She threw a hand out to encompass the wall of men. "They move about too much and block my line of sight." She looked around and saw the squire's lips compress as his gaze moved from the men to the castle, then to the middle ground where Ranulf would meet her brother.

He was wavering, Lizanne realized, and she pressed the advantage. "Pray, Roland, grant me this."

"Very well." Slowly, he guided his mount to the far left edge and positioned them diagonally across from the castle and just in back of the men.

Craning her neck to look down the forward rank, Lizanne saw that both Walter and Geoff had moved back and left Ranulf alone before the gathering. He faced outward, staring ahead, helmet in place, chain mail hood drawn beneath his chin and buckled.

It was exactly how she remembered him from the day he had returned to Penforke for her. He was perfectly matched for Gilbert. Or perhaps not. Although her brother had learned to adjust for his lameness, it was a certain disadvantage that could mean his downfall when faced with a man like Ranulf.

Still, she was surprised by a sudden inner calm, the unexpected emotion fueled by certainty that she would be able to put an end to this senseless duel.

Then the portcullis raised, and a single horse and rider rode out onto the drawbridge. Behind him, the portcullis fell back into place.

Gilbert. Did he see her? In her green dress that blended with the greenery behind, it seemed unlikely. Turning her head, she looked to where Ranulf guided his own horse forward at a slow canter.

Do it now!

She gasped loudly and fell forward, draping herself over the horse's neck in as close to a dead faint as she could manage.

"Lady Lizanne!" Roland pulled her limp form back against him.

Inclining her body to the side, she allowed herself to begin a downward descent. As expected, the squire focused on keeping her astride, shifting her back over the midline of the horse's neck.

Wondering if any of the others had yet noticed his predicament, she gave a low moan and shifted her weight opposite.

Roland muttered as he steadied her with one hand, then he carefully swung out of the saddle, surely that he might pull her safely down beside him.

Lizanne shot upright, brought her leg up, and thrust it against his chest. As the force of her kick sent him backward into the grass, she called, "Forgive me," and grabbed the reins. Digging her heels in, she spurred the horse past the ranks of men and heard their surprised utterances as she shot forward.

Knowing Ranulf would try to stop her, she stayed to the far left as she guided Roland's mount through the long grass toward Gilbert. As she drew nearly level with her husband, she worked a hand through her hair and released its long braid. It was calculated, for when Gilbert saw the black tresses, he would know it was she.

A moment later, Ranulf bellowed, "Nay!" and she knew he had seen her.

She looked to him, saw him change direction and urge his destrier to a full gallop to intercept her, while behind his men rode rapidly across the glade.

"Faster!" Lizanne urged her mount, arcing inward as Ranulf gained on her, all too aware her precipitous course was drawing them dangerously close to the castle's walls and that soon they would be in range of arrows.

She returned her gaze to Gilbert and uttered a cry at the realization Ranulf would reach her first, her brother yet too far off and Roland's horse no match for her husband's beast.

Still, she pushed onward, determined that, if nothing else, she would delay them long enough to speak to Gilbert and explain before the two men she loved were locked in mortal combat.

As Ranulf neared, she altered her course to gain extra time, jerking the reins and guiding the horse back to the left, toward the moat. The move gained her only seconds, for suddenly Ranulf was alongside her, his arm tearing her from atop her mount.

She shrieked as he dragged her across his leg and onto the fore of his saddle. Her tailbone struck the pommel, but she had little time to dwell on the pain before the air around them was displaced with a shrill whistle.

Ranulf's body was flung backward, sending them both flying through the air with his arm clamped around her. It was he who took the brunt of the fall to the damp-softened ground, his breath that slammed out of him and rushed past her ear.

It took Lizanne several moments to regain her bearings, and when she did, she twisted around in Ranulf's hold. Though he did not completely release her, she was able to slide off and kneel beside him.

Ignoring the sound of approaching riders, she swept her gaze from his pain-stiffened face to the feathered shaft protruding from the links of his hauberk. Just below his right shoulder, blood seeped through the chain mail and spread outward.

"Ranulf!" She cupped his face between her hands.

His lids lifted. "Lizanne." He shifted his gaze to the shaft, then back to her. "Why?"

Tears flooding her eyes, she swallowed. "I did not want this. I wanted only to speak to Gilbert, to explain. You would not allow me to."

His eyes flicked past her and she followed his gaze to where Gilbert was fast approaching, then beyond to where Ranulf's men rode to his defense.

With a groan, Ranulf sat up, pushed Lizanne away, and snapped the arrow to a point just above its entrance.

Lizanne reached to him, but he pushed her away again. "Ranulf," she pleaded, "we must needs tend your wound. You will lose too much blood if it is not seen to."

Another arrow sliced the air as he straightened and reached for his sword. It missed him by inches, cleaving the ground to his left.

"Nay!" Lizanne scrambled upright and launched herself in front of him as he awkwardly used his left hand to draw his sword.

Knowing Gilbert's men would not fire upon him with her in their path, she tightly wrapped her arms around her husband's waist and clasped her hands together at his back. Through her bliaut and chemise, she felt his life's blood soak through to her skin.

"Get back!" Ranulf growled, trying to shake her free. "I do not need your woman's skirts to shield me."

She met his angry gaze. "I would not have you die for me. Pray, do not do this!"

Momentarily rising above rage, Ranulf searched her lovely, fearful face, and it struck him that she could run from him now. But she did not.

"I care for you," she whispered. "Do not ask me to explain. I just do."

"Lizanne!" Balmaine called. "Move away from him!"

Ranulf looked to the man who reined in and leaped to the ground. Sword in hand, Balmaine advanced on them. He was tall and broad, a hitch in his gait that Ranulf could use to his advantage just as his opponent would use the advantage of the arrow wound.

Ranulf returned his gaze to the woman he would risk all to have. "I was wrong," he said. "You *are* worth dying for, Lizanne Wardieu." He bent his head, brushed his mouth across hers, then thrust her so forcefully away that her hands broke free from his waist.

Before she could recover, he swung his heavy sword up. And scowled, though pain was less responsible for his expression than the ungraceful movement. The familiar weapon felt unfamiliar and awkward in his left hand.

The barrage of arrows from atop the castle's walls kept Ranulf's men at bay as the two opponents advanced on one another. But just as they drew near enough to assume stances to set their blades against one other, Lizanne ran past Ranulf and threw herself in her brother's arms.

God's blood, this woman of mine!

However, neither would Balmaine allow her to thwart him, for he gave her but a brief hug before firmly setting her away and continuing toward the man from whom he intended to draw blood.

"Gilbert!" Lizanne grabbed hold of his sword arm. "Stop this now. Ranulf has done no wrong."

Her words had the desired effect, halting her brother who looked down at her, a puzzled expression transforming the determined set of his face.

"Is this not the man who tried to defile you?" he demanded.

She shook her head. "It is not."

Her brother's head snapped back as if he had been struck. "What? Look at him!" He pointed his sword at where Ranulf had halted. "Does he not have the pale hair you described? Is he not the same breadth and height you spoke of?"

She inclined her head, then looked over her shoulder at the man she had wed. "But it cannot have been him."

Her words rocked Ranulf. Did she truly, finally believe him?

Balmaine's gaze sped between his sister and the man she defended, and Ranulf almost felt sorry for him as he surely struggled to reconcile his belief in Ranulf's guilt with his sister's unexpected behavior.

And then Lizanne dealt another blow. "He is my husband, Gilbert."

Her brother took a step back, and the breath that exited his mouth was so harsh Ranulf thought his men behind him must have heard it. "You have wed this..." He locked eyes with Ranulf. "...cur?"

"I am Ranulf's wife."

He swung his gaze to her. "You were forced into marriage?"

She hesitated. "The king wished it so—"

"The king! So for this he delayed my departure from court."

"I was given a choice," she hastily added. "And I chose Ranulf." She drew a deep breath, placed herself squarely before her brother, and lifted her chin. "And I choose to stay with him, Gilbert. I will not be returning to Penforke."

Her brother looked past her.

Battling weakness from the loss of blood, feeling sharp, tearing pain radiate outward from just below his shoulder, Ranulf held his gaze.

"Answer me this, Wardieu," Balmaine said. "Did you or did you not lead a raid against an encampment near Penforke four years past, and in doing so, slaughter nearly all?"

"I did not." Sword growing heavier, Ranulf gripped the hilt tighter.

"Has my sister not accused you of this deed?"

"She has."

The man's fists clenched and color rose.

"Can you not see he is hurt, Gilbert?" Lizanne entreated. "Have a care and let us take him within where I may tend his wound."

Her brother was slow to respond, and Ranulf guessed the man was measuring his opponent's state, likely aware it was only a matter of time before the last of Ranulf's strength abandoned him. But, finally, he said, "We must needs speak further on this, and he is no good to me dead—yet. Mount up, Baron Wardieu."

Ranulf was torn between outright refusal and his need to stem the blood that now stained nearly the entire front of his hauberk. He looked to Lizanne who had turned to him with a tremulous smile, then lowered his sword and signaled his men to ride forward.

"Nay!" Balmaine barked. "Only you."

Ranulf narrowed his eyes upon him, his surge of anger bringing with it a renewal of strength. "'Tis my home," he snarled, "and I will take with me whom I wish."

"Then I cannot allow you within." Balmaine planted his legs apart.

It was Lizanne who decided the matter. She ran past Ranulf and, a few moments later, led his destrier forward. "I will not go without my husband," she said. "Surely there can be no harm in allowing him an escort?"

Balmaine was not pleased, but he grudgingly nodded. "He may choose two."

"A dozen," Ranulf countered.

Balmaine shook his head. "Six."

Ranulf signaled for Walter to ride forward. Then, returning his sword to its scabbard, he awkwardly mounted the destrier and reached a hand to his wife.

"Lizanne," Balmaine called, "you shall ride with me."

"I will not." She slid her hand into Ranulf's.

Balmaine's jaw bulged, but he turned and, shortly, mounted his own horse.

Inside the inner bailey, the small party was greeted by Balmaine's men who quickly relieved Ranulf's escort of their weapons. From among the gathering, a small, fair-headed woman emerged.

"Ranulf!" his mother, Lady Zara, hastened forward. Halting alongside the destrier, she reached up and gripped her son's thigh. Her eyes widened as she took in his blood-soaked hauberk, so intent upon it that she did not seem to notice the woman seated before him.

"Mother." He laid a hand upon her smaller one. "You are well?"

"Of course. But you...What has happened?"

"A flesh wound," he assured her, though he knew it went deeper than that.

"We must needs get him inside," Lizanne said. "He has lost much blood."

Lady Zara shifted her gaze to the other woman and blinked as if surprised to see her there. And then her eyes narrowed, and Ranulf knew she had guessed this was the one responsible for all the trouble.

"Get you down from there!" his mother demanded. "I will see to him myself."

Lizanne stiffened. "'Tis I who will tend him, for I am a healer—and his wife."

Lady Zara stumbled back a step.

Fortunately, Walter was quick to gain her side. Leaning down from the saddle, he laid a hand upon her shoulder. "Come, Lady Zara, 'twill be explained later. First we must see to your son's well-being."

Walter and Geoff assisted in Ranulf's dismount. Though still conscious, increasing weakness forced him to accept the succor offered.

It was Lady Zara who led the way through the donjon to the lord's solar. Once Ranulf's men lowered him to the bed, Lizanne pushed her way past them and tossed orders across her shoulder as she leaned over Ranulf to examine his wound.

When his mother started to protest, it was Walter who again quieted her and pulled her aside.

"I will also need a cauterizing iron once the shaft is removed," Lizanne said, voice exceedingly calm in view of the task that lay before her. "And set a fire."

"You are truly a dangerous woman to associate with," Ranulf murmured as he peered at her between the narrow slits of his lids. "Methinks I may yet die for you."

She smiled weakly. "Not this time, Husband."

He tried to return the smile, then closed his eyes and sank into a deep, painless sleep.

21

"WHERE IS YOUR son?" Philip demanded of the woman whose hard work in the service of the Charwycks had aged her far beyond her forty and some years.

Unnerved by his sudden appearance, Mary cowered against the rickety table upon which she had been kneading dough when the baron's son had flung open the door and entered her small cottage. Though it had been many years since last she had been so near him, she still held no liking for him. After all, he was to blame for her son's wild, sometimes vicious disposition. Too many years of Darth's impressionable youth had been spent in the company of Philip Charwyck.

And now that Philip had been given control of his family's estates, though his father yet lived, life at Medland had become very difficult for its people. The past two years had seen much hunger and sickness among the common folk. Fields that should have been producing abundant food for the winter lay fallow. Only those who had been given plots of land by the baron—the villeins—had enough to eat and with which to barter. But even they despaired, for Philip Charwyck was not averse to taking from his people that which his neglect failed to provide for his household. The old baron's son had no conscience.

"M-my son is in the fields, milord." She clutched the skirt of her apron to her ample bosom.

Scowling, Philip stepped closer until he stood over her. "Then fetch him."

She flew out the door, scattering coarsely ground flour from her hands as she went.

Philip turned to watch her lumbering flight toward the fields. When she disappeared from sight, he propped himself against the table and pinched off a large piece of the pasty dough. He popped it in his mouth, then another pinch. He was a good ways through the dough before the mismatched duo appeared in the doorway.

Entering ahead of his mother was the large man called Darth, his dirty pale hair pulled back and secured at the nape of his thick, corded neck.

"Milord, ye wished to speak to me?" he asked as he moved to stand in the middle of the small room that immediately shrank around him.

Philip wiped his hands and strode across the short space. He put his face near the other man's and inspected the weathered features that spoke of years of heavy toil in sun and wind, then gripped Darth's chin and turned his head to the right, then the left. Confirming what he had already guessed, he issued a short bark of laughter and stepped back.

"Well, Baron Wardieu," he enunciated the name, "what do you in the fields working like a serf?"

It was Mary, Darth's mother, who first responded to his query— giving a small cry before collapsing to the floor in an unsightly heap.

Immediately, her son was beside her. "Mother!"

She moaned and blinked her eyes open and shut again.

With a grunt, Darth lifted her and carried her to her pallet. He laid her down, then settled himself beside her.

Philip set himself upon a stool to watch as Darth lightly slapped Mary's cheeks and called to her in a gravelly, unrefined voice that bore no resemblance to that of the one he resembled in nearly every way.

Darth turned his ebony eyes toward his lord and, for the first time, Philip noted intelligence in the man's face. Perhaps too much.

"Ye called me Baron War...dieu," he said, testing the name upon his tongue. "What mean ye by it?"

Philip leaned forward and pointed to the woman who fearfully stared at him. "Methinks your mother can best answer that."

Darth looked down at her. "Ye know what he speaks of?"

Mary shook her head.

Philip heaved a sigh. "I know not the details, but she does. Mayhap I can refresh her memory."

"Go on," Darth urged.

"To the north, at Chesne, there is a baron by the name of Ranulf Wardieu. You know the name, do you not, Mary?"

She swallowed loudly and turned her face toward the wall.

"Oddly," Philip continued, "the man has hair as fair as Darth's and eyes every bit as black. He is as tall and nearly as wide. And were it not for your son's hard years in the fields, one could say the two men were, in fact, identical. Twins. Now do you remember, Mary?"

The woman looked around and up at Darth. "I know not of what he speaks!"

If not that the big man was present, Philip was sure he would have beaten the hag. "The way I see it, either Darth is of noble birth, or his brother is of peasant stock. Which is it?"

She struggled to sitting and gripped her son's arm. "Darth, I must needs speak with ye alone," she said, lips trembling and white-edged.

Face hardening, Darth demanded in a voice grown as cold as the first frost of winter, "Answer him."

Tears beginning to roll down her full cheeks, she whispered, "I can explain, son."

He shook her hand off. "Then explain."

"'Twas so long ago," she muttered and lowered her head to stare at her bent, fleshy hands. "I was barely six and ten—"

"First answer this," Darth interrupted, "am I of noble or peasant birth?"

She reached up and grasped his face between her palms. "You are my son."

Again, he pushed her hands away. "Answer me!"

She looked past him to the open door of the cottage. "Noble birth. You are the second-born son of Baron Byron Wardieu."

Darth shoved to his feet. "Who bore me? You?"

"Nay." She began to sob. "Lady Zara Wardieu birthed ye."

"Then who are ye, the woman who has called herself my mother all these years?"

Content to let the scene play itself out without his interference, Philip silently observed the two, certain there were useful revelations yet to be spilled.

"Though I did not give birth to ye, Darth, I am yer mother. Is that not enough? Have I not cared for ye and loved ye as only a mother could? Have I not—?"

Darth growled, waved her words aside. "Who are ye?"

Mary closed her eyes. "I am the misbegotten sister of Lady Zara. I was her husband's leman."

Philip was fascinated by the anger that bunched Darth's muscles, thickened his neck, and made something terrible of a face that surely frightened the woman who had stolen everything from him.

"How came ye by me, *aunt*?" Darth shouted. "Did my mother abandon me?"

Mary shifted her cumbersome body and lowered her feet to the floor. With a great heave, she stood and faced him.

Philip did not think there was anything ugly about tears—indeed, often found them pleasing—but those that streamed the woman's face made him rethink his opinion. They were really quite unsightly.

"I gave birth to Lord Byron's son the night before Lady Zara birthed ye and yer brother," she said. "My child died the next day, and I was heartbroken. Ye understand, don't ye?"

Darth sneered and she hung her head.

"Then here Zara had two fine, healthy boys when she needed but one to give Byron his heir. I hated her. She had everything I wanted— noble birth, beauty, and Byron." She drew a deep breath. "So I switched my dead boy for one of hers—you, Darth. It was simple, as my babe looked so much like ye. Then I left. Hardly since have I thought of it. I raised ye as if you were from me own body—"

"And reduced me to a commoner!" Darth caught her shoulder in a grip so tight she cried out. "I am noble! Look what your greed and jealousy have done to me, old woman."

"Ye were second-born! There would have been naught for ye."

"Naught? 'Twould surely have been better than this existence. I could have become a knight and made my own fortunes."

"Ye know not what ye say. Ye love me! I am yer mother."

"A lie!" He thrust her away and she toppled onto her pallet.

Quickly, she gathered herself and scooted back into the corner where she began to weep loudly.

Darth rounded on Philip. "Why tell me this?" He jabbed a finger at him. "Yer up to somethin'!"

Philip rubbed his stubbled chin. "Four years ago, you served me well. Somewhat." He could hardly forget that both Gilbert and Lizanne Balmaine had lived. "I would but repay my debt to you."

Darth stared at the one who had set aside their friendship—if that was, indeed, what it had been—following the raid upon the Balmaine camp.

"And so," Philip continued, "I have a proposal for you." He stood from the stool.

"What would that be, milord?"

Philip raised his eyebrows, smirked. "'Tis no longer necessary to address me as your superior. We are, after all, nearly equal as nobles. Call me Philip."

As once he had done...Darth moved nearer him. "Well, Philip, what is this proposal?"

Philip crossed to the door. "We will speak elsewhere. And bring your possessions, for 'tis not likely you will return to this hovel."

Mary shrieked and stumbled up from her pallet. "Do not leave me, Darth!"

Philip laughed, strode outside.

What followed as Darth gathered his belongings was sobbing, pleading, clinging, cursing, and more sobbing, but when he finally stepped through the narrow doorway for what he promised himself would be the last time, the only thing that flung itself at his back was blessed silence.

Sack flung over his shoulder, he strode to where Philip sat languidly atop a thick-limbed stallion.

The man who had brought all to light looked from Darth to the cottage, smiled crookedly, and said, "Follow me."

Shortly, in a secluded area beside a swiftly running stream, Philip dismounted and seated himself on the moist bank.

Darth slung his sack to the ground and lowered himself a short distance away.

Leaning back, Philip clasped his hands behind his head. "Would you like to claim that which was stolen from you—perhaps more?" he asked.

Darth grunted. "'Tis a question that hardly bears answering. Think ye I prefer to live out the rest of my years doin' the stinkin' work of a commoner?"

Philip grinned. "I was merely prefacing my proposal."

"And what is this proposal?"

Philip closed his eyes, turned his face up to the sun. "'Tis simple. You shall become the baron of Chesne."

"That does not sound simple. What of this brother of mine? Is he not the baron?"

"For the moment."

"How am I to take the title from him?"

Philip met Darth's gaze. "You know the answer to that."

Darth snorted. It had been a foolish question, for in his youth he had too often been in the company of Philip Charwyck to not know the means by which he should dispose of another. "We look alike, my brother and me, ye said."

"Were it not for the hard life you have needlessly suffered, old friend, it would be impossible to tell you apart."

Darth probed a hand down his face, feeling the sun- and wind-cut ridges. His resentment over the blow his life had been dealt burgeoned. "How am I to kill him?"

"How would you like to kill him?"

"First, I would meet him."

"Ah, sentimental." Philip sighed. "But you most certainly will meet him."

"When?"

"Soon, but worry not. I will be at your side."

Darth nodded. "What do ye think to get out of this fer yerself?"

"You know me well, old friend. I want only one thing—the baron's wife."

"That is all?"

"'Tis enough, though I am sure your deep gratitude will serve me well for years to come."

Of course. "Why is this woman important to you?"

Philip sat up and propped his arms on his raised knees. "I want her for my bed. And there is the matter of revenge that is my due for an insult she gave me."

Certes, she would rue the day she had dared. "She is beautiful?"

"She is, though I should be the one asking the questions, for you know her better than I. After all, 'twas you who bedded her first. Tell me, how was she?"

Darth shook his head. "I know not what ye speak of."

"Of course you do. Do you not remember Lady Lizanne Balmaine?"

Darth startled, and Philip slapped his thigh and sprang to his feet. "Aye, the same. Ironic, is it not, that she would wed a man who looks exactly like the one who violated her? I look forward to having the full story from her myself. And soon."

Darth did not know how to respond, but he did know he could not tell Philip the truth—that the wench had knocked him senseless before he could have his way with her. "Why do ye want her now," he asked, "when ye did not want her before?"

With a swagger, Philip came to stand over him. "Had I known she would become such a beauty, mayhap I would not have been so hasty in trying to dispose of her." He grinned, propped his hands on his hips. "Are you with me, Baron Wardieu?"

22

THE FIRST LIGHT of dawn was etching its warm fingers across the walls when Ranulf opened his eyes to the familiar surroundings of his solar. At first, he thought these last weeks were a dream, but when he turned his head and saw Lizanne, he felt a surge of relief.

He considered her smooth profile where she sat in a chair, head propped upon crossed arms resting on the mattress. Even in repose, she was the loveliest thing he had ever seen.

Still, she was exceedingly pale, the dark smudges beneath the sweep of her lashes standing out in sharp contrast. Further, running from her temple down to the curve of her jaw was what appeared to be dried blood. His.

He looked to the clean bandages secured over his wound and wondered at the absence of pain. He would have expected terrible discomfort after such an injury. Instead, there was only a dull throb.

Recalling his former jailer's praise for his lady's gift of healing, he returned his gaze to Lizanne. Gifted, indeed.

Moving slowly so he would not awaken her, he lifted a lock of the black hair spread over the coverlet. Free of the weight of the mass, the strands sprang to life, finding a new shape as they curled around his fingers. He smiled and lifted another lock, watched it also coil.

A sound from the hearth stilled him. Lifting his head, he looked beyond the foot of the bed to the chair filled to overflowing with the watchful Gilbert Balmaine.

For what seemed minutes, the two stared at one another until Balmaine slid his leg off the arm of the chair and stood. He threw his shoulders back, rolled his head side to side, and walked forward.

Ranulf slowly lowered his head to the pillow and watched the man's approach, hackles rising the nearer he drew. Seeing the anger in Balmaine's erect bearing, Ranulf wondered what weapon might be at hand with which to defend himself. He supposed a fist would do.

"Thanks to my sister's skills," Balmaine said quietly as he halted alongside her, "it appears you will suffer little from your mishap. A pity."

Feeling a muscle in his jaw jerk, Ranulf glanced at Lizanne. "You do not trust me alone with my own wife," he said, his voice husky as he struggled to keep it low.

Balmaine's eyes narrowed. "Not when your wife is also my sister."

As if the silent battle waged between them could be felt, Lizanne stirred, murmured something, and turned her head on her arms before returning to her exhausted sleep.

Gilbert held Wardieu's stare a moment longer, then bent over his sister and gently lifted her from the chair.

She grasped a handful of his tunic and nudged her face against his chest as if seeking his warmth. But it was not *his* warmth she sought, Gilbert knew, and a moment later it was confirmed when she murmured, "Ran."

Jealousy crept through him. After their father's death, never had she called for anyone but her brother, but now there was another in his stead.

As it should be, he told himself, *as I feared it might never be for her.*

During the long night, Gilbert had discovered there was something very different about his sister and grudgingly conceded it seemed right. It was as if time had turned about, reversing some of the effects of that nightmarish night they had shared four years past. Disturbingly, though, he was unsettled by the loss of its burdensome familiarity, having too long lived with it.

What had happened between Lizanne and this man? he wondered, as yet having no explanation from her. The only thing he knew for certain was that she cared deeply for Wardieu, perhaps even loved him. And it infuriated him. Wardieu was still the enemy and would be until it could be proved otherwise.

Gilbert walked to the other side of the bed and carefully lowered his sister to the mattress. "She has not left your side since you were brought here," he said as he flipped the coverlet over her and tucked it around her.

He straightened and returned to the chair she had slept in. Settling into it, he leaned back and clasped his hands on his chest. "If you are up to it—and you appear to be—I would hear from you the circumstances that led you to take my sister from Penforke."

"She has not told you?"

"Nay, though I do have it from my people that it was not unprovoked. She abducted you from Langdon Castle, did she not?" He could not help but savor the glimpse he was afforded of Wardieu's shame at having been bested by a woman, and resented that it did not linger longer upon his face.

"That is how it began," Wardieu said low. "I do not think, though, now is the time or place to discuss it."

"My patience is worn nearly through, Baron Wardieu." Gilbert sat forward. "What is it? You fear you may not be able to control yourself?"

Wardieu ground his jaws. "Methinks neither of us will be able to control ourselves once started."

Gilbert stared the man down—or tried to, for Wardieu was obviously in no mood to be intimidated.

Gilbert heaved a sigh and dropped back in the chair. "Then we will wait until Lizanne awakens," he said and began the habitual kneading of his leg muscles.

When Lady Zara, accompanied by Wardieu's man, Sir Walter, entered the solar a few minutes later, Gilbert rose and crossed the chamber to stand with his back to the fireplace.

"Leave, Baron Balmaine," Wardieu said, pinning him with his black glare. "I would have time alone with my mother and Sir Walter."

Gilbert shrugged. "When we have settled this matter between us, you will have your privacy, not before."

"Then let us settle it now." Wardieu flung the covers aside and was off the bed so quickly it was hard to believe he had suffered as great an injury as he had. However, as he pushed past his mother, his stride broke and he slammed a hand to the end bedpost to steady himself.

"Ranulf!" Lizanne sat up, sprang across the covers to the foot of the bed, and dropped down beside him. "You should not be out of bed," she said, gripping his arm.

He jabbed a finger in Gilbert's direction. "I want you out of here. Now."

Gilbert started to smile, but as he sized up the man whose torso was bare but for the bandages covering his injury, he found himself more given to a frown. "The scar," he said, staring at Wardieu's unmarred abdomen.

Lizanne swung around. "I have told you, Gilbert, 'tis not him."

She had been explicit in every detail of her assailant, down to that telling scar. But Wardieu bore no evidence of it.

"We can talk while Lady Zara visits with her son," she said and turned back to Wardieu who shook off her hand and returned to the bed.

"What goes?" Lady Zara demanded. "Of what scar do you speak, Baron Balmaine?"

Gilbert glanced at the woman, looked back at Wardieu as he lowered to the mattress and Lizanne stepped near to draw the covers over him and satisfy herself he had not further injured himself.

Shortly, Gilbert and Lizanne withdrew from the chamber. After giving instructions to the two guards posted outside, he grasped his sister's elbow and guided her down the corridor.

Without warning, she halted and, when he turned to her, launched herself into his arms and began to cry.

Bewildered, for he had not seen her in such a state in a long time, he smoothed a hand over her hair. It was some minutes before she quieted and lifted her flushed face to his.

"I am sorry." She unclasped her hands from his waist. "This is all my fault. I was foolish to act so rashly, should have waited for your return before—"

"Shh," he hushed her. "Let us walk outside, and you can tell me everything."

Lizanne nodded and took the arm he proffered.

The castle's garden was lush with the scent of roses, and there was every shade imaginable, from the deepest to the palest.

"'Tis the work of Lady Zara," Gilbert explained as Lizanne looked about in wonder.

"How?" She buried her nose in a full bloom that was just beginning to shed its abundance of soft, velvety petals.

Gilbert shrugged. "I do not know how she does it, but surely as you have a gift for healing, she has a gift for flowers." Over the past days, he had come to admire the strong-willed woman who was Wardieu's mother. She was fire, this small lady. In fact, were she younger, he thought he might have considered taking her to wife.

Eyes bright, Lizanne moved bush to bush, smelling and touching. "Even the king does not have roses as fine as these," she exclaimed.

Only when she had been a girl had Gilbert seen her take interest in such things, so he was surprised by her enthusiasm over something that had nothing to do with weapons or strategizing.

"You have changed," he said, feeling a loss that he knew was rooted in selfishness.

She looked around. "Have I?"

He stepped forward and placed a hand against the small of her back. "Come, we will walk, and you will tell me of this Ranulf Wardieu."

Though the garden was not large, they spent the next hour covering every inch of it as she poured out her tale, beginning with her encounter with Wardieu at Langdon Castle and ending with how she had wrested Squire Roland's mount from him in order to disrupt the duel.

"Oh, Gilbert." She shook her head. "Why the dramatic gesture of sending a lock of Lady Zara's hair? It so infuriated Ranulf."

"I thought it might." He nearly smiled in remembrance of how he'd had to steal upon the lady to clip a piece free. Discovering too late what he had done, she had turned her wrath upon him with the force of a sea-blown storm. Narrowly, he had escaped the kick that had aimed to unman him.

"'Twas cruel of you," his sister said sharply.

Gilbert stopped and pulled her in front of him. "I was taking no chance of Wardieu running with you."

"But he—"

"I had to get you back. The thought of failing you again..." Realizing how quick his breath was coming, he dropped his hands from her, closed his eyes, and determinedly slowed his breathing.

Lizanne stared at her brother. She felt his pain and knew he had too long carried this burden as she had allowed him to do with nary a protest. And she was deeply ashamed. The king had been correct in his estimation of her.

She laid a hand on his arm. "You did not fail me, Gilbert. There was naught you could do to prevent what happened." She steeled herself for his reaction to what she would next tell. "And I no longer regret it—at least not where I am concerned."

He opened his eyes, barked, "What say you?"

She squeezed his arm. "If not for that night, I would now be married to Philip. As I discovered at court, he is not a kind man. Indeed, there is something quite cruel about him. He..." She lowered her gaze. Should she reveal what the man's final words had alluded to?

Gilbert lifted her chin. "What are you not telling me?"

"Philip," she croaked. "Methinks 'twas he who ordered the attack upon our camp. I am nearly certain of it."

Gilbert stared at her, slowly shook his head. "You speak nonsense. Who has filled your head with such outrageous lies? Wardieu?"

"Nay, not him. Philip Charwyck himself." In a rush, she told him of that last audience with the man who had been determined to make her his leman and the words he had spoken that had caused everything to go dark. When she finished, the fury upon her brother's face made her flinch.

"He is the one responsible," Gilbert ground out.

"Certes, he knows of the man who..." She swallowed hard. "... resembles my husband."

"Has Wardieu a brother?"

She blinked. "This I do not know. He has spoken little of his family. And, truly, I did not even consider the possibility." And for that she was ashamed, for it seemed the only solution.

"Then we shall ask him." Gilbert turned and strode away.

Though Lizanne's legs were long, their reach could not match his. However, with a bit of running, she caught up with him and accompanied him back inside the donjon.

Lady Zara and Walter were leaving the solar when the two of them stepped off the stairs.

Without explanation, Gilbert took Ranulf's mother by the arm and pulled her with him past the guards stationed on either side of the chamber.

Lizanne threw an apologetic look at the stupefied Walter and followed her brother inside and closed the door. Almost immediately, a ruckus commenced in the corridor outside and, a moment later, Walter burst inside.

"What is this?" Ranulf thundered, though not from the bed where he ought to be.

Lizanne followed his voice to where he was seated in an armchair before the fire, but before she could order him to return to bed, her brother spun around and shouted, "Out!"

"I will say who is and is not permitted in my chamber!" Ranulf growled.

Gilbert looked to him. "'Tis a private discussion I mean to have. I want no interference from that one." He pointed at Walter who was struggling to free himself from the guards who had taken hold of him.

"He may stay," Ranulf said in a dangerously level voice.

"He will go," her brother countered.

With growing trepidation, Lizanne watched as Ranulf's eyes narrowed to slits. "I have said he will stay, and he shall."

Knowing that, regardless of her husband's injury, it was only a matter of time before blows were exchanged, Lizanne stepped to where her brother stood with Lady Zara. "It can do no harm to have Sir Walter present," she said. "He can be trusted."

The determined set of his jaw told that he was not about to waver.

However, Lady Zara was not put off. "Let him stay," she said softly and touched Gilbert's hand.

Lizanne looked sharply at the woman and, when she caught the strangled sound behind her, glanced over her shoulder at Walter whose face reflected rage.

"Very well," Gilbert said and dismissed the guards with a nod. Then, Lady Zara on his arm, he advanced on Ranulf.

Lizanne waited for Walter to draw alongside her before following. Noting his dark scowl and recalling the advice he had given her at Westminster, she murmured, "Where Lady Zara is concerned, do you lead with your heart?"

The man startled so violently, she thought he might be having a seizure. However, he quickly recovered and turned remorseful eyes upon her. "Too often my head," he said.

Pleased at having solved the puzzle, she nodded and went to stand beside Ranulf who now wore a thick robe. "You are feeling well?" she asked.

"I was," he said, mouth set thinly as he stared at Gilbert.

Gilbert seated Lady Zara in the chair opposite Ranulf, then stood beside her. Rather forlornly, Walter positioned himself to the side and between the two chairs, but his eyes never left Ranulf's mother.

Gilbert broke the uneasy silence. "Have you a brother, Baron Wardieu?"

Ranulf blinked, looked to Lady Zara who had gone rigid. "I have no siblings—that I know of. Why do you ask?"

Gilbert folded his arms across his chest. "There is the matter of the man who committed an atrocity against my family for which, it seems, you have borne the blame. Though my sister says it cannot have been you, you match her description in every way."

"Except the scar." Ranulf's eyebrows rose into the hair brushing his forehead.

"Aye, except that."

"Lady Lizanne," Lady Zara leaned forward in her chair and pinned her new daughter-in-law with eyes as black as her son's. "You are saying there is another who resembles my Ranulf?"

"Aye, so nearly identical that I mistook my husband for that one, which is why—"

"Tell me of this encounter," Lady Zara urged.

Lizanne drew a sharp breath, gripped the back of Ranulf's chair. "I do not wish to speak of it. Suffice it to say there is another."

The lady stared hard at Lizanne, then sat back. When next she spoke, her voice knew sorrow. "I gave birth to twins." Her eyes moved to her son. "Ranulf was firstborn, Colin second."

Feeling herself sway, Lizanne held tighter to the chair.

Anguish etched Lady Zara's face. "Mayhap, 'tis Colin."

"Colin is dead, Mother," Ranulf said sharply.

She clasped her hands before her face, nodded. "He died within hours of his birth."

"Then what is this nonsense about it being Colin?" Ranulf demanded.

His mother shook her head, then reached to Walter. Immediately, her son's vassal was at her side, grasping her small-boned hand in his larger one.

"I never even held him," Lady Zara said, more to Walter than anyone else, eyes awash with unshed tears. "Byron said the child was diseased, but mayhap 'twas not Colin after all."

Loathing the pain this conversation was causing his mother, Ranulf decided he'd had enough and shoved to his feet. "Ridiculous speculation! I will hear no more of it."

"But 'tis possible," his mother protested. "Do you not see?"

"What I see is that you are becoming distressed for naught."

"Nay, mayhap Colin was stolen from me."

Silently cursing the weakness that washed over him and the wound that throbbed alarmingly, Ranulf shook his head. "Who would dare such a thing? Be sensible, will you?"

"Know you of any other children born before or shortly after yours, Lady Zara?" Gilbert asked.

"Enough!" Ranulf shouted and took a stride toward the other man, one that caused him to sway and threatened to send him crashing to the floor.

Once again, Lizanne set herself between them. "Pray, Ranulf"—she turned a hand around his arm—"sit down ere you fall down."

Since collapsing before the insufferable Gilbert Balmaine was the last thing he wished to do, Ranulf warned the other man, "I have not finished with you," and allowed Lizanne to urge him back to the chair. However, before she could move to stand beside him again, he caught her wrist and pulled her down onto his lap.

Amid her protests, he said, "You are where you belong, Wife," and looked to her brother whose nostrils flared and color ran higher. "All right, Mother." He turned his attention back to her. "Let us end this speculation. Were there any other children born during the same time?"

Lady Zara nodded. "Aye, Byron fathered another—on my illegitimate sister, Mary."

Ranulf stared, wondered how many more blows he might be made to suffer this day. He had known of his dead twin, but never had he heard of his mother's sister.

"When I discovered her betrayal, and Byron's, I demanded she leave Chesne." She sighed. "But she had no place to go, and Byron convinced me I should let her remain until her babe was born. He promised that then he would send her south. She hated me, though I did not know it until after she had lain with my husband and got herself with child. 'Twas torment day in and day out to see her about the castle. She flaunted her pregnancy and openly speculated on which of us had been impregnated first...whose child would be Byron's true heir."

When she dropped her face into her hands and began to cry, Walter moved nearer and laid his other hand on her shoulder. It was some minutes before she offered him a weak smile of gratitude and continued.

"Mary birthed a son the day before Ranulf and Colin were born. As promised, she was gone from Chesne when I recovered sufficiently to see my Colin given a proper burial."

Lizanne was the first to break the silence. "Lady Zara, forgive me, but do you know the name Mary gave her son?"

"Of course." She gave a bitter laugh. "She named him for Byron's father, D—"

"Darth," Balmaine supplied.

Lady Zara gasped. "That was his name."

"'Tis him," Lizanne breathed. "The name of the one who led the raid against our camp."

"Then it was Mary's son you buried, Lady Zara," Balmaine concluded. "She who likely took your second-born with her to Medland, Charwyck's home."

That man's name snapped Ranulf back to the present, and he sat forward so suddenly he nearly dumped Lizanne off his lap. "Charwyck? What has he to do with this?"

Balmaine looked to his sister. "You have not told him?"

Ranulf pulled her chin around. "'Tis the reason you collapsed at the palace, is it not? What have you withheld from me?"

She tried to pull free, but he held tight—until her struggle caused her elbow to bump his wound. At his groan, she stilled and slumped against him. "I could not tell you. I had to first sort it out." She twined her fingers in her lap and stared at them. "Philip was not explicit," she continued in a voice so low Ranulf was not sure how much the others heard. "He simply said you bore a resemblance to another—a common villein—and then he disappeared. 'Twas so confusing and frightening to think he might have been responsible for the attack, to think he would go to such lengths to avoid wedding me."

"I will stain my sword with his blood!" Ranulf bit.

"The knave is mine," Gilbert countered, "as is this Darth."

Ranulf's mother leapt from the chair. "If 'tis my Colin, you will do no such thing, Gilbert Balmaine. He is my son and cannot be held accountable for those things another surely forced him to do." She turned to Ranulf. "Is that not so?"

He looked from her to the woman he held in his arms. "We will have to see," he said. "Some things can be forgiven. Others?" He shook his head, then eyed Balmaine. "We will do this together. When I have recovered sufficiently, you and I will meet Charwyck and demand satisfaction for the pain he has inflicted upon our families."

Balmaine snorted. "Then you had best be recovered within the hour, for I ride this afternoon." He turned on his heel and stalked to the door.

"How do you propose to get past my men?" Ranulf called, bringing the other man to a halt.

Balmaine returned and halted before Ranulf. "I shall place Chesne back in your hands. Your men can have no objections to allowing us to leave peaceably."

Ranulf smiled. "Of course not—providing they have a good length of rope with which to string you from the nearest tree."

Balmaine's hands turned into fists.

"You may as well accept it, *Brother*," Ranulf said, "for 'tis the only way you will leave Chesne alive."

The man's face reddened.

"Please, Gilbert"—Lizanne slipped off Ranulf's lap, stepped near her brother—"do not do this alone. Wait for Ranulf."

"You do not trust me?" he bit. "You think I will fail you again?"

"I do not. But as my husband, and a man terribly wronged, he has the right to go with you."

Balmaine stared long at her, then shifted his gaze to Ranulf. "A sennight, then."

"Nay, a fortnight," Lizanne said. "His wound went deep."

Her brother was nearly trembling with whatever he struggled to contain. "Very well, a fortnight. Then I ride—with or without you, Wardieu." He turned, crossed the room, and slammed the door behind him.

23

✧

Over the next several days, Ranulf remained distant with Lizanne, angry with her for having kept her knowledge of Philip from him. He allowed her to tend his wound but was otherwise withdrawn. Between Lady Zara, Geoff, and Walter, all his other needs were met without so much as a single request made of her.

It pained Lizanne, but she refused to give in to the easy comfort of self-pity, accepting Ranulf's anger as his due.

During that time, the tensions eased between her brother and him. From a distance, she watched their mutual animosity evolve into a tentative alliance. Though pleased, it also made her feel more of an outsider, especially since they always set aside their conversation in her presence.

Sleeping on a bench in the great hall, a coarse woolen blanket her only companion, she got very little sleep, though more because of her whirling thoughts than discomfort.

Each day, she determinedly set about familiarizing herself with the castle and its people. Though disheartened by her reception, she was not surprised that, as the sister of the man who had laid siege to Chesne, the castle folk were less than friendly.

They snubbed her, going out of their way to avoid being near her. Even Gilbert's appearance could not clear a room faster than hers. It did not seem to matter that she was their lord's wife. And Lady Zara, who had warmed only slightly, was short with her and ofttimes argumentative. It took very little intellect to discern that, until the woman accepted her, Ranulf's people would not.

Once satisfied with exploring the castle, Lizanne spent hours in the outer bailey, watching with longing as Ranulf's and Gilbert's men tilted at the quintain, practiced archery, and fiercely tested each other's sword skill. With nothing else to occupy her, she contented herself with analyzing the mistakes made by the competitors and visualizing what she would do differently. It sustained her. For awhile.

In the evening of her fourth day at Chesne, feeling the forced distance between Ranulf and her had gone on long enough, she climbed the stairs to the solar.

Softly, she closed the door behind her, leaned back against it, and contemplated Ranulf's still form that lay in shadow upon the bed. Unnerved, but determined, she gathered her courage, crossed the room, and began to shed her clothes. When only her thin shift remained, she folded back the covers and slid in beside her husband.

She felt him stiffen when her thigh brushed his, but she moved closer.

"What are you doing, Lizanne?" Irritation was evident in his voice.

She pulled the covers up over her shoulders, lifted her head and, in the bare light of the room, met his sparkling gaze. "I am your wife now. It should not be necessary for me to seek accommodations elsewhere."

"So, you grow weary of sleeping in the hall with the others. Is it too cold or too crowded?"

She bit back the prideful response that was the first to make it to her lips, shook her head. "'Tis too lonely."

He was silent a long moment, then slid his fingers into her hair and cupped the back of her head. "I did not know you wished to be here with me."

She shivered. "I do."

"Why?"

"A wife should sleep where her husband sleeps. Otherwise, 'tis not likely there will ever be peace between them."

"And you want peace?"

"Verily."

Ranulf stared up into her shadowed face. At that moment, it would not have taken much for him to cross the line he had drawn between them and satisfy his baser needs, but he held himself in check. "What convinced you it was not me who committed those crimes against you and your brother?"

She sighed. "Sir Walter told me I must lead with my heart. And my heart told me it was not you."

Walter had said that? Stern, serious Walter who rarely led with anything but his head? What magic had Lizanne worked on him to bring forth such flowery, poetic advice? Of course, Ranulf was not blind to the bond between his vassal and his mother, but it had always seemed more friendship than anything else—at least, until the day Lizanne had revealed the missing piece of her conversation with Charwyck and his mother had held tight to Walter's hand. However, Ranulf had been too taken with anger and frustration over Lizanne's revelation to expend thought on what his mother and vassal might feel for one another.

Lizanne's next words pulled him out of his reverie. "Even before we wed, my heart was telling me this, but I would not listen. I was too frightened." He heard her swallow and wondered if she pushed down tears. "And though I continued to deny your innocence when I saw you did not bear the scar, inside I knew. Ah, Ranulf, I am sorry."

He drew her head down to his shoulder. "As am I for the suffering my family has caused yours. But why could you not have told me this sooner, Lizanne? So much pain it would have saved us both if you would have revealed your grievances against me when I took you from Penforke."

She drew a shaky breath. "In the beginning, I was certain it was you, and I knew such a villain who was also a nobleman was far more dangerous than one born a commoner—that he could not possibly allow one to live who knew his secret. I thought you a murderer and..."

Her body convulsed with a sob, and then came tears.

Ranulf held her, stroked her hair, and whispered soothing words. When she calmed, soft hiccuping all that remained of the expression of her anguish, he said, "No more, Lizanne." He lightly drew his hand down her spine and up again. "Henceforth, you will not cry over this. 'Tis done."

She lifted her head, and he felt her gaze seek his. "You forbid me the comfort of tears?"

"I do not like it when you cry."

It was not his intent to anger her, and yet when he felt that emotion stir between them, he was not at all averse to it, for it meant she would be fine. She was too fiery to be otherwise.

"Then I will be finished with crying—for now. However, if I must do so again, I shall."

"You would defy me? Your lord and husband?"

"'Tis not defiance!" She sat up on her knees at his side. "You cannot tell someone when to turn their emotions on and off. It is more complicated than that. I am no puppet, and if you expect me to behave as one, there will never be peace between us."

Ranulf could no longer contain his laughter. It rolled out of him and carried around the chamber.

"Why do you laugh?" she demanded.

He sobered as quickly as he could. "I am pleased with you, Wife."

"Pleased with me? As the king forced you to this marriage, I would not think you would be pleased at all."

Sliding a hand behind his head, he peered up at her shadowy figure. "The king did not force me, Lizanne. I chose to offer for you."

That silenced her, and when she finally spoke again, her words were not much more than breath. "You told me you had declined."

"I changed my mind."

"Why?"

He shrugged. "It is something I am still sorting out for myself."

Lizanne stared at him, longed to see his face that might reveal if his struggle was the same as hers had been before she had accepted it was love she felt for him. She sighed. "That is good—one less thing for me to feel guilty about."

Ranulf chuckled and pulled her back down beside him.

She settled her head on his shoulder and placed a hand to his chest to feel the beat of his heart.

Shortly, his voice came low to her. "Each time you look upon me, will you remember what that other one—my brother—did?"

Lizanne did not immediately respond, not because she did not know the answer but because it was more easily answered than she would have believed. "When first I laid eyes upon you at Lord Langdon's castle, 'twas as if only yesterday it had happened. Now it seems a very long time ago. Mostly, I see only you."

"It is unfortunate such a tragedy brought us together, Lizanne, but I am grateful for it."

She pressed nearer. "Ranulf?"

"Shh. Go to sleep. We will have our wedding night later."

She started to protest his conclusion, but realized she would not be believed. And rightfully so.

She closed her eyes. However, though her mind was fatigued, sleep did not come, for she remained too aware of the warmth of her husband's body. Nor did it help that he lay awake as told by his shallow breathing and the brisk beat of his heart beneath her palm.

Certain the only way she would sleep this night was apart from him, she lifted his arm from around her waist and moved to the edge of the bed.

To her surprise, he followed and curled his body around hers. It felt wonderful, but it was worse than before.

"I wish you would not do that, Ranulf."

"What?" he asked near her ear.

"Touch me without…touching me."

"I but wish to hold my wife."

"But I cannot sleep for being so near you. And, it seems, neither can you. So why do you further delay our wedding night? Is it because of your…" She cleared her throat. "Is it because of your first wife?"

Ranulf tensed against her back. "What of her?"

"She has not been long dead. Do you still love her? Is that why you will only hold me?"

She felt and heard the breath move in and out of him, then he rose up and turned her onto her back. "You know not of what you speak," he said, his face nothing but shadow above hers.

"Then tell me."

After a long silence, he said, "God forgive me, but I cannot even mourn Arabella's death."

Lizanne nearly startled. "Why?"

"She was a cold, conniving woman, and more than once unfaithful to our marriage vows. She did not come to me a maiden, though she claimed to be one."

Lizanne was almost fearful of her next question, but she needed to know the fate of her own marriage. "And you, Ranulf? Were you faithful to her?" After all, his father had not been faithful to Zara.

"I was, though Arabella and I lived separate lives—did not even share sleeping quarters."

Lizanne could not hold her relief inside, expelling it on a breath that sounded loud even to her own ears. "Then I will not be expected to share you."

Ranulf's fingers touched her neck, lightly feathered down to her collarbone. "Only if I must share you, and I have no intention of doing so. You are mine."

"But Arabella—"

"I did not want her any more than she wanted me. You, I want, Lizanne, more than I have wanted any woman. Do you understand?"

Berating herself for daring to hope he might declare his love for her, she nodded and told herself his desire would be enough. But it would not, and she was grateful for the dark when tears filled her eyes. "If Arabella does not hold you from me, what does?"

He lowered his head and brushed a kiss across her lips. "You, Lizanne. I have been waiting on you."

"Me?"

"For your consent, madam, and not merely consent by obligation."

Remembering when she had declared she would never willingly accept his touch, her anguish eased. Telling herself it mattered not that only she loved, she said, "I give you my consent, Husband. And not out of obligation but..."

"What?"

How she longed to say *love,* but the old Lizanne—the one before Ranulf Wardieu had spilled the pieces of her single-minded world and rearranged them around him—would not let her. And so she spoke what was also true, though not nearly as deep, "Out of want, Ranulf. I want you."

A moment later, his mouth was on hers again, and it was no brush of the lips. No quick end to it. No restraint. And no regrets, not even when Gilbert walked in unannounced the following morning and roared at finding them asleep in one another's arms. It was some minutes before he calmed sufficiently to resheathe his sword, and only when Lady Zara appeared and suggested a stroll in the rose garden did he remove himself from the solar.

Fortunately, Ranulf was quick to distract his wife from her embarrassment, and the two of them spent the morning abed.

24

AFTER A FULL sennight, Lizanne still felt like an outsider. Though she cared for Ranulf's injury and had spent these last nights in nuptial bliss, there were still so many hours of the day to fill that she thought she might go mad with restlessness. She had tried, repeatedly, to take part in the running of the household, but Lady Zara was still far from accepting of her presence.

In the end, there was nothing left for Lizanne but to spend her free time with Duncan, Gilbert's squire. At the back of the donjon, away from others' eyes, they set up targets and practiced archery.

To her chagrin, far too often the squire's skill exceeded her own. It would not have been so bad, but she had taught the young man to shoot, and she was bothered by her failure to so much as match him.

She complained that she had not practiced in weeks and her chemise and bliaut were too cumbersome. Good naturedly, Duncan loaned her chausses and a tunic, but it was hours of practice that sharpened her aim.

It was not long before Geoff and Roland discovered their secret and persuaded Lizanne and Duncan to give them instruction in the proper use of the bow. Lizanne, knowing Ranulf would disapprove if he discovered she was practicing, secured a promise from both squires that they would say nothing of it.

So it was that Geoff forgave Lizanne for the imprudence of her act in attempting to end the duel between Ranulf and Gilbert and once more offered his friendship. Grateful to have someone else to talk with, Lizanne set about making an invincible archer of him. He did not disappoint her.

Roland, however, was a different matter. He had been sorely shamed by Lizanne's trickery. Though he accepted her instruction, he stubbornly withheld his camaraderie until the day the four of them traipsed about the wood in search of prey.

Each with hares tied from their belts, they emerged from the trees.

"A good catch," Lizanne called over her shoulder where she strode ahead of the others, so taken by the thrill of the chase that, not for the first time, she had to remind herself it was not becoming of a hunter to cavort. Fortunately, no one could fault her for a long stride. And, hopefully, none would fault her for putting meat on the table—

A great snort sounded, and before she snapped her chin to the right, she knew what it portended.

"Run!" Duncan shouted as the wild boar rushed at her.

Gathering her wits, Lizanne threw a hand over her shoulder to draw an arrow from her quiver. And found it empty as her brother's squire had surely seen it was. For a long, precious moment, she could not move but then, still grasping her bow, she set her limbs to flight through the long grass.

Louder and louder, the animal's angry wheezing grew, faster and faster the beat of its hooves as it closed the distance between prey and predator.

Certain she felt its hot breath on the backs of her legs, Lizanne pumped her arms harder.

Then the boar screamed, a tortured, high-pitched sound that cleaved the air before blessed quiet fell.

Lizanne whirled around and stared at the shuddering beast that lay feet from her, an arrow protruding from its side.

The bow fell from her hand and she dropped to her haunches in the wake of a world nearly torn asunder. Seized by a fit of trembling, she lifted her head and focused on the squires who ran toward her. Roland was in the lead, and she guessed it was his arrow that had felled the beast.

"You are well, my lady?" he asked as he hunkered beside her.

She nodded but could find no words to reassure him.

"Can you stand?"

She held up a hand in silent appeal for him to wait, then looked to where Geoff and Duncan had halted alongside the dead animal.

"God's wounds!" Geoff exclaimed. "You could have been gored—"

"Splendid shot," Duncan cut across the other squire's words, then placed a booted foot on the boar and wrenched the arrow from its carcass.

Shakily, Lizanne raised herself and was grateful for Roland's grip on her elbow.

"You are well, my lady?" he asked again, concern lining his face.

Lizanne turned into him and wrapped her arms around him, so incredibly grateful that she could not speak past a tongue grown thick.

Awkwardly, the young man patted her back until she drew away. "You saved my life," she said. "I thank you."

As it turned out, a sentry upon the walls of the castle had seen the spectacle play out and raised the alarm. Thus, Gilbert arrived shortly thereafter.

Jaw clenched as if to hold back angry words, he drew Lizanne away from the kill that would put much meat on the table, lifted her onto his horse, and headed back to the castle.

They were crossing the drawbridge when Lizanne summoned enough courage to turn and offer her brother a tremulous smile. "Methinks Roland will forgive me now," she said. As soon as the words were out, she regretted them.

Gilbert reined in and turned her around to face him. "Do you play some silly game, Lizanne?"

She blinked. "You think I asked that boar to chase me?" She shuddered in remembrance. "I was truly frightened. At first, I could not even run."

"Then why so satisfied?"

She was reluctant to explain, but she knew he would not allow his question to go unanswered. "Because I made something good out of something bad. Roland has been angry with me for deceiving him when

I tried to prevent the duel between Ranulf and you. Mayhap I took my fright further than necessary, but surely you understand..."

He appeared unmoved by her appeal.

She looked at her hands. "Pray, do not tell him, Gilbert. I would not have him hate me."

"What I ought to do is paddle your behind. Or better yet, I should let your husband see to your punishment."

She gasped. "You would not!"

He sighed, shook his head. "Your secret is safe with me. However, if he does not yet know, Wardieu is bound to find out about your hunting. I think that will be sufficient punishment."

She huffed. "What is wrong with it? You have not objected before."

"Aye, and I was foolish to allow you so much free rein. You have no business behaving as if you are a man, Lizanne. You are married now and, God willing, will bear children before long. You are a woman. It is time you start behaving as one."

She could not speak past the lump in her throat. She did not think she had ever seen Gilbert so angry with her. It could not get worse. Or so she thought.

Ranulf appeared upon the drawbridge, face hard as he swept his gaze over the men's clothes she wore, harder yet when he looked to the empty quiver protruding above her shoulder.

Clothing aside, Lizanne knew well the image she presented. Her hair had all but come undone from the braid to which she had earlier set it, flying out in all directions and falling into her eyes. Too, her face was smudged with mud from when she had raced through a large pool of stagnant water to intercept that last hare. It was not the image a baron— any man—wished to have of his wife.

"You do try my patience," he finally spoke. "Now come down from there."

She held out her arms, but he stepped back, refusing to aid in her dismount. His message was clear. If she was going to behave like a man, she would not also enjoy the benefits of being a lady.

Snapping her teeth, she twisted around and slid partway down the horse. She dropped the last feet to the wooden planks, turned, and faced her husband.

Ignoring the warning sparkle in her eyes, Ranulf leaned forward and cut the ropes from which her game was suspended from her belt. He tossed the rabbits up to Gilbert, resheathed his dagger, then closed a hand around her upper arm and marched her past the disapproving castle folk.

He did not slow, not even when they entered the great hall. His mother, Walter at her side, stood when they walked past and raised her eyebrows.

Ranulf raised his own and his mother very nearly smiled.

Pulling his wife behind him, he mounted the stairs and traversed the corridor. Upon entering the solar, he released Lizanne, closed the door, and waited for her to turn to him.

She accommodated him, tossing her hair back and crossing her arms over her chest. "Now I suppose you shall lecture me on hunting."

"After you have removed those filthy clothes."

She glanced down at them. "I will not."

Ranulf had no intention of arguing with her. However, when he stepped toward her, she pivoted and ran to the far side of the bed. He stopped, stared, considered what her next course of action would be. When he took another step forward, she remained unmoving except for her eyes that followed his progress.

"Lizanne," he said warningly.

"Ranulf."

He came around the bed and stopped again. Though there remained less than two easy strides between them, still she did not move.

He lunged.

She bounded onto the bed and sprang to the floor on the opposite side.

Still somewhat encumbered with his injury, Ranulf followed.

She was just passing through the door into the corridor when he caught her arm and pulled her back inside. He slammed the door and pinned her to it with his body.

"You truly thought to escape me?" he demanded.

Head tilted back against the door, she shook it. And smiled. "I very much intended for you to catch me."

He frowned.

"Admit it." She poked him in the ribs. "You enjoy the hunt as much as I. Would you deny me the same pleasure, my lord?"

"You do not take this seriously," he growled.

She laughed. "I do not, for I refuse to let you ruin a perfectly good day. I enjoy the bow, and as I would not ask that you give up your weaponry, I think it unfair for you to ask it of me."

There were so many things he wished to say to her, but the only one that came out sounded weak. "You could have been killed!"

Her face was slow to sober. "Aye, but I was not."

He saw the light of fear in her eyes as if she harkened back to that too-recent incident. Then it was gone, replaced by another of her captivating smiles as she attempted, without much tact, to entice him out of his anger.

"Do tell. What would you have missed most?" She raised herself onto her toes and lightly blew in his ear. "The excitement I bring to your life? Or my arms around you at night?"

He pulled his head back, but the moment he looked into her eyes, he was lost. With a groan, he claimed her lips.

Shortly, he drew her toward the bed, but he did not press her back upon it. Instead, he released her, retreated a step, and swept his gaze up and down her wretchedly clothed body.

Lizanne looked down herself. "Not very appealing, hmm?"

"Indeed." He walked around her and considered her backside.

She swung around. "What are you doing?"

He raised a hand to quiet her, ran his gaze down and up her again.

"Are you inspecting me?" she demanded.

He reached forward and pulled her tangled hair over her shoulder. "Something will have to be done with this mess."

She slapped his hand away. "How dare you!"

It was Ranulf's turn to laugh. "'Tis not as if I do not owe you. Surely you remember subjecting me to the same in the king's presence?"

She caught her breath, smiled sheepishly. "I suppose you have been waiting for the right moment to repay me."

"I would not say I have been waiting, but this opportunity was too good to let pass. Consider yourself fortunate *I* chose to do it in private."

"You are considerate, my lord."

"So I am." He stepped near again, kissed her. "As you find pleasure in hunting," he said, "I will not speak against it. However, in future, I shall accompany you."

She reached up and cupped his face between her hands. "Then I shall find all the more pleasure in it."

25

❧❦❧

Near the end of the stipulated fortnight, Ranulf declared himself fit to ride south with Gilbert. Together, the two men made plans to leave in two days' time.

With growing apprehension, Lizanne watched the preparations and escalation of training for Ranulf's and Gilbert's men.

All this for me, she thought and wished there was a better way. Although the worry over Ranulf and Gilbert slaying one another had abated, she now had the worry of Philip Charwyck, a threat she took quite seriously.

As all three squires found themselves occupied with their lords, she spent much time brooding over the matter. When she had broached the possibility of accompanying Gilbert and Ranulf, she had been met with such angry opposition on both sides that she had fled the hall.

Now, seated atop the outer fence of the corral, idly stroking the muzzle of the great stallion that blew softly into her hand, Lizanne was too intent on the training yard across the way to notice she was approached until a hand touched her knee.

Looking down from her perch, she saw it was Ranulf's mother.

"Lady Zara." She gulped, drew her hand from the horse, and clasped it with the other. Immediately the stallion nudged her shoulder, pushing her sideways and forcing her to transfer her hands to the fence railing to remain upright.

"You have a way with horses," Lady Zara said. "That one is far from being broke, yet he comes to you without fear."

Blinking at the cryptic compliment, Lizanne glanced at the animal that stood watching her with great, doleful eyes. "I had thought him broke. He seems gentle enough."

The lady smiled, not a full smile, but it was a beginning. "Try mounting him once, then——" She shook her head. "Nay, I should not even propose that in jest, for methinks you would try."

"You are right." Lizanne eased herself off the fence. "You wish to speak with me?"

Lady Zara placed a hand on her daughter-in-law's arm and guided her away from the corral. "I have received word there is a young child in the village not far from here who has broken his leg, and that it may need to be removed. I thought, perhaps, you would like to accompany me."

Lizanne halted. "You trust me?"

The look the lady gave her said the question was absurd. "You have proven yourself skilled—far more than I. My son behaves as if he never sustained an injury."

Lizanne smiled. "Of course I shall accompany you." However, in the next instant, her enthusiasm shadowed. "Do you think Ranulf will mind if we go? He has forbidden me to leave the castle's walls."

Lady Zara frowned. "I do not need permission to see my people. Ranulf is accustomed to my visits to the villages. Besides, we will have a proper escort."

"Very well. I must needs gather my medicines, and we can set off."

"Be quick about it," Lady Zara said to Lizanne's retreating back.

Their escort was more formidable than it would have been had Ranulf not caught word of their intent. To their ranks, he added a score of armored knights and men-at-arms and chose Walter to lead them.

Staring up at Lizanne where she was mounted and ready to depart, he pushed his hair back from his sweat-streaked face. "Lizanne, pray do not test Sir Walter. Regardless of the child's condition, I want you back before sunset. Now, give me your word you will follow his orders without question."

She smiled down at him from atop the wonderfully spirited mare she had been given to ride. "You have my word."

Ranulf removed his belt, slid the sheathed dagger off it, and handed it to her.

Recognizing it as her own, she eagerly accepted it. "Thank you, Ranulf—my lord." She lifted the hem of her skirts and slid the weapon in the top of her hose before he could protest her lack of modesty. Then she gripped the pommel of her saddle and bent toward him. "If you do not know it, Husband, I have lost my heart to you." At his look of disbelief, she smiled, leaned nearer, and kissed him before all. "I love you, Ranulf Wardieu." As she drew back, she stared into those black eyes that yet reflected surprise. Then, straightening, she prodded the mare forward.

It had cost her much to speak those words knowing he would not return them, but it was as if, in saying them, a burden had been lifted from her. It was done and could not—would not—be undone. Ever.

As she nosed the mare beneath the raised portcullis, she ventured a backward glance.

Ranulf stood where she had left him, hands on his hips as he stared after her.

Due to the nature of their excursion, they rode at a pace that was far from leisurely, and Lizanne thrilled to it. It seemed ages since she had been in control of a worthy mount. The wind in her face, the steady, rhythmic movement of the mare, and the smell of the land, all combined to send her senses soaring.

At the village, Sir Lancelyn, Gilbert's vassal, assisted with her dismount. Until that moment, she had not realized Gilbert's men were among those chosen by Ranulf to accompany Lady Zara and her. It seemed a good sign of the two men's newly formed alliance.

She smiled at the familiar face, then pulled her bag of medicinals from the saddle and hurried after Lady Zara, who was being led to a small hut at the edge of the village.

Inside the one-room dwelling, it was dim, and a small boy of no more than four summers aged lay moaning on a straw pallet, his mother on her knees beside him.

"Lady Zara," the pretty young woman exclaimed and scrambled to her feet. She rushed forward and touched her lady's arm.

Ranulf's mother placed a hand over the other woman's. "I did not know it was Lawrence who was hurt."

She nodded, looked to where Lizanne stood upon the threshold with Sir Walter at her back. "'Tis a healer you have brought with you?"

"Aye, Becky, this is Lady Lizanne. It is she who healed my son."

The young woman gasped, took a step back. "And no doubt caused his injury," she said.

Though Lizanne knew dislike when she saw it, she refused to waste time on it. The boy came first.

She stepped past the woman and lowered to her knees beside the child. "I will need more light," she said as she stared down at him.

Whimpering and clutching at his leg beneath the coarse woolen cover tucked around him, he raised feverish eyes to her.

Lizanne smiled reassuringly and laid a hand upon his moist forehead. "You will be all right," she said softly before turning to her bag and removing a stout vial.

The boy was too weak to protest when she placed the acrid powder on his tongue. Within minutes, he drifted into a blessed, drug-induced sleep.

Gently, Lizanne pried his fingers from his leg and bent near to examine his injury. In spite of the protrusion of bone, the leg was not as bad as feared. With careful attention and prayer, she was confident it would heal completely and he would suffer no lasting ill effects.

While he slept, she cleaned and reset the leg, spread a sweet-smelling unguent over the stitched flesh, and applied a heavy bandage around the splint. Throughout, Lady Zara assisted, while Sir Walter and Becky stood to the side watching.

Afterward, while the child continued to sleep peacefully and the sun moved toward its final descent, Lizanne pressed a packet of medicine into Becky's hand and took some minutes to impress upon her the importance of keeping the leg clean and covered.

Becky followed Lizanne outside to the waiting horses. "Mayhap you will make Baron Wardieu a good wife," she conceded with a small smile once Lizanne had mounted her restless mare.

"I intend to," Lizanne said. "I will return in two days' time to check on your boy. Do not forget that he should lie abed throughout—even if you must tie him down."

Becky nodded and stepped back as Sir Walter called for them to ride.

Lizanne urged her horse forward and sidled up to Lady Zara.

"You did well," the older woman said with a smile. "They will respect you now."

Feeling she had also earned Lady Zara's respect, though the woman did not seem ready to admit it, Lizanne smiled in return.

They were within a few leagues of the castle, the sun just touching the horizon, when a large group of riders appeared. At its head was Ranulf, his pale hair flying out behind him.

"He worries too much," Lady Zara laughingly called to Sir Walter.

Spurring her horse forward, Lizanne overtook the knights at the front of their escort. Though they stayed close behind, none tried to stop her. Out of breath, she reined in just short of the oncoming party and beamed up at her husband when he came alongside her.

He did not smile back.

She frowned and opened her mouth to speak, but no words came out. A moment later, she screamed.

26

❧❧❧

THOSE TERRIBLE BLACK eyes Lizanne remembered too well bored into hers as his lips parted to reveal yellowed teeth.

Reflexively, she jerked on the mare's reins as Darth reached for her. The high-strung animal reacted instantly, turning aside and rearing, its hooves cleaving the air.

Lizanne draped herself over the horse's neck and clutched at the tangled mane. She held on and, when the animal settled back to earth, eyes rolling, ears flattened to its head, dug in her heels and snapped the reins hard.

Hearing Sir Walter raise the alarm, she jerked her chin around as her horse lunged forward and saw his men draw their swords, close formation around Lady Zara, and turn their mounts to flee the greater number of men facing them.

Unfortunately, there was nothing they could do for Lizanne, who had set her own course far to the right of them.

The assailants surged forward, spreading outward in an attempt to enclose the smaller group. If not that other riders emerged from the cover of the wood, escape would have been possible.

Cursing loudly as a circle was drawn around them, Sir Walter signaled for his men to gather at its center.

Crouched low over her horse, Lizanne sped ahead, eyes trained on the opening between two riders. Knowing that if she could make it, she had a chance to reach Chesne and give warning, she fought down the fear boiling in her belly and held on.

As she passed between the two horses, her mount brushing heavily against the one on the left, the soldier astride lunged for her. And missed. But what he could not do, the well-placed arrow of another did, embedding itself in the mare's side.

The animal screamed, reared, and flailed as it twisted sideways.

Lizanne groped for purchase as the reins were torn from her hands, then plummeted to the ground. Her head hit something, and though it did not render her unconscious, it left her pained and dazed. However, she was given no time to recover, for the soldier who had tried to wrest her from her horse was upon her and dragging her to her feet.

She swayed against him, lifted her head, and stared at the mounted riders on all sides. So many…

Shakily, she probed the gash beneath her hair, brought her hand forward, and winced at the blood staining her fingertips.

"Surrender or the lady dies," a familiar voice rang out above the clamor of restless horses and men.

Philip Charwyck! Lizanne swept her gaze over those gathered and searched the ranks for a glimpse of him but could not pick him out from among the other armored men. With their mail coifs, they all looked much the same.

She turned her attention to where Sir Walter and his men clustered around Lady Zara. Lady Zara herself sat unmoving atop her horse, gaze fixed on her second-born son.

Lizanne felt her pain. Here was the son stolen from her all those years ago, and now he returned a villain. And he had not even acknowledged her presence although her hair, so like his own, revealed she was his mother.

"Lay down your arms!" Philip ordered when Sir Walter remained irresolute, "Or I will spill her blood where she stands." He separated himself from the others and spurred his horse toward Lizanne.

She threw her chin up, glared at him when he came alongside her and motioned for the soldier to release her.

With a shove that sent her stumbling forward, the man complied.

Philip reached down and ran the back of a gloved hand over her cheek. "What? No warm welcome for your lover?"

Lizanne jerked her head back.

"Tsk-tsk," he clicked his tongue, then he lunged and caught hold of the hair at the top of her head.

Deciding she could afford to lose a few strands, she strained backward and lashed out, striking him with her bloodied hand and soiling the front of the sleeveless tunic he wore over his hauberk.

He retaliated by wrenching her hair and striking her across the face.

Lizanne heard the distressed murmurings of Sir Walter's men but knew she stood alone. Ignoring the pain, she swung her hand up again and aimed for his eyes.

Philip knocked her arm aside and pulled harder on her hair, nearly lifting her off her feet. "I will tame you, shrew," he growled.

Eyes flooded with tears of pain, she slammed her knee into his horse's belly.

The destrier protested loudly and jumped away, but Philip did not release her and she stumbled and fell against the animal.

With a satisfied snort, Philip leaned down, threw an arm around her waist, and lifted her. Being no small thing easily hauled up the side of a horse, especially by a man not much larger than herself, Philip struggled. In the end, it was only with the help of one of his men that he succeeded in seating her on the fore of his saddle.

She strained away from him, but he pulled her chin around and slammed his mouth down upon hers, proclaiming to all that she belonged to him.

But she did not, and that knowledge made her grow still. Though he surely expected her wrath when he lifted his head, she smiled thinly, then made a show of dragging the back of a hand across her mouth and spitting on his boot.

"You taste of sewage, Philip." That earned her another slap.

Lord, she thought, *I am not going to be a pretty sight when we get out of this.* She only prayed they would...

"If needs be, I will kill her," Philip threatened again and pulled his dagger. He touched its point to her neck, drew it down her chest to her abdomen. "Now, if you wish Baron Wardieu's wife to live, throw down your weapons."

In the silence, Lady Zara's voice carried across the cool air. "Do as he says."

As it darkened into night, the interlopers and their prisoners covered much ground before immersing themselves in a thick wood. And still they rode.

Hours before dawn, they came to a clearing that was deemed suitable to set up camp so the horses might rest a few hours before continuing on.

Halting his destrier in the middle of the field, Philip shoved Lizanne off his horse, sending her sprawling in the grass.

"That," he said, amid his men's laughter, "is for the spit."

Lizanne sank her fingers into the soil but squelched the impulse to throw the clumps at Philip lest she find herself trampled beneath his horse's hooves.

Slowly, she got to her feet. As she wiped at her soiled skirts, she felt the dagger's hilt where it was hidden in the top of her hose.

"Do not exert yourself, Lady Lizanne," Philip said. "I will want you alert when you come to me."

More laughter.

"Bernard," Philip called, "put her with the others."

Lizanne wanted to resist the large man who gripped her with such force she winced, but common sense bade her cooperate. To infuriate Philip further would only bring her closer to the time when he would attempt to violate her. And the best place for her now was with the others. Hopefully, they would discover a way to free themselves.

While the camp was hastily erected, the hands of all the captives, with the exception of the two women, were firmly bound behind them. Then they were corralled together into a pen constructed of ropes wound around a grouping a trees. About the perimeter, Philip set a good number of guards. He was taking no chances.

Knees drawn up beneath her chin, Lizanne sat next to Lady Zara, on whose right sat Sir Walter. All around them were Ranulf's and Gilbert's men.

Several times during the past half hour, Lizanne had tried to talk with Lady Zara, but the woman was too preoccupied with following her second son's progress about the camp. Thus, Lizanne turned her thoughts instead to finding a means of escape.

"So alike," Lady Zara finally spoke, voice filled with sorrow, "yet so different."

Lizanne looked at the woman who appeared much older in the flickering light of torches. "One good, one evil," Lizanne said.

Lady Zara closed her eyes, nodded.

Lizanne touched her arm. "He has not yet spoken with you?"

"Nay, he spurns me, though me must know I am his mother." She was quiet a long moment. "Tell me more of this Philip. What does he want with you?"

Though it certainly did not take Lizanne's mind off the threat of the miscreant's violation, she acquiesced, starting at the beginning and ending with her final confrontation with the man at King Henry's court.

Lady Zara touched the largest of the two swellings upon Lizanne's face, causing her to wince, then edged nearer her daughter-in-law. "You must not give in to him." Her voice was but a whisper. "Do you still have the dagger Ranulf gave you?"

"I do."

"Good, and I have mine."

Lizanne startled. "Have you?"

Lady Zara nodded. "We must needs be wise in this. Do you think you can use yours on Charwyck when he comes for you?"

"Aye," Lizanne said without hesitation.

"And could you make your way back to Chesne?"

Having paid attention to the course Philip set, Lizanne was familiar with her surroundings. "I could."

"Then listen well. You must get to Ranulf and lead him—"

"I shall need a horse."

Lady Zara shook her head. "'Tis not likely you will be able to obtain one without being caught. Nay, you must run. I know you can do that."

Lizanne nodded.

"Ranulf cannot be far," she continued. "No doubt, he has divided his men, and they are this moment scouring the area. When all is quiet, I will see that the ropes are cut from our men. If we have surprise on our side, mayhap 'twill be possible for us to escape as well. Otherwise, it is up to you."

"I will bring Ranulf back—and Gilbert."

Lady Zara placed a hand over Lizanne's. "You are my daughter now. With a mother's protectiveness, methinks I judged you too harshly. For this, I apologize."

Lizanne smiled, her tongue too clumsy to reply.

"And for the pain my family has inflicted upon yours," Lady Zara continued, eyes glimmering with tears, "I beg your pardon. Had we but known..."

Lizanne squeezed her hand. "You could not have. 'Twas a cruel deception played on both our families."

Lady Zara summoned a small smile that returned a measure of youthfulness to her face. "He loves you."

Lizanne blinked. "Ranulf? He told you this?"

"Not in words, but I have seen it in his eyes."

Lizanne drew a deep breath, looked out across the camp. "Methinks you are wrong, Lady Zara. Your son but desires me."

"'Tis you who are wrong, Daughter. Never did Ranulf feel toward his first wife as he does you—or any other woman. Do you love him?"

"I told him as much before we left for the village."

"How did he respond?"

"He did not." She sighed. "Forsooth, I did not give him the chance to."

Lady Zara opened her mouth to say something, but closed it when the captives began to murmur amongst themselves.

Her second-born son approached.

With a suddenness that startled Lizanne, Ranulf's mother gave her a fierce hug. When she drew away, Lizanne felt the sharp, cold steel of the small dagger Lady Zara had slipped beneath her hand. "'Twill better serve Walter," she whispered, then turned toward Darth.

When he came to stand over them, he stared at the woman who had birthed him, his jaw set in a hard, thrusting line.

It was Ranulf, yet not him…

Panic skipped through Lizanne as she peered up at that face, terrible memories beckoning her to come play with them. Swallowing convulsively, she lowered her gaze to his booted feet and concentrated on getting her breathing under control even as she concealed the second dagger in her shoe.

"So, ye are the woman who bore me," Darth finally said.

Lady Zara pushed to her feet. "Aye, and you are my Colin."

He laughed. "Colin. Better than Darth, methinks. Noble."

"You were stolen from me." Lady Zara's tone was apologetic.

"And now I am returned to ye, Mother. Rejoice in the miracle that has brought us together again." He shifted his gaze to Lizanne, nudged her with his booted foot. "I never finished with ye, wench. Mayhap when Lord Philip is done, I might have another taste of yer sweetness."

Bile rose as Lizanne met his stare. "That would first require that you remain conscious."

He stiffened, but forced a laugh. "I shall. And mayhap ye will as well." He took hold of Lady Zara's arm. "Come, we have much to talk about, Mother."

Immediately, Sir Walter gained his feet. "Nay!" he shouted and ran forward though his hands were bound behind his back.

Darth swung around. A dark smile splitting his features, he slammed a fist into Sir Walter's face and sent the smaller man backward.

Sir Walter's men lunged upright and surged forward.

The guards raised their weapons, but the captives did not stop. However, it took but one arrow through the chest of the man nearest Darth to squelch the uprising.

Lady Zara cried out and struggled to free herself from her son's hold, but without success.

Having scrambled to her feet, Lizanne ran and knelt beside the fallen soldier.

Moments later, his lids lowered and he shuddered out his last breath.

Hands clenched upon his chest, she felt the burn of tears as she stared into the still face of one of the two who had guarded her during those first days with Ranulf. Little more than a dozen words had passed between them, but she felt his death straight through.

And then came anger. She thrust to her feet and crossed to where Sir Walter sat, a number of his men gathered around him. Bound as they all were, they were unable to offer aid. Thus, Lizanne stepped over them, made a space for herself, and knelt beside Ranulf's most esteemed vassal.

"Evil," Walter croaked, his broken nose gushing blood.

"Lie back." Lizanne pressed her hands to his shoulders. When he resisted, she put her full weight behind her and lowered him to the ground. Then, lifting the skirt of her bliaut, she wadded it and pressed it to his face to stem the blood.

"You and I are quite the pair," she said a short while later when she helped raise him to sitting and saw both his eyes were blackening.

Sir Walter looked past her to search out the area beyond. "I will kill the miscreant if he harms one hair upon her head," he growled.

Not for one moment did she doubt him.

"How could you?" Zara demanded. Clasping her hands hard in her lap, she shifted on the fallen log so that not even her skirts touched the man who sat beside her.

"Had ye lived the life I have," her son said sharply, "ye would not find it so hard a thing to do."

"'Tis wrong—in the eyes of God *and* man."

"I am not my brother," he said gruffly, "though I shall soon enjoy all manner of the life he has had these many years while I toiled in the fields." He grinned. "'Tis only fitting that I now become the baron of Chesne, is it not?"

Fear gripped Zara more tightly. "What of Ranulf?" she asked, willing herself to meet those dark eyes. Now that she looked close, they were not really all that similar to Ranulf's. The color was the same, but the emotions expressed there were as unlike Ranulf's as day was unlike night. Summer unlike winter.

Colin—though it seemed he truly was this Darth—looked to the campfire. "Ranulf," he spat. "Philip has plans fer him."

"Then he will try to kill the man who is your brother," Zara said, knowing better than to phrase it as a question.

"If 'tis not him, it will be me."

Zara felt her face begin to crumple. At long last, she had her second son, knew him now to be a grown man, and he was cruel. If it would gain him the barony, he would take Ranulf's life. He would take from her that which she held dearest.

She dropped her chin to her chest.

A hand that, surprisingly, had some of the warmth of Ranulf's, fell to her shoulder. "No harm will come to ye, Mother." His voice was almost gentle.

She lifted her head and looked at him through tears. "'Tis not for me I grieve. 'Tis for Ranulf. And you. That you could not have loved each other as 'twas meant to be. That your heart is so cold and ways so cruel."

He glowered. "Had ye toiled as I have all my life, worked till yer body screamed in agony, neither would ye look so fairly upon this world."

Despite what he was, her heart ached for him. "What was it like, Colin?" she asked softly.

He sneered. "Never enough food to eat, so ye had to steal from another to fill yer belly. Ever too much work to be done, so ye never could get enough sleep. Always too cold or too hot. Always saying 'aye' to the lord no matter what he asked of ye—"

"Is that why you attacked the Balmaine camp—for Philip?"

"Aye, he promised me a share of the dowry wagons and my own plot of land did I do it fer him."

"And you did."

"I am no fool!"

"Did he give you what he promised?"

A muscle leapt in his jaw. "I failed him. He gave me naught but blood upon my back."

"And you think he will give you Chesne?"

Her son's eyes narrowed to suspicious slits. "I will not fail him this time."

A chill passed through Zara. Though it was not truly his fault he was the way he was, her second son was evil. It was Philip Charwyck's—and Mary's—fault. "Tell me about Mary," she said.

"The hag is dead."

Zara stared at him, something telling her she did not want to know the answer to the question that rose to mind. Still, she had to ask. "How did she die?"

As if suddenly uncomfortable, he shifted on the log. "She fell. Fell and broke her neck, methinks."

Zara drew a deep breath. "Tell me you did not do it, Colin."

He wet his lips, shrugged. "I would think ye'd rejoice in knowing she is dead. She did steal me from ye."

"That she did, for which I do not know that I can ever forgive her, but I would still have the answer to my question."

His face twisted into an ugly mask of hatred. "When she tried to stop me from leaving with Philip—cried that I was her son and owed her for all the years she cared for me—I pushed her." He spat upon the ground. "I was angry. After all, 'twas her deception that caused me to suffer all these years."

Zara longed to return to her tears, to shout at the injustice of it all. Not only was her son a thief and a ravisher, he was a murderer. He was so different from Ranulf that the only thing the brothers had in common were their looks, and even that had been corrupted by the different life her second-born had led. She had only ever known such great sorrow when she had been told of Colin's death nearly thirty years past.

"Ye are disgusted," he said.

She shook her head. "I am saddened for the life you were forced to live, pained that you seek your brother's death so that you might obtain all that is his. Have you no feeling for Ranulf?"

He gave a shout of laughter. "Think ye he would welcome me at Chesne? Nay, he seeks my death as surely as I seek his."

"'Tis not true! Ranulf has said no such thing."

"He need not say it fer it to be true."

"He is not like that."

"What of his wife? Ye are telling me he would not seek to avenge her honor?"

"There was naught that occurred between Lady Lizanne and you. She stopped you—do you not remember?"

"Aye, well I remember, as I remember laying low her brother, though I did not lay him low enough. And for that, I gained two dozen stripes across my back." He grunted. "I should have severed his head from his neck. Had I to do it again, I would not make the mistake of leaving him or his sister alive."

"Do not say that!" Zara exclaimed, still harboring hope she might find some way to set her second son on the right path. "It is not too late, Colin." She gripped his arm. "Help us escape Philip Charwyck, and all will be dealt with fairly. This I vow."

He pushed her hand away. "Fair would be to take my life for the crimes I have committed, and I do not wish to die. Nay, Philip will secure Chesne for me, and then I will have what is rightfully mine."

Zara nearly pointed out that it was not rightfully his, but it would only rouse him further. "Philip will see you dead, Colin. It is not only

Lady Lizanne he desires but Chesne. He is not the kind of man to settle for a woman when there are riches to be had as well."

"Ye lie. Chesne will be mine!"

Zara shook her head, the reserve of love in her heart for this unknown son beginning to shrivel. He was of her body, but not of her soul, as much a stranger to her as any other.

"If Ranulf dies," she said, "so will you, for Philip cannot allow you to live knowing what you do about him. You have only one chance to save yourself. Aid us."

For a moment, he looked to be considering her proposal, but then he laughed. "Ye are as deceptive as yer misbegotten sister."

Her shoulders slumped as she accepted there was no way to reach him. It was up to Lizanne.

"Now," Darth said, "ye will tell me everything about Chesne."

She pressed her lips tight, turned her face away, and looked to where the others were held captive. She would say no more.

27

THE COMMOTION PORTENDED ill. Thus, when Lizanne turned, she was not surprised to see Philip in the midst of his men. They were laughing, crowing, making lewd, suggestive comments as he headed toward the captives.

And now he comes for me.

Lizanne retrieved Lady Zara's dagger and slipped behind Walter as unobtrusively as possible. Praying she would not cut him in her haste, she sliced the weapon up between his bound wrists. The ropes fell free.

"Keep your hands behind your back," she whispered, then slid the dagger up his sleeve and closed his fingers over the hilt. "'Tis Lady Zara's. I only regret I cannot leave you mine as well, but methinks I will need it myself." She clamped her mouth closed as Philip caught her eye.

"Come!" he called, waving her forward.

"I will bring Ranulf," she murmured as she pushed to her feet. Shaking her head at the men as they moved to shield her, she weaved her way toward Philip.

When he took hold of her and guided her across the camp, she did not protest.

"If you do not fight me," he said as he drew her past the campfire, "mayhap I will keep you to myself."

She halted, forcing him to turn to her. "I am resigned to my fate. Do with me what you will."

He regarded her with suspicion before a smile made its way across his face. "I am glad we understand each other." He stepped forward and lightly touched the bruises on her face for which he was responsible. "It does not please me to have to mark you."

Just barely, she contained the inner cringe that threatened to manifest itself outwardly. "Then you will not hurt me again?" she asked in as submissive a tone as her constricted voice allowed.

He brushed the hair back from her face. "That is in your hands."

"Then I need not worry on it."

Looking satisfied, Philip drew her forward. As they stepped amongst the trees, he announced himself to a guard posted there before pulling her deeper into the wood.

"This will do." He released her, unclasped his mantle and, eyes never straying from her, spread it on the fallen leaves. Then he unbuckled his sword belt, but not the one upon which a dagger was hung.

Clenching her teeth, she began to work the clasp of her own mantle and was glad to be shed of it when she let it fall from her shoulders—one less thing to get in the way.

"You seem eager, Lady Lizanne," Philip said.

Oh, I am.

She glanced at him. Though having only the waning moon for light, she could not be certain he was smiling across the space between them, but she thought it likely.

"Now your bliaut," he said and lowered to his mantle.

As she pretended to struggle with the laces, she said, "You know I have always loved you, Philip. When you broke our betrothal, I was deeply hurt. For that, I chose Ranulf over you."

"As thought."

She nearly snorted at how quick he was to believe that had been her reason.

"What takes you so long?" he snapped an instant later.

She threw her hands out to the sides. "My laces are knotted." Not a lie. She had made sure of that. "I shall require your aid." She stepped forward, lowered to the mantle with her back slightly turned to him, and raised her left arm to provide access to the laces.

As he set to them, she slid a hand across her thigh and lower leg, then up beneath the hem of her skirt and closed her fingers around the dagger's hilt.

Philip tugged, cursed, growled, then wrenched at the material that tore beneath his impatience.

Sending up a silent prayer, Lizanne swept the dagger from its sheath. She did not care where she buried her blade—arm, shoulder, chest, abdomen—providing it incapacitated him sufficiently to allow her to escape.

She felt the displacement of air as she swung the dagger toward him, next the slam of his hand upon her wrist as he arrested her assault inches from his heart.

With a bark of anger, he threw her onto her back and rolled atop her. Catching hold of her other wrist, he pressed it hard to the ground, then forced her dagger-wielding hand high above her head and slammed it against a rock.

Despite the terrible pain, Lizanne refused to release the dagger. It was the only thing that might save her, so thoroughly pinned was she that, no matter how she writhed, she could not raise a knee with which to unman him.

Cursing now, Philip raised his chest slightly, released her other hand that was empty of a weapon, and began to grope for something at his waist.

Though Lizanne was quick to use her freed hand to scratch at his face and neck, a moment later, the point of his own dagger was at her neck.

"You can die now or later," he said, saliva flecking her face. "Which do you choose?"

She stared into his dark gaze and knew a truth she wished she did not—better death now than after what he would do to her. "Now," she said.

The name he flung at her was vile. Worse, was the force with which he once more slammed her hand against the rock.

She cried out, and cried out again when her bruised and bloodied fingers spasmed and lost hold of the dagger.

Philip laughed, a crude, rasping sound. "'Twill not be easy to keep you, but I will. For awhile."

He sat back and, straddling her, lifted his dagger from her throat and considered its blade that was touched by the first light of dawn. "Now, let us see if we can think of an appropriate punishment for you." He shifted his gaze to where she lay still but for her attempt to recapture her breath. "As I do not think I could stand to look upon you were your face any more spoiled than 'tis, I will have to be creative."

So swiftly that Lizanne barely saw him move, he put his blade to the waist of her bliaut and sliced it up through the material, parting it to reveal the chemise beneath.

"Are you not frightened?" he demanded when she remained unmoving.

"Are *you* not frightened of what my lord husband will do to you?"

He drew a sharp breath, but before he could physically express his anger, an alarm sounded from the camp, audible even at this distance.

Ranulf? Or were Walter and his men attempting an escape? It mattered not. What mattered was that it caused Philip to rise from her.

"Do not move!" he yelled, waving his dagger at her as she started to sit up.

Struggling to calm herself, Lizanne watched as he retrieved his sword belt and fastened it around his waist. He drew the sword from its scabbard, returned the dagger to its own scabbard, then hauled her to her feet.

Leaving his mantle behind, he pushed her ahead of him through the trees. At a safe vantage point from which to observe the camp unseen, he dragged her to a halt and pressed the edge of his sword against her neck to ensure her silence.

In the soft morning light, Lizanne saw the mayhem caused by the arrival of Ranulf's and Gilbert's men, but she did not have time to search out either man before Philip dragged her back through the trees.

Muttering curses, he forced her to a run. Fortunately, she was not without recourse, stumbling and tripping at every opportunity.

They had not gone far when Darth emerged from among the trees, Lady Zara seated before him on one of two horses.

"Lizanne!" Ranulf's mother cried as her eyes took in her daughter-in-law's dishevelment.

Darth tossed the reins of the second horse to Philip, then yanked his mount around and spurred away.

Philip ordered Lizanne up ahead of him, mounted behind, and set off after Darth.

"Nay!" Gilbert bellowed.

Ranulf, too consumed by his own inner raging over the fate of his mother and wife, retrieved Lizanne's mantle from the ground where it lay near another—doubtless, Charwyck's. Tensely silent, he swept his gaze around the area in search of any clue that might lead him to the two women.

Naught. So they would ride south—

Nay, Charwyck was too clever to continue that course. East, then. The easy terrain would aid his flight, though it would offer little cover.

As he turned on his heel, a glint among the grass caught his eye. He reached down and lifted the object from the base of a rock. It was Lizanne's dagger, but no blood dulled its shimmering blade. Clenching the hilt, he closed his eyes. It had been his fervent hope she yet retained it. That she didn't could only mean Charwyck had discovered it beneath her skirts, confirming Gilbert's belief that his sister had been violated.

If Charwyck had not been a dead man before, he was now. Even if it took Ranulf the rest of his days to track him down, he would see the life drained from the miscreant's body, drop by stinking drop, for there were only two women who fit inside his heart, and no greater offense could have been dealt him than to steal them away.

The admission surprised—and yet did not surprise—him. And in that moment, he accepted what he had been wrestling with for days. He loved Lizanne. It was not simply infatuation and desire as he had tried to convince himself, but a new emotion that went far beyond the bounds he had previously set. If only he had told her...

Gilbert was still hurling curses to the sky when Ranulf noticed dark spots on the gray surface of a rock near where he had found the dagger. He wiped his fingers across it, stared at the blood that was only now beginning to dry.

Giving no thought as to how it had come to be there or whose it might be, he pivoted, grasped Gilbert's arm, and urged him toward their horses and the men awaiting their orders.

"They cannot have gone far," he said, showing the evidence to his brother-in-law.

Gilbert's eyes widened as he stared at Ranulf's stained fingers. "God's rood!" he shouted and ran to his destrier.

Ranulf quickly divided his men, sending the smaller of two groups south before leading the larger one east. They rode hard, at last converging upon a level meadow that stretched for leagues before rising to gently rolling hills.

"There!" Ranulf shouted when he spotted the riders—two indistinct forms upon the crest of a distant hill, one topped by a flash of pale hair.

Abreast, he and Gilbert swept forward, their men close behind. Though their quarry had the advantage of distance, it would be short-lived, for their mounts carried two each—a hindrance that would see them overtaken.

As they drew near, Charwyck looked around, shouted something to the other man, and both horses veered hard right toward the wood where, doubtless, they hoped to immerse themselves and evade capture.

It was not to be. As the pursued descended to level ground, the pursuers swept around them.

Charwyck and Darth reined in alongside each other and considered the many who would see them dead.

Ranulf sought and gained Lizanne's gaze where she was held by Charwyck on the fore of his saddle. In spite of her beaten face, the wild joy in the eyes with which she regarded her husband gave him hope that the worst had been spared her—but then he looked lower and saw her torn bodice. And knew that not even the ripening of his blade with his enemy's blood would satisfy him. Nor would it satisfy Gilbert whose tension evidenced he had also seen.

It was stark pale hair and glittering black eyes probing his that stole Ranulf's regard from Lizanne. So like—nay, identical—to him. His heart thundered as he stared at the man who pressed a blade to the small woman before him, and a chasm opened within him as he attempted to reconcile that the knave was also his brother.

He lowered his gaze to his mother who sat before Darth. She did not look well, her face pressed to her lost son's chest, arms drawn up around her head. He did not think she knew what transpired, but perhaps that was good, for it would save her from what must follow.

"Let us pass, else they die!" Philip shouted, pressing his blade to Lizanne's midriff as his horse pranced nervously.

Ranulf exchanged glances with Gilbert. Then, swords drawn, they broke formation and urged their horses forward.

"I have warned you, Wardieu!" Philip yelled.

Still they came, avengers who had set themselves the license of God.

"Release them," Ranulf demanded, "and prepare to die."

"'Tis your wife and mother who will die if you do not allow us to pass!"

At fifty feet, Ranulf and Gilbert reined in.

"Would that it could be any other way…brother," Ranulf said to that other one who, like Charwyck, was without armor. He dismounted and, as he removed his own hauberk, announced, "'Twill be a fair duel."

Gilbert dropped down beside him and also shed his hauberk. Then, swords before them, they advanced on their opponents.

"Come down, Charwyck," Gilbert's deep voice echoed around the hills. "Or are you faint of heart?" When his taunt was met with silence, he laughed. "Know you how to wield a sword, man?"

Surprisingly, it was Darth who first took up the challenge. He set Lady Zara's limp form over his horse's neck, swung out of the saddle, and turned to face Ranulf and Gilbert.

"Coward!" Lizanne spat over her shoulder.

"Quiet, wench!" Philip snarled.

"Do you think you can hide behind a woman's skirts the rest of your days, Charwyck?" Ranulf asked. "Be warned, there is no shield tax that can save you from the service required of you this day."

In the silence that followed, Charwyck turned a shade of red not unlike vermilion. Still, it was some moments before he dismounted, blessedly leaving Lizanne astride.

"Now you will earn that title you seek," Charwyck said to Darth.

Breathing easier, Ranulf met Lizanne's gaze and nodded for her to move clear.

She guided the horse to Lady Zara, took hold of the other horse's reins, and murmured something to the woman who continued to lean upon the animal's neck.

Geoff and Duncan rode forward to meet the two women. Though Geoff's sword was drawn, Duncan, as usual, carried his bow, an arrow nocked in place.

Ranulf's squire took charge of Lady Zara and guided her horse behind the ranks of men. Though Duncan tried to do the same with Lizanne, she shook her head, refusing to relinquish the reins. The squire threw Gilbert a helpless look, then settled his bow across his lap, removed his short mantle, and leaned sideways to drape it over her shoulders.

Ranulf assured himself she was safe with the squire at her side and looked to his brother-in-law. "Which will you take?" he asked, offering him first choice.

"Darth." Gilbert pointed his sword at the pale-haired man.

It was surely not the one he wanted, but it was a wise choice as Ranulf had hoped it would be. Gilbert had good cause to question how Ranulf would deal with his newfound brother and was taking no chances—ensuring justice was done.

"Very well," Ranulf said, "but first I would speak with him.

Gilbert nodded and shifted his regard to Charwyck.

"Come, Brother," Ranulf said, moving toward Darth. "Let us speak ere we do battle."

Darth looked uncertain but acquiesced, following Ranulf a short distance away from the other two.

Each with their swords before them, the two brothers faced one another and studied the other's face. At first, it seemed to Ranulf as if he stood before a large mirror, but the differences soon became clear and he felt a pang of regret for the hard life reflected in his brother who had grown up beneath the warped tutelage of Philip Charwyck.

"Would that I could have known you, Darth—Colin," Ranulf said. "That it could have been different."

"'Twill be! Chesne will be mine, and ye will be dead."

Ranulf shook his head. "Chesne is mine, though *had* things been different, I would have shared all with you."

Darth's mouth twisted. "Ye lie as much as our dear mother."

Ranulf glanced at where Lady Zara sat unmoving upon her mount, then to Lizanne. Back stiff, his wife watched their exchange, her dark hair lifting in the cool breeze.

Justice would be done—for her, for Gilbert, for all those who had fallen at the hands of his brother in the name of Philip Charwyck.

"I speak the truth," Ranulf said, returning his attention to Darth, "but 'tis too late now." It was a risk he took in turning his back on the man, but Ranulf pivoted. With long strides, he crossed toward where Charwyck awaited him and briefly paused to clasp arms with Gilbert.

"No mercy," Lizanne's brother said, meeting Ranulf's gaze, then continuing past him.

Two would die this day, Ranulf knew, but which two would live? Determined he would not be the one to spend his life's blood upon this field, he readied his sword and advanced on Charwyck.

Lizanne prayed. And prayed. What followed was bloodier than expected, for Ranulf's opponent was more than simply proficient with a sword. He was expert. Darth was a different matter, but not to be taken lightly. What he lacked in finesse, he redeemed in sheer strength and unpredictability, which proved dangerous for Gilbert whose speed and maneuverability was hindered by his lame leg.

Labored grunts and groans filled the air, curses were hurled like flotsam upon the waves, and blows were exchanged that left each man staggered and bleeding.

As Lizanne swung her gaze from Ranulf to Gilbert, she saw her brother parry a thrust that would have severed his head from his neck had he not anticipated it. Wrath roared from him, and he countered with a swing that sliced through the other man's sword arm.

Darth stumbled back, grasped at the gaping wound from which blood flowed. Though his sword was of little use to him without the strength to guide it, he held it aloft as Gilbert cautiously circled him. And then her brother was upon him, sword thrusting, triumphant shout rolling like thunder over his opponent's passionate death cry.

Lizanne nearly doubled over with relief. Gilbert was safe, now she had only Ranulf to worry about.

She swept her gaze back to him and caught her breath when she saw him falter in his battle with Philip as he glanced at where Gilbert stood over the body of his brother. In the next instant, his opponent made up the ground earlier surrendered by dealing a blow to Ranulf's side.

"Nay!" Lizanne cried.

But her husband remained standing. With a shout, he deflected the next blow and forced Philip back a pace, then another. Steel rang upon steel with increased vigor as he sought and found the other's flesh, repaying tenfold each injury done him.

Finally, Philip reeled backward, dropped his sword, and fell to his knees.

Victory at hand, the world soon to be set right again, Ranulf touched his sword to the man's chest. "And now it ends," he ground out.

Clutching his gut, Charwyck threw his head back. "I yield!" he shouted for all to hear, then slowly smiled.

Ranulf tensed. "Either way, you die, be it by my hand or the king's order. My question is, will you die honorably, or as the poltroon you are?"

"I shall take my chances with Henry," Philip retorted.

Ranulf pressed the point of his sword more heavily to Philip's chest, causing the man to sway backward. But one push was all it would take to end this now and forever.

"You would kill a fallen knight who has offered himself up to you, Baron Wardieu?" Charwyck challenged his honor.

Ranulf clenched his jaws, battling with the conflicting inner voices that seemed intent upon tearing him in two. Finally, assuring himself the miscreant would meet the same end either way, he gave honor its due.

"Get up!" he ordered.

As Charwyck rose, holding a hand to the wound that had been his undoing, he taunted, "I had your wife, you know."

Ranulf nearly leaned into his sword, but stopped himself. Every muscle straining, he lowered his sword.

Charwyck laughed and straightened.

Stepping behind him, Ranulf thrust the man ahead of him toward Gilbert. His anger was so consuming that he was unprepared when Philip rounded on him, arm thrown back, the newly risen sun glinting off the blade he held.

Before Ranulf could swing his sword up, Charwyck convulsed where he stood poised to release his dagger. A moment later, he toppled forward, an arrow shaft protruding from his back, blood spreading over his tunic.

Ranulf knew.

He raised his gaze and found the master archer whose accuracy and unhindered reflexes had spared his life. The bow still extended, Lizanne faced him from atop her mount.

Ranulf stepped over Charwyck's inert form and went directly to her. As he neared, she lowered the bow, giving him his first close look at her.

'Tis not the time for rage, he reminded himself. Although he had seen she had been beaten, he was grateful he had not known the extent, for it could have clouded his judgment, and it might be he who lay dead on the field—as had very nearly happened before his brave, indomitable wife had stepped in.

Holding her gaze, he halted beside her mount.

With a strangled cry, she tossed the bow to the ground and slid off the horse into his waiting arms. Clinging to him, she wept against his chest.

Ranulf held her and stroked her hair. Even when her brother appeared and spoke soothingly to her, she refused to relinquish her hold on her husband.

Gilbert turned and crossed to where Lady Zara remained atop her mount.

"'Tis over," Lizanne finally said, raising her tear-streaked face to Ranulf's.

He gently cupped her cheek. "It is indeed."

"What of your injuries?" She started to pull back as if to examine them, but he kept hold of her.

"Naught that cannot wait," he assured her.

"Can we go home to Chesne?"

He smiled. "Aye, Wife. Home." Then he lifted her into his arms.

Geoff was waiting with his lord's destrier, a broad smile upon his face.

Ranulf set Lizanne in the saddle, mounted behind her, and drew her back against him. "I love you, Lizanne Wardieu," he spoke the words he had thought never to utter to any woman.

Her head came around. "Truly?"

He lowered his head and kissed her. "With everything I am and everything I shall be with you at my side." He drew back and looked into the shimmering green pools of her eyes.

"Have you loved me long, Ranulf?" she asked with wonder.

He had to laugh. "It seems as if forever."

"But when did you discover it?" She reached up and played her fingers through his pale hair.

"Methinks 'twas when you crawled up that accursed tree and refused to come down, though I did not realize then that was what I felt. You see, I have had little experience with loving."

"As I have had little. But then, we are just at the beginning, are we not?"

He nodded. "Aye, years and years ahead."

"Forever," she murmured and lowered her head to his shoulder.

He urged his destrier forward and, at a leisurely pace, preceded his men back toward Philip's camp where, he was confident, Walter would have everything under control.

"I have something for you," he said some minutes later and removed the dagger from his belt. "For such a valuable weapon as this"—he placed it in her hand—"you seem to have a difficult time keeping possession of it."

She ran a finger over the hilt. "I fought him," she murmured.

He felt every muscle tighten. "I do not require an explanation. 'Tis behind us."

Lizanne sat straighter and raised the dagger. "Though I did not get the chance to carve him with this, it did serve its purpose."

Ranulf stared at the hand with which she gripped the hilt. From wrist to fingertips, it was scratched, gouged, and bruised, and he knew Charwyck had beaten it against the rock in order to take the dagger from her. "Then he did not—?"

She shook her head.

He released his breath, lowered his head, and kissed her soundly. "Why do I continually underestimate you? 'Tis you who saved my life, and for which I will be ever grateful now that I have you."

A mischievous glint shone from her eyes, and her dimple emerged. "Then you will not object to my practicing weaponry occasionally?"

"If it pleases you, Lizanne Wardieu, you may instruct every last one of my men—especially in the use of a bow."

28

"A GIRL," RANULF breathed as the perfectly formed infant was placed in his arms. Cradling her carefully, he touched the silken hair sprouting in abundance from the small head.

"Flaxen," Lady Zara murmured, standing on tiptoe to view her granddaughter. Cooing softly so as not to awaken her daughter-in-law, she placed a finger in one miniature flailing palm and smiled at the child's strong grip.

"Do you think she will be as beautiful as her mother?" Ranulf whispered.

"Of course. Save for the hair, she has the look of Lizanne."

"Do share," his wife said from the bed.

Ranulf stepped around his mother and lowered the bundle into Lizanne's waiting arms, then he kissed her.

As he straightened, she peered at her babe and breathed, "Oh, she is beautiful." As she had barely had time to focus on her child before exhaustion had overtaken her following the birthing, it was her first real look at her daughter.

"Gillian," she pronounced. "We shall call you Gillian."

Ranulf frowned. "What kind of name is that?"

She kissed the crown of her daughter's head, then settled back upon her pillow and smiled at her husband. "Since I can hardly name a girl Gilbert, 'tis the closest I can come to honoring my brother."

Ranulf looked to his mother, but as if realizing he would get no support from her, he resignedly plowed a hand through his hair. "You are certain?"

Lizanne nodded. "As she has your surname, 'tis only fair she has one of my family's names. But you may choose a name of endearment, if 'twould please you."

Ranulf lowered beside her and took her hand in his. "I must think on this a while. 'Twill have to be something wonderful lest she not care for her given name."

Lizanne chuckled. "Oh, she will like it all right."

"I must needs tell Walter," Lady Zara said. "He was as nervous, I think, as Ranulf." She turned, hastened to the door, and went in search of her husband.

Lizanne beckoned Ranulf closer. "Now I would have a real kiss."

Eagerly, he complied.

Gillian gurgled, and he drew back to stare into the eyes of the gift Lizanne had given him.

"You are not disappointed she is not a he?" Lizanne asked.

He touched the new pink skin of his daughter's hands. "Never."

Gillian whimpered, her round face slowly brightened, and she began to thrust her legs beneath the swaddling cloth.

Lizanne and Ranulf looked at each other in silent question. Then, with a grin, Lizanne turned the babe in her arms and settled the little one to her breast. It took coaxing and several failed attempts, but at last Gillian set about satisfying her hunger.

"You have sent word to Gilbert?" Lizanne asked.

Ranulf was slow to answer, his attention upon his daughter. When Lizanne nudged him, he said, "Aye, ere long he will know he is an uncle."

"Do you think he will come?" Worriedly, she nibbled her bottom lip as she reflected on her brother's latest troubles with the Charwyck woman, Philip's sister.

Ranulf shrugged. "Mayhap not straightway, but he will come."

"'Tis that Charwyck woman again, is it not?" Lizanne grumbled.

He nodded. "It seems she is not making this easy on your brother."

Lizanne fingered Gillian's soft hair. "'Tis a pity she did not get word of Philip's death until after she had taken her nun's vows."

"Gilbert will no doubt survive," Ranulf assured her.

Then the subject was forgotten as they immersed themselves in the wonder of their child.

"Are you truly happy?" Lizanne asked later when their daughter slept and Ranulf stretched out beside her.

He propped himself up on an elbow and drew a finger down her throat. "Very." He met her gaze. "Now I have two worth dying for."

Excerpt

THE UNVEILING

Age of Faith: Book I

12TH CENTURY ENGLAND. Two men vie for the throne: King Stephen, the usurper, and young Duke Henry, the rightful heir. Amid civil and private wars, alliances are forged, loyalties are betrayed, families are divided, and marriages are made.

2

THERE WAS BUT one way to enter Wulfen Castle. She must make herself into a man.

Annyn looked down her figure where she stood among the leaves of the wood. And scowled. Rather, she must make herself into a boy, for it was boys in which the Baron Wulfrith dealt—pages who aspired to squires, squires who aspired to knights. As she was too slight to disguise herself as a squire, a page would be her lot, but only long enough to assure Jonas was well.

Still haunted by foreboding, though it was now four days since it had burrowed a dark place within her, she dropped her head back against the tree beneath which she had taken cover and squinted at the sunlight that found little resistance in autumn's last leaves. If only her mother were alive to offer comfort, but it was eight years since Lady Elena had passed on. Eight years since Annyn had known her touch.

A thumping sound evidencing the wily hare had come out of the thicket, Annyn gripped her bow tighter and edged slowly around the tree as her brother had taught her.

Though the scruffy little fellow had not fully emerged, he would soon. She tossed her head to clear the hair from her brow, raised her bow, and drew the nocked arrow to her cheek.

The hare lifted its twitchy nose.

Patience. Annyn heard Jonas from two summers past. Would she hear his voice again?

Aye, she would see him when she journeyed to Wulfen Castle where he completed his squire's training with the mighty Baron Wulfrith, a man said to exercise considerable sway over the earl from whom he held his lands.

Annyn frowned as she pondered the Wulfrith name that brought to mind a snarling wolf, her imagining made more vivid by the terrible anger the man was said to possess. Since before William of Normandy had conquered England, the Wulfrith family had been known England to France for training boys into men, especially those considered seriously lacking. Though Jonas's missives spoke little of that training, all knew it was merciless.

The hare crept forward.

Hold! Jonas's voice, almost real enough to fan her cheek, made her smile, cracking the mud she had smeared on her face as her brother had also taught her to do.

She squeezed her eyes closed. Thirteen months since he had departed for Wulfen. Thirteen months in training with the feared Wulfrith who allowed no women within his walls. Thirteen months to make Jonas into a man worthy to lord the barony of Aillil that would be his as Uncle Artur's heir.

The hare thumped.

Annyn jerked, startling the creature into bounding from the thicket. *Follow, follow, follow!*

She swung the arrow tip ahead of the hare and released.

With a shriek that made her wince as she did each time she felled one of God's creatures, the hare collapsed on a bed of muddy leaves.

Meat on the table, Annyn told herself as she tramped to where her prey lay. Not caring that she dirtied her hose and tunic, she knelt beside it.

"Godspeed," she said, hoping to hurry it to heaven though Father Cornelius said no such place existed for animals. But what did a man who did not know how to smile know of God's abode? She lifted the hare and tugged her arrow free. Satisfied to find tip and feathers intact, she wiped the shaft on her tunic and thrust the arrow into her quiver.

She stood. A catch of good size. Not that Uncle Artur would approve of her fetching meat to the table. He would make a show of disapproval, as he did each time she ventured to the wood, then happily settle down to a meal of hare pie. Of course, Annyn must first convince Cook to prepare the dish. But he would, and if she hurried, it could be served at the nooning meal. She slung the bow over her shoulder and ran.

If only Jonas were here, making me strain to match his longer stride. If only he were calling taunts over his shoulder. If only he would go from sight only to pounce upon me. Lord, I do not know what I will do if—

She thrust aside her worry with the reminder that, soon enough, she would have the assurance she sought. This very eve she would cut her mess of black hair, don garments Jonas had worn as a page, and leave under cover of dark. In less than a sennight, she could steal into Wulfen Castle, seek out her brother, and return to Aillil. As for Uncle Artur...

She paused at the edge of the wood and eyed Castle Lillia across the open meadow. Her disappearance would send dread through her uncle, but if she told him what she intended, he would not allow it.

She toed the damp ground. If he would but send a missive to Wulfen to learn how Jonas fared, this venture of hers need not be undertaken. However, each time she asked it of her uncle, he teased that she worried too much.

Movement on the drawbridge captured Annyn's regard. A visitor? A messenger from Wulfen? Mayhap Jonas once more returned for willful behavior? She squinted at the standard flown by the rider who passed beneath the raised portcullis and gasped. It belonged to the Wulfriths!

Though the men on the walls usually called to Annyn and bantered over her frightful appearance, her name did not unfurl any tongues when she approached the drawbridge.

Ignoring her misgivings, she paused to seek out the bearded Rowan who, as captain of the guard, was sure to be upon the gatehouse. He was not, but William was.

She thrust the hare high. "Next time, boar!"

He did not smile. "My lady, hasten to the donjon. The Baron Wul—"

"I know! My brother is returned?"

He averted his gaze. "Aye, Lady Annyn, your brother is returned."

So, neither could the renowned Baron Wulfrith order Jonas's life. She might have laughed if not that it boded ill for her brother's training to be terminated. Though of good heart, he had thrice been returned by fostering barons who could no more direct him than his uncle with whom he and Annyn had lived these past ten years. Thus, until Uncle Artur had sent Jonas to Wulfen Castle, brother and sister had been more together than apart. Soon they would be together again.

Silently thanking God for providing what she had asked, she darted beneath the portcullis and into the outer bailey, passing castle folk who stared after her with something other than disapproval. Telling herself her flesh bristled from chill, she entered the inner bailey where a half dozen horses stood before the donjon, among them Jonas's palfrey. And a wagon.

As she neared, the squire who held the reins of an enormous white destrier looked around. Surprise first recast his narrow face, then disdain. "Halt, you!"

She needed no mirror to know she looked more like a stable boy than a lady, but rather than allow him to mistake her as she was inclined to do, she said, "It is Lady Annyn you address, Squire."

Disdain slid back into surprise, and his sleepy green eyes widened further when he saw the hare. "Lady?" As if struck, he looked aside.

Annyn paused alongside Jonas's horse and laid a hand to its great jaw. "I thank you for bringing him home." She ran up the steps.

The porter was frowning when she reached the uppermost landing. "My lady, your uncle and Baron Wulfrith await. Pray, go quick 'round to the kitchen and put yourself to order."

Baron Wulfrith at Lillia? She glanced over her shoulder at the white destrier. How could she not have realized its significance? The baron must be angry indeed to have returned Jonas himself. Unless—

William's unsmiling face. The lack of disapproval usually shown her by the castle folk. The wagon.

Not caring what her appearance might say of her, she lunged forward. "My lady, pray—"

"I will see my brother now!"

The porter's mouth worked as if to conjure argument, but he shook his head and opened the door. "I am sorry, Lady Annyn."

The apology chilling her further, she stepped inside.

The hall was still, not a sound to disturb God and His angels were they near.

Blinking to adjust to the indoors, she caught sight of those on the dais. As their backs were turned to her and heads were bent, she wondered what they looked upon. More, where was Jonas?

The hare's hind legs dragging the rushes where the animal hung at her side, she pressed forward, all the while telling herself Jonas would soon lunge from an alcove and thump her to the floor.

"'Twas an honorable death, Lord Bretanne," a deep voice struck silence from the hall.

Annyn halted and picked out the one who had spoken—a big man in height and breadth, hair cut to the shoulders.

Dear God, of whom does he speak?

He stepped aside, clearing the space before the lord's table to reveal the one she desperately sought.

The hare slipped from her fingers, the bow from her shoulder. Vaguely aware of the big man and his companions swinging around, she stared at her brother's profile that was the shade of a dreary day. And there stood Uncle Artur opposite, hands flat on the table upon which Jonas was laid, head bowed, shoulders hunched up to his ears.

Annyn stumbled into a run. "Jonas!"

"What is this?" the deep voice demanded.

When Uncle's head came up, his rimmed eyes reflected shock at the sight of her. But there was only Jonas. In a moment she would have him up from the table and—

She collided with a hauberked chest and would have fallen back if not for the hand that fastened around her upper arm. It was the man who had spoken. She swung a foot and connected with his unmoving shin.

He dragged her up to her toes. "Who is this whelp that runs your hall like a dog, Lord Bretanne?"

Annyn reached for him where he stood far above. He jerked his head back, but not before her nails peeled back the skin of his cheek and jaw.

With a growl, he drew back an arm.

"Halt! 'Tis my niece."

The fist stopped above her face. "What say you?"

As Annyn stared at the large knuckles, she almost wished they would grind her bones so she might feel a lesser pain.

"My niece," Uncle said with apology, "Lady Annyn Bretanne."

The man delved her dirt-streaked face. "*This* is a woman?"

"But a girl, Lord Wulfrith."

Annyn looked from the four angry scores on the man's cheek to his grey-green eyes. *This* was Wulfrith? The one to whom Jonas was entrusted? Who was to make of him a man? Who had made of him a corpse?

"Loose me, cur!" She spat in the scratchy little voice Jonas often teased her about.

"Annyn!" Uncle protested.

Wulfrith's grip intensified and his pupils dilated.

Refusing to flinch as Jonas had told her she should never do, she held steady.

"'Tis the Baron Wulfrith to whom you speak, child," her uncle said as he came around the table, his voice more stern than she had ever heard it.

She continued to stare into the face she had marked. "This I know."

Uncle laid a hand on Wulfrith's shoulder. "She is grieved, Lord Wulfrith. Pray, pity her."

Annyn glared at her uncle. "Pity *me*? Who shall pity my brother?"

He recoiled, the pain of a heart that had loved his brother's son causing his eyes to pool.

Wulfrith released Annyn. "Methinks it better that I pity *you*, Lord Bretanne."

Barely containing the impulse to spit on him, she jumped back and looked fully into his face: hard, sharp eyes, nose slightly bent, proud cheekbones, firm mouth belied by a full lower lip, cleft chin. And falling back from a face others might think handsome, silver hair—a lie, for he was not of an age that bespoke such color. Indeed, he could not have attained much more than twenty and five years.

"Were I a man, I would kill you," she rasped.

His eyebrows rose. "'Tis good you are but a little girl."

If not for Uncle's hand that fell to her shoulder, Annyn would have once more set herself at Wulfrith.

"You err, child." Uncle Artur spoke firm. "Jonas fell in battle. His death is not upon the baron."

She shrugged out from beneath his hand and ascended the dais. Her brother was clothed in his finest tunic, about his waist a silver-studded belt from which a sheathed misericorde hung. He had been made ready for burial.

She laid a hand on his chest and willed his heart to beat again. But nevermore. "Why, Jonas?" The first tear fell, wetting the dried mud on her face.

"They were close." Uncle Artur's low words pierced her. "'Twill be difficult for her to accept."

Annyn swung around to face those who stared at her with disdain and pity. "How did my brother die?"

Was Wulfrith's hesitation imagined? "It happened at Lincoln."

She gasped. Yesterday they had received tidings of the bloody battle between the armies of England's self-proclaimed king, Stephen, and the young Henry, grandson of the departed King Henry and rightful heir to the throne. In spite of numerous skirmishes, raids, and deaths, it was told that neither man could claim victory at Lincoln. Nor could Jonas.

"Your brother squired for me. He was felled while delivering a lance to the field."

Despite her trembling, Annyn held Wulfrith's gaze. "What felled him?"

Something turned in his steely eyes. "An arrow to the heart."

All for Stephen's defense of his misbegotten claim to England.

She sank her nails into her palms. How it had pained Jonas to stand the side of the usurper when it was Henry he supported. And surely he had not been alone in that. Regardless of whose claim to the throne one supported, nobles vied to place their sons at Wulfen Castle. True, Wulfrith was Stephen's man, but it was said there was none better to train knights who would one day lord. If not for this silver-haired Lucifer and his thieving king, Jonas would be alive.

"He died an honorable death, Lady Annyn."

She took a step toward Wulfrith. "'Twas for Stephen he died. Tell me, Lord Wulfrith, what has that man to do with honor?"

As anger flared in his eyes, Uncle Artur groaned. Though Uncle also sided with Stephen, he had been aware of his nephew's allegiance to Henry. This, then—his hope of turning Jonas to Stephen—among his reasons for sending his nephew to Wulfrith.

Amid the murmuring and grunting of those in the hall, Annyn looked to Wulfrith's scored flesh and wished the furrows proved deep enough to mark him forever. And of Stephen who had pressed Uncle to send Jonas to Wulfrith? Whose wrongful claim to England had made the battle that took Jonas's life?

"Again, were I a man, I would kill your beloved Stephen."

While his men responded with raised voices, out of the darkness of his accursed soul, Wulfrith stared at her.

"Annyn!" Uncle strangled. "You do not know of what you speak."

"But I do." She turned her back on him and gently swept the hair off her brother's brow.

"Pray, Lord Wulfrith," her uncle beseeched, "do not listen—"

"Fear not. What has been spoken shall not pass from here."

Annyn looked over her shoulder. "My uncle is most grateful for such generosity from the man who bequeathed a grave to his heir."

Wulfrith's lower lip thinned with the upper, and his men objected more loudly, but it was Uncle Artur's face that stayed her. His torment pushed past the child in her and forced her to recognize it was not Wulfrith who staggered beneath her bitter words. It was this man she loved as a father.

She swallowed her tears. She would not further lose control of her emotions. After all, she was four and ten winters aged—a woman, though her uncle defended her as a girl. If not for his indulgence, she might now be wed, perhaps even with child.

She closed her eyes and drew a deep breath. When she lifted her lids, Wulfrith's harsh gaze awaited hers. "We wish to be alone," she said.

He inclined his head and looked to Uncle. "Lord Bretanne."

"Lord Wulfrith. Godspeed."

Despising the baron's ample shoulders and long-reaching legs, Annyn stared after him until he and his men passed through the door held by the porter.

"You should not have spoken as you did," Uncle said, though the steel in his voice would forge no sword.

Jonas's death had aged him, had stolen the breadth of shoulders on which he had borne her as a young girl.

Pressing her own shoulders back, she stood as tall as her four feet and some inches would stretch. "I know I have shamed you, and I shall endeavor to earn your forgiveness."

He mounted the dais and put an arm around her. "All is forgiven." He turned her to Jonas.

As she looked at her brother, a sob climbed up her throat. Reminding herself she was no longer a girl, she swallowed it.

"An honorable death."

Uncle's whispered words struck nearly as hard as when Wulfrith had spoken them. Though she struggled to hold back the child who incited words to her lips, she could not.

"Honorable! Not even eight and ten and he lies dead from serving a man who was more his enemy than—"

"Enough!" Uncle dropped his arm from her.

"Can you deny Jonas would be alive if not for Stephen's war?"

Anger met weariness on his brow. "Nay, as neither can I deny he would yet breathe if Henry, that whelp of Maude's, did not seek England for his own." He reached past her, ungirded Jonas's belt, and swept up his tunic. "Look!"

She did not want to, longed to run back to the wood, but that was the girl in her. Jaw aching at the force with which she ground her teeth, she dragged her gaze to the hideous wound at the center of her brother's chest.

"What do you see?" Uncle asked.

"A wound."

"And whose army do you think shot the arrow that put it there?"

Henry's, but—

"Whose, Annyn?"

Henry's, but Stephen—

"Speak it!"

She looked to her quaking hands. "Henry's."

He sighed, bent a finger beneath her chin, and urged her face up. "Stephen may not be the king England deserves, but until a worthier one appears, he is all there is. I beseech you, put aside Jonas's foolish allegiance to Maude's son. Henry is but a boy—barely six and ten—and unworthy to rule."

Unworthy when he led armies? Unworthy when—

She nodded.

Uncle stepped back. "I must needs pray."

As she ought to herself, for Father Cornelius told it was a long way to heaven. The sooner Jonas was prayed there, the sooner he might find his rest. "I shall join you shortly."

As her uncle turned away, Annyn saw the captain of the guard step out of a shadowed alcove. Had he been there when she entered the hall? Not that any of what had been said should be withheld from him, for he also had been like a father to Jonas. Did Uncle know of Rowan's presence?

She looked to her uncle as he traversed the hall and saw him lift a hand to his chest as if troubled by the infirm heart that beat there.

Panged by the suffering of the man who had been good to her and Jonas—far better than his brother who had sown them—Annyn silently beseeched, *Please, Lord, hold him hale.*

A moment later, she startled at the realization that she called on the one who had done nothing to protect her brother. Thus, it was not likely He would answer her prayers for her uncle.

When the old man disappeared up the stairs, Annyn drew nearer the table and reached to pull Jonas's tunic down. However, the V-shaped birthmark on his left ribs captured her gaze. Since it was years since the boy he had been had tossed off his tunic in the heat of swordplay, she had forgotten about the mark.

She closed her eyes and cursed the man whose charge of Jonas had stolen her brother from her. Wulfrith had failed Jonas. Had failed her.

When Rowan ascended the dais, she looked around.

The captain of the guard stared at the young man to whom he had given so many of his years, then a mournful sound rumbled up from his depths and he yanked down Jonas's tunic.

For fear she would cry if she continued to look upon Rowan's sorrow, Annyn lowered her face and reached to straighten the neck of her brother's tunic. If not for that, she would not have seen it. Would never have known.

She looked closer at the abraded skin deep beneath his chin. What had caused it? She pushed the material aside. The raw skin circled his upper neck and, when she traced it around, it nearly met at the back.

Understanding landed like a slap to the face. Wulfrith had lied. An arrow had not killed Jonas. Hanging had been the end of him. Why? Had her brother revealed his allegiance to Henry? More, who had fit the noose? Wulfrith who stood for Stephen? It had to be. And if not him, then surely he had ordered it.

Annyn whipped her chin around and saw that Rowan stared at what she had uncovered.

Bile rising, she stumbled past him and dropped to her knees. When the heaving was done, she wiped her mouth on her sleeve. "What will Uncle say of Wulfrith and Stephen now 'tis proven Jonas was murdered?"

Rowan sank deeper into silence, and she realized that, though Uncle's heart might abide the honorable death of one he had loved, Jonas's murder would likely ruin it, especially as he had sent her brother to Wulfrith in spite of Jonas's protests.

If not that she loved her uncle, she would have hated him. "Nay, he must not be told." Feeling as if she had aged years in these last moments, she stepped past Rowan and pulled the misericorde from her brother's belt.

Frowning over the pommel that was set with jewels to form the cross of crucifixion, she wondered whence the dagger came. She would have noticed such a splendid weapon had Jonas possessed one. Was it of Wulfen? It mattered not. All that mattered was revenge.

Vengeance is not yours, Annyn. Jonas's voice drifted to her from six months past when he had come home for three days. *Vengeance belongs to God. You must defer to Him.*

Her anger at the visiting nobleman's son who had set one of her braids afire had faltered when she heard Jonas speak so. He, who had so often shrugged off God, had found Him at Wulfen. Considering Baron Wulfrith's reputation, it had surprised her. And more so now, having met the man and discovered his lie about Jonas's death.

False teachings, then. A man like Wulfrith could not possibly know God. At that moment, she hardly knew Him herself. For days, she had prayed He would deliver Jonas home. And this was His answer.

She squeezed her fists so tight that her knuckles popped.

How she ached to make Wulfrith suffer for the bloodguilt of her brother's death. She knew vengeance was God's privilege, but she also knew it had once been the privilege of surviving family members.

Would God truly strike her down if she turned to the ways of the Old Testament? Revenge *was* the way of the world—certainly the way of men. Revenge begat revenge, as evidenced by the struggle for England's throne.

She nodded. How could God possibly deny her, especially as He was surely too busy to bother with such things himself? Were He not, He would not have allowed what had been done to Jonas.

Splaying her fingers on her thighs, she glared at the ceiling. "Vengeance is *mine*, and You shall just have to understand." A terrible, blasphemous thought crept to her tongue, and she did not bite it back. "If You are even there."

"Annyn?"

She looked to Rowan whose talk had turned her and Jonas to Henry's side—Rowan who would surely aid her. If it took a lifetime, Wulfrith would know the pain her brother had borne. Only his death would satisfy.

It had been necessary. Still, Garr Wulfrith felt the stain of young Jonas's death.

He reached for the hilt of his misericorde and too late realized he no longer possessed it. *That* had *not* been necessary.

Berating himself for the foolish gesture, he lifted a hand to his cheek where Jonas's shrew of a sister had scored his flesh. So the girl who looked and behaved like a boy had also turned. Though Artur Bretanne remained loyal to Stephen, somehow his brother's children had found Henry. For that, Jonas was dead. And hardly an honorable death as told.

Remembering what he had done the morning he found his squire strung from a tree, he told himself it was better that the truth of the betrayal die with the betrayer. No family ought to suffer such dishonor, not even a family that boasted one such as Annyn Bretanne. Thus, he had falsified—and now felt the brunt of God's displeasure.

Save me, O Lord, from lying lips and deceitful tongues, his mother would quote if she knew what her firstborn had done.

For this, Garr would spend hours in repentance and pray that this one lie did not breed, as lies often did—that after this day, he would know no more regret for having told it.

He looked over his shoulder. Though it was the receding Castle Lillia he sought, Squire Merrick captured his gaze. A promising young warrior, if not a bit peculiar, he and Jonas had served together in squiring Garr. At first there had been strain between the young men who both aspired to the standing of First Squire, but it had eased once Jonas was chosen. In fact, the two had become as near friends as was possible in the competitive ranks of the forty who sought knighthood at Wulfen Castle. But, as Merrick now knew, friendships often had false bottoms.

Garr shifted his gaze to Castle Lillia. He pitied Artur Bretanne. The man would be a long time in ridding himself of his niece, if ever, for who would take to wife that filthy little termagant who had but good, strong teeth to recommend her?

Of course, what man took any woman to wife other than to get an heir? Women were difficult, ever endeavoring to turn men from their purpose. However, as with all Wulfrith men who preferred warring over women, especially Garr's father, Drogo, Garr would eventually wed. Forsooth, he would have done so three years past had his betrothed not died of the pox.

He turned back to the land before him. Once Stephen secured his hold on England, Garr would find a wife of sturdy build whom he could visit a half dozen times a year until she bore him sons to raise up as warriors—men who stood far apart from ones like Jonas.

An image of the young man's death once more rising, he gripped the pommel of his saddle. How could he have been so wrong? Though he had sensed Jonas's allegiance to Henry, he had used it to put heart into the young man's training. After all, how better to make a man than to give him a powerful reason for becoming one? The aim was not to turn one's allegiance, though sometimes it happened. The aim was for the squire to give his utmost to his lord, which was of greatest importance in battle.

But the strategy had failed with Jonas—fatally. A mistake Garr would not make again.

Telling himself Jonas Bretanne was in the past, dead and soon buried, he released the pommel. As for Annyn Bretanne, she would put her loss behind her. All she needed was time.

About The Author

TAMARA LEIGH HOLDS a Master's Degree in Speech and Language Pathology. In 1993, she signed a 4-book contract with Bantam Books. Her first medieval romance, *Warrior Bride*, was released in 1994. Continuing to write for the general market, three more novels were published with HarperCollins and Dorchester and earned awards and spots on national bestseller lists.

In 2006, Tamara's first inspirational contemporary romance, *Stealing Adda*, was released. In 2008, *Perfecting Kate* was optioned for a movie and *Splitting Harriet* won an ACFW "Book of the Year" award. The following year, *Faking Grace* was nominated for a RITA award. In 2011, Tamara wrapped up her "Southern Discomfort" series with the release of *Restless in Carolina*.

When not in the middle of being a wife, mother, and cookbook fiend, Tamara buries her nose in a good book—and her writer's pen in ink. In 2012, she returned to the historical romance genre with *Dreamspell*, a medieval time travel romance. Shortly thereafter, she once more invited readers to join her in the middle ages with the *Age of Faith* series: *The Unveiling, The Yielding, The Redeeming, The Kindling,* and *The Longing.* Tamara's #1 Bestsellers—*Lady at Arms, Lady Of Eve, Lady Of Fire,* and *Lady Of Conquest*—are the first of her medieval romances to be rewritten as "clean reads." Look for *Baron Of Blackwood,* the third book in *The Feud* series, in 2016.

Tamara lives near Nashville with her husband, sons, a Doberman that bares its teeth not only to threaten the UPS man but to smile, and a feisty Morkie that keeps her company during long writing stints.

Connect with Tamara at her website www.tamaraleigh.com, her blog The Kitchen Novelist, her email tamaraleightenn@gmail.com, Facebook, and Twitter.

For new releases and special promotions, subscribe to Tamara Leigh's mailing list: www.tamaraleigh.com

55086206R00184

Made in the USA
Lexington, KY
10 September 2016